A TREASONABLE GROWTH

A TREASONABLE GROWTH

RONALD BLYTHE

This edition first published in 2010
by Faber and Faber Ltd
Bloomsbury House, 74–77 Great Russell Street
London WC1B 3DA

Printed by Books on Demand GmbH, Norderstedt

All rights reserved
© Ronald Blythe, 1960

The right of Ronald Blythe to be identified as author of this work
has been asserted in accordance with Section 77 of the
Copyright, Designs and Patents Act 1988

This book is sold subject to the condition that it shall not, by way of
trade or otherwise, be lent, resold, hired out or otherwise circulated
without the publisher's prior consent in any form of binding or cover other than
that in which it is published and without a similar condition including this
condition being imposed on the subsequent purchaser

A CIP record for this book is available from the British Library

ISBN 978–0–571–26913–6

Our authorised representative in the EU for product safety is
Easy Access System Europe, Mustamäe tee 50, 10621 Tallinn, Estonia
gpsr.requests@easproject.com

For Christine

And, worst of all, a treasonable growth
Of indecisive judgments, that impaired
And shook the mind's simplicity . . .

    William Wordsworth: *The Prelude*

1

MR WINSLEY himself let him in—and so immediately. How was that? Had he been watching and waiting? Had he been balanced upon one of the small armorial chairs prinked around the hall?—wicked, slippery, inhuman chairs with recessed rings cut in their seats for top-hats, and looking like frustrated commodes. Was he *so* intent on being the first to welcome a raw new master to the School that he could descend to the frigid hall and station himself behind the orange calix of a Morris lily, which was the one clear segment in the bubbly glass window of the huge front door? It seemed that he was.

'Charles,' Mr Winsley said, holding out his hand.

'Richard,' corrected Richard, and at the same time resenting this uncalled-for warmth.

Mr Winsley nodded agreeably. Just as you wish, he implied. Charleses and Richards, they came and they went and they left a little instruction behind them. Unqualified teachers gypsying about from St This to St That's, with their clothes and references scrambled together in fibre suitcases and their neckties vivid witnesses to the well-established tradition of their calling. 'We like to think of ourselves as one big family at Copdock House,' he said. 'We have to be an institution, of course, but I hope you will discover for yourself that none of us subscribe to the grisly portentousness of that word. But come in, come in.'

Richard said: 'I should have let you know which train——'

'Let us know——? But you did, dear boy. You did! This is Stourfriston! When our guests do not materialize on the nine-seventeen, then we switch our trust to the two-thirty. Thank God, we have never had the worry of what they call a "good service."' Mr Winsley rose compulsively on the balls of his feet and swayed. He had a pear-ish thinness of trunk and short fat legs. His habit of tiptoeing was his, now unconscious, way of protesting against the injustice of his physique. 'Leave your bags for Darwin—against that chest I should think. They won't get in the way there.' He led the way across a high, dark hall with a certain amount of ritual. Occasionally he even went so far as to jerk an elbow or a thumb towards particular features of it, like an anxious guide in Chartres or Knole who suspects a faldstool is not getting its fair share of wonder. Note the stairwell, Mr Winsley insisted and Richard saw a huge ochre core capped by a purple dome and festooned with photogravure reproductions of Great Paintings. In the landing window just above his head, a north Oxford St Sebastian flaunted a delicate biscuit-coloured nudity. About three feet up from the skirting ran a bas-relief dado of plaster marigolds. Dotted about the floor were satchel-laden settles. A large crocketted hatstand held one dirty cap and some ancient visiting cards tucked in its deleterious mirror.

At the stairs Mr Winsley paused and said: 'It was, you see, her home. . . .'

'Before it was a school?'

'Before she *made* it into a school.'

'I see . . . I hope Miss Bellingham is well,' Richard added politely, thinking it odd that she hadn't wanted to see him. Her signature on the letter appointing him had been the only real indication of her existence—that and her name on the door-plate. Mr Winsley had conducted the interview and it had been unflatteringly obvious that he had not only been the lone candidate, but the single applicant. When he had written to Quentin, telling him that he had got the job, Quentin had replied, 'Oh yes, there had been a Miss Bellingham and she had founded some kind of prep school, but surely both were dead as Hannah Moore?' But Mr Winsley was looking at him queerly.

'Miss Bellingham *well*, did I hear you ask?'

'I just wondered as she wasn't at the interview——'

'She is in excellent health, thank God.'

They were passing fire-extinguishers and buckets of sand, the latter liberally spattered with spit marks. The floor was ceramic, its colour liver-red. Here and there, sanguinely adrift, were a few portrait tiles of the Angevin kings, their necks awry, their limbs gravely dislocated. The banister-rail was a phalanx of cast-iron asphodels. The almost unerring bad taste of nearly everything the School contained coalesced into such a single-mindedness of wrongly applied aesthetic principles that the result was in some frightful way admirable. Say what you like, thought Richard, taking it all in all, it's *something!*

'I've seen the School lots of times, but only from the outside —usually when Quentin—he's my brother—and myself were on the way to Cambridge.'

'You couldn't have,' said Mr Winsley quickly, 'it can't be seen from the station.'

'I—we were bicycling, Sir.'

'Bicycling . . .' Mr Winsley puffed innuendo into the word.

'And it was a long time ago.' Now that he considered it, there was something, well otiose, about bicycling to Cambridge —particularly where Quentin was concerned.

Mr Winsley looked comforted. 'Ah, yes,' he said, 'boys' energies!' He smiled and the blue and vermilion veins webbed across his cheeks tilted and crinkled into small deltas of apparent sagacity.

They came to a chocolate-brown door embellished with more asphodels, this time in the form of copper finger-plates. It opened with a similar clairvoyance to the one in the hall and showed Mrs Winsley, a little, shining-eyed woman burdened with an intricate cushion of greying-gold hair, the front of it impolitically blued.

'My wife. Minna, this is Mr Brand.'

'At last,' she said and a pronounced smell of cooking told him why. The Winsleys, knowing that there was not such a thing as a restaurant car on the train, had waited lunch. It was ten to three. He hardly knew what to say.

'Charles knows Stourfriston, he says,' Mr Winsley began and Mrs Winsley opened her foolish doll's eyes wide and said: 'Oh really! You sit here will you, Charles.'

'It's Richard——'

They laughed explosively at one another and Mr Winsley said: 'Now don't you take any notice of Minna; she's forever getting names wrong.'

'Cadman . . .'

But Mr Winsley only went on laughing and Richard, recognizing the merry apologia which conceals the disastrousness of so many marriages, the too-jolly laugh, the boisterous void of certain conversations, felt it best to add his own grin and say nothing more. The food was welcome and they meant to be kind. He ought to leave it at that.

'Your brother—did I hear you mention that he was at March?' Mr Winsley was asking.

'He is the Senior English master there.'

'Indeed,' Mr Winsley said, and then, 'March . . .' his tone implying, yes, yes, I know March—one of those too public public schools!

Mrs Winsley pressed her chignon and said hurriedly: 'The news is dreadful, isn't it. I expect you've seen the papers this morning. They're going to have another blackout test on Sunday night. I still remember the last time, you know!' She gave a little triumphant chuckle as though scoring some sort of historic point.

'We've got to have our measure of safety, my dear,' insisted her husband. He bared his rose-pink dentures at Richard in a demand for corroboration. He was bending over the casserole and disturbing its contents with small, inquisitive thrusts of a fork and tablespoon. 'Yet,' he went on, 'it would be criminal on our part for us not to appreciate just a little of their point of view—' Here a slight gesture of dissent, or perhaps, embarrassment from Mrs Winsley caused him to sweep the hand with the fork in it in her direction. 'I'm not saying anything more than what was said at the Lorrilows' on Wednesday night, now am I, Minna? You see', he went on, switching his allegiance to Richard, *'we* can breathe! There is Australia—New Zealand. Rhodesia. *We* don't have to be squeezed up as they are, a great and growing nation, between the Baltic and the Northern Latin bloc. Now if you ask me, Herr Hitler . . .'

'Caddie—not now, darling. Everything's getting cold. . . .'

Mr Winsley, looking displeased, turned to Richard and asked abruptly, 'What made you decide on our little school—eh?'

Why? That was a good one! Richard felt like offering his own disillusioned laughter to the general spurious enjoyment. Graceless answers flipped their way through his brain. One, it was two hundred a year. Two, because, unlike Quentin, he didn't possess a degree, which cut out March and any of the more or less decent schools. Three, destiny. Wasn't he the kind of person who was born into a Copdock of one sort or another? Hadn't he the perfect background? There was a margin of so-called 'decent employment' for the offspring from country rectories, and it included amateur schoolmastering. At first Richard had made a mistake about this. He had forced his way into a bank thinking that he could scoop and lick and count and weigh like anyone else and still have time to work out rhyme-endings, or jot down his impressions of people and life. He thought of Charles Lamb on his office stool and even of T. S. Eliot, whose poetry seemed to have landed him in a boardroom. But something had gone wrong. He hadn't been able to divide himself properly. Eventually he left and they presented him with a note-case because he had been with them just over the year. A leatherette note-case—that's what one got for flying in the face of destiny. . . . Yes, the bank had been a distinct mistake. Now it occurred to him that he had picked on its alternative too precipitously. There was something quite wrong about Copdock, wrong in the most subtle, the deepest dyed sense. Above Mrs Winsley's head he noticed the windjammers anchored forever in their water-colour sea—becalmed and benighted in a gentle waste where it would always be sunset and evening star. . . . Nine ebony elephants trundled across the lid of the piano. Two bronze youths wrestled with two wild bronze horses. Each of these things appeared to him at that moment to be offering a more romantic solution to the problem of what he should do. Where he should go. In the middle of the mantelpiece a simpering girl swung time away under the French clock. He saw that Mrs Winsley was so interested in his reply that she had stopped eating and her fork was poised so that it reflected against her tight waxen throat.

'Well for one thing I've always liked Stourfriston itself—'

Mr Winsley, looking even more displeased, dug away at his food. It was clear he had hoped for some sort of enthusiasm. This constant lack of enthusiasm in others was the chief reason for his being always so irritably upon the defensive. But Mrs Winsley was saying, 'It's not much of a town—would *you* call it much of a town, dear?' Her eyes shone with flattering enquiry. Richard saw that she had made it her rule never to know the answers. She was twisting a strand of white beads round and round as she spoke. Every now and then her hands would drop the beads and fly to her hair as though some nodule of its elaborations was about to drop off. Her attitude was almost oriental. She had become, over the long years of her marriage, as compliant and as agreeable as a meringue. It was obvious that she would give her soul to keep the peace.

'*I* like it,' her husband said sharply.

'Oh, I *like* it, Caddie; I was just wondering why Char—why Mr Brand did.'

'Merely because of its size, Mrs Winsley. It's something like five thousand, isn't it?'

'Something like that, but Caddie will know.'

'Five thousand, three hundred and seventy,' pronounced her husband oracularly.

'There!' she said, pleased.

A sudden uproar cut across the meal. An uninhibited descent of the bare stairs outside the door of an avalanche of clattering feet, caused the room to tremble like matchwood. Mrs Winsley, who had affected to be distracted by a clumsy movement of the luncheon table, remained quite unmoved by this racket. She went on eating placidly. Mr Winsley, chewing hard, looked from his watch to the gilded girl and said: 'Half-past. Bateson's late again.'

'Mr Bateson is to be your neighbour,' Mrs Winsley smiled. 'We're all very fond of him. He's our coach.'

The row stopped and left a torpid silence in its place. There was a moment of revelation as a wink of sunlight strove to pierce the dirty window, a moment when Richard thought he was about to discover the secret of Copdock, of its boxed-up rooms, of the same air being used over and over again, of experiences emasculated by repetition and used until they were threadbare; of the strict precautions taken to see that nothing ever actually happened. The interview had been like that, uninquisitive—decorous almost. Yet at the same time insisting that whoever it was who was offered and who accepted the post, should also realise that they had been offered (and must accept) Copdock, lock, stock and tradition. New brooms, new methods—new anything—just weren't called for. Acceptance was what was required. At the time Richard thought it quite easy to comply with such conditions. After all, he didn't want to be a schoolmaster, he wanted to be a writer and Copdock would have the same long holidays as any other school. Just the thought of his writing made him feel much better. This was only a job after all. He must remind himself of this whenever he felt depressed. He said: 'I heard—only the other day, as a matter of fact—that my father knew Miss Bellingham a little. They met occasionally at meetings of the Archaeological Society in Ipswich. I . . . I'm quite looking forward to seeing her.'

Mr Winsley turned on him with extravagant interest. 'Oh, are you?' he said, and his tone implied, I'm afraid she's hardly likely to be doing the same with regard to you!

Mrs Winsley hurried in with her kindness. 'She's awfully old now, that's why she never comes down, you know.' Did the ghost of malice haunt her words? Richard couldn't be sure.

'She's eighty.' Behind his sturdy spectacles Mr Winsley's eyes flickered and swam like minnows. 'It's a great age and in Miss Bellingham's case, a great achievement . . .' And then, more indulgently, 'When *I* came to Copdock, Miss Bellingham was forty, just forty! . . . think of that!'

Richard tried not to think of it, but ages and dates added and subtracted from each other in his brain. Forty years ago Mr Winsley was twenty-four—or thereabouts. Mrs Winsley, too. And what about Bateson? They said he was the coach, but it still didn't prevent Richard from imagining some venerable figure heeling down the turf with a rheumaticky foot. 'And Mr Bateson . . .?' he enquired.

'When did Bateson come, Minna?'

'The Jubilee, Caddie—surely you remember!'

Before Richard could hide his disappointment—it was, as Quentin had implied, a hopeless, helpless, senile dump after all—Mr Winsley was saying, 'Nineteen-thirty-five—so long! That's over three years ago. It's incredible!'

Relieved, Richard muttered something about Bateson obviously liking Copdock since he hadn't wished to change and was going on to say that all he himself wanted to do was to settle down in some job where he felt he was going to be of real use—in fact, a conciliatory little speech to set his own and the Winsleys' minds at rest; when he was prevented from doing so by the sudden fear in Mr Winsley's face.

We all have words which lacerate, if they do not destroy, our peace of mind. They taunt us from hoardings. They forsake their context and leap out of the newspapers at us. If they are on the page of a book we see them before any others. They describe our hopes and our guilt. 'Change' to Cadman Winsley had proved itself to be a desolatingly haunting word. It rang in his ears like a faulty bell—*change*—sinuous, nasal; a syllable suspended over him as threateningly as a Damoclean sword. One day it would really fall and he would be destroyed. Deep down, deeper than the virile declamation of his tobacco-yellow moustache, or the contentment declared in the rise of his high, soft, indulgent little belly, or in the arrogant fluttering of his pale eyes, there lurked his buried self. And what a self! Another individual who was, in his way, as much 'Cadman Winsley' as the touchy elderly schoolmaster who concealed him. This creature thrived on a diet of words like 'battle—banner—soldier—regiment—glory' O the brave music of a distant drum! General Wolfe, it is said, would rather have written an elegy than win his war. Mr Winsley would have given ten years of his schoolmastering life to have been gazetted as Major Winsley . . . He had preserved his boyhood visions, sepia in tone, since they derived from those excellent pencil drawings in old copies of the *Illustrated London News*; in which a certain gallant officer marched, galloped and fought. Sometimes as he sat in class, he saw it all, even now—the troopships behind him and in front of him, the Residency lights. One day, he used to tell himself, I shall change. But, of course, he had never changed and now the very word terrified him. Since his decision to make the best of things as they were, he no longer cared to picture them as they might have been. And he wouldn't have to—except for 'change'. Why did people always have to drag the thing up? Just when he might be happy and somebody! Instead of replying he said moodily,

'You'd better see your room. I expect you want to unpack.'

This reminded Richard of his luggage left downstairs in the hall, his father's old suitcase still lettered J.L.B. and a small canvas affair marked 'Stella Brand'. Grossly inadequate luggage it now seemed, small and paltry and not even personal.

When he said that his books were coming by Carter Paterson it was more to cheer himself up than to semi-apologise to the Winsleys.

'It is true what we hear—that you write?' asked Mrs Winsley shyly. She cringed in her chair while a stout middle-aged maid rattled the plates together.

'A bit. I haven't really begun . . .' He felt like a liar. Hoping to be and being were too-widely distributed states for the sort of unqualified assertion he had made at the interview. Mr Winsley didn't help matters by rubbing his papery hands together and insisting, 'Nothing wrong in that; we all have to begin.'

His room was at the back. It was quite big. There were two long cold windows in one wall and the floor glittered with linoleum. A sparse rush mat by the bed skidded crazily when he walked on it. Their breath—Mr Winsley had followed him in, carrying the canvas bag because Darwin couldn't be found —rode out on the frigid air in long sad plumes.

'That fire's simply splendid when it gets going,' Mr Winsley said. He kicked it with the toe of his boot and the grey mantels fell forward in an atrophied honeycomb. "A shelf for your books—when they arrive.' He banged a shiny primrose ledge.

Then he turned to a majestic wardrobe with glossy doors and a romping pediment topped by a mahogany urn. 'And your clothes in here. Well, Richard, I trust you will be happy with us.' At the door he turned and said rather solemnly, 'Tea is served in Big School, but you may like to come down at supper-time as it's your first day.'

Left alone, Richard held a match to the desolate grate. Nothing happened. The mantels clinked like dead cinders. By sprawling at full length on the floor, he found the meter which was under the bed. He pushed all the pennies he had in and when he struck another match was rewarded by a blinding boom which at once settled down to a comfortingly sibilant drone. He lit the light then hung his clothes up. In the huge mirror fixed to the gargantuan wardrobe he saw himself, darkish, squarish and, in a wispy moment of self-revelation, younger somehow than he imagined. And much, much poorer. He put everything away except the letter which said:

                Copdock House Preparatory School for Boys
                Stourfriston,
                Suffolk
                2nd December, 1938

Dear Mr Brand,

I want you to know how delighted I am with the results of last Monday's interview. Discussing the matter after you had left, Mr Winsley and I came to the conclusion that it would be of the very greatest assistance to us (and possibly of help to you yourself) if you could come to the School at once. It would mean that you could make yourself familiar with our ways and so begin the new term in January . . .

The letter then went on about other sundry details, including one or two oddments like 'did he know that George Gissing often came to Stourfriston' and that 'swimming in the river was quite safe now' and was signed, largely and blackly, 'Freda Bellingham.'

There being nothing else he could possibly do, he looked out of the window on to a large, surprisingly private, garden. Three ancient cedars linked their pyramidal darknesses together at the end of a lawn. Beyond the cedars, glimpsed through their trunks, were sagging tennis nets. Beyond the nets, a high, severe red-brick wall. The wall, because of its quite extraordinary height, hid most of the neighbouring houses. But buildings further away could be seen and the result was an architectural skyline balanced on a dull rose base which for those living in the back part of the School was lavishly decorative. It was an excellent view to have, redemptive and atoning. Richard traced the row of spires, gables and chimneys and felt better. He particularly liked the rear of the Corn Exchange, upon the roof of which sprawled a couple of heroic plaster labourers with their arms hugging sheaves and their hands clasping sickles. They became for him the crown of this bricks-and-mortar frieze as they stood there with their backs to him amongst the snowy pigeon dirts and chipped plaster stubble, two saffron Corins, *circa* William the Fourth. And the garden itself was nice, he admitted. Even in December. Even in the half-dark. But then he had always rather enjoyed Victorian gardens and gloomy evergreens. The latter were limitless—banks and tiers and thickets of them converged to make a truly formidable shrubbery. Laurels dripped and the clock on the parish church struck four. Down below, immediately below, sour flower beds lay in the tenuous grip of box hedging which, in spite of nearly half a century's incursions by desolating boys, still wound itself crisply in the Tuscan formality with which Miss Bellingham's father had originally contrived it. To the left was a purple glass conservatory. To the right, a muddy paddock with goal-posts. In a letter which he wrote at a small inkstained kitchen table, 'a desk in your room' Mr Winsley had said, he described all this to Quentin. Then he went down to tea.

2

A BOY might see Miss Bellingham a dozen or so times during his stay at Copdock, unless some persistent offence qualified him for a particular audience in the abundant terror of her room. Twice a year she showed herself publicly: in May when she walked between parents and sisters scattered over her lawn in the fickle sunshine to sit under the cedar, like Paris under Ida, to judge the annual attainments; and in December when she entered her mother's old drawing-room, now Big School, to make a speech about Christmas and duty and love. Boys who remembered little else of their schooldays remembered Miss Bellingham, and more particularly than her decrepit presence even—her voice. Intensely loud and much accentuated, by some art it also contrived to be moving, sweet and very feminine. It even made them feel that something was missing when, later on, they made their own morose encounters with women. The mystery, perhaps.

A visit to her was a journey to a goddess. Although she had adopted rooms in the servants' quarters, there wasn't a tread on the scrubbed deal stairs that was not hieratic. Parents with any qualms that this elderly blue-stocking might put into the heads of their quaking offspring ideas other than those needed as a foundation for the minor professions of country life, erred in two ways. The first because they had been conceited enough to imagine that anything remarkable should be hidden in such dull clay; the second that even if by some miracle it *did*, that the old, cold glance of Freda Bellingham would help to raise it up. The truth was she disliked boys. There was nothing perverse in her dislike, nor self-pity because she herself was maiden, nor was it because they spoilt all the best rooms of Copdock House, where she might have sat in peace if her money hadn't run out. She simply had no use for sketches, roughs or anything in the making. What she demanded was a good full canvas, not to mention a reasonably gilt frame. To Miss Bellingham boys were embryo men and nothing more. They were incomplete and, she suspected, inhuman. For her their personalities didn't exist. Their pain was an unpleasant snivelling. Their joy was a guffaw. They were nobbly green fruit bumping against the learned bough waiting for what seemed to her at times, endless summers before they were ripened. Like green plums, their skins might glow, but they remained essentially nasty.

She sat now opposite Mr Winsley. They were carolling down below in the street 'We Three Kings of Orient are . . .' But there were a great many voices. 'Is it a choir?' she asked. She forced a hand behind an ear. Her ears were big, with brown, dragging lobes. Above their expansive, almost shameful nakedness, flared a *bouffant* mass of white and beautiful hair. Her fingers spreading down the arm-rests of her chair were the palest flecked gold and might have been, in the poor light, the carved rosewood terminals themselves.

'I thought I was going to die today,' she said. Her lids crept up like shutters and she trapped Mr Winsley in her glaucous gaze.

'Oh don't say it! You musn't say it!'

'Do you imagine at this stage one *chooses* what to say? These things happen to me so I mention them.'

'But you are feeling better now?' It was as much a statement of fact as a question.

'Better? Worse . . .? I don't ask myself those kind of things, Cadman.'

She bent forward and smoothed the multifarious coverlets of rucked crochet which held her in the chair.

'Did he arrive?' she asked.

'After luncheon.'

'So he didn't get any?'
'Minna waited.'
'Minna!' repeated Miss Bellingham disparagingly.
'Do you know what she said today?' said Mr Winsley. ' "Why aren't *I* ever given something to do?"—She meant she herself, you know!—I really think she meant it!'

Miss Bellingham laughed too. Her lips fled back and showed darkness. It was the mirth of a mask. 'You *were* a fool, you know, Cadman,' she said, but without rancour. 'I suppose Minna liked him?' she added.

'I think so.'

'Do you?'

'I suppose so—why not? He's like all the rest, of course; he thinks he's going to make a big bang in the world . . .' Mr Winsley snuffled and passed a cold finger over the little delta of veins which ran down the tip of his nose.

Miss Bellingham sank back into the buttony comfort of her chair. Her jaw worked slightly as it always did when she was absorbed in thought, grinding away with a gentle mandibular insistency. Mr Winsley watched her. He hadn't sat. He now leaned against the cluttered bookshelves and swung one foot backwards and forwards with unconscious grace. A tall oil lamp with a blue glass stem threw a ball of light between them. Miss Bellingham's lids, half closed, hid all her eyes. Once or twice she ran her hand up over the shawls in a stiff little clawing movement before she let it rest among her beads and once she turned and stared long at the jalousie fidgetting against the window.

'I arranged that he should take the fourth and fifth for everything except maths and physics,' said Mr Winsley. The silence irked him. It emphasized an existence beyond the limits of his knowledge, a delicious enfeeblement of blood and resolution which was the penumbra of the end. Those futile scrabblings of her fingers against the chair! The way she indulged dissolution! He could shake her. He hoped he wouldn't be as selfish when his time came!

'My dinner was cold tonight,' she complained suddenly.

'I'm sorry. Minna must see Ellen at once.'

'Ellen—?'

'She's the new cook—the one we hired last week.'

'Why do you say "we" when she's obviously some inefficient slut that Minna found!'

'But you *did* see her.' Mr Winsley's face grew owlish in his intensity to convey conviction.

Miss Bellingham said: 'They're using the top landing again. I heard them. *I won't have it!*'

Mr Winsley could not explain. He read all along the top row of the bookcase opposite. *The Psychology of the Poet Shelley* by Edward Carpenter. *Cities* by Arthur Symonds . . . *The Transactions of the Seldon Society* . . . Marie Bashkirtseff . . . Octavia Hill . . . *Leaves of Grass* . . . *Who's Who* 1911 . . .

But Miss Bellingham was recovering. Her liveliness when she remembered it was huge. She jerked up now and tried to reach something on the table. Mr Winsley picked up letters, papers, pamphlets—a book to help her. 'Allow me,' he repeated over and over again, blind to how much it maddened her, this getting-in-the-way politeness of his that was only a damned nuisance. She dashed whatever he proffered from his hand. He let her do so with joy. Her sudden strength set his fears at rest. She found what she was looking for. It had slid down the side of the chair. She clutched it firmly, a broad white envelope exquisitely addressed to herself.

'Paul is coming home,' she announced.

Mr Winsley was speechless.

'In fact, he *is* home,' went on Miss Bellingham. 'He's at Brown's Hotel and will be coming down to Sheldon after Christmas. He invites advice. Here, see for yourself.'

She threw the letter and it fell to the floor. Mr Winsley dived to retrieve it like an adipose gannet avid for the least information.

'Is it a secret?' he enquired.

'Read it and see.'

'My dear Aunt,' he read.

'Or I might almost say, my dearest, dearest Egeria, if I were normally given to such excesses. I'm in London. Are you surprised? And will you be amazed when I tell you that I intend very soon to be found only at Sheldon? I'm *miserable* about it, of course—not for dear Sheldon but for being hurried along by all these armies, for being *pushed out*. It is generally believed in Sicily that it *must* come in the spring. I pray not and the British Government evidently believes not—or so people say on trains. But things are *bad* and I thought to come home now would be to do so less precipitously than later on. The Harveys have left too—in fact we all came together. It was terrible getting rid of things and packing things and saying farewell to the garden. Allessandro wept, I wept, Father Guiseppi wept—such a flood! But even if there isn't a war, I think that the time has come to consider Sheldon. I'm fifty-three.

Did I tell you we saw Hitler? It was at Mainz last October. But surely I would have told you. But it is possible I forgot, so here is the description once more. The general, all-over impression, as you might say, is mycological. A flocculent puffiness pushing out a policeman's coat. The wonder is his voice, of course; harder than anything imaginable. And coming out of his soft little body, it's as marvellous as flames spurting from a sponge. Do you remember a particular type once described as 'common'? Well he is that. They roared and roared and I'm sorry to say that we almost did too. A roar is so infectious! We ached *not* to and ached at the same time to be sick. An uncomfortable confliction, you must agree!—but I mustn't bore you.

Is there a soul in your estimable employ who could help me get my books and things straight at Sheldon?

Tomlinson's have just taken the last volume of *Charon's Cox*—I'm glad to see the going of it. *Scrimshanks* is being re-issued. (*Again*, you will say.) The B.B.C. want *The Woman Who Meddled*—but without its sequel. So they shan't have it.

I'm pleased to be coming back to Sheldon. Yet sad. It means that so much is over. Love,
Pauly.'

'Well?' she said, exasperated by his silence.

'You know that I'm pleased,' answered Mr Winsley defensively, 'why must I say it!' He had put on his glasses to read the letter and his pupils were enormous.

'The advice, Cadman . . .'

Mr Winsley thought he saw light.

'It is very true that I have little time these days, but if there is anything that I can do to help Sir Paul you know that I will only be too pleased.'

Miss Bellingham twisted round suddenly. For a moment it looked as if she was going to get up. She did so sometimes. It always staggered him, mostly because the exertion that brought it about was so concentrated as to appear saurian in its strength. But now she just turned to face him. Her half-sealed eyes took in his fat little legs, his neatly inclining shoulders and the black bone buttons winking down his waistcoat. Her lips crept back in the new outlandish mirth she allowed herself these days. She laughed and he let her.

'How did you find out that he writes?' she asked at last.

Mr Winsley did not reply.

'Sulks,' she said.

He glanced at the clock. It was nine-twenty. 'Time you were resting, my dear,' he announced primly. The jalousie had worked free at last and was clacking wildly against the wall. He opened the window to fasten it and the December wind ravished the cloying heart of the room. He caught the shutter and fixed it.

'Well,' cried Miss Bellingham, 'how *did* you find out?'

'Hush . . .'

'It doesn't seem to me such an extraordinary question,' she complained, but in a more controlled voice.

'There's no mystery—he told me. Or rather he told Minna. You know her naïvety—she asked him outright.'

'And he said yes?'

'He blushed, if I remember.'

Miss Bellingham was touched. 'Well he's different to Pauly. Pauly wrote things when he was twelve and we were all forced to read them. And when he was twenty he'd buy up nearly the whole issue of a magazine that happened to contain one of his tales. You'd never have called Pauly indifferent about what he wrote!'

'Or modest either,' retorted Mr Winsley with distinct asperity.

'That old middle-class thing!'

He looked down at her, catching at a ghostly flirtatiousness. Bending arcoss the chair, he patted her hand.

'You've got to rest,' he scolded in a babyish, chin-chucking voice.

'You were a fool, Caddie, weren't you? Say you were!'

'I must get that shutter mended,' he said in a highly-concerned way.

'First a doll and now a doormat—but it's what you must have wanted!'

'Is there anything else?' asked Mr Winsley, moving about, piling up flocky little cushions, tidying books and papers, placing two sleeping tablets in a stained Rockingham saucer and last of all, tugging a curtain back and revealing a big, untidy bed.

There was a long pause. Miss Bellingham had retrieved *The Times* from where it had fallen behind its rack and now her hands crackled through it like trapped birds. Her hair in contrast with the newspaper was whiter than ever. Above her head, a clock built into a model of St Martin-in-the-Fields went tuk-tuk, tuk-tuk. Deep down in the chasm of the street a car purred by.

'Caddie.'

'Mm?'

'Caddie—it's the last time. Tell me, did it *really* seem so truly—utterly . . . impossible . . .? *Then*, I mean?'

'Why do you ask?' he said sharply, but not unkindly. 'The whole point surely is that it was *then* and not—not later. Isn't that the answer? Anyway, why bring it up again now?'

Miss Bellingham toyed with a sleeping pill. She moved it gently across the painted saucer, pushing it on from rose to rose with a varnished nail.

'You always did get out of things,' she retorted equably.

It is your plight that you make not the faintest attempt to, thought Mr Winsley. 'Sleep well,' he said.

He was at the door when she called, 'Cadman!' She had clambered out of the chair and was bunching her hair between fluttering fingers. Shawls strewed the carpet. 'Tell Mr Brand that I would like to see him now.'

'Now?' he expostulated.

Miss Bellingham didn't answer. Without looking again he knew she was aspen with her curious, sudden, decrepit anger.

★

'And this,' Bateson was saying, 'is Big School.' He flung wide a door like a guide announcing the Medici apartments. He climbed on a desk, struck a match and lit the gas. The room swam up out of the night. It's really rather fine, thought Richard, in spite of a sour chilliness which spread a damp bloom over everything. Four long naked windows looked out to the street. There was something immensely theatrical in their moon-flooded bareness. A dais stood at the far end and on the dais, a pale, scratched table. To the right was an upright piano, its pedals trod to wafery gold. Over the piano was a photograph of Queen Alexandra wearing dozens of necklaces. A mouse sped into the skirting. Bateson grabbed a ruler and lunged at it wildly, then lifting a desk-flap he said: 'There's a particular squalor for every age; the immediate prepubescent for example. Take a look.'

Richard saw a cooking-apple with large brown bites in it, a torn *Euclid,* a pen inexplicably impaling a Swan Vesta box, a truncheon of torn *Wizards,* a spongy publication called *The Hangman's Daughter*; nibs, rubbers, a gnawed cap . . . a slab of unthinkable toffee.

Bateson shook his head. '*Nature morte* indeed,' he said. He closed the lid. 'Now you know what you're in for!'

'How many pupils are there altogether?' asked Richard.

'Sixty-one.'

'Oh yes, sixty-one—I remember Mr Winsley telling me now. I suppose that it's full? It would have to be, I mean, to make it pay?'

Bateson heaved himself up to his handsome height from where he had been lolling across the back desks. The gas arm hissed a warning just above his neat head.

'You're not trying to tell me that there's money in it, are you, old boy? Listen to me; Copdock's a goner. Finished. I mean it! It's had its moments and there have been enough shekels rolling in to keep the Belle in gin and vermouth, but for heaven's sake don't be an ass and kid yourself with things like "seats of learning" and "Alma Mater". All that you are going to find here are the rags and tatters of academic opportunism.'

'You tell me what comes next then,' said Richard, a little dashed, but amused.

'Next,' repeated Bateson. 'Company, sharrrn!' he bawled at the benign blackboards. 'That's what's next.'

'I don't believe that—not entirely.'

'I don't *want* a bloody war,' said Bateson, suddenly aware that it might appear that he did.

'What is it that you don't want, Bateson?' asked Mr Winsley coming in unexpectedly. His white, narrow face was set with irritation. 'Incidentally, have you two been properly introduced? Tom Bateson—Richard—er—Brand . . .'

'We were discussing the war,' explained Bateson.

'But there isn't a war.'

'Ah, but there might be!' retorted Bateson with mock enthusiasm. 'Brand is clever, you know. He's just been explaining the stained-glass window on the stairs. It's by Forester or somebody who was a follower of Burne-Jones. Did you know that? Nobody ever told *me*.'

'It's a memorial to Miss Bellingham's sister, Lady Abbott,' said Mr Winsley.

'It's very good,' added Richard, feeling it was time to praise something. He was about to say, 'of its kind,' meaning of its period, setting, place; but Mr Winsley was staring at them in turn, gathering up all the objections in reach and doing so with an ominous, pouncing kind of silence. He saw himself as a custodian of the past and it was something that he just wouldn't put up with, this wilful toppling down of earlier values. When it was obvious that Richard meant what he had said Mr Winsley was a trifle mollified.

'Before I forget it, Brand,' he said heavily, the change to surnames the phantom of his disfavour, 'Miss Bellingham wishes you to go to her room.'

Richard was appalled. It was like waiting for an operation for months and months and then somebody saying, 'Oh, and before I forget it . . . if you could just step along to the theatre we could do that little job now . . .' His new-kid feeling came back with a rush. In the sparse interval caused by his astonishment Bateson turned out the light. Mr Winsley was talking to him, telling him where to go.

'Don't remain too long. You mustn't tire her.'

Unnecessary, thought Richard. Well, get it over. But since she had waited so long, couldn't she go on waiting until tomorrow, say? Bateson, whether out of inquisitiveness or kindness, followed him. That was a relief, but not for long.

'Bateson,' called Mr Winsley (Bateson was obviously in favour), 'Bateson, about that vaulting-horse. Oughn't we to be able to fix it up a bit . . .?'

Bateson disappeared through the patched baize door and Richard was alone. He found the room easily enough. It was just a matter of going up and up. He knocked warily at first and when there was no reply, more firmly.

'Come in!' It was faint. He wasn't certain whether he heard it or imagined it. She was placing a book, face-downwards, on her lap. Behind her the tall oil lamp rose up like a moon. Her hair, bright in its death, rushed up towards it in an albescent flood. Richard couldn't see her face.

'Sit there, will you,' she said.

The chair was too small. Too low as well. His legs stuck up like scissors. By his side was a table quite mountainous with dusty letters and curling yellow bills on crazy spikes. Miss Bellingham held out a hand which, with its delicate orange and purple blotches and the watery shrine of her rings, was like a knot of withering blooms. Richard stood up and took it gently. He expected it to be as soft as flowers, but it was as hard as wood. Before he could sit again, she seized a tray covered with dirty cups and plates and said: 'This is in our way.'

He put it on a platform of encyclopaedias piled up on the floor and took good care when he came back to sit in the far-side chair. But not for long.

'No, *here*, Mr Brand.'

So he took the uncomfortable seat again.

'I like to think that people are happy,' she said. Two gnat-sized flecks of light in the twin hollows of her face showed that she was examining him.

'I'm sure I shall be,' answered Richard, thinking that she had sent for him to make conventional conversation about his appointment.

'Why?' asked Miss Bellingham.

This was disconcerting.

'Well I wasn't really happy at the bank,' he confessed.

'What bank?'

'Goodyear's—at Ipswich. It was my first job—I—I wrote all about it in my application.'

'I expect you did,' Miss Bellingham answered tartly.

The huge marble clock chimed ten. Richard felt extraordinarily tired. He felt, too, that his weariness must extend to everything about him, to the cramped room, to the old woman with her restless face. To the books, to the pictures slung against the walls with a tangle of cords.

'Perhaps you would rather I came back in the morning . . . It's late now . . .' he began.

'Now?' she said, 'Morning? What's the difference to me? Can you tell me that?'

Richard smiled to hide his slight embarrassment.

'Unless you mean that you are tired!'

'No, not at all,' he protested. But he was. Deathly. Why, he couldn't think.

'The duties cannot be called onerous, Mr Brand. The secret is to work steadily, *patiently*, through the syllabus, with enthusiasm if you like, but not with fervour. The two are different, you know. I have always distrusted fervour. Young men who have that generally have bad breath as well! You must keep order, of course. Enforce the *utmost* politeness, because in the long run that is the most to be hoped for in the type of boy who passes through Copdock. What did Wordsworth say? "The youth, who daily farther from the east must travel, still is Nature's priest." Well, nobody could be more wrong at times than Wordsworth. Those smelly creatures you will be paid to instruct are grossly natural—and so quite un-priestly. It speaks for itself, doesn't it? *Why* did I do it? Well, you may well ask that.'

But Richard was too bewildered to ask anything. His eyes wandered about the room in a game of their own. One long gilt, two maple, one chipped gilt, a looking-glass—that didn't count; a freckling of miniatures in ebony rings . . .

'You admire pictures?' she asked. 'That one there is a Samuel Palmer. Copy-cat,' she added obscurely.

'It's a good one,' said Richard, straining to see it better without getting up.

'How do you know—are you an expert?'

He sank back uncomfortably, sensing mockery.

'Well are you?'

He shook his head. 'I meant that I like it.'

'And so what you happen to like is good?'

'I don't know, but isn't that the way most people make their assessments . . .?'

'Quite likely—and so accounts for the amount of bad taste in the world, I suppose.'

'Perhaps if I saw it in the daylight,' Richard said, stepping back from the conversational quagmire. He thought Miss Bellingham's head nodded a little. He noticed her face for the first time. She had moved and the lamp rained down on it. There was a stain under each eye like a cicatrix and her neck was scrabbled together in some seemliness and held tightly in a stiff *broderie anglaise* band.

'I have been young, of course, but never beautiful.'

He felt like somebody discovered peeping. I must get out, he thought; hurry away from this guttering life. Toothpaste might drive the atmosphere of the room from his mouth, but how would he shake it from his clothes! All tomorrow it would nudge him, this sweet stale room so blatant in decay. Besides, she *saw* so much! Every particle of a thought was seized on by her greedy perception.

'Whereas,' she continued with a certain limited daring '*you* might be said to be both . . .'

A gulf-like silence parted them. Unperturbed, Miss Bellingham leaned out of her chair and began to search about her in a rather desperate way. Her hands straggled feebly in the recesses of the upholstery and then through contents of a green velvet bag slung from clicking tortoise-shell handles at her side.

'I've lost it,' she said, 'No, no—here it is.' She pointed. It was on the floor, Sir Paul's letter in its fine white envelope with the stamps stuck on anyhow. She took it from Richard and waving it at him said: 'People are so kind to the really old; they tell them everything. It is because they expect to discover some discretion at the end. Being a writer you will have half an understanding of such things, Mr Brand.'

'It wasn't in my references,' smiled Richard. He felt a bit better. He wondered how she had found out about his writing.

'It would hardly need to be. We asked for no talent beyond those required for the working of the syllabus.'

'I only wondered how you knew—how Mr Winsley knew?'
'Oh, *he* guessed,' she said. 'He's a great guesser. Not that you are likely to do much in the next few years; you're not the type. Paul now, he's my nephew,' she squeezed the envelope and it cracked open, 'he was always so much *doing* that he found inaction superfluous! A change, you must admit, to the usual order of things! He wrote *Tiger-moth* when he was fourteen . . .'

Richard listened, but with half an ear. A wind had sprung up and wound itself dreamily about the window, bringing with it a welcome sense of isolation. It reminded him that he was free, that this room, Copdock, Stourfriston itself were only conventions; that beyond them were mountains and seas and illimitable hazards and rewards. It was like reading Shakespeare or like Quentin's habit of saying 'Where will it all end . . .?' by which he meant a cry of mock despair, but which made Richard feel extraordinarily optimistic. Where? Why it might be anywhere! It was exhilarating. It was the other thing which made him sad; the unending regularity and what people called 'security'. When the wind flagged he heard her voice. She became for him just a poor old woman chattering about the past and about her family. He paid little attention, although sometimes he smiled and nodded. She was talking about books. Had he read Sir Paul Abbott? What a question! God! what wouldn't he give for *that* kind of ability! Now it was nephew again. Nephew and the celebrated Sir Paul, they grew one in the same breath; they parted. They were twin orbs moving across each other, illuminating then obliterating each other. Nephew was gold—*very* precious it seemed, by the way Miss Bellingham spoke of him. Sir Paul was purple (but only in the very best sense). They swam together in the stream of her talk and just when they might be said to be one and the same, nephew spun free; a relation only.

'My sister's only son,' she explained with her eyes fixed on something over his head.

Why am I so tired? Richard wondered. Sleep was fast becoming more than a nodding acquaintance. It had certainly been a long day. He found it hard to believe that parts of it were this particular day at all. Breakfast at Lafney for instance. Was that today? The bookies in the train? . . .

Weren't they years ago? But she was asking him something. He must grab at consciousness. He did so and the effect made him jerk forward in a way that it was impossible to hide. He felt for his handkerchief, straightened his tie—anything than let her see that he was dozing—and coughed.

'If you see Matron,' said Miss Bellingham, interrupting her more important conversation, 'she'll set you up with a gargle.'

'Sorry,' he muttered.

'You see,' she went on with extreme clarity, 'Sheldon's been shut up since nineteen-twenty-seven. There's been a housekeeper of course, but there will be a great deal to do—much more than ordinary servants can cope with. You could catalogue, couldn't you? He says, Pauly, you know,—well I'll read it to you.'

Miss Bellingham's nephew and Sir Paul Abbott suddenly became one. Snap! It was incredible! Just wait, thought Richard, wait until I tell Quenny! They had both known about Sheldon, of course, and of it belonging to Sir Paul. But he had never lived there and the house, spread goldenly behind a deep screen of parkland, watched time and traffic trundling by, uncared for, uncaring, its beauty undiminished by neglect. Richard and Quentin had propped their bicycles up against the palings and stared at it and Sheldon had stared back from all its regular windows. Lady Abbott had been a Miss Bellingham then? Neither he nor Quentin had supposed that, although it was the sort of thing Quentin usually knew. Richard was now quite painfully awake. What was Miss Bellingham saying? Nothing. She was waiting. It was his turn. (But Quenny—wait till he heard! The best they could muster at March was a self-published poet, a Mr Gridbitter.)

'When would Sir Paul like me to see him?' he asked.

'It could only be on a Sunday, couldn't it' retorted Miss Bellingham pointedly. 'What am I to say—that you would like to? That you will?'

'I should like to very much,' answered Richard.

'Then I shall just say that.'

'Will you? Thank you.'

'Don't be too ready with your thanks.'

'But it's exactly the kind of thing I should love to do,' he protested, not at all nervous of her now, but unhappy about the ease with which she switched from consideration into malice.

She let his eagerness pass. She placed her cold, hard little fingers together and bent them weakly in and out. 'Now tell me,' she said, 'you write too? Or you want to? Is that it? We'll get this point straight first, shall we? You're a writer, an embryonic one, if you like, but that's better than being the other kind—*manqué*, you know. But there, you're too young to be *manqué* anything as yet. Do you hope to be married Mr Brand?'

'Blast, blast!' he thought. She was remorseless. There were old women like that in Lafney. There was nothing they couldn't ask. He smudged any directness in his reply by rising and stroking the chair cushions straight. The clock said ten-to-eleven.

'Then don't leave it too long,' she insisted in a vague, accusative voice. 'Pauly put it off and *put* it off—and now there's nothing to stop him traipsing across the world a hundred times if he wanted to. Nothing *affectionate*, you know.'

In the silence that followed, Richard walked gently to the door. The dying fire winked across furniture and pictures. Miss Bellingham in her tangle of stuffs—the formal sheen of the top half of her dress, the crochet shawls—sat motionless. Yellow lamplight poured across her hair. The walls were lively with photographed eyes. Stunted hyacinths in an earthenware bowl sent up a few sweet nodules of bloom in their black ring of earth. The carpet was spattered with letter-paper. Is there anything more? he wanted to ask, knowing there could be very little.

'Are you off, Mr Brand?'

'It's late,' he answered gently.

'I trust that you will like Mr Winsley.'

'Oh, yes.'

'And Mr Bateson's your neighbour, I'm told.'

He waited.

Miss Bellingham wagged her snowy head, a pensive gesture at once marquise and senile. Her hands began to pluck at Sir Paul's letter, slipping from her lap. She crammed it back into its envelope.

'Well then, that's settled, is it? We'll take it you've come—and come to stay.' She shrugged as a wisp of humour possessed her. Holding up her hands, she held out her skinny fingers wider and wider until they looked like stripped fan-sticks. 'Not to say, outstay,' she added mordantly.

Richard didn't notice Mr Winsley at first. It was dark on the landing. Then he heard a sound like outraged mice. It was Mr Winsley's nails in a furious tattoo against a window-pane. A second later he had brushed past him, said nothing, flung wide Miss Bellingham's door without knocking and disappeared. Walking slowly, Richard went down all the carpetless stairs until he found his own room. It was icy.

3

EDWINA BRAND paused when her duster reached the automatic calendar. She stared at it and the calendar returned her gaze with a dull malachite intensity. Of all the rubbish in this room, she thought irritably, that thing wins hands down by its utter futility! How could one have any faith in a date that one had brought about oneself? A stud was pressed and a day, a month, a year even, fled by; indicating no predecessor, intimating no future. This morning for instance it said 'Friday 4th January 1939'—but who was going to prove it? It would have to be on the purest assumption that she would have to believe that Sunday was the sixth when the Crawfords were coming. Quentin had given it to her, she recalled; a birthday or a Christmas. She lifted it to see. 'For Mummy from Quenny on her 100th birthday. X X X.' That was Quentin, even then! He told one nothing. She passed on, dusting idly, not very well, hardly shifting things; books, shepherdesses, silver cups—the last fairly explicit regarding its origins (Trim House, R. L. Brand, 1934), mats, more books, and photographs in living frames. Then she arrived at a looking-glass and observed herself very privately.

Odd, she thought, how one never saw it approaching. Her hair, for instance, surely it was only that peculiar fawny colour early in the morning? She didn't have hair like that all day? It used to be so bright. Lovely! Edwina gave her nose a searching scrutiny. Then her eyes. Her eyes, she decided, now quite lost in reflections, *they* were still charming. There was loyalty for you! Something at least which had stood fast in all the fading and awaying . . . It was an agreeable discovery. Leaning forward in her faintly-mocking appraisal, she avoided the thin, tired skin at her throat, so white, so pitifully soft, and gazed fully into the depths of her own dark vision.

'Hopeless, if you ask me.'

'Quentin!' Edwina was really mortified. She would have said that something was in her eye if she were more practiced in fibs. Instead she sought to cover her embarrassment by fingering the ornament on her dress and giving brave little jabs to the puffy wings of her hair. 'Why must you always come down in your dressing-gown?' she scolded. 'It really is an unpleasant habit.'

'How witty we are this morning,' Quentin replied, flicking the knotty end of a trailing rope girdle out with his feet . . . 'It *is* a habit, although I disagree about it being unpleasant. How on earth did you guess? I bought it off a boy who is a spoilt Buchmanite.'

'What is he now?' asked Richard, pausing to shiver as he made his way to the downstairs bathroom.

'He is a very private secretary.'

'Hurry, Richie!' shouted Edwina from the kitchen. She was darting to and fro with knives and plates. 'Scrambled eggs, porridge if you can bear it, but *do* hurry! You know there's no help today and Stella feels she must come home again this week-end *and* the Crawfords coming as well! Christmas,' she wondered aloud, grappling with toast and slotting it home in the rack, 'is it worth it? It's taken me about an hour just to pick up the cards and put them down again. And awful heaps of half-eaten things.'

'Did I hear you say "Crawfords", Mum?'

'Oh shut up, Quentin! There are times,' she continued with random belligerency as she made her way to the sink, when schoolmasters' holidays can seem most dreadfully protracted.'

Richard left them to their affectionate war. It had been going on for years now and he knew it could never stop since it concealed some more terrible belligerency. The bathroom glittered with its frugal amenities. It wasn't a very good bathroom but it was the wildest luxury after the gurgling horrors of Copdock. But any bathroom was a fine place where Richard was concerned. It was not that he shared Quentin's animal lust for comfort. There was a different reason. In this warm, white cell he found he could think, which for him meant, dream. There it was, a tiled, be-towelled sanctuary in which a steamy anchorite might indulge his imagination. There was no past and no future; only a moist, warm, delicious present. The steam grew into a chiaroscuro of ideas. Words flooded up, effortless, strange, eclectic, shining. They came, but alas they went. It was hopeless trying to write words down in a bathroom. Richard had tried and you couldn't. He shaved thoughtfully with the bath taps thundering in his ears. What was it that brought Quentin and himself home, he wondered for the hundredth time, drawing pink lanes through the soap with his razor. Or, rather, what was it that didn't take them away? Of course there was March and Copdock, but neither he nor Quentin was really in either place. They were here, in Lafney, in 'The Portway', an absolutely ugly little villa hanging above the sea which had become their home after the move from the rectory. And even The Portway showed a lack of continuity in its externals only. Inside it might have been the rectory all over again. Nothing had changed. There wasn't a chair which didn't creak with reminders and the tables were positively expansive with anecdote. He had only to take Christmas Eve. He had been sitting on an awkward armless little chair, limp after so much Copdock and Quentin's more discreet reminiscences of March. His mother sat opposite and Quentin read, his hands to his face and his eyes glinting methodically as they fell from line to line between parted fingers. Suddenly Richard heard it, a sound no louder than the destruction of a campion on a summer's day. Pop! went the present.

He was where he was, in the same chair, but the chair was in the rectory. It was Christmas and the room smelt foody and full. The chair, he remembered, gave him great discomfort. He was pressed somehow too near its rail of carved walnut roses. Quentin and the other children were jiggling round him in fierce glee. They were yelling, 'Mrs Brand . . . Mummy . . . Dick hasn't pulled his cracker! He hasn't. Look, it's here

... he won't!' He had wanted to save it, Richard had lied. But Quentin knew why. He knew everything—always the real reason behind frightened behaviour. 'Pull it now—*now*!' he had insisted. Then Richard had screamed, a terrible noise so cut off from himself and his usual placid control that its unreality was terrifying and for a minute he found himself listening to his own temper with disdain and detachment, as though it was someone else's. When the shame asserted itself, crawling across his flesh in a burning rash, he had tried to blot the whole room and life itself out, by throwing his body against the plump upholstery, drawing in great lungfuls of its musty breath. His tears had stained the tapestry unicorns and for consolation he had counted the tight buttons over and over again. There were ten. Until that particular moment on Christmas Eve the small grief had vanished. It had been swirled down stream like a straw of hurtful experience in the welter of time.

This was only one reminder. There were countless others, indigenous to that life and to this. There was Richard's childhood and the man he was now. Did Quentin feel such things? There was no sign that he did. But then Quentin was chameleon, donning colours so lavishly in his outward dissemblings that he could hide behind a brilliant panache and so be Quentin all the time. Quentin was sure of himself because he was sure of others. As for Richard, he had never been sure of anything. There lay their difference.

The bathroom wasn't working at all well this morning, Richard decided. It was making him morbid. He rushed through the rest of his toilet and then into breakfast. They had started. Edwina observed him covertly as he sat down. It was a habit of hers these days to allow herself a generous helping of awareness where other people were concerned. As the rector's wife she had been too nice for too long. If she was apt to stare somewhat at times, it was only to insist that she should not be deceived. Yet she was—as indeed she was bound to be since her unworldliness was of the chronically myopic kind. At this very moment she was convinced that she saw both Richard and Quentin. But, of course, she didn't. The two young men battling for *The Times* were just her 'boys', her adorable ungainly children. So she continued, blessedly oblivious of the reality of keeping open house for closely-related strangers.

People, Edwina recalled, were inclined to say that Richard had a 'nice' face—meaning that it was open and frank and unobjectionable, and that also its unfinished look made it sufficiently identical to so many other young English faces for it not to give reason for worrying speculation. Not so Quentin. People behaved very differently in his case. His decided beauty quelled them. Neither could they ignore it, it was too factual, too apparent. It was so decidely off-(or on-) putting that it usually had the effect of a remarkable blemish. It divided his aquaintanceship into those who were extra kind and those who were extra cold. He really was terribly sweet, thought Edwina, blind to all this. But then they both were. She wouldn't make favourites. She loved them equally. Nobody would take them for brothers, people also said. Edwina answered that she was pleased to hear it. But since she did not add her reason for such a peculiar reply, which was that she felt dreadfully sorry for the 'alike as peas' kind of family, so many repetitions of eyes and chins and noses merely making her flinch, the statement was generally regarded as one of her more gnomic utterances. Edwina gets vaguer and vaguer, they said.

But there was nothing obtuse in what she wanted to say this morning. 'I really don't know quite how to broach this,' she confessed, digging a server into the ham and eggs.

'Oh, just as it comes,' answered Quentin airily.

'Not *this*,' retorted Edwina, giving the food a jab. 'You know I'm worried stiff about your future—I'm serious now,' she insisted. 'You also know that neither your father nor myself ever wanted to force you into any decision which was other than your own. Oh, dear!' she said—the toast rack had slipped sideways and carefully emptied itself among the coffee things—'Richard, it's going to have your cup over any minute! What was I saying—? Oh, yes; the future.'

'But not at breakfast, not *now*, at any rate' said Quentin.

'What's wrong with now?' demanded Edwina.

'It's so early for one thing.'

'But is it? You're twenty-five. When Dads was twenty-five . . .'

'I'm twenty-four. I shall be twenty-five *next* Friday. Time is one of the quantities one should never be liberal with. There's a man here,' he went on in his quick clever voice which seemed to dote on irrelevance, 'who after thirty-one years as the Secretary of Gray's Club has taken Buddhist vows and now lives in solitude with fifteen hundred monks in Tibet.' He rattled the paper in her direction.

'Quentin, dear, do listen. If I seem to be talking particularly to you, it's because yours is a different position from Dick's. You had Cambridge, and, to be quite blunt, you should have gone on.'

'Gone on to Ely, I suppose you mean?'

'Well,' enquired Edwina, the hint of defence in her voice, 'isn't that what you wanted to do?'

'Yes—when I was eighteen.'

'Then what stopped you?'

'Do you really want to know?' he asked.

'No, no!' retorted Edwina hurriedly. She blamed herself. She might have known that any prolonged talk with Quentin on such a subject as his future was out of the question. He grew more and more outlandish in the things that he thought he could say. It needed all her concentration at times to misinterpret them. 'I won't say,' she went on, 'that being ordained was *all* your father hoped for. You know he would have been the first to insist that you should be absolutely free in such a matter. But I've got to see you settled—both of you if it comes to that.'

'I'm settled enough,' announced Richard with deliberate irony. The extreme seediness of the Copdock appointment fell all about him like a scrofulous cloak discarded by a vindictive prophet. All this concern about whether Quentin became a parson—God help them! But what of himself?

His swift depression was obvious.

'Copdock isn't a *public* school,' said Edwina soothingly, 'but it's an awfully good school of its kind. I've heard people say it's a very unusual school. You could say it has distinction . . .' She paused, exhausted by what she liked to fancy was her debate. Peering over the glittering rim of her cup she regarded these children of hers and decided that their charm, like the grasshopper's, could be a burden.

'Winsley actually runs it,' said Richard in a sudden desire to cover up his real discontents in front of his brother.

'What does she do then?' asked Quentin.

'The Belle . . .?'

'The Belle,' repeated Quentin. 'Is she, would you say . . .?'

'You know she's as old as the hills; she's eighty-six.'

Quentin shuddered.

'She's awfully nice. Witty too. She knew Maria Montessori. I like her,' he added. Having made a stand for Copdock he felt it was his duty to exploit it.

'Of course you do,' said Quentin evenly, splurging a golden hill of marmalade into his toast, 'But then you're so 'nice' yourself. You're as generous as a hamper. Something for everybody.'

There was a suggestion of a storm. It drifted across to Edwina who had given up her argument to read her letters. She hoped that they weren't going to quarrel. But the oleaginous kindliness of the season was having its effect so far as Quentin was concerned. He wanted to break out. She could tell it by the frigid poise of his head, a stance he had carried forward from childhood.

'There was a man at Trinity rather like you,' Quentin was saying. 'His name was Munsen-Orle, no actual friend, but a near acquaintance. He was so damned—sorry, Mummy—*polite* for one thing. He just couldn't refuse an invitation, however boring. He was jolly nice to old ladies. "I can't manage Tuesday," he once said to me, "It's my night for visiting Mrs Teeming—she used to be the postmistress of Royston, you know." But it might equally well be a duchess. And once he introduced me to a dear little man in King's Parade. "I expect you know Mr Herbert Wells," he said. That was fine, but the very next day he insisted that I accompany him to the Dorothy Café to have tea with a posse of hikers all set for determining the Hog's Back. A pomander, you might call him, with relationships sticking out in so many directions that they made it quite impossible to get near to the heart of Munsen-Orle himself. . . .'

He's away, thought Richard, a backwards journey to all those spirited Cambridge evenings. Would he always talk like that? It was all right now, but later the words would rattle like pebbles in a can. 'It's because you only believe in a tight, right little circle,' he accused. Yet it wasn't true and he knew it. To do that meant that you were scared, and Quentin, when it came to it, had the most alarming courage.

'N-n-no . . .' answered Quentin consideringly. 'All I want to know—and I really want to know—is *why* you have to go about with all those dreary people that we hear of. *Why* sit in pubs making up to the bores, why, if I may say so, foster relationships with those you are in fundamental enmity with? I only want to know . . .'

'Fundamental *what* . . .?' asked Edwina, surfacing from the post. Her letters were too equable to have such words as 'fundamental' anything lumbering through them. She stuffed the one she was reading back into its envelope.

'He means Bateson, I suppose,' said Richard.

Quentin did not answer.

'Oh!' said Edwina in a suddenly disinterested voice. The conversation assumed an immediate pointlessness where she was concerned. It was just the children arguing. She began to clear away. 'Anyway,' she added, 'what could Quenny know of Mr Bateson?'

'Lots,' said Quentin. 'Haven't I had him for every meal— Tom Bateson, the jolly old coach, all beer and bonhomie!'

'So it's how does Bateson fit in with my conception of poetry and life. Well, if you must know, this type fits in very well.'

'Concessionally speaking, of course,' said Quentin with lively mockery.

It was here at this point that Richard should have begun to lose his temper. But he didn't. It was becoming one of those things which needed an effort to bring them off. 'What about your own friends?' he retorted, knowing that here he was at a great advantage. Quentin's friends were the shadows of shadows: myriad, but unsubstantial. They must be since nobody had seen them. They wrote prolifically. Quentin's forwarded post was a revelation and a wonder to the Lafney post-office staff. But he let little of what they wrote out into the common air. Occasionally a bold name would tumble from his talk with a regrettable jingle, like a penny speeding up the aisle. They got from him only the smallest of small change.

'What happened to that nice boy who came here just after you both took Schools?' enquired Edwina.

'Marston,' said Quentin. 'Africa—Colonial Service.'

'Does he like it?'

'I've no idea—I suppose so.'

'But didn't he want to paint? . . . I seem to remember him saying so.'

'Well, he can paint in Africa—jolly good place to paint.'

'Do you hear from him? That's all I wondered,' persisted Edwina. 'Oh, look here,' she added in the swift fluster that so easily overtook her, 'it's ten—or nearly!' She whisked the mats together and so discovered Sir Paul's letter. For a moment she was certain it was one of those cream embossed envelopes bought over the counter. Friends frequently wrote to her from hotels and post-offices in an excess of remembrance following some little jaunt. Her glasses had hid themselves. Holding the letter close to her nose, she made out the accomplished hand. 'Richard,' she said, almost reluctantly, 'it's for you.'

It was a brief letter, polite, concise and unambiguous, but he read through it twice before answering Quentin's unspoken question.

'It's from Sir Paul Abbott.'

'He has some punctuation difficulty, perhaps?' Quentin's mockery, however, was for once bereft of his driving energy. He pushed away from the breakfast table and stood up, tall and most deliberately casual. The cigarette bouncing on the lid of his silver case jumped like a nerve. He seemed to be groping for something, a word, a reason. 'How—why?' he asked outright, because if what Richard was saying was true, it was so extraordinary.

'Well, read it.' Richard flicked the stone-grey page across the table.

' "Brown's Hotel," ' read Quentin out loud—'The handwriting! Like the Recording Angel's! "Dear Mr Brand, I am writing at once to thank you for listening so sympathetically to the proposition I put to my aunt Miss Bellingham just before Christmas. The task won't be wearisome—or I trust that it won't—only a matter of getting things back into their proper places, books and papers which cannot be left to any ordinary help. But I'll say no more in this note than to beg you to come to Sheldon and see for yourself. I leave this hotel on Tuesday next. Would the *following* Tuesday suit you? Please come to dinner then. Sheldon is four miles from Copdock, not at all as the crow flies, but you will find it, no doubt. Take the St Edmundsbury Road.

Yours sincerely, Paul Abbott . . ." '

*

Stella arrived at six. She was the eldest of the Brand children by a number of years. In all, in her appearance, in her interests, her job and her far too desperate loyalties, she should, one felt, have added up to some dull accord. She was the kind of person you *expect* to find complete. She should have been a fugue, close-knit and sustained, against whose endless contrapuntal the wilder themes and grace-notes of her more erratic brothers might have soared with effect and impunity. But she wasn't. Her own enviable poise was maintained by too much common sense. It excluded every scrap of the uncommon kind and she could be ungenerous and rather cruel without knowing it. From similar dark burnt-gold eyes as Quentin's she saw only a workaday world which caused her few complaints. Quentin found her particularly bewildering. He wasn't even certain that he liked her. Her huge sanity floored him. The difference was that he had a hundred answers to every question posed by life and Stella had but one. It was the obvious one, of course. Quentin now took good care not to ask his sister's opinion of anything that really mattered to him, but he would endure, with a rather flinching smile, her blunt little observations on subjects he found expendable.

Nor was she beautiful. All the Brand features were present in her neat, practical head; the squarish nose, the fine rich eyes—but when added up they amounted to an actual plainness. Clothes, make-up, even a faint interest in how she appeared to others, might have lessened this. But Stella didn't care. Not remotely. Yet it still was quite mystifying that she wasn't beautiful, that is, until you accepted the fact that beauty of person is a diffuse quality, a merging of bone and spirit, flesh, colour and the imaginative heart. Stella certainly kept all her wits about her, but nicely pigeon-holed. They didn't coalesce into a personality. She used her mental equipment like so many efficient gadgets. And finally, she was never really *changed* by what she thought. Her reaction to practically everything was cerebral, certainly, but it was the cerebration which could be ascribed to a highly gifted carpenter. She had very lovely, very white hands.

They heard her turn in at the gate in her small old, shuddering Austin.

'I'm brimming with news,' she announced. She flung her hat and rug down on the couch and hurried to the fire.

'Don't start! don't start!' called Edwina anxiously, running in and out with water glasses, side-plates and napkins. She adored Stella's gossip. It was all gossip should be, surprising, accurate and straightforward—unlike Quentin's unfathomable small-talk or, for that matter, Richard's unwilling conclusions.

'Help me,' said Stella, 'there's lots more.'

Among the laurels the Austin shone yellow-paned like a little lit-up room. The back seat was a mountain of papers, vacuum flasks, food tins, maps, books and leathery things. There was also a sparkling ebony-bright tin helmet marked W.

'The typewriter,' she said. 'Carry that, will you, Dicky.'

'You're not going to work?'

'I must. I've got to give a talk at Harrods.'

'Harrods . . .?'

'It's called "Reading trends for adolescents"—it's their National Book Week, or something.'

Stella was famous. She lived in a windy flat in Ipswich and wrote stories for girls. They had been enormously successful. The actual grand sweep of her achievement still startled her. The 'Petunia' books had caught on. They had certainly accumulated. One every six months she found was nothing and now their titles made a long, solid slip in the publisher's catalogues and a hefty wedge in the public libraries' card indexes. Even more miraculous were the astonishing cheques drifting through her letter-box. Just for this! she would beam to herself, shuffling the day's scrawling effort together as the constant breeze carried in the cheerful cretonne from the ever-wide window. She looked around her girlish eyrie. The plaster rabbits hunched along the mantelpiece glowed cosily. Stick by us. they seemed to say, and we'll jolly well stick by you. For Stella there was small effort needed in complying.

'What do you think?' she asked in her easy, rather rushed voice when they were at last all settled, 'I've told Dicky just now—I'm giving a talk at Harrods.'

'A talk at Harrods . . ?' Quentin rocked gently. A talk at Derry and Toms . . . 'If it's successful,' he enquired, 'shall you be taking it on to the Home and Colonial—or perhaps Swan and Edgars might like it. The possibilities are infinite . . .'

'*Everything* isn't funny,' Edwina declared.

Stella explained.

As they bickered, Richard ate silently. All through the meal Sir Paul's letter sent out a crisp morse in his pocket. He would have liked to tell Stella before she was led away into Quentin's fantasy of the oblique and the embellished from which she would return believing nothing. Or to get the news in before his mother thought of it. But Edwina was eating hurriedly with one eye on the clock.

'It's an awful pity,' she said, 'just when you're all home together, but I've got to leave you for an hour or so. I've promised to attend a meeting, an evacuation committee at the Infirmary. I shan't be long.'

This was just the sort of remark to have set off Quentin's nervous, whooping mirth. '"An evacuation committee,"' he repeated, '"at the Infirmary . ."' Yet he didn't. Instead a curious change came over him. His face grew suddenly tormented. 'All these ridiculous preparations!' he cried, 'all this interference! Why can't everybody talk of something else?' For a moment he hesitated, unable to go on, then, with his face oddly white and set, he hurried from the room.

'But . . .' said Edwina helplessly.

'Don't worry, Mum,' said Stella in a particularly comfortable voice. 'It's really,' she added with unusual discernment, 'because he feels all these directives personally—you know, all the gas-masks, conscription talk, evacuation, trenches in Hyde Park. Poor Quenny! the ladders are being propped against his precious ivory tower!'

'He's entitled to his life,' said Richard, not meaning to be sententious, but suddenly seeing Quentin's predicament very clearly.

'We all are, dear,' replied Edwina vaguely. It's my fault, she thought. I'm clumsy. How funny they were when you came to think about it; not Stell, of course—just the boys. If only she knew what it was all about. If only someone would *tell* her! She sighed because she knew no one ever would. The fact that she would be always in the dark, however, allowed her a little self-justified anger. 'Why, anyway, should Quentin think of himself so very particularly? If *he* couldn't bear the word "sandbag"—why should we? One had to!' Castigating Quentin was such a luxury so far as Edwina was concerned, that having begun it she used it as an opportunity to wail a bit herself. 'He's *exasperating*!' she declared. 'You've no idea what it means to have him in the house for a month! I feel as though I'm putting up with the ways of a foreigner—funny little ideas, you know.'

But even as she spoke, Edwina felt her affection, a unique one in Quentin's case, rising within her in a violent sap of warmth and love. But she was still rather furious, so that when her compassion, rising higher, met a descending force of reason, she merely grew irritable and her eyes smarted till she had to dab them, and her voice, rambling on rather wildly, went on accusing him in a tone of blunted tenderness.

'I'll have a word with him,' said Stella when she could. 'It's not surprising that Quenny gets het-up at times—I do myself.'

'I don't believe *that*!' said Edwina in a voice she knew must sound appallingly jolly all at once. 'If only we were all like you—how wonderful!'

'Aren't we counting some perfectly awful chickens before they're hatched?' Richard asked. 'I think I'll go out. See you soon.' He felt he must get out of The Portway at all costs.

'There, now—Dicky's gone!' lamented Edwina. 'It was me. I did it. . . .' She searched for her handkerchief and found it, which was a great comfort. 'Well, I *have* to attend the evacuation committee.' Feeling so very responsible for the conversational cloud, she felt it only right to point out that her argument had been backed by realities.

'Off you go then,' said Stella, who had a positive flair for being impossible.

*

Richard walked slowly from the house along the top road until it joined the Town Steps. The night was brilliant, though the moon was hid. And almost warm except for brief jabs of an icy wind thrown up from the sea. There was a bench at the top of the Steps. He flopped down and stared at the glittering sea. The Town Steps, forty or fifty of them, swept away in a torrent of shallow treads, the long steep flight broken into at intervals by platforms made of black flints. A narrow chasm sundered the cottages at the foot of the steps, cutting through not only the cliff face, but also the grim red-brick terraces which ran in triple alignment to the beach. Looking left he could just see the Moot Hall, its Tudor chimney-stacks monolithic against the stars. The sea seemed to be both below and above him, a great jetty breast of water pressing up to the firmament. Coasters, looking sacred in their anchored stillness, balanced perilously on the horizon, their illuminations, larger, lower stars. Richard could just make out the danger signs. The Greek letter held high over the deep had a curious bitterness. As well as warning, there was something kill-joy in its angularity. It should have been a good place in which to think, he thought, looking down at the huge glinting bar of water topped by its enormous dome of night. But he couldn't think. He could only remember, which is a different thing. Also it was too cold. He got up and walked slowly to Church Road.

There was a warmth about Church Road no weather could alter. It turned in a slight arc away from the bleakness, the skidding shingle and the January wind, suffering a more tolerable gloom cast by holm-oaks and yews and the extravagance of its gothicized villas. The clipped shrubs were traps for the sou'easters and trembled incessantly with a victim cold. But in summer everything was reversed and Church Road provided a cool alley of rigid shadows beneath the conifers. It was oddly colourless, considering the blazing vividness of the sea front, though hardly ever misty or indeterminate. Only here and there would be a flower drawn up by the shade to a prodigious height to nod above a stately gate. Sometimes the gates, ajar, would reveal a short harsh sweep of gravel cutting through the poor blond grass. There would be a weather-vane, a sundial (*Horas non numero nisi Serenas* or, more blatantly on Alderman Sproutly's house, 'Time is money') a hothouse, or sawn-down tubs flauting stunted orange trees. The road had other, nicer distinctions as well. No guest-house advertisements ever marred its sombre gardens and only rarely, an agent's board. Its residents never drifted. They stayed and stayed. They were Lafney's true anchor in a sifting society. Their roots were deep even if they consisted mainly of the turnip kind. The smell of permanency drifted out across the gardens from expansive bay windows; a mixture of much-polished belongings, too-treasured and over-guarded as well as the more stagnant essence of trivial snobberies. The rectory was in Church Road. In whatever way Edwina thought of it, The Portway on the Long Terrace must always seem quite a come-down. Not that she cared; but the Church Road people did. To have lost her husband was quite sad, they thought, but to be obliged to give up Church Road was a tragedy pure and simple. Edwina grinned and bore it and fitted her massive mahogany into tiny rooms, receiving more sympathy for this than for the death of her husband. The Church Road people called and called. It seemed that they would never tire. Suddenly Edwina rebelled. She gave up not only Church Road but Church too. Everyone thought she must be ill, but she wasn't. She was reading novels—hundreds and hundreds of them. They improved her conversation greatly, which in turn inaugurated her great friendship with Mrs Florence Crawford. The secret of their friendship was that they had absolutely nothing in common, a fact they had neither of them suspected until Edwina's spiritual backsliding.

But Richard, as he trudged along, was on much earlier ground. He remembered struggling to keep in step with his father, a scrunched-up surplice under his arm, and sometimes there was Quentin, too, walking precisely and delicately, not kicking up the pine-needles like himself. He dragged the toe of his shoe along the choked gutter now and was pleased with its little harvest of larch cones, yew dust and the lacy skeletons of lime leaves piling up on top of it.

At the church gate he stopped. The tombstones looked elegant in the moonlight, rosy when they were of granite, and a pale damp blue where they were marble. The church itself, so exaggerated and underlined with night, with pinnacles prinked with stars and all its windows swagged with shadows, was most enticing. He tried the door and it was locked, so he walked round the gravestones instead. The Reverend John was buried near the vestry wall. 'John Launcey Brand, M.A., for thirteen years rector of this parish . . . Until the day break . . .' It was rather frightful when you came to think of it, reflected Richard, that when the poor old man was thought of at all, it was in a somewhat horticultural connection. '*French* marigolds . . . ?' Edwina would wonder. 'Would they make a nice border—they wouldn't hide the book, at any rate . . .' (There was a large white alabaster volume to contain the Reverend John's brief credentials). Or, lamenting the nasty rain-stained chips of marble, 'I do wish we'd had grass and crocuses . . .' Although the Reverend John's name leapt from page after page of yellowing registers, letters, or the mussed-up records of the diocese, all direct pronouncement of his existence lead inevitably to a seed catalogue. He might have been Ada Poulsen. Actually, at that moment as Richard looked down, his father was a wiry ring of variegated holly.

4

ON Sunday Edwina rose early, that is at eight, and began as she always did, to rush through the day. She had never quite got used to her alarming freedom. Soon the tufty hats would bob past the window and the bell would toll, but not for her. There was no help for it—she just didn't care! All *that* passed away with the Reverend John.

The Crawfords came at about half-past twelve, Florence first, so assured, so *bouffant*, so sweepingly marine (she was Rear-Admiral Crawford's widow), that she looked like a figure-head on leave. There was the same undeviating purpose about her and one felt that she hadn't so much lived her life, as weathered it. Mary followed.

Mary Crawford was a waster, there was no doubt of it. She allowed her days to trickle away. She poured life into the ground, as it were, negligently, hardly touched. She had some beauty, but she could never see it. She seemed to exist only for her own deprecation. She had been wonderfully modest as a young girl and had been much commended and praised for being so. It was right at the time, as well as being rather miraculous. But later on, instead of dropping it and promoting herself a little, she did the reverse. Her self-examination had grown so huge, it was like the narcissus legend in reverse, and now she couldn't see her face for her faults. This mortification or wilful blunting of her good points extended to her mind as well. And her clothes were a wilful disaster, baggy tweeds in whose humiliating contours she rejoiced, like a saint in a hair shirt. Mrs Crawford helped Mary in all this—which isn't hard to believe, since such a monumental indifference could hardly have resulted from a single nature.

Florence had her reasons, which, whatever they may have been in the past, were now unblushingly selfish. Having got Mary through what she called 'the treacherous twenties', she saw less reason than ever she did before why Mary should marry. If she had ever shown any sign of having *wanted* to, it would be a different matter. But where was the urge? Had anybody ever seen it? Florence doubted it. If the idea ever came up now, it would be gimcrack—not the real thing at all. In fact, she was doing Mary a Christian service in stalling it. She would be wretched, unhappy; Florence knew she would! Anyway, why should she give up her company now? It would be most unfair. And it was all so worrying, she told Edwina. Alliances which would have been thought pathetic in her own day, now cropped up in the press with depressing frequency. There *was* a time, she recalled, when a mother could sit back and be secure in the knowledge that her old age wouldn't be just a desert of boringly dutiful letters if she had preserved one daughter from the scrum and got her safely through to her thirties. But now she often read of women of forty and over getting married—and for the first time! It was clear that she would need all the fortitude she could muster. The men were to blame, she supposed. Their object in marriage could not be quite the same as it was when she was a girl.

They lived in a large curved house of saffron plaster—the sort of house which was advertised as a 'watering-place residence' at the time of Copenhagen. It was on a hill above Lafney and a slight convexity on the sea side gave it an air of rather wistful impermanence. Both Richard and Quentin knew

Meridian House well. And Stella could even remember having tea with Rear-Admiral Crawford, a fact which at once invested her with some brooding, epic quality in her brothers' eyes. It whisked her out of their decade once and for all. Stella was in some way veteran, they decided. She had taken tea with the bas-relief in the south aisle; that sunken cheek, flaccid even in marble; that niggardly chin already browning with age. Stella had seen it move, heard it munch 'All little girls like seed-cake'. She hadn't. She was six and she loathed it, but for Quentin's sake she remembered all she could and retailed the story with a fond retrospective aplomb—like old Countess Guiccioli summoning up Byron. Quentin used to peek through his fingers during the Magnificat, absorbing the Admiral's thin nose, his breast puffed out with stony honours and the elegant blindness of his polished eyes. He imagined him, a thin, disdainful figure, on the bridge, on the small lawn at Buckingham Palace, at the races: but wherever it was, never without the proud, tacking majesty of Mrs Crawford in his wake. 'True and faithful' read the inscription, which was generally assumed to be patriotic.

Edwina enjoyed her friendship with Mrs Crawford more than she had enjoyed anything before, and as far as sheer actual enjoyment went, more than her marriage. But Mary she was sorry for. It worried her terribly to see her getting vague and floppy and to hear her running herself down with the wilfulness of clockwork. And when Mrs Crawford joined in, giving encouraging twists to the denigratory mechanism as it were, she was nonplussed. Rectories are thrifty places where things are nursed along to their proper ends and the proper end of Mary Crawford should have been the chancel step. It was agony for Edwina to watch Mrs Crawford spreading soap on it.

'What about Stella?' demanded Mrs Crawford defensively one day and was told that Stella had 'interests'. Mercifully the retaliation was not extended to include Richard or Quentin. If it had been Edwina would have been really in a plight. There were those things in their natures which she wouldn't at all mind having changed, but she was certainly not going to discuss them with Florence Crawford. There was a fault, and Edwina knew it; a basic error, though nothing you could call cardinal, which, when everything else was added up, always produced an odd total and it wasn't necessary to be a sibyl to spot it. Florence Crawford saw it; she wasn't blind. Babies, she had decided long ago. Nothing to worry about from that quarter. Anyway, Mary was thirty-two.

They were altogether now, as they had been so often in the past, in the over-furnished, under-aired drawing-room of The Portway. Luncheon had gone off very well. They all ate too much in the reaction against the frugal reaction towards Christmas gorging. Quentin stared at Mrs Crawford's heavily-powdered throat. How reckless it was!—a sweeping, blushing isthmus of flesh the colour of mashed strawberries descending from her chin to a barely veiled disaster. Only a small gold pin, like Horatius at the bridge, prevented a fate unimaginable. It wrought with the scrabbled veil with determined, panting clasps. Round her neck Mrs Crawford sported a tumble of gold chains. They held her lorgnette, a tiny golden pencil, a little golden locket and a clackety heap of other trinkets.

'We'll take the coffee through—shall we!' Edwina had suggested brightly.

'Lovely,' said Mrs Crawford insincerely. She hated moving. She could never do it without real consideration and effort. 'I do so love your little drawing-room, Edwina.' She lied this time in an attempt to comfort herself. The Portway generally made her feel desperately gloomy and the drawing-room most of all. It gave her claustrophobia. 'If only Edwina could see how *awful* it is!' she complained to Mary. The poorer people were, the more they furnished their rooms! But it was nice to be with dear Edwina.

'I like this house altogether,' she declared plangently. She walked across the hall, her fleshy back arched forward so that the chains fell out in front of her in bright swinging loops.

'It *is* a pretty house,' agreed Edwina, who thought it was. 'The boys painted the dining-room? did you notice, Florence?'

'Very practical,' admitted Mrs Crawford. 'D'you know that, Mary? Quenny and Dick painted the dining-room.'

'They're really both quite practical,' said Edwina, 'but it's the latest thing for young men to appear not to be, you know.'

'Now Stella,' said Mrs Crawford, sinking into an armchair, 'you're practical. You must talk to Mary. Not that I think of you as impractical, my dear,' she nodded heavily in Mary's direction, 'but Stella with her story-books and things has got the right idea.'

Mary bent over the little gilded cups. There was a soft bloominess in her movements. Her small white and pink hands touched the silver and porcelain with a deft tenderness. Her wrists were incredibly pale. 'Do you mean I should get a job?' she asked.

'No point in that,' retorted her mother quickly, refusing to be drawn.

'Then you want me to write books?'

'You know you don't write,' said Mrs Crawford, making it quite clear that whether one did so or not it was entirely a matter of choice. 'Edwina knows what I mean.'

'I thought Mary did all the gardening,' interrupted Richard. 'Doesn't she do the flowers and the greenhouse?'

'She needn't,' said Mrs Crawford shortly, 'Humpson's paid for that.'

All at once, as though it were something doled out with the coffee, a fearful pedestrian languor invaded the room. There was silence, not a relaxing peace, but a dearth of interest as though a porridge of boredom had been poured over the delicate fare of conversation. And the sun, which until that hour had hung against the window with a token warmth, faded away into wet mist. It grew drearily dark. Edwina wondered if she should light a lamp or two. Instead, she poked the fire. A log turned over luxuriously like a sleeper and sent out a sudden dream of brilliance. The flames, no longer subservient to such a weakly, pleading sun, shot out gloriously, turning the piano into a box of nervous gold, firing the candlesticks and jagging the plates and ornaments with limpid, running fissures. Mrs Crawford lay in her chair in a heap of helpless grandeur. Her chains slid and shone. Quentin sat on the dark carpet, curiously disembodied like a very old portrait in which only the hands and the waxen face can be seen. Mary leant forward, warm and rich as velvet. Her eyes were smudged away, yet this very indefiniteness added to their blueness. They were almost the only colour other than gold and black in the room. Outside, a grey sea made a grey sound as it slumped up the shingle. Richard stretched. His feet went on and on until he could barely see them. Oh God, oh God! he thought, what next? What a life!

Mrs Crawford must have been afflicted with a similar despair for she, too, struggled to an upright position as though she had to defend something, or somebody. The gardener would do. Wasn't he constant? Wasn't he a dependable relic of that other world which had once moved so effortlessly on its well-greased axis? When you came to think of it, God how things had changed!

'We'll never get another Humpson,' she reflected solemnly.

'How right,' muttered Quentin, 'two would be terrible.'

'Sorry?' Mrs Crawford said loudly.

Feeling responsible for the cloud, Edwina struggled from her own particular morass in a last effort to divert.

'I knew I had something to tell you, Florence. Sir Paul Abbott is coming home. He—'

'But we saw it—it was in the personal column—I mean the Court Circular in *The Times*. Mary saw it and read it out.'

'Oh,' said Edwina rather dolefully. 'I didn't know it was news. I thought it was still gossip. Anyway, Dicky's going there won't be in *The Times*.'

'Why?' enquired Mrs Crawford, mystified. 'Has he left the new school already?'

'It's not an actual job,' said Richard. 'I shall know more about it after I've had dinner with Sir Paul. He says to meet him on the twentieth.'

Mrs Crawford didn't attempt to hide her amazement. Nor yet her incredulity. She paused, open-mouthed, wonderingly, like someone who has been the frequent victim of 'wolf! wolf!' But Edwina hardly noticed. The room, till then so deep in weariness, now trembled with enquiry. Even she realized that she had made few statements in her life whose results had been so gratifying. Quentin didn't help matters. He left the carpet and perched himself on the revolving piano stool from which, long and limply curling, he surveyed the company like a contemplative fern. He didn't say a word, but watched everyone with an almost spiteful avidity.

'There'll be a great many people on the way home,' said Mrs Crawford as flatly as she could. 'It's a sort of reverse of rats leaving a sinking ship.'

'But not in Sir Paul's case, surely?' said Stella.

'Why not in his?' declared Mrs Crawford in a tone that was as near to rudeness as she could get away with. The young people were beginning to madden her this afternoon. Why couldn't they make themselves scarce . . .? It was Edwina who was her friend, not her extraordinary brood. 'Because he's a writer, I suppose you mean? Isn't it ridiculous when you come to think of it, how any man could prefer New York to Sheldon! Sheldon was where he belonged, and Sheldon was where he should have stayed. I'm told it's a shambles because of the neglect. When I used to go there in old Sir Eric's time . . .'

'He doesn't live in New York,' said the fern putting out a tentative frond in an uncongenial climate, 'he lives—or lived, we shall have to say now, in Marsala.'

'Is that in France or Italy?' enquired Mrs Crawford, as if she welcomed the information.

'It's in Sicily.'

'I always understood it was New York,' said Richard, politely taking sides—'not Marsala, of course, but where Sir Paul lived.'

'Well he doesn't,' answered Quentin abruptly. The fern had lost its delicacy and had unravelled into a robust leaf which threatened to disturb the complacent air around it. 'Did your letter come from New York?'

'It came from London—from Brown's. I told you.'

'Things must be worse than we thought,' said Mrs Crawford, not without enthusiasm. She dismissed a winning picture of herself bossing a servile host of females at the Mansion House. The great rooms were functional with trestles. They sorted out surgical appliances, matched up crutches, devised strange slippers for shattered feet. The telephones buzzed, the Admiralty, the War Office—Balmoral perhaps—why not? Who is to limit dreams? She tore herself away from such a luring prospect with infinite reluctance. 'Do you know, Edwina,' she added in a tone of appropriate grief, 'I simply can't help wondering what we'll all be doing this time next year . . .'

'I know what I'll be doing,' said Mary lightly, 'cleaning up the borders.'

'Let us hope you are right,' her mother said darkly.

'Oh I'm certain Mary's right!' said Edwina.

'Of course Mary's right,' insisted Quentin. Leaning back precariously on the piano stool, he lit a cigarette, then noticing Mary's stare of unconscious intensity he flicked the silver case open again.

'Do you?' he asked.

'No thank you, Quentin—never.'

'Never?'

'Never,' she smiled.

'You're as bad as Dicky—he hasn't any vices.'

'That doesn't make him deficient, does it?' Mary turned slightly to include Richard in her amusement. He was the only one of the Brand children she didn't actually fear a little. Quentin quite terrified her. His pastel-fine head and restless hands gave her the same apprehensiveness as when she dusted the Miessen cabinet. Sooner or later the situation would prove to be too delicate for her. The image would splinter in her too ponderous grasp and then there would be no more communication, no more talk; just a passing nod for old time's sake. And Stella? Well, Stella was really admirable. It was what she intended to be, and would have been, except that her very determination prevented it. She was almost free of complexity. She didn't have to adapt herself to the generalised codes and credences; she actually thought that way. She read the *Daily Telegraph* from cover to cover with pleasure and profit. She was a founder member of Readers' Union and she listened to all the Proms on the wireless. She gave advice, but of that stalwart kind which is too apparent for any but the quite insensitive to act upon. Not that Mary hated Stella; she didn't. She didn't even dislike her. Her attitude was self-protective and rather withdrawn. Stella thought she was shy and a bit feeble, and patronized her a little on these accounts.

So that left Richard—Richard who was young enough for Mary to have led by the hand round the garden of Meridian House and so was not even a playmate! There was the predicament which must always confront her where the Brand boys were concerned; her few extra years and their carefully sustained immaturity. It could never be bridged, not by herself, that is. It would mean the most awful energy and she simply hadn't got it.

'I went to Sheldon once . . .' she said in her easy uncaring voice.

'It was years ago,' said her mother quickly, 'you couldn't have remembered a thing.'

'On the contrary, darling—*everything*.'

'What, then?' asked Quentin.

'It was quite a long time ago—I really went to see the church, they say it's haunted—and on a table just inside the door I found a book called *The History and Antiquities of Sheldon in Suffolk* by a Sir Gerald Abbott . . .'

'Sir Stephen,' corrected Stella.

'Well, Sir Stephen. Anyway the book made the house sound much more fun than the church, so I called.'

'On Sir Paul?' asked Richard, rather astounded.

'On the housekeeper—Sir Paul wasn't there even then—and she showed me round.'

'Yes,' said Quentin, 'and what did you see?'

'Oh, nice things and ghastly things and a Gainsborough with a roly-poly Sir Paul lolling against a stile in a park and a Sargent of a terribly plain woman—'

'The Belle's sister,' interrupted Richard. 'Miss Bellingham you know, of Copdock.'

Mary nodded. 'That's right, I expect so.'

'Is it a big house, enormous, I mean?' asked Richard.

'Quite enormous but not vast—not Chatsworth.' Suddenly the torpid after-Sunday-dinner-ness became too much for her. 'I'm going out, I think.' she said. 'Anyone coming? Do forgive me, Mrs Brand—Mummy, you don't mind do you?'

Mrs Crawford budged a little in the depths of her chair. To go out; how futile! she implied. But do, do if you must. Don't consider me; that would be too much! 'Don't be long,' she said.

'We'll walk to the Martello,' said Richard, rising as well.

Pleased, surprised rather, Mary said, 'All right, let's.'

★

They walked along the front. The sea, so upright when viewed from the town heights, was supine on the level. It faltered sluggishly at the breakwaters before gathering its strength to rip up the shingle in a little spurt of boredom. Its voice was *slub*—and then *slub-slub* as it parted at the tide points. At each retraction the beach clucked and clinked as its flints shifted, exasperated, it seemed, by their endlessly nudging propinquity. Groynes humped themselves up out of the water, black and hirsute with rubbery weeds. Summer was only an orange crepe sole, a rag, still striped and blue; the blanched T of a child's spade, a belt; a coconut scalp with matted dun hair. This on one side, their left, as they made for the Martello. On the other side were the hotels with towels sausaged-out along the ledges where the sashes joined to keep the wind away. Inside, the bedding would be curled up in an obese slumber of its own. Cut-glass vases would be stowed away in cupboards. The windows, bellying forward, caught at each facet of the cold. Peering in the biggest of them, the 'Royal Snape', Richard saw the inflated furniture sprawling across the carpet like spruce whales; fat couches and chairs, desperately floral, wallowed in an Axminster flood. I think I hate this place, he thought; I *think* I do. . . .

'I suppose we have to go all the way to the Martello?' said Mary.

'I suppose we do,' he replied. 'But why, don't you want to?'

'We might get blown away.'

'Will you be cold?' he asked, at once solicitous. He felt hot still. The close room, so lately deserted, still hugged him.

'Not a bit,' she fibbed. 'I just thought we might find it rather dismal, that's all.'

'If we go the other way, it will only be another kind of dismalness.' He meant Church Road.

'Oh, yes,' she agreed.

They trudged on in silence in the pearly light until they reached the place where the ordinary path joined the sea-wall and where, if you wanted to go on, you had to walk Indian-file. Perversely, the wind which was cutting up and down the blank streets, was almost non-existent on the gaunt neck of shingle leading to the Martello tower. Richard went in front. Walking exactly behind another person can be as curiously rewarding as watching them asleep. Richard's striding, balancing back-view amused Mary at first; then it obsessed her. That is, she couldn't see anything else—only his gawky walk and the breeze prising up his hair in a solid mass and the way one arm kept flinging itself towards the sea and the other kept still.

'It's a silly question,' he suddenly cried, shouting rather and half-turning round—there wasn't a soul nearer than the men in the lightship glued for ever to the skyline,—'but do you wonder, Mary, if we shall *ever* be any different—me, you, Quenny; Lafney if you like?'

'What do you expect me to say at this minute! I'm far too busy keeping my balance.'

'On the wall . . .?'

'On the wall!' she laughed. 'I know,' she shouted back, 'horses—it's the only way if you want to talk.' She caught up with him and precariously eased herself abreast.

'Watch out! You'll fall . . .'

'Not if you hang on . . .'

We can't, he wanted to protest. It's not just a matter of size, it's a matter of *time*. You can't go back to another age, another condition; it won't fit.

'Don't be pompous, Richard,' insisted Mary. 'Hang on—or I really will go over the edge!' She was laughing rather breathlessly as their arms caught at each other's waists. The position was absurd. It was far from companionable and farthest of all from being 'horses'. Once she looked convertly to see if he was angry, but his head inclined non-committally towards the sea and in its winter-vague profile there was little to be read. She felt a tension, but put it down to this childish, foolish impulse of hers, although she was wrong about this.

'How the hell do you stand it?' he burst out. 'Hometown! All the awful fuss kicked up by nobodies going nowhere!'

'Shussh!' she said. 'You can't be wild at such close range!'

'Oh, I'm sorry.'

'Stand what, anyway?'

'Well, this afternoon for instance—*all* the fiddling afternoons if it comes to it.'

'How do you?' she retaliated, feeling uncomfortable.

'That's it!' said Richard. 'I can't—I don't. I'm really snarled-up inside all the time.'

Mary laughed. 'Don't worry about that at least. Nobody would ever guess.'

'Poor you,' replied Richard. He tightened his arm consolingly. Poor you because I'm behaving like an ass. We'll forget it, shall we? It's just what with Quenny going about like an exposed nerve, and Mummy in blinkers, and Stella being the world's good sort . . .'

'Where do you come in—is that it?'

'Where *do* I?' he asked. 'Perhaps you can tell me?'

'Let go, will you,' she said, 'we're just coming to the slippery part—' She clambered on to a rock. Her coat was crushed where his arm had been. 'It's quite plain,' she continued, 'you come in when all that family of yours goes out. After all, there's no earthly reason why one's relations shouldn't be dropped just a little, particularly since one can never be accused of having taken them up in the first place! What's more, it's not necessary to be heartless to do it.'

'Well . . .!' said Richard, who was dumbfounded.

'I know what you are thinking,' said Mary, bending over and brushing sand from the hem of her coat—'the pot calling the kettle black and all that sort of thing. But it's not quite the same. Not really.'

'I disagree.'

'Of course you do!'

'I suppose,' he said slowly, 'I need love . . .'

'You need a separate world,' Mary agreed. The wind, rising slightly, filled up the space between her collar and her throat. She felt it uncomfortably, like a cold halter. They were picking their way through the ruined periphery of the outer fortification. It sagged across the beach like huge, dank hunks of fruit cake.

'Do you have one?' he asked.

'Yes,' she said surprisingly.

'It must be a very private one.'

'Oh—it is!'

'Then I suppose I must have one too . . .'

'I doubt it from what you say. If you have it's not much good to you since it obviously doesn't present a refuge from the public one. But perhaps I'm wrong to insist on a private world in your case. I'm different. It's essential to me—I couldn't go on without it. You and Quenny—I hope you don't mind me saying this—you and Quenny might mistake its purpose. I mean you might use it for a sort of bolt-hole. Well you did *ask* me. . . !' She protested, seeing the frowning, bewildered look on Richard's face.

'Because we're scared?' he said. They had reached the tower and had followed its inwardly inclining wall until the wind was defeated.

'Not scared, lazy,' said Mary. 'You enjoy a kind of incompleteness—it's an American trait, really. I can't imagine where you both picked it up! You just can't be bothered with being grown-up. It's awfully dangerous to stuff all the fullness of life away in some old drawer, because you'll need it badly one day and when you do it's quite likely to come out all the wrong shape.'

'Well!' he expostulated.

'Oh, I'm terribly, terribly sorry Dicky—I'm a lecturer; how awful!'

He had an urge to be cruel. 'The same might be said of you—haven't you stuffed life away?'

She considered for a moment. 'No,' she said, 'I don't feel that I have.'

'Why do you seem to care so little—about everything?'

'I do care,' she said, rubbing her neatly gloved fingers against the rough brickwork. 'Perhaps it would be more obvious if I were more vain.'

'You're vain about not being vain,' Richard replied as woundingly as he could. The Christmas miasma, the blank horizons wherever he looked, the feeling of fifth-rateness, filled him with a little-boy temper. He wanted to kick somebody, so it had to be Mary. Of course he was sorry the minute after.

Mary flinched to prove her vulnerableness then became very grown-up indeed.

'I have no wish to quarrel, Richard,' she announced. She removed a glove to find her watch. It was back-to-front on her wrist and to see it she had to bring her arm up close. For a second her hand opened out, white and tendril-like, to the darkening sea. Each finger was capped humbly with a discoloured cross-hatching, the stigmata of her worthy interests, gros point and gardening. He felt he could almost hate her again for this, violently and irrationally.

'Let me see,' he demanded rather wildly. He seized her hand and brought it round until the little dial glittered against his eyes. It said four o'clock. He remembered it vividly, because at that precise moment, without rhyme or reason, the hand was lying in his own and his mouth was pressing against hers. The unsuspected sweetness of her flesh shocked and amazed him. It was like kissing soft, damp, sweet flowers. In his rough grasp her mussed-up tweeds were more than ever an outrage to the body they sheltered. Velvet, he thought. He imagined it slipping against the round soft smoothness. Her face was as cold as stone. He touched it with his lips, then the rich bunchy hair near her ears. An outlandish notion occurred to him. He laughed gently. 'People are just as young as they taste,' he said.

Mary pulled herself free. 'What?'

'Never mind.'

'But I do mind. What right have you to make me go on and on with all that advice, or whatever you like to call it, and then show yourself so alarmingly self-sufficient? You've made me feel like a natural history mistress who has come to grief over the birds and the bees! Why *were* you so beastly to me just now—you were, you know.'

'Well at this moment you do rather sound like the natural history mistress—all this scolding.'

She stared at him uncertainly. She hardly knew what to think. These last few minutes had made him a stranger. All that had preceded it; their mutual childhood, their families, the sparsely featured parallels of their individual existences which had run side by side for so long, were all gone; quashed by this confused embrace.

'We shall have to get back,' she said. 'What was the time when you looked?'

'But you looked too.'

'It was just a gesture. I can't see a thing without my spectacles.'

'I should say it's five.'

'*Heavens!*'

He put out his hand. 'Don't rush—not now . . .'

Mary didn't answer. Gradually, gently, as though finding herself very precious, she made her way down the tumbled masonry. Richard followed. Above their heads, the Martello tower, already brim-full of night, grew indefinite and dark in its outward shape and became one with all the neglected monuments of the earth. The wind piped shrilly through its meagre windows. A mile away, Lafney winked with lights.

'It's a horrible place,' he said, catching up with her.

'What!' She was surprised. 'The dear old Martello?'

'Hundreds of men died in it. They had cholera or something and the local people wouldn't allow them any help.'

'But when, Richard?'

'After the Napoleonic wars, of course. You don't think that it's just an ornament, *that* place?'

To be truthful, she hadn't thought of it as much more.

'Urgh!' she said, shrinking from his timing for the retailing of the fact, rather than its historic truth.

They walked along side by side until she thought it too grotesque. It made her feel like a housemaid on an evening out so she walked in front and Richard followed. Lafney lay ahead, a grey wedge of diminishing habitations locked under dripping slates. She thought of Stella and found herself full of envy. Her astuteness, her downright professionalism seemed to her all at once desirable. Stella had triumphed over messy things like love and friendship and could now look forward to a cheerful prospect of breezy flats and long, matey holidays. Oh, to be Stella! thought Mary. She felt common sense coming on like influenza. It was her age again, she decided. It was the sort of thing you might contract easily at thirty-two ... Time ... time! she sighed. Which reminded her; she must straw the funkias. Frosts could be expected now.

Back on the front, a star came travelling to meet them, a slow-travelling star regularly pausing to touch-off further stars. It was old Baggotty the lamplighter on his bicycle; a wambling municipal acolyte.

'Goo' night, Miss Crawford,' he said. 'Mr Brand ...'

They strolled back to The Portway, gravely apart, through a purple ravine of mid-Victorian dwellings. The glow from the drawing-room window was prophetic of the snugness inside.

'Shall you go back to Copdock on Monday?' she asked—as if there was a choice in the matter.

'*Next* Monday,' he answered.

'We'll be seeing you before then though, at Meridian, I mean?'

'Of course,' he replied, but too emphatically as though he must remind himself to be loving.

5

RICHARD made two visits to the Crawfords before he returned to Copdock and neither of them could really have been called a success. It was true that there had been only six days left. Florence was unerringly formal. She thought that by being so she was braking the scurrying wheel of change. She forbade one just 'dropping in'. A call was a call, but a meal was a well-considered invitation.

'But I don't *want* lunch,' he had insisted on the telephone. He heard Mary's laugh, a bit stifled, but gay all the same.

'And Quentin's asked too,' she said slowly, then waited to hear what effect this would have.

'He can't come,' she heard Richard say with disappointing evenness. 'He's off to London.'

And he was. With ruthless politeness he had turned in his trim Lafney harness and was away, fled to some mysterious address as unexplained as it was unenquired of ... All Edwina had said was, 'But how *can* you go to town dressed like that?' This was because Quentin wore a kind of fancy-dress of very old clothes at home; his shirts gaped, his slacks slipped in grubby folds round his thin hips and he affected a disastrous hat. But he had waved her quiet. He had some things where he was going, he said, and since he had made a similar remark the previous summer before setting off to Edinburgh, Edwina imagined caches of suitable clothes existing for him all over the country. It was all a puzzle to her—and a worry. She liked him well turned-out—he paid high dividends in that sort of thing—and his affected sloth bored and affronted her. Her protest had no effect; that is how he went, over-muffled, with his delicate features poised above the dirty Trinity scarf like an ivory on a hassock.

Stella went too, but that was to be expected. She left in a swirl of impending activity, so that there must be no mistaking that hers was the full life. No day could ever be too long for her, no minute too precious. She stuffed both with her remorseless energy. She rushed off now, the slam of the car door as vociferous as her intentions; Harrods, a playlet for Children's

Hour, an invitation to visit Stockholm where 'Christabel in Camberwell' had been made into a play and was fantastically successful. The Austin leapt at her touch and headed knowingly for the flat in Ipswich, boisterous with its own private gale, where the cute china animals she collected flaunted their dinky scuts. 'Give me air!' beseeched Stella aloud to the monkey mascot bobbing from the windscreen wiper. A week-end with her brothers made fearful inroads on her tact, which was limited at the best of times. She was pleased about Richard's job however. He had gone straight from school into an Ipswich bank, where his listlessness had become a byword. Not that he was lazy. He did all that he had to do. But his unconcealed boredom was so evident that it became almost an affront to those of his colleagues obliged to consider their job as the *raison d'être* for their earthly existence. 'He isn't settling down,' lamented Mr Jude, the manager, to Stella one day as they met in the Buttermarket. So she had had a little talk with Richard. 'But you *must* know what you want to do!' she had expostulated. 'Everybody does—even if it's deep-sea diving!' But all Richard had said was, 'might he have the window shut? Her flat was icy—did she know?'

And then there was Quentin. He never came near her and that she found was more worrying than being pestered. She loathed secrets of the smallest kind and to have a whole life tucked away, and a brother's life at that in which she felt she had full shares, was maddening, to put it mildly. Well, now she was away from them both and that was a relief. Quentin would go on being Quentin, she supposed, and Richard would now feel that, with Copdock, he wasn't outclassed in some way. She drove on, with heavy accomplishment, to Ipswich.

'And Stella?' asked Mary—'but then I needn't enquire . . . She's buzzed off?'—this appearing to be so exactly the right way to describe her going.

'Just this minute, as a matter of fact,' Richard said.

'Well I'm glad.'

'Oh, *are* you?'

'Very,' she said. 'Very, very, very . . .'

'Darling,' said Richard. The word jangled wildly on the line. He must ring off. The instrument was no longer a receiver but had become a kind of bakelite Dracula feeding on his words.

If he held it up a moment longer its avid mouth would suck rash promises out of him. 'Wednesday then. Good-bye.'

'What?'

'I said Wednesday—and thanks awfully, Mary...'

'Dear Richard,' she said, sounding vaguely disturbed, and rang off herself, though very gently.

*

Do houses outstay their purpose like so much else?

The real fault where Meridian was concerned was that its functions were abused. Its pleasures—and its sole reason for being built at all was to give such things—were frankly seasonal. It was a summer house. It could even be (with a little give and take on both sides, such as well-considered fires, wind-breaks under the south rowan spinney and its windows all shut up tight as a tomb), a *spring* house. But never an autumn house, and never, never a winter house. Its bellying plaster and affected impermanence was a mood and even in summer, to live in it day after day, climbing its shiny leap of stairs; banging its pretty, frail doors by their handles of oval, fluted brass; meeting too frequently the wreathed Pompeiian faces on conduit, lintel and chimney-piece and altogether encountering a surfeit of grace wherever the eye might turn, was apt to carry with it a sense of prodigious waste. There was too much key-pattern. One expected to run into Sir William Hamilton so frequently that it became frustrating not to do so. It was too apparently tasteful, in fact too gluttonously so. To live in it year and year out was like a solid diet of ptarmigan, or emptying something or other to the drains—*Château Yquem* perhaps. And yet it wasn't a big house, nor even truly splendid of its kind. Brighton is covered with such structures, and so is Hove. But in Lafney, where such architecture as there was crawled parallel to the shingle in a triple rash of grocer's Victorian, Meridian flashed like a jewel. There it sat, on its tuffet of lawns, beaming with its pre-meditated distinction. Its function was to be marine and marine it would be for as long as one rain-grey slate hugged another. Stealing noises from the immense poplars flanking its walls, Meridian re-diffused a delicious whisper-from-the-conch, creak-o'-the-rigging, yell-of-the-cormorant mood. Florence Crawford's taste may have mauled the interior a bit but it remained all-glorious without; pink and grey, with a porch as Greek as Euston and two tidy rows of wobble-paned windows.

Richard, however, saw it with disappointment. It was just one more thing that had turned out to be shabbier; less lovable that he remembered it, if only for the reason that it had once been so greatly loved. He looked up the sun-spattered garden front to see Mrs Crawford plunging along the terrace. Her right arm was extended agreeably to the sea. She might have been the over-afflicted Mrs Jordan making a last desperate appeal to her single-minded Hanoverian prince, except that Mr Yockery was too tall, too bending, too pin-like altogether for the latter's excessive rôle.

'Blast!' thought Richard, 'Old Yockers . . .'

The Reverend Francis Benedict Yockery, A.K.C., had taken up all that had been laid down by the Reverend John Brand at the latter's early death. Not only the parish duties, but a welter of chairmanships, a morass of committees; the Archaeological Society, the Cottage Hospital and, more than these, a paternal interest in Edwina's children. 'Send them to me,' he advised her, 'in their hour of need . . .' But it turned out that their needs were small. In fact Quentin and Richard had proved to be almost offensively out of 'need'. Mr Yockery watched them grow up with increasing disapproval. Had Edwina only *listened*—for he blamed her, of course—how very different might not her sons' characters have been! So many admirable traits, observed by Mr Yockery when they were really young, had stopped dead in their tracks, so to speak. So much promise of the angelic kind, all gone, all gone! Take Quentin, who had proved a really promising brass-rubber; why had he so frankly declared at fifteen 'that he couldn't look another Crusader in the face'—such a silly remark, anyway, Mr Yockery had decided at the time. As for Richard, there had been very real ground for hopes there. He had served the Eight o'clocks regularly and immaculately until, at almost the exact same age, he, too, had defected.

Mr Yockery might hardly have noticed it except for an innocent little pleasure he permitted himself. He enjoyed searching through the choir's cassock pockets as those demure garments hung from their pegs in the rich violet gloom. It was surprising what he found—not that he minded, he only needed to *see*. Bits of string, bits of plasticine, cigarette cards, gnawed indiarubbers, spongy segments of the Sexton Blake Library; in all an innocuous enough haul, endearing rather than distressing. He put it all back neatly and went away convinced that his knowledge of human nature had been thereby increased, if only by a hair's breadth. But one day in Richard's cassock he discovered *The Garden of Khama*, and if that didn't show which way the wind was blowing, what did? Sexton Blake was 'healthy'. But Indian poetry . . . and in the vestry. He had wagged his narrow head sadly.

'If ever those boys need a father's guidance, it's now,' he told Edwina severely.

'You can try,' she had answered. And he had, and failed—utterly.

Robbed of one patrimony, Mr Yockery tried another. He was very High, point-lace and incense, processions and a distribution of persuasive pamphlets to explain such things. The inhabitants of Lafney were on the other hand insular and prodigiously memoried when it came to their Puritanism. They suffered the rector's tan and purple statues, his gold, board-like cope, his ardent prostrations and even a Mass bell, but when he demanded a spiritual parenthood and expected them to address him as 'Father', they rebelled.

'*Father* Yockery thinks that we're having the mildest January since the Armistice,' shouted Mrs Crawford, spotting Richard in the drive. If he wants to be called that, let him! was her attitude.

Richard waved to show that he understood and made his way up to them. Where was Mary, he wondered.

'No Quentin?' asked the rector.

'You know Quentin's gone to London—I told you,' Mrs Crawford said.

'You did . . . you did!' conceded Mr Yockery. A dim kindliness played over his face.

'Stella's gone off too, I hear,' she added.

'Yes, she left this morning,' said Richard.

'I understand Stella's doing wonderfully well, **wonderfully** well!' said Mr Yockery. He nodded in the direction of a leaden vase in incontrovertible harmony with all he said. Self-agreement elongated his jaw, drew down his nose, softened his gaze. He gathered in congratulatory bouquets from every source, from the winter heliotrope as it happened at that moment.

'Why,' he declared, sniffing soundly, 'you've got some of *this*!'

'It's been out ever since Christmas,' said Mrs Crawford.

'Wonderful! Wonderful!' said Mr Yockery.

'You'll never believe it,' Mrs Crawford declared, gathering up her chains in a rich haul, 'but when we mowed yesterday —last time, thank heaven—there were daisies out still.'

'A daisy!' reflected Mr Yockery. He stared ahead of him with the sweet inanity of a Holman Hunt apostle. 'A daisy . . . the Eye of Day . . . fancy that, Richard!'

'When my husband obtained his first captaincy . . .' Mrs Crawford was commencing obscurely when a silvery jingle occupied the little cupola high up on the roof. 'Luncheon,' she said. At the too-gracious door she turned and speaking to nobody in particular, added, 'I maintain that it's still possible to keep up one's standards if one has a mind to . . .' She moved a hand vaguely in the direction of the dining-room.

At that moment Mary came through with Hibble, originally the parlourmaid, now everything. Mary, in spite of the effort she had made with her clothes, was too busy to look really pleasing. She wore a light blue woollen suit with some rather big milky-looking beads. They lay at her throat, cloudy, opaline; contrasting dully with her white, clear skin.

'Ready at last!' she announced, reserving a small private nod for Richard. 'Sorry to keep everybody waiting.'

They ate slowly, the conversation anaemically attuned to Hibble's despising presence—despising because of the presence of the rector. Hibble was Wee Free, or something of that sort. Helping Mr Yockery to sprouts was as bad as nourishing the Devil where she was concerned. She did so now, plobbing them sadly on to his plate, more and more—and still he was silent. At last his hand fluttered. I knew it! Hibble thought— he eats and eats, that one! She passed on, heavy with her hate, to Richard.

'Now,' said Mr Yockery, 'let me hear all the news. Where

shall we start? What is your news — eh, Mrs Crawford?'

'Mine? I've forgotten what it's like to have news—I suppose that should indicate a wonderful contentment. I think you had better ask Richard. He's bursting with news.'

'We *know* Richard's news, or the gist of it,' said Mr Yockery.

'There's not much more to tell so far,' said Richard. 'I went to Copdock a week before they broke-up for Christmas—just to get the hang of the place and I start teaching as soon as they go back.'

'What shall your subjects be?' enquired Mr Yockery. A goatish glimmer made its way along the moist rims of his eyes.

'English, I suppose.'

'You suppose . . .?'

'It's a very small school and there's not a lot of specialization. I shall be responsible for English and on a roster for practically everything else.'

Mr Yockery's head sagged and his hands crawled over the tablecloth in search of mustard, pepper, the salt. 'And what,' he enquired with snuffling deliberation, 'are the qualifications requisite for being on . . . a *roster* . . .?'

'None—in my case,' said Richard shortly. Old Yockers wasn't going to bait him, even if he thought he was! An earlier detestation of that leaping Adam's-apple returned to him in full force. If he'd known who was going to be present for lunch he would have found an excuse for not coming. Too late now, he would just have to keep a check on himself.

'Do they make you comfortable?' asked Mr Yockery, rather as though Copdock was an hotel.

'It's not bad.'

'Tell me about Winsley. Is *he* well, would you say?'

'Quite. But I didn't realize you knew one another.'

Mr Yockery paused before he looked up. 'There is no reason why you should have,' he said. 'We were young together, you might say.'

'I must tell him that I have seen you,' Richard said.

'*Must* you?' said Mr Yockery. 'If you must, you must, I suppose . . .'

'Well, not if you would rather I didn't.'

Mr Yockery's large, limp, too-scrubbed hands paused for a

second from their pea-baiting, mutton-piling preoccupation. He was considering. His eyes did little sums of addition and subtraction. What should he lose; what might he gain, they indicated. He cleared his throat and gulping rather, said, 'Second thoughts, do tell him. It is just possible that he might like to know.' Turning to Mrs Crawford, he explained, 'You knew that Cadman Winsley and myself were up at the House together, didn't you, Florence?'

Richard was too surprised by the 'Florence' to take overmuch notice of the answer. He glanced at Mrs Crawford and then at Mary.

'Quite true,' insisted Mr Yockery with a fearsome playfulness. 'You ask Winsley. He was going into the army, or so we all thought then. He even went to a crammer's but nothing came of it. I wonder why . . . Or do I?' he added maliciously.

Mrs Crawford's rich bulk shook a little at this. Her fingers among the wine-glasses expressed a submerged glee. This was gossip as she adored it; tentative, cruel and shaded with a flimsy esotericism sufficient to stir the wits of the semi-informed and to fox the rank outsider. She looked first at Richard and then at Mary and was a trifle angry to see them unaffected and eating. If people were not going to rise a little to the implications of the game, they—Father Yockery and herself, might just as well be alone. She leant across and rang the bell with marked resentment.

Hibble arrived and lunged about the table with florid hands, collecting plates and tureens; dinging the servers together. Richard stopped breathing when she reached his place. A compelling fancy from his childhood forced him to believe that Hibble smelled. He was ashamed to believe this, and wrong too, as it happened. Hibble, in spite of her frumped skirts and screwed-up hair, maintained a sweet and distinct freshness. None the less, she took so long to clear the plates near himself that he thought he was going to burst. At last she moved away, to return with Mrs Crawford's octagonal Bristol-Delft fruit-plates, which she scattered before them with a certain adroit recklessness.

'Anything else?' she demanded to know.

Mrs Crawford looked up, the hint of battle in her eye. She

had a sneaking admiration for Hibble's daring at times, but she wasn't going to have it flaunted in front of guests.

'Lovely, Hibble,' said Mary quickly. 'No, nothing more, thank you.'

Hibble left the dining-room rather sharply. The victory had been altogether too shadowy for her to be really sure of it.

'I suppose that you think Copdock's a pretty awful school?' said Richard, taking a pear gingerly from the pyramid of fruit in the middle of the table.

'I don't—not a bit,' denied Mr Yockery. He jabbed an elaborately engraved knife into the soft flesh of an orange. 'And who am I that I should say anything which might reduce another's sense of vocation . . .?' He wiped his long limp fingers on his napkin. 'I suppose you *do* feel it to be a vocation . . . I am sure I *hope* you do.'

'It's a job,' said Richard shortly.

'I like to think that life's task is a little more than that,' replied Mr Yockery sententiously. '*Jobs* always make me think of sculleries.'

'A vocation . . .' began Mary hesitantly, still in her role of appeaser.

'Exactly, Miss Crawford,' said Mr Yockery quickly, never doubting that she was on his side. But his formal use of her name was something a great deal more than mere politeness. He pronounced it to ensure her isolation from the charmed circle of his own and its adjacent generations. She was too young by far to enter that enjoyable and ever-reminiscent world he so assiduously cultivated. And in any case, she was a woman, and he didn't care overmuch for women. Mrs Crawford was different. She was sixty, so that made her something more than just a woman. He liked women to be rising sixty, for by then they could shed their more deplorable femininity and could even be mildly clubbable. Florence Crawford was proving herself a godsend to him. Mr Yockery admired her most sincerely. Besides who would have thought that so much of their individual pasts had impinged and had so delicately collided across half a century! Hardly a day passed now without one more thing in common being added to their recollections.

Plumbing the well of experience they discovered Canon Huntington, Oberammergau in 1921—a common occasion, though severally enjoyed—*Sinister Street* and their tallying views on it, and most miraculous of all, Florence's own discovery that they must be cousins of a sort. The last argument he had found hard to follow, but it was a fact that Tothills of the Bedford breed existed for both of them. Alliances of a more lasting kind had been founded on less things in common. And far beyond all this—Florence comforted him. He was tall and gaunt and grey; aspen with a natural asceticism that a lifetime of good feeding had not corrupted. One might say that he was one of Nature's Savonarolas, whereas Mrs Crawford, without a doubt, was one of Cheltenham's Helen Fourments. How often had not Mr Yockery longed for the symbolic comfort of that splendid breast! Marvellous and matriarchal she had always appeared to him. Only to see her, he considered, was sufficient to make the ethics of Delphi of Cnidus truly admirable. How wrong the reformers had been when they swept away the great mother-figure from English worship! In fact he wasn't sure if this had not been the very worst thing which had happened to the nation, that is if one left out the 1870 Education Act. Talking of vocation, he wondered if Florence might marry him.

'I would like to think that too,' said Richard. 'To be certain of one's vocation must be the nicest kind of smugness.'

'Aren't you sure then?' enquired Mr Yockery bleakly.

'Not a bit, I'm afraid. I really want to write, so Copdock will have to go on being just a job.'

'In the newspapers. . . ?'

'Oh, yes, in the newspapers—in anything.'

'I knew a writer once,' announced Mrs Crawford in her curiously noisy voice. 'His family was terribly nice—you remember the Pawseys, Father?'

'St Alban's?' said Mr Yockery quickly. This was wonderful! Another little bit of jigsaw past in place! He almost heard the click as he fitted it.

'St Alban's,' confirmed Mrs Crawford. 'In fact, I believe Mrs Pawsey's still there, but *he's* dead, of course.'

'It must be Nicholas Pawsey—the son, I mean,' said Richard. 'He writes in the *New Statesman*.'

'I suppose he has to live,' said Mrs Crawford.

'He writes awfully well . . .'

'So he should,' she retorted. 'He was sent to Oxford.'

God! thought Richard. It just couldn't go on. It was unendurable! How on earth did Mary stand it! He glanced across and saw her chipping away at a hard-looking sliver of apple with the pretty detachment of a squirrel that fancies itself alone. A crystal quiet surrounded her. This irritated him. How was he to be any kind of knight-errant and slay her immense boredom when she possessed sufficient weapons and courage of her own? To make things worse, her self-sufficiency was just enough to be exacting. It made him furious—until he remembered the long schooling she must have had to produce it. Then he forgave her. Doing so brought a new tenderness. He had a sudden desire to run his fingers through that fine rich hair, to touch her softly shadowed throat with his mouth. He would rescue her—crystal quiet, or no crystal quiet. He held his breath.

Hibble was splashing out the remains of the slightly sour hock. Her gesture was one of libation combined with an upstart pity. She poured too high and made it sound like the last drop. They were damned, she was thinking to herself, and everlasting night was waiting for them. In a little while . . . in the twinkling of an eye. . . . Then (for herself) the endless ease of Glory, the eternity with her feet up. . . . Blessed were the meek after all, she decided. Mr Yockery's, at last barren, plate fell to her like a trophy.

'No one really knows what is going to happen,' Mary was saying. She spoke from her vantage place, from the half-amused platform of her detachment. The room, its glass and furniture and winter flowers and those who inhabited it were her whole existence, yet it was obvious that at that particular moment she found them expendable. The vicious little observations of the older people were of no more meaning or importance than the wisps of bog-cotton which blew about the same well-polished room in the summer-time. Now and then she glanced at her mother, not even askance any more at Mrs Crawford's ostentatious sociability with its arid and accomplished 'conversation'. It was only when Mrs Crawford began to throw out opinions which could be hurtful with that faint coarseness which comes to the elderly did Mary start. Then her tolerance lapped over into a stare of warning. She could only be snubbed now in certain permitted ways; not anywhere, anyhow, as she used to be.

'Richard is right, I think,' she went on, her eyes on the table so that all she could see of him was the urbane reflection of his hands in the shiny wood. 'How can anyone say that "I shall do this" or "I shall do that" for the rest of their life— Surely the time has passed when a person calmly picked out a convenient niche in the world and calmly sat himself down in it. . . .'

'You think that?' said Mr Yockery sardonically. He didn't much like this kind of talk. He preferred to imagine that his own age carried with it its own privileged eminence; that its standards were still the criteria of taste and conduct, not picturesque, nor anachronistic. Besides, there was another reason for his uneasiness. Like Quentin, he dreaded war. He couldn't face disturbance of any kind. To combat the newspapers and the present sort of talk, he cultivated a wan optimism, a tiny self-deception that was just sufficient to keep his contentment ticking over. 'I trust, Miss Crawford, that you're not yet another person who believes that there is going to be a war?'

'Perhaps not,' she replied vaguely. 'In some miraculous—or dishonourable—way there may not be. Who can tell!'

Mrs Crawford didn't trouble to hide her disappointment. For her, nineteen-sixteen had been the golden time. Might not equivalent perils reproduce it? She was sorry for the dead, of course. One should be. But did not even *they* gain a trifle in the golden sense? Their names would not be nearly so bright a colour had they lived. She recalled it all as surgingly glorious —and golden. People were improved by the most varying conditions and she had been at her best in a holocaust. Terror did not drain her; nor the usual fears. It was Lafney which did that; Lafney with its bleak calm and orderliness. If something didn't break out soon she didn't know what she would do. Anyway, wasn't it good for the men? She seemed to remember being told something of the sort.

'Well it's much too pleasant an occasion to worry ourselves with such things!' said Mr Yockery. 'Thank you, my dear Florence.' He gave a little bow which wasn't quite a charade.

Mrs Crawford nodded and smiled and boosted the big, loose colourless knot of hair at the nape of her neck. 'There's coffee to come.'

Hibble brought the coffee in, but already doled out in thimbly cups, which was something more to irritate.

'We'll have the pot too, Hibble,' said Mrs Crawford.

Instead of showing her temper to the maid she turned swiftly to Mary. See—she's done it again! flashed her heavy, accusing eyes. Suddenly she felt bored and angry. She thought that Mary was getting more out of these occasions than she did herself. Like endless other people—even those of the most harmonious kind—she had a sudden longing to have the house to herself. 'What are you going to do this afternoon?' she demanded, as if she couldn't get them out of the place soon enough. It was a dismissal to make quite clear her own unshareable plans.

'I hadn't thought—What will you do, Richard?'

'Me——? Pack, I suppose.'

'Oh, yes, pack,' she said rather miserably.

'It won't take me long,' he said, retreating before her forlorn statement. He felt as she did, the immediate worthlessness of everything and beyond this the flutter of some unuttered invitation; a quality affecting the sound of her voice, and not what she was actually saying, which was exactly what he most enjoyed—the entrée to a ready-made situation. A confusion of trust, innocence and lassitude ruled out any real combative side to his nature. If and when something happened to him, it was because some accident or coincidence precipitated him in that particular direction. He rarely struggled towards the change of his own free will. Others generally set the scene he was to inhabit. Going to Copdock had been like that. An advertisement in *The Times Educational Supplement* would have had no effect whatsoever. It had to be Stella's bank manager's friend's word-in-the-ear and the interview that wasn't an interview, since the result existed before the examining. After that, the easing of himself out of Ipswich and into Stourfriston had been comparatively painless. Too painless perhaps—that was the danger of living other people's plans. This is where he envied Quentin, because Quentin fought wildly for what he wanted. In fact, made himself nervous and ill with all his striving and perfecting. The miracle was, that with all Quentin's effort and his own monumental insouciance, the two of them had, on the face of it, come out pretty level. The conditioning factor being, of course, 'on the face of it'.

Now another landscape spread itself before him. Or perhaps, a gardenscape. At any rate he didn't have to brave mountains or swim seas to get to it. He wouldn't even have to cope with a new language because presumably they would use the words of a lifetime. There it was, screened only by the flimsiest trellis, the unfamiliar wastes of love. If he withdrew a little at first, it was because of the shock of discovering the object of desire where he had least expected it to be. 'Let's walk along to the Martello . . .' he would have suggested, except that was too much like going over old ground. There were few walks in Lafney worth the taking. The town was all on a line with the shingle reach and the wind knifed along it, all the winter and early spring, slicing up talk and well-being.

'The dyke, then . . . ?' he suggested, as if they had both of them considered and rejected the other proposal.

'The dyke?' asked Mrs Crawford. 'It hasn't broken again, has it?'

'Of course not,' answered Mary. 'We're going for a walk. Nobody minds, do they?'

'You know it has nothing to do with me, what you do or where you go,' Mrs Crawford retorted. The reality of the occasion quite failed her. It was after luncheon and the children were going out and the grown-ups were staying at home. That had happened often enough in the past, God knew! If there were many more days like this she thought she might go mad. Perhaps it was time she organised something—A.R.P., nursing . . . evacuees. But *how*—in Lafney? It was so tight, so complacent; a nincompoop could organise the whole place to the hilt in a jiffy.

Only Mr Yockery suspected the broad truth of their departure, and that in a purely habitual way. His age and his prolonged isolation from affection made him follow desire in others like a star. He had an oldmaidish zest for matchmaking.

'If I don't happen to see you again, Richard, you'll remember me to Winsley, won't you.'

'Certainly.'

'Oh, you were about to tell us, Father,' cried Mrs Crawford, swivelling round in her chair with sudden interest. 'You were saying earlier on—oh, what was it we were discussing before Hibble came in—do you remember, Mary?'

'I don't think I do. Was it about Richard's going to see Sir Paul at Sheldon . . . ' She realized the magnitude of her mistake as soon as she had made it. She looked at Richard, her mouth parted with unsaid apology.

'Yes, of course!' declared Mrs Crawford. 'Sheldon! I knew there were hundreds of things we should be discussing—And now everybody's going out. What a pity!'

Richard made an attempt to strangle any further talk by pushing back his chair, but it moved silently on the thick carpet and Mr Yockery, dragged back from his own ungovernable little thoughts, echoed, 'Going to Sheldon . . . ?' It was surprising how the reiteration of the word by so many nosey tongues had debased it. Sheldon had seemed the most charming name for a house in Miss Bellingham's room. Now it hummed with innuendo. Unsuccessful with his scraping chair, Richard held out his father's heavy silver case, hoping that that might stem further questions. Mrs Crawford accepted a Gold Flake and smoked it in her ugly, inexpert manner—the way women may have smoked in the beginning, holding it with too many fingers and exhibiting a garish clot of rings.

'Yes, I heard that Sir Paul was on his way home,' said Mr Yockery. He turned his pale narrow head in the direction of Mrs Crawford in a self-conscious effort to give an absolutely unequivocal impression. 'I'm a great fan of his,' he added. 'I think I must possess everything he's ever written.'

'Including *The Solitary Height*?' asked Mary.

'Including that rare masterpiece indeed,' replied Mr Yockery sententiously.

The situation was saved—or restored. A wavering harmony though nothing to boast of, returned. So did Hibble, cross and unrung-for, but with that unerring clairvoyance which told her 'they were done'.

'I'll just get my warm coat,' said Mary in a slightly confused voice.

'You'll come back and have some tea, won't you?' insisted Mrs Crawford in her loud insincere hostessy way.

'In that case I won't say good-bye,' nodded Mr Yockery, pleased with the prospect of an extension of the occasion. There were fifty hours in every one of his days. He took his place at Mrs Crawford's side and became lost at once in that particular fantasy. What security he found in doing so! Even she was gratefully pleased with the care with which he conducted her from the room.

6

THE car was Mary's idea—an immediate one, although she toyed a little with other suggestions just for the look of the thing. Because she had put off telling her mother that they intended to take it—a slight weariness at having to explain her flimsiest actions year in and year out had produced its own little pall of dishonesty (she found actual lying forced up an almost physical nausea inside her, so she now shied away from that and relied entirely on silence with its mixed bag of answers), they eased the vehicle from the gig-house with an apprehensive casualness. It was an Alvis. It had a fine, bright dashboard and high, cold, slippery seats. Through the clean lunette made by the windscreen wiper on his side, Richard took in the intricately stacked lumber which lined the place. Beginning with trunks, too immense ever to have gone anywhere, it mounted with a sad profligacy of colourless basket furniture, damp books and bursting saddles. Like a grotesque cornucopia spilling out the essence of its decade, a large gentian-shaped gramophone horn swung forlornly from a rafter. Over everything—even competing with the chilly leather and petrol reek of the Alvis—there lingered still the sweet ineradicable hint of horses.

She backed the car gingerly.

'It needs a jolly good clear out,' he said.

'I know,' she answered limply. There was barely room to put a matchstick between the front wing and the chest faintly inscribed 'Commander R. St. J. Crawford, R.N.' She got out and closed the door herself, a bit resentful over his criticism of something for which she had a fondness. Of course it needed a clear out. Wasn't one absolutely surrounded by this haphazard loot from the past, things that nudged and reminded one all the time? Of course it should be tidied away, outlawed from sight and memory. Yet it never would, because the result would not be order, but a void. Her own life had so far been too quiet for her to feel that she could take a broom to her experiences and start afresh. They were all too frugal, too cherished. She hoped that the mere fact of her loving him would not lead him to believe that all she had gone through, trivial though it might seem, was *nothing*. The vein of richness, the novelty even, in the new situation was wonderfully exciting to her, but for it to be anything other than just *that*, she must be sure that he liked what he actually saw, and not what his conceit or his imagination envisaged. She locked the garage door. How complete I am when it comes to being truly underhanded, she thought. From the corner of her eye she saw Richard lolling in his seat with the door wide open, looking a bit quelled and embarrassed that she should be doing everything. She climbed in and the car swung a little on its springs in the way she used to find so luxuriously thrilling as a child.

'I was looking at all the thingummies,' he said, fingering the dashboard; 'how beautifully they're made.'

'You've seen it all hundreds of times before.'

'Thousands, if you like,' he retorted a little sharply, reacting to the vague irritation in her voice, 'but does that prevent me seeing it in a quite new way at this moment?'

She smiled, catching at the retreating choke inexpertly. She enjoyed his being faintly put out. His good manners—extreme politeness is, after all, but one aspect of cowardice—could be exasperating.

'You mean that we didn't even think of it as an Alvis before?' She scrubbed against her window with an old piece of yellow rag.

'Oh no. It was something far more interesting.'

'Like an early morning start to a holiday? Or a picnic?'

'Dunwich!' he said triumphantly. Dunwich had always been the outing *par excellence*. The Alvis, crammed with the Rectory children; Mr Brand, with his fearfully tired merriment; Edwina, too nicely hatted and gloved; Mary, a big, self-conscious summery girl in her teens and in front, Mrs Crawford herself driving with meticulous style and with an aplomb more suitable to reins than to gears; would descend on the little place with something like a whoop. 'Couldn't we go there now?'

'Now?' She pretended that it hardly mattered where they went. 'Let's get out of Lafney for a bit, that's the chief thing.' She let go the brake and the gentle tremor of the moving car brought on a rush of happiness as illogical as it was unfounded.

'Oughtn't we to round by the back drive?' he asked, remembering Mrs Crawford.

'Why?'

He was unable to check himself. Subtlety was degenerating into obtuseness. He floundered. 'I thought she—your mother might see us—might wonder at us taking the car, I mean. We did say we were going for a walk . . . '

She knew this was true, but refused to be reminded of it. The very fact that Richard was insisting on doing so in his muddled, lame way, only heightened her deliberation. She turned the car in a swift, too-generous arc round the front lawns and noticed with perverse satisfaction that her mother *was* staring out of the drawing-room window. It was a second only, in which Mrs Crawford's features, set against the black opaque oblong of the window, glowed snowily like the negative of a snapshot.

'We won't have to open the gates,' she said in an even, pleasant tone which was really an apology. 'The little runner things got stuck when they tarred the drive last summer.' He nodded, but didn't answer and as she manoeuvred her way through the town, she forced herself to see him as she thought he would want to be seen. He was more vulnerable than she had reckoned and he could still sulk—in which case, she decided, he must be more involved with childhood than she had credited. Men were. The complex fusion of cruelty and love, immediate reality and protracted romanticism, never quite left them. When women were adult, they were so in a way a man could never be. If by any chance a man *did* approach this kind of maturity he at once became suspect. To be really grown-up meant—in the popular fancy at least—some lessening of his maleness.

As though he followed this argument, Richard pulled himself up from his slumped position and said, 'Here, let me have a go.'

'It's not quite like an ordinary car,' she said unwillingly. 'You have to know it.'

'You forget that I do know it.'

They were on the coast road now. Behind them, Lafney, its slatey little core a smirch of one grey on the lighter, more drained greyness of the sky, looked trivial and neglected. She drew in to the side and heard the tyres scrunching over the shingle and saw the disturbed gulls waddle off across the seer, shrivelled-up plantains and heard the sea aching against the beach. They got out and changed seats and at once she found herself unexpectedly glad.

'I take it that it's to be Dunwich,' said Richard, pulling out a badly-folded ordinance survey map from the string rack over their heads. A few poor brown flowers fell from its creases.

'But haven't we decided on all that?'

'Have we? Okay. If you say so.'

Taking great care because he thought she might be still in her highly critical mood, he drove on, saying, 'Then Dunwich it is.'

'Honestly, you'd think we were off to Xanadu!'

They both laughed at this. It was so obviously true.

'I can't ever remember it being anything like an adventure before,' said Mary. 'I think they took us there because there was never anything to do except bathe and eat buns. Quentin was always bursting to get to Southwold just because it had a pier and deck-chairs.'

'Did he?' asked Richard, '—was he, I mean. You seem to remember more of those days than I do.'

It was a hint that she should remember no more, but it didn't offend her in the least. 'I know . . . ' she said with surprising contentment. 'Richard . . . '

'Mmmm?'

'Oh, nothing!'

'In that case,' he answered, regarding her with amusement,

'we'll blame old Yockers. He's rather flattened us out, hasn't he!'

'He may have,' she admitted, 'although I don't mind him really, do you?'

'I've come to the conclusion that I don't mind anybody *really*. Real minding presumably comes later—don't you think?'

She acknowledged that it did, or that it might, though rather hesitantly and vainly attempting to extract any note in her voice that she cared personally. A state forest came into view; acres and acres of shivering little larches planted with military precision in the sandy gorse wastes leading to the sea. Washed up on a slight mound was Blythburgh church, the bare bones of Gothic, yet defiantly exquisite still, as fresh as a gull and as brittly perfect as starched Mechlin.

'Oh, *isn't it lovely*! Go slower—don't you always love it, Richard!'

He stared at it obediently, though acknowledging to himself that it was a too-familiar loveliness ever to genuinely stir him again. The Parthenon must be a pretty hackneyed sight to the Athenians. At the same moment he saw her face, turned away to the cold landscape, her eyes very bright and the skin over her cheek-bones, taut and crisp with a delicate wintriness. Her beauty relieved him. It existed—he hadn't fancied it, although he had been nearer to it a thousand times more often than he had to the famous beauty of this building. The miracle was that he could have ever considered her without such a beauty! The too-cambered lane sent them lurching towards each other. His leg fell across the gear heavily and jostled against hers.

She said, 'I'm longing to have a walk,' and stretched away from him, both the movement and the words drawn from her by some priggish involuntary reaction she was unable to control. 'How funny to come here in winter—it was always August before . . .'

'It'll be muddy.'

'I wasn't quite thinking of that.'

He remembered that he had said nothing in the way of thanks for the lunch; worse, that in some way he had caused her to apologize for her mother and the rector. Now that he came to think about it, it hadn't been so bad—amusing really. Quentin would have extracted *his* ounce of pleasure from it. 'Old Yockers was in pretty good form,' he said.

She looked at him quickly, surprised to find him still thinking about something which seemed to have happened a hundred years ago. 'Mr Yockery——? He isn't so bad,' she said defensively.

Richard caught at her mood. 'He must be awfully lonely.'

'I expect he must be,' she replied flatly, making it plain now how little she cared. 'Look!'

'What——?' He craned towards to the windscreen.

'It's gone.' It was a squirrel.

After this, harmony became the high essential. Richard discovered himself slipping into the new situation with easy complaisance. The simplicity of it appalled him. He tried to force his imagination along towards an ardency which would at least add to his self-respect, but the more he did so, the more his amiable languor persisted. He could even be faintly amused, and this proved his detachment as nothing else possibly could. He wondered what Mary was thinking. When he saw her face and its pensiveness in the imperfect mirror made by the stripped hedges darkly glowing behind the windscreen, he was vain enough to identify its expression with his own mood. She can't get over it either! he thought. She thinks it's astounding! Her stillness deceived him. He thought that she must be controlling a sort of gaiety, such as his own. He turned sharply to the right and the Alvis made a bee-line for the shore, but coasting first along the rim of a waste of sodden bracken. They passed the bare shape of the Priory gate, strung up in the frigid air like a well-picked Gothic wishbone. A few yards further and the Alvis drew up knowingly by the sullen dunes.

'Brrr!' he said, 'I think it looks awful—I think I'll stay here ... ' He leant back in his seat to help pull the deep fur collar of her coat snugly round her ears, finding it essential to touch her.

'It makes me cold—even in summer,' she confessed in a dull, abstract voice. 'Perhaps because it's no place. It's nowhere. It was, but it isn't. It's like an old woman tottering to the grave under the weight of her great name. She knows, and the whole world knows that she's the last of the de-somethings. But yet she might just as well not be. There's nothing left to prove it, no lurking distinction, no beauty, no wit, nothing at all. This is Dunwich—but what proves that?'

'The Priory might.'

'You find that sort of ruin anywhere.'

'I know—the bones!'

'Oh,' she protested, as if against a new coldness. 'The bones —I'd quite forgotten them . . . I don't suppose we could see them?'

'Why not—except it will be terribly muddy.'

'You're always saying things like that,' she accused him. 'Are they for me or for yourself—yourself, I think. You must know by now that sort of comfort means nothing to me.'

'You're sharp: you shouldn't be. And you're far too literal. There has to be this kind of padding in life to keep it from being all deeds and—and . . . ' He turned away, more injured by her unannounced little stabs of brusqueness than he could possibly explain. She had the power immediately to cast him down. He heard her speaking, in a quick, light, uncomprehending way which might almost be called insensitive, until he understood that her sudden hardnesses were really no more than rapid plots to maintain a new degree of happiness. It was not himself that she was fighting, but the entire pattern of her own uneventful life.

'No,' she was saying, 'I simply can't agree. I've had quite a struggle to keep *my* head above the upholstery!' She gave him a quick smile to acknowledge the absurdity of their metaphor as well as to admit that she *had* said some word out of place—although heaven knew what it could be—she was sorry. They had the long, damp bonnet of the Alvis between them. The historical sense crept back into her mind. Where they stood, where reeds carried on their barren little penance, whipping and cutting across each other everlastingly; had been a street, an aisle, a court. Where they stared over the gravely gorging sea, there had once been roofs and spires and hopes. Fat cold porpoises surfaced where the bishop's gardens had sunk, and in the second in which their silence multiplied, a few more grains of England fell and were sucked away by the tide. The mere inexorable ritual of it could present greater fears than any they might contrive, as it could also, were it heeded, ravage and isolate their love. With such a desolation flaunting its strength before her she was utterly contrite for her burst of nerves had temper. She wanted to rush round to his side, take him and kiss his mouth; to feel that certainty of contact—there was always this immense distance about him which lent him a spurious innocence—which only his body provided.

Richard said: 'We never thought of it as 'Dunwich' exactly when we came for picnics. It was just a decent place to paddle.'

'Yes,' she agreed pacifically, 'and isn't that just like all historical knowledge? It forces such dreary truths upon one! We were right the first time—it is a good place to paddle . . .'

'And nothing more?'

'Of course not—not if we didn't happen to know it.'

'Then what about the bones?'

'They were just one more thing we didn't know about.'

'*They* must have known, Daddy and Mrs—your mother.'

Mary shrugged and laughed and said: 'Come on. I'm freezing.'

'Quenny knew,' said Richard.

'He did?' And then because she did not want their talk to develop into yet more reminiscence she added, 'Oh, *Quentin* . . .' It was the dismissal of history again as well as a cue to the way they should be behaving.

Richard walked beside her. His hand was on her shoulder. She felt it hardly at all where his palm gripped the padding in her coat, but the tips of his fingers burnt against the softness of her arm. She was silent with sheer unanswerable joy of where they were and how they were, and could scarcely believe it when she heard him proposing a return to the car.

'We don't *have* to see the bones or Dunwich. We can go back up the lane—anywhere. What does it matter!' He thought she was depressed by the place, and her stillness an expression of her boredom. He never thought that his steadying hand across the rucked dunes existed for her as an embrace.

She listened to him, a little at cross purposes with what he was saying and the reason for him saying it, before realizing with a tiny pang of regret that it *did* matter—where they went, that is. Dunwich became the city of destiny, even allowing for the fact that barely one brick of it still nudged another. They had come to it and it was for Dunwich to decide their whole new conduct, whether it was to be furtive or revealed; the world faced up to, or the world retreated from. To run away now was unthinkable. What did it matter what degree of mortality surrounded them? It was ridiculous and inconsequential. In Lafney it was the living, at Dunwich, the dead. Given the choice, who is to say that the latter may not prove the least formidable? Her intelligence told her all this, but her stomach revolted against the idea of hanging over the cliff-face and seeing that terrible débris.

The path along the cliff crumbled at every step and grew muddier at every turn. It crept up over her shoes and was so sticky she was obliged to walk with her feet rather apart with a coarse inelegance which made Richard laugh. She managed to laugh as well, but privately she found the wet sludge more nauseating than she could say. Once she floundered helplessly and after that he held her above the waist and she tried not to resent the certain, yet half-conscious exploratory touch of his hand beneath her breast. It was this above all which she despised in herself, the way she flinched at any physical move in this intoxicating new situation. They reached the cliff-top and there it seemed less wintry. What was left of the church lurched towards the sea with an almost voluntary energy from every haggard corbel and chamfered arch. Much of the building was already drowned and the rest must soon follow. The flints would be released at last from their mortar and the facing-stones made smoother than any mason's shop could ever contrive them. A little cropped meadow covered the cliff, oddly green for January, in fact rather May-ish. There were swags of blackberry and intricate thickets of blackthorn which shook stiffly when the wind passed. A few yards from the church was a single tombstone on which was engraved, very sedately, 'In loving Memory of Thomas Easey who departed this life August 22nd, 1828. R.I.P.' A low curtain of cobblestones which had once been the Priory wall ran crazily for many yards to the extreme right and so still afforded a gaunt compound where pigs and poultry might scratch and wallow in safety.

Richard spread his mackintosh on the cliff edge and then himself on top of it. The bones, a long sand-stained layer of them, were about three feet down. They reflected a pale ochrous light and were like a costly filling which had failed to stay the inevitable corruption of the land. Mary crouched at his side and together they looked silently at the poor slender little knuckles of arm and thigh laid low like vanquished sceptres; the scattered reels of the vertebrae from which all meaning had long since been spun and a leaky basket of ribs through which sand and earth trickled remorselessly. Poised on a ledge, a small neat skull fixed its huge gaze upon an austere view.

She drew back when at last she saw this.

'No—no—I can't . . . '

'At least we've seen what we came to see.'

This blunted truth sent her spinning back into her earlier isolation. He laid at her feet with a sprawling, tense grace, with his head dangling above the splitting graves and with a kind of avid stillness. 'It's too horrible . . . ' she protested, 'too real, too actual. If *that* is everything, why make any effort . . . anywhere . . . Why struggle?'

Richard found her genuine concern rather enviable. It was the kind of thing he had attempted to feel himself a thousand times, but the genuine emotion had always become adulterated somehow by what he could only call 'poetry'. Just when he was about to touch on an immediate experience, a sort of literary mattress descended between himself and it, and then what he really felt was something he might just as well have read, often with more profit and less inconvenience. He scrambled to his feet and picked up his coat. To reintroduce the warm, reasonable, living world he took both her hands in his own and kissed her, not on the mouth, but on her brow; a soft, dragging kiss of uttermost tenderness. The wind rushed up and around them, sweeping her skirts strongly against the back of her legs and she was unable to distinguish this embrace from his own, so that she discovered herself suddenly surrounded and hedged about with desire and sweetness. For a tumultuous second they remained standing there with the cold, noisy air swirling Richard's and her own heavy clothes together like the rumpled finery in a baroque apotheosis. Gulls appeared, thrown up to their peaceful height from some more clamorous squalor on the beach itself. They howled and ranted and injected their own terrible exhilaration into the moment, before they fell back screeching to the sea. Oh Mary thought, closing her eyes, This is all and everything. Lafney is dust and there is dust below us, but this is the rich, the tangible, the living thing! I love him—I love him ... But she said nothing, not daring to. Instead, with a tentative restraint which she half-guessed might please him, she drew his head down a little towards her own, then further, so that they laid side by side in a Janus completeness, looking up and down the long grey coast. It was absurd and wonderful. To maintain the nonsense, she moved her hand to the side of his face until she felt his ear, like nervous ice, and at this revelation she was able to tug herself free, pull the edges of her coat over her skirt and laugh happily.

It was then that he bewildered her by a grim gaiety of his own.

'Do you think it's very old?' he asked.

He was looking over the cliff's edge again, finding nothing there but the ingredients of another sensuous situation.

'The skull?' she enquired wonderingly. 'No, not very. The sea is supposed to have reached the eighteenth century part of the churchyard. His king was probably George the Third.'

'Or hers——'

'Yes—or hers.'

'I think I'll get it.'

'What?'

'I shall be O.K. I shan't fall,' he said, mistaking her anxiety. 'If I do, it's only loose sand and the worst that can happen is that I shall get into a bit of a mess.'

'But I don't want it—it's a revolting idea.'

'Why?' he demanded. He had turned and was looking her full in the face. '*Why* is it revolting?' And then when she was unable to answer, made all at once silent and wretched by his flippant attitude. 'It's macabre, it's strange—it's affected if you like; but it's not revolting.' He knew he was being unreasonable, that this was only a hint of how he would always repay devotion because devotion for him meant a prison of sorts and that he *must* have freedom—even freedom from love. Yet he hated himself for hurting her—and then began to hate her for existing to *be* hurt. All loathing is a trick done with mirrors which must inevitably reflect back to ourselves.

She was terrified and chastened by his unreasonableness. 'Then don't fall,' she advised weakly.

'No.'

He looked for the moment as if he might apologize or even kiss her. Then, fastening his coat carefully to prevent its catching, he swung his legs over the wet edge of the cliff and lowered his body until his feet came to rest on a little sinking hump of clay bellying out above the sea. Below were the dunes against which the waves slid in coldly unctuous scallops. The gulls were outraged and struck about the sky. The skull was near his knee. He could feel it. Clinging with one hand to a gorse root, he put his hand down and took it. It was like bird's nesting. He remembered then how his hand would pass lightly over every kind of roughness until, with a faint sensual tremor, his fingers would discover the warm, delicate eggs. Only this time the egg was chilly and unreasonably heavy—it was full of sand. It fell from the grave to his hand easily and once he had moved it so far, he felt bound to accept it as some monstrous award. Getting back wasn't so easy. He managed to button the skull inside the top of his coat. When at last he gained the neat, grassy headland it was to discover a more recent desolation. Mary had gone. He saw her in the distance, her head jerking and nodding as she stumbled back to the car. He thought, she's furious. Quite forgetting about the state of the path which was the cause of her flouncing movements.

At that moment he would have tipped the skull back to where it would so soon have fallen, to the lonely beach. Mary's grief was so evident that the skull became just an enormous reminder of his own selfishness. All at once he loathed it. He took it from his coat with disgust and immediately a quantity of smooth, summery sand poured from it, ritualistically, like the dust from a fissured sermon-glass. With the sand was spilt the horror, and when it was all gone, he felt that what remained described some curious aspect of beauty. The skull was fragile and warm. It was the colour of much-used chessmen and it awarded the January afternoon with a startlingly brash smile from its small, level teeth. The eyes alone maintained their awe. Their darkness was insupportable. He tried to forget this as he hurried back to the Alvis.

'I'm really sorry,' he explained. And he was.

'I was just a bit cold,' she said defensively. It was the truth; the most awful cold had possessed her for a moment. 'Where is it? Did you manage to get it . . .?'

He revealed it casually. 'The sand has proved quite a reasonable preservative.' This was an old way-out of his—the endowing of an emotional act-of-the-moment with motive and consideration. 'I'll just shove it under the rug at the back.'

'No—let me . . .' She put out her hand, but drew it back at once, although certainly not meaning to flinch. Then she saw that it was quite beautiful, so clean and tidy and really so unsuggestive of misery that it might have been the delicate basis of some work of art that had crumbled away. In this way she could touch it. 'It's light—how light!' she said.

'It was full of sand which ran out like sugar.'

'Oh, *poor* young man!' she exclaimed, all at once ridiculously happy. 'Do you think he was a sailor?'

'Or poor young lady—Do you think she was a tart?'

'It will have to be reasonably romantic if it's to come with us in the car—either that or something purely scientific. We could say he was Edward- something and that he went twice round the Cape before dying of love for an Ipswich no-good. Why it's as plain as the—' She stopped abruptly. It was a mistake to play up to a false situation, or to other people's sense of exaggeration. People always knew when one forced oneself along in their own particular brand of facetiousness and it never came off. The better one did it, the more care the imitated one took to hide his awareness of it. It was so flattering. And there was the extra felicity of hearing the imitator do quite badly what one did extraordinarily well oneself. This was Richard's kind of nonsense. Coming from him it would have been acceptable. She watched rather sadly as he placed the reason for it in a corner of the back seat and threw a fold of the Inverness rug over it. Sliding across into the driving-seat, she revved the engine busily.

It was getting dark when they came to the purple rift of lane which cut across the main road like a transept and he said, surprisingly, 'Right.' More surprisingly still, she tugged the wheel and went right. And when he said, 'Stop—Mary . . . will you . . ?' she did this too, only with a kind of bewilderment which sent the car rocking against the verge.

As he kissed her, with an efficiency she had not suspected and now could hardly bear, she thought, I won't—I *won't*! This is the worst thing I have ever done, this making plain of my needs, this exposure of them—She wanted to fight back against such a disturbing new enemy. Everything in her nature told her that if she did—and overcame there would be peace once more. Order and design, her ease and her awful tranquillity. Instead of this strength, however, there was a delicious ease of body in direct conflict with her mind, so strong in fact, as to master thought; to subdue it, even efface it. He was selfish because he was young (ten years younger, she thought —or almost) and he would destroy her contentment (and that was the lowest estimate at which she could assess her happiness) and she would now be wretched and miraculously happy in alarming succession; but wretched mostly. Worse, people would witness her destruction because she could never hide it; her mother would treat it cruelly, because she would be frightened and would dread losing her. It would have to be something to do with *him*, she considered, some failing which would be intolerable to her and revealed suddenly, that could effect her release. Nothing within herself could save her. If only some vulgarity could be found to repel her—something equivalent to the outrageousness of a face-slap which follows up an hysterical collapse! But there was nothing present which she did not long for, nothing to make her drag herself free from the whole idea of love—not even the conviction she held that Richard did not yet love her. He wanted her and idiotically enough, this made her glad. Like somebody from whom a deeply personal experience is being extracted by subtle questions, or a patient who must submit to a great pain or die, she withdrew her imagination from the vaster issue and took refuge in immediate trivia. First in Richard himself. His hair, which looked so fine and soft, was hot and coarse, she discovered, and his face was unexpectedly firm and cool against her own. It felt like fruit. Then the car gadgets—the brake rubbed shiny by all those stops and starts, the silver flower-holder caught against the windscreen by its sucker—it used to flaunt a carnation in her father's day; now it was full of matchsticks . . . Moths, petals, white scraps of those old carnations were coming towards her now, whirling and twirling sadly. She watched them gently, saw them withering against the windows, saw them die, before she interpreted them correctly as a few soft stars of early snow. Night swelled the conifers and laid a bloom on the tarmac. An owl, hustling into action, was caught with threatening fidelity in the side-lights before the forest swallowed it in its maw.

'Richard . . . my dearest . . .'

'You mustn't speak—you don't have to, you know.'

'Because of waking you up?' she asked quietly. His extraordinary stillness hung over them both like an enchantment. After the adroit, sensual way in which he had kissed her, he was lying in her arms like a child.

'You'll come to Copdock?' he asked.

She smiled in the cold darkness. 'I might—but only on speech-days.'

He sat up abruptly and sighed. 'Well you can't say that a little silence isn't a novelty in our case?'

'Ours—?'

He saw his mistake, but was bound to explain.

'Quentin's, mine.'

'I wonder why you should imagine yourselves so much alike—you're not really, you know.' Then, when he didn't answer, 'You'll be off pretty early tomorrow—?'

'First train; the eight-seventeen.'

The everyday world rushed in on her. 'If we're sensible—' she began. It was a plunge at rationality, yet the words died the second she uttered them, they dropped about her clumsily, calamitously, even. She thought of the future. The word 'prudence' entered her head and she was ashamed to find herself contemplating it with contemptuous amusement. Ashamed because she was being derisive about an aspect of her nature all too familiar to her. Prudence was like fear, she thought. If you were born with it, you don't get rid of it in a hurry. It was essential to her whole peace at Meridian that nothing was said, nothing observed. Her mother would be the first to concoct some kind of pity if she found out, and that would be intolerable. He *must* be silent. She demanded it with a little desperate glance, because how could she possibly *say* it! But she needn't have worried. Both Quentin and Richard were naturally furtive, even Edwina only getting as much of their lives as they thought possible for her. Neither of them liked to think that he deceived. It was all a matter of not saying. It was an option of shadows and cheerfulness, or of clarity and pain. Stella alone was crystal. She evoked the image of a full-length glass in which was reflected the unanswerable conduct of a hockey captain.

Now he was taking her hand, holding it up to his face, absorbing its whiteness and the pale red paint so carefully applied to her long, narrow nails; opening and closing her fingers with a proprietary sensuality. Then, to atone for this crude examination, he began to kiss her wrist. 'That's better,' she felt she ought to say—as if her hurts were to be healed as easily as that!

'No,' she protested, when his hand wandered about the huge buttons fastening her coat.

'But I love you . . .' he said in an astounded, muffled, voice.

I'm too aware, too conscious, she thought. If only I didn't see myself failing, hear myself saying these grotesque things! Instead there was her own voice adeptly returning the appropriate sentences. 'I love you,' she was saying, effortlessly, meaninglessly; like a charm against the plague. But there was one immediate consolation. For the first time in her whole life she felt no longer alone. Shadows from the past coalesced with the uncertain present, nudging each other with the awful familiarity of passengers who have travelled for years on a regular bus route. I could have had this before, she deliberated—it wasn't love in its actual, longed-for state. It was really (and here she shrank, even to think of it), a very ordinary need. She had been abstemious and grudging in her treatment of it, and really it should have dwindled to very little. Yet it had not. Desire had been in hiding—a coward most likely and had now been discovered. She faced it as a stranger, with neither relief nor concern, seeing it as she saw everything else at that moment, with a hideous detachment. That is why she could tolerate the tense exploration of the hand near her breast; why, although she trembled, she did not flinch. Only she wished with all her heart that it had not been *him*, Quentin's brother, Edwina's child and, not so long since it seemed, her own frequent charge. Lovers should be strangers first. It was better so.

Between his caresses and his words—the same words, cruel and consoling, which were little more than an abracadabra requisite for the occasion, she saw the snow, or rather, felt it; flake after flake falling against the car and against her mind, as well as two bright parallels of it streaming from the headlights. Watching it descend was like a drug. Each settling speck of it helped to submerge reality. Soon there would be only this faultless whiteness covering everything, like a huge, clean paper upon which they might write anything they liked irrespective of what had been scribbled down before. It occurred to her, sadly and wryly, that it was only their immediate needs which were identical, her own halting and deperate, and his a sort of languorous greed. This then was an 'affair' . . . Her muddy shoe played nervously above the accelerator. I must be *convinced*, she insisted to herself. How—? By touch? By words? Perhaps if she could see him, that would infuse some truth into her realm of doubtful shadows. Drawing his head gently round towards the snowy light, she watched and waited. His eyes flickered across her own, intimate and amused.

'Richard . . .' she hesitated.

His amusement declared itself blatantly.

'Oh!' she cried, hurt and bewildered. Her hands fell away from him like lead.

Contrite beyond all words, he gathered her to him and when at last he thought he could explain, he did so in a vague, ordinary manner as if by destroying the warmth in words he might divest them of their meaning.

'It was just the way you held my head—it made me think of the skull . . .'

'*That* made you laugh?'

'It should have made me weep, of course—*Timor mortis conturbat me*—as they say!'

'Oh not yet!' she protested—'if that means what I think it does. Anyway, let's forget about the skull. And talking of forgetting, what is the time?'

'Six-ish.'

'*Heavens*!' She fumbled for the starter with abstract fingers. 'Here—let me.'

She shook her head. The car shuddered and ran forward over the unmarked snow. Driving with exactitude and rather slowly, she took care to observe the stripling forest and how the roadside trees, like a guard, dipped shade after shade before her. The mere fact of driving soothed her. She not only felt equable once more, but anxious that Richard should remember only the best of her, and that he could not do this if he still imagined that her temper had deserted her at Dunwich.

'What will you do with it?' she asked casually.

'Take it back . . . perhaps.'

'Oh, you won't do that!'

'If I don't, I shall keep it. I might have it on my desk.'

But already there was the burden of it, the regret of children after they have carried bluebells too far and the long, nude stalks have become accusative and hateful to them. He would liked to have tipped it out into the darkness—it would lodge somewhere under the blackthorns, happily and for good— but being adult brought its own onerousness and he couldn't. Honour insisted that you stood by what a passing mood had ravished. The skull, lifted from its trickling, gritty context, was his. No one was likely to claim it of him; neither church nor state. Even the sea's interest was limited to the indiscriminate appetite which caused it to feed on all it embraced. His motives for stealing it had been strictly poetic and that was that.

A searchlight waggled an admonitory finger in their path. Another joined it and at once both became yellow antagonists jousting austerely in the barren sky. Lafney appeared, first the new bungalows, obsessed with their niceties of rockery and nomenclature; then the station sizzling with the six-forty, the engine hissing like a great hot bug; then the church, outrageously picturesque with every twitch of its Gothic titivated with winter; then the streets, modestly pretty and lastly, Meridian itself—alone incensed by the wind, the cold and the general bitterness, and aching for blossom and a gaudy sea.

'It's because I always associate life with literature—that's why I do certain things. When I pinched the skull I wasn't thinking of taste, I was thinking of Donne.'

'So you equate all your behaviour with books?'

'A good deal of it.'

'You may have to change your ideas,' she smiled, nodding in the direction of the searchlights which were now feeling their way through the thinner clouds with a kind of golden prurience.

'I don't see why,' he demurred. 'Wars have always had their word-spinners. When you come to think of it,' he added, 'what do either of us know about the last one beyond its actual literature? Only music—rubbishy music: and poetry that was indignant and fine, but is awfully dated now. Yet we know it couldn't have been remotely like that—that's the funny thing about writing of any sort, the worst or the best. It can't ever say *exactly*.'

Mary said: 'Wars ... books ... you're tying me up in knots. I think I must be in a peculiarly stupid mood.' She laughed to imply some sort of compliment. Then, more seriously, 'I expect it will be just the same next time. Civilization always likes to follow a precedent when it stages its massacres, don't you think? The more ritual there is, the less feeling of guilt. They'll even dig trenches again—you'll see—although death was often less disgusting than life in them. I remember Daddy talking about it, the trench idea, and how it broke the spirit. How awful: I sound like Dean Inge!'

'You think that they'll prefer a trench to any newfangled battlefield?' he asked.

'It's the devil they know,' she answered a little wearily, immeasurably saddened by the way the conversation was going. The sadness made her weak. Privately to herself she was thinking, it won't be the discomforts and horrors that will get me down if it does come; it will be the *talk*! She wanted to rest, to collect herself and to collect, too, every aspect of this curious day, which, at the moment, sprawled so bewilderingly in her brain. She was now committed to some other situation than the one she had awoke to this morning. She must examine it and herself as well.

'Did you want to come in again?' she enquired hesitantly.

He liked her for asking this. Here was a devotion to his own private feelings which sheered away from formal politeness. From now on they would have this particular kind of intimacy.

'Not really—I've got to pack.'

'Yes, you have. I wish we could just sit and talk. It's because I'm so frightfullly tired all of a sudden. I want to talk, but I have nothing to say.'

'Good night, dearest Mary.'

She heard the door crunch dully as it fell against the snowy bank of the drive and felt the night assail their close, tobacco-ridden comfort with its glittering astringency. He bent across to kiss her and she knew it to be the last of the warmth. Straight ahead, in the direction they faced, Mrs Crawford switched on the dining-room lights and immediately the geometry of three tall windows ruled its problem over the snow. They watched her generous darkness pass from window to window, then Richard left.

The car had slipped a vague regretful yard or two before she braked, wondering how she should call him. But he had remembered and returned in time to spare her lifting the skull from its snug tartan nest. The rug had faintly polished it to a primrose glimmer of bone and blackness.

7

It was a week before he wrote in any way properly. During that time Mary had written twice, not letters in the actual full sense of the word, but a sentence or two that were like inky antennae reaching up from Mrs Crawford's too-blue paper. He expected these notes, was pleased to get them and replied lightly in the same vein. When he did write at last—a double page of typing-paper—it was because for the first time since he returned to Copdock he felt morose and wretched. There is little so depressing for the newcomer to a scene than for him to be urged towards a hearty participation in its threadbare loyalties. If it was just a matter of reassuring the boys, Richard wouldn't have cared. That sort of conduct was all right. But Mr Winsley was attempting to extract homage to Copdock itself. In his letter to Mary he complained,

'This *is* a fearful hole after all, not in any physical sense, that is: I can eat the food and my gas fire keeps me fairly scorched—but in some other, hard-to-explain way. The teaching, you feel, is a game to hide a more violent activity. *Now*, of course, you're going to say something about people with nasty imaginations! But it's true all the same. The marvel is that anything happens in the school sense at all; yet it does. The class-rooms are neat, although they look a bit improvised and the old man squeezes a few more chaps through Common Entrance every year. Don't ask me how it is done, it just *is*!

'Much warmer today and slush everywhere. (Why, I wonder, do I write you this kind of stuff?) Shouldn't I be more fond, although that isn't quite right. I really mean, shouldn't I set free the fondness I feel, so that it rushes across the paper and fills up every word like a little well of love? I'd do that even, if I thought you wouldn't smile and go bustling off to see what your bad tempered old Hibble was up to. Anyway,

Much love,
R.

P.S. Our relic has had to go on to the hat-shelf in the wardrobe. It's too reproachful as a paper-weight. Would one be prosecuted for sending it through the post? I just thought that perhaps ... Quenny ... He loves surprises!'

The letter was a duty done. Strolling out to post it, he ran into Bateson who at once insisted on their going to a pub. Pubs were Bateson's peculiar terrain. Once inside them he felt safe and secure. The more stifling the bar, the easier he breathed. They were his way of forgetfulness and his cosy remembrancer. He was never so happy, so little at variance with life, as when he plunged into their kindly cocoon of obfusc conversation. The 'Golden Fleece' was full. The painted china handles of the beer-engines rose and fell with bright authority. Smoke lay ravelled against the electric bulbs and hung about the leather-backed seats like the wraiths of dead customers.

'A pint?' suggested Bateson.
Richard nodded.
'Cheers,' Bateson said carefully.

The pub was full and kindliness crept through its various rooms in a treacly stream. The till rang triumphantly; little asterisks of profit flew gaily from its bell. A huge varnished fish, a pike, ogled them from a single glazed eye and above the roaring fire hung an oil painting of a gaunt racehorse with spindly fetlocks and crazed nostrils. Two brewers' looking-glasses, opposite each other, carried Bateson's image on and on through a whole suite of mysterious bars, accompanied each time by the faithfully reflected pike. The evening papers, the *Standard* and the *Star,* lay unopened on the rosewood piano.

'The Winner isn't keen on the staff showing up here,' said Bateson. 'It's not so much drinking that he's down on as any of us giving loyalty to anything outside the limits of the school itself. Or that is what I suspect.'

All around them the mouths talked or sipped and the hands wagged eloquently; but the eyes remained curiously divorced from either interest. They just watched. And the landlord, a tall slender man until it came to his belly, which pressed forward like a sleek globe just above his belt, stared most of all.

'The same, gentlemen?' he enquired and their glasses tottered in his ginger-haired fist.

'The same,' said Richard, and Bateson muttered,

'I give it a year—a year at the utmost.'

'What, the school?'

'The war—the school—life as it is.'

'You do . . . ?' asked Richard, too eagerly. He had rolled into this job and was also slipping fecklessly and with too little passion into the Lafney situation. The idea of war at that moment flickered with a lurid romantiscism, like the lightning quivering across Toledo in an El Greco picture. That was how it must always appeal to the young, he thought, recognizing in his own callousness a crude release from too many loving hands and later on, a rough and inevitable glory. How Bateson would shine! His was the hero-martyr type to an almost ostentatious degree. If it came, the whole youth of England would wish to look, stand and move like Bateson. Talk like him as well, throwing away their intentions in a series of short, brash, slang-raked little sentences. It would be the Batesons' hour; the Batesons would lead and inspire because the Batesons could *act*!

Bateson at that moment was thinking hard. He had the sort of features which, when not animated, set themselves with a parvenu ease into the highest roles of taste, intelligence and distinction. A physical accident had endowed him at birth with most of what blood, brains and striving might in the normal way have taken centuries to amass. He was fool enough to be rather ignorant of this and would often put up a great fight with his flimsy learning, where a mere charming gesture would have seen him through. And this, of course, only added to his charm. He was like the immensely rich whose dividends increase so helplessly. He moved his glass round and round in a shiny beer ring on the bar. His hand was pensive and priestly in its whiteness—the kind of hand which never needed washing and which made few involuntary movements.

'I might as well tell you,' he said, 'I'm thinking pretty seriously of signing-on——' and was rewarded by Richard's immediate look of interest and concern. 'Oh it won't be for a month or two,' he explained. 'I don't intend to just clear out and upset the old apple-cart.'

The landlord tilted his narrow head at this and tut-tutted regretfully. 'The news *was* bad,' he agreed. His missus had just been listening to the nine o'clock. Hitler was moving troops about and he himself had been digging a hole in the garden all the afternoon to put an air-raid shelter in—although he thought it was a complete waste of time in a place like Stourfriston. The old men seated round the bar, farm-workers, labourers; yet entirely unidentifiable as to the specific purpose to which their long, calm lives had been put, heard the landlord silently, their eyes light coloured and staring with the peculiar fixity of the victim. Peace, war—it was all so far out of their hands that there was nothing they could say. They bought more beer and returned with it to their settles to drink it with grave politeness.

'Won't they have quite a bit of difficulty in getting someone in your place at the school?'

'Certain to have,' replied Bateson flatly, and Richard, looking at him, was bound to agree that it didn't matter. The school had served its purpose by providing for its founder's wants for half a century. Now, *Vale!*—or very shortly that. Miss Bellingham, in her cluttered eyrie, was already tying up time-stained runs of the *Quarterly* and *Hibbert Journal*, cremating in the grate letters, bills and notes and anything else likely to gratify an avid executor; shaking her books and astonishing herself with the prophetic inaccuracies of the press-cuttings that fell from them; drinking brandy whenever that whim took her and altogether faintly rejoicing in the frugal finale of a selfish life. Although her total migrations may have taken her no further than 'the blue bed to the brown' she was content. She had had power and some bizarre affections. Now, when she was ready, she would depart. She would not be 'taken'—she would go. Miss Bellingham regretted one thing only; that at a time when life was promising to be inordinately amusing, she must leave it. Upstairs in her hot, smothered room she practised an unseemly laughter at the expense of Mr Winsley as he waited, rusty gown spread out to catch his academic windfall, knowing that he would only receive a sucked orange. Bateson, old Canon Ribbs, who took part-time scripture; prim, careful, unwedded Mr M'Tooley, the maths master—even Richard himself, so late to the scene—could all see what Mr Winsley was utterly blind to—the fact that Copdock House School was finished. That is, of course, if he did not possess a singular vision of his own—*Nimium ne crede colori; fronti nulla fides*, as he might prefer to explain it—and had high hopes of instilling new life into the ramshackle place. Yet one only had to take a quick look at Mr Winsley to realize how unlikely it would be for him to instil life into anything. He hadn't enough puff left to improve a balloon.

'What will you join?' asked Richard. 'The Army?'

'Oh, of course.'

'A county regiment?'

'Yup—if I can.'

'But you've got a commission in the Terriers.'

'Two pips,' admitted Bateson, 'they'll help.'

The landlord swayed with admiration and the old men cringing on their settle regarded Bateson's almost fatuous good looks with little blinks of awe and wonder from their wet, blue eyes.

'If you ask me,' said the landlord, 'it'll be the spring. I give it the spring. What do you say, Charlie——? I was telling of these gentlemen here, I give it the spring.'

Charlie, a stout brooding individual, nodded and the rest of the old men rocked with their mute sagacity.

'The sooner we had a showdown the better,' Bateson declared, causing more mandarin assent from the tired, windshriven faces on the settle. There was a heightened interest in the absurdly blue old eyes as Bateson spoke and it was obvious that he was already the hero. The spring, it seemed, suited everybody.

Listening to these beery generalizations, not one of them so profound that it could silence the businesslike bell, or the satisfying *plob*! as a dart entered the board, Richard began to think rather grimly of his predicament. What was he doing here, in Stourfriston, he wondered, if, as they were saying, there was going to be a 'showdown'? Why wasn't he doing what he liked in these last few weeks which marked the beginning of the end? Perhaps he ought to have gone abroad, or tried to write a book, or just done something quite simple, though satisfying—like tramping and sketching in the Hebrides. Being an expert when it came to procrastination, the wastefulness of even lolling against the bar of the 'Golden Fleece' now occurred to him as something he ought not to be doing. There would only be time from now on for him to think about essential things. The book on the rug and the fire he had left burning in his room came back to him. He was no longer in control, he realized—not without a feeling of relief. So now he could give up huge issues, such as whether it was a mistake his coming to Copdock, or whether Quentin would continue to shine at his expense. He could just *be*. Fate had turned into a big hand in which the world lay with no more stability than if it were one of those Christmascracker games consisting of a glass-fronted pill-box around which small silver balls hurtle hopelessly unless by chance they happened to get caught momentarily in this hole or that. If that was all that he had to say in the matter, why did he struggle? What was going to happen to him could neither be planned for nor rejected it seemed. It would just—happen. Soon—perhaps in the spring as they all seemed to think—the palm in which they lay so helplessly would shake and send them all rushing helter-skelter round the periphery of disaster. The enormity of discovering himself on the brink of a great historical tragedy was too novel, too confusingly gay and sad for him to dread it. Quentin dreaded it whole-heartedly he knew. What on earth *would* happen to Quenny he wondered? Bateson's clear, authoritatively-vowelled voice drivelled on. It wasn't boastfulness on his part; he just hadn't the energy to keep silent. Beer and the watchful company had robbed him of all that. He was enjoying himself. He chattered with disarming gaiety about the Jerries and the Maginot defences and air warfare until even the old men began to lose sight of the ghastliness of what they had once endured and recollected their own bewildered soldiering as a 'bit of a spree'. So it went on until closing-time.

They returned and got into the school the back way. The path by the garden-room-cum-Gymnasium was a welter of unswept snow. Limp swags of it flopped from the eaves.

'Can't make it out,' said Bateson—his feet had just become entirely and unexpectedly soaked—'all this thaw. You listen to the forecast? I could have sworn they said it was going to be a brass monkey night.'

Copdock was steeped in its own special darkness. Here and there a window glimmered with a puny light. The wind felt its way along the tall Victorian walls like an inquisitive hand, touching the shutters and interfering with fastenings and sashes. On the far side the assured silhouette of a Sheraton chair cast against an oiled silk blind caught Bateson's eye.

'What luck,' he said, 'the Winner's gone up!'

But he hadn't. He was crossing the hall attired rather monkishly in a bunched-up Jaeger dressing gown, its cord trailing and writhing in his wake like a sorry adder. His hair, clapped raggedly above each ear, looked like a pair of old brushes. He wore his spectacles and when he passed the clock he stared over them with a mixture of despair and accusation. The only light in the hall came from a gas-arm held out against the fanlight. There was a nice sense of the historic in its little tongue of flame. It illuminated them all—including Mr M'Tooley, who manifested an unsuspected elegance of paisley robe swirling about his crisp pyjamas in spite of the fact that he was visibly shuddering with cold. As they entered, Mr Winsley jerked to a standstill and Mr M'Tooley turned with one of those small classical gestures he could not subdue, like 'Ha! Who calls?', which had the effect of turning his paisley into something more praetorial. Then Mr Winsley shuffled unhappily towards them, his ankles glimmering feebly like peeled sticks inside his unlaced boots.

'We're sorry . . . ' began Bateson in a rather dumbfounded voice. This was the scene he had dreaded for a long time. The Winner's ire at his harmless little jaunts had boiled over—probably because he'd taken young Brand with him, he thought. Oh well . . . He shrugged in an effort to set his philosophical detachment in motion. Why should he worry! How much longer was all this going to last anyway? He waited for the prim reprimand. But in vain. Mr Winsley's nervous fingers which danced so accusingly against the dirty cuffs of his dressing-gown were directed in their very evident despair against a higher intrusion on his peace.

'She was so well,' he insisted, 'such a wonderful *colour* . . . '

'The doctor will soon have some good news for us,' said Mr M'Tooley in his neat voice.

Mr Winsley looked at Bateson. 'I went up as usual,' he explained, 'at five, you know, and there she was, writing letters, stamping them herself—with *energy* . . . '

'I am sorry,' said Bateson, who was actually relieved.

'Can I do anything?' enquired Richard, whose newness at Copdock coupled with the general way in which he was being ignored was beginning to make him feel *de trop*.

'You?' Mr M'Tooley asked with a little fluttering laugh.

'Doctor Manderville is with her now,' explained Mr Winsley more kindly. 'But you could do the rounds for me. All the lights and the doors and the windows. Make sure they're all right, will you, there's a good fellow.' And then, 'No—no—You'd better stay with us,' as Bateson made a move to escape as well.

An electric torch stood on a cluttered Pembroke table. By its side laid a gigantic bunch of keys. Each key had a label, made from one of those shapely tags drapers use and scribbled on in Mr Winsley's efficient hand.

'Do I lock everywhere?'

'Of course not,' said Mr Winsley in an amazed tone, 'just the outside doors. But all lights, mind. And have a look in the dormitories.'

Relieved to be able to escape from such a tense little situation, Richard picked up the torch and began to wander with a mixture of aimlessness and diligence from room to room and from floor to floor in the somnolent honeycomb of the icy school. First, the ground floor. The kitchen reeked of stale bread, the scullery of washing-up water and the passages leading to them, of both. When he played the torch over the walls, it showed a thin glaze of malefaction imperceptibly creeping to lower levels before it collected itself and fell with a fulsome drool on to the tiled floor.

He opened each of the main classrooms and peered in, flashing the light round yards and yards of cream distemper, a dull, soiled cream which, because of its hint of dampness, returned a muted lambency of its own. Lower down, under the cream distemper, there was a dado of horizontal stripes and key-pattern worked out in ochre and deep brown paint. Above the dado, which decided an arbitrary division between art and the work-a-day world, a few highly familiar faces stared out briefly before returning to darkness: General Gordon, the 'Infant Samuel', a wistful Tuke youth poised goldenly over Carbis Bay, the examiners in 'When Did You Last See Your Father?' and King George V—the latter looking, perhaps, as kings will never look again. The blackboards, a little less dark than the night, made grey rectangles that were invisibly suspended above the trench-like desks. The frosted globes depending from the gas-mantles hung from their iron settings in big smeary pearls. Now and then Richard paused and hoisted a window up. The sashes closed with a thin shrill scream. On the first floor he put his head inside the Common-Room where the torch, like an informer, fell upon the huge dusty table and picked out the ashtrays which were all very full and looked rather like sordid reliquaries. There was also a copy of *Passing Show* and of *The Times Education Supplement*, the last with its middle page half made-up into spills, as well as a twopenny bottle of ink and a quantity of surprisingly good-looking writing-paper headed 'Copdock House Preparatory School for Boys, Stourfriston, Suffolk'. Richard helped himself to

a fair bundle of this and shoved it into his pocket.
He was yawning almost constantly—the beer was having its effect—and his head was beginning to feel like an old flock cushion. He felt so tired, he could hardly remember climbing up another staircase when he found himself outside the flimsy partition leading to the junior dormitory. He entered silently. The room was at an angle to the rest of the house and was lined on one side with long, narrow windows that almost touched. A wintry glimmer showed itself at each one. In the barely-realised light, he made out two rows of prim iron bedsteads tapering away into darkness, each one, in its extreme solitariness, like a small, breathing grave. The children sent up a constant, infinitely tender protest from their crumpled sleep. Little mews and sighs melted against each other before they became lost in the general torpid oblivion. One boy spoke and Richard started; something about a pony . . . a pony—and then there was a grateful slurring back into incoherence. He tiptoed out and closed the door.

Further along the passage, on his way to the senior dormitory—there were only the two and these divided by another of the snake-like corridors with which Copdock House was riddled—a boy passed him, walking with a curious gravity along the crippling coconut matting, his bare white feet strangely impervious both to the coarseness and to the cold.

'Good night, Sir.'

'Good night, Sanderson—your windows O.K.?'

'I'll look, sir.'

'Right—Good night.'

'Good night.'

Then he went to bed. The next floor was staff quarters and the next—well he would hardly be expected to answer for the security *there*. He wondered vaguely if Miss Bellingham was very ill. And so he might have slept, with that deadness which threatens a breakfast reckoning—the beer pleaded inside him like poppies—had not he possessed a positive genius for being startled. Before this—just before, as a matter of fact—he had blinked into the shaving-glass and reflected, my God! you'd have thought I'd sunk a gallon of the stuff at least . . . The extreme tiredness he had attributed to the stuffy little pub, coupled with Bateson's essential dullness, was the true reason for it he supposed. It had broader credentials actually. One was Copdock House, which, like a lump of much used blotting paper, still had some power left to mop up a fair amount of the human spirit. The second was mainly to do with the geographical position of Stourfriston itself. The town lurked in a wooded hollow and was trapped into loitering mists by a loop of shallow river. Where at Lafney every puff of wind was as bright as a new sixpence, the climate of Stourfriston just accumulated, the stale undermost, drugging the senses until the mind no longer even attempted to ward off its importunate languors.

He was huddled on the bed, rather than in it, when Mr Winsley entered. Mr Winsley knocked first, of course, but because Richard had not the slightest doubt that it was Bateson returning to enlighten him a little about the business downstairs, he appeared, with a book resting on his knees, at a far greater ease than he felt. Even then he would have slid somehow to his feet, but between his sleepiness and his astonishment, he was vaguely conscious that Mr Winsley was forbidding it. He was holding his hand out nervously, and with soothing, extended and conciliatory fingers, was insisting how sorry he was; how *very* sorry.

'On the face of it, merely a whim, you might say,' he explained uncomfortably. 'She had a bad turn and it frightened her. Her wish for company is really quite normal in the circumstances. Anybody would desire the same . . . ' A sharp, querulous note was forcing its way into his voice. 'I said that you would be asleep, that it was late, but—and I can tell you this now—time means nothing where she is concerned. She has put it by. It has become expendable—if you know what I mean—so now there is nothing to regulate her demands. That is why Mr M'Tooley and myself think it would be kind if you would go to her.'

'Of course . . . ' Richard agreed unhappily. 'Poor Miss Bellingham,' he added politely, while all the time a disgruntled rebellion deep down inside him insisted that he was a fool, that all this had nothing to do with him. What if the mechanism of Copdock *was* limping along to its last few academic shudders —was *he* to blame? Could he, even with the maximum of truthfulness, remotely care? And why couldn't old Winsley understand that the amount of loyalty to be handed back in exchange for one's first month's salary was infinitely small *any*where. A slate couldn't slip on the huge roof without the Winner feeling the pain of it. But with himself it was different. He still remained outside Copdock emotionally. It was only its two hundred a year which counted, that and a sort of relief that he was settled. So what else except 'poor Miss Bellingham'——?

'Better get some things on,' Mr Winsley insisting impatiently. 'I'm sorry, you know, Brand. It's a whim of hers that she should chat to someone, so you had better more or less dress.' He searched through the inch-wide crevasse where the ginger plush curtains failed to meet and added rather sadly, 'It's begun to snow again.'

At the insignificant door leading to Miss Bellingham's room, Mr Winsley said, 'I should just knock and go in, that is what I should do; just knock and go in.'

Which is what Richard did, first putting up a hand to set his tie straight, rather quickly because any hesitation would soon have degenerated into panic; only to discover that in the rush he'd forgotten to put on his tie and that his collar gaped in a wide summery V. At the same moment, a nervous, not quite voluntary motion of his other hand had flung the door rather unceremoniously open and there he was, inside, with the door being rapidly and efficiently snapped behind him by Mr Winsley. For a second he was a child again at Meridian, holding his breath, closing his eyes against Hibble's imagined horrors. But here again his instincts were unjustly malignant, bracing themselves against sights and odours that would never come.

She wasn't even in her bed, but sat very upright in the roomy armchair. Her feet were propped up by some unseen hassock and her lap was full of papers. A voluminous welter of rumpled embroideries swamped her, which he later interpreted as a *peignoir* of sorts, but of such grubby richness that it might have served time in a museum. Minutely-sewn glass beads, and small lumpy nodules of thread-work and the terrible manner in which it refused to conceal a thick, soiled linen nightdress, gave it the *grande tenue* claims of a robe at a rather licentious court. Fold after fold of it muffled, yet could not hide her gaunt and rigid person. Her hair, he noticed, was still a wonder, whisked up above her polished brow like an immensely successful meringue in the lightest, spunaway pinkish-gold mass. Amber trifles rollicked below the dragging, cerise-tipped lobes of her ears. Her fingers were helpless with rings as she made futile efforts to use a small cheap cigarette-lighter. It worked at once when Richard took it and as the soft grey smoke surged between them, she declared,

'*Isn't* this fun, Mr Brand!'

'I am glad that you are feeling better,' he replied in a perplexed voice.

'Better——? That strikes me as being a rather rubbishy word, if you don't mind my saying so! Sit there, will you. No there—where I can see you.'

The fire burnt away behind him, its heat, pleasant at first then uncomfortable as it gathered at a point in the hollow of his back.

'Now,' she said, 'tell me just what you were doing when they came to fetch you—playing tennis, one might suppose.'

Richard smiled, tugged at his shirt and said, 'I think I was reading.'

'Ah,' sighed Miss Bellingham, 'I often think that! How else could one say that one had read all this'—she waved a stiff hand to include the heaped-up bookshelves—'and yet remember so little of their contents! There, see that one?—No, more to your right; yes that. *Hudibras*, isn't it? I was twenty-three when I thought I read that. And where, do you suppose—at Vézèlay, which is in France, you know, and in Burgundy to be particular. We were all staying there, Clare—that's my sister, our Aunt Winely and Norah Township, as she was then. They had gone for a walk so I took *Hudibras* up behind the church and sat down in the cold grass and turned the pages over and over and *thought* I was reading! But I wasn't, of course. I was watching the monks lolling on the wall. Such dears! So young! They made me think of charity boys as they sat with their knees tucked up under their cassocks and their faces staring out to Auxerre. You don't know Auxerre, I suppose? All the monk boys had a tonsure about the size of half-a-crown. I remember thinking it the most elegant disfigurement—until we went to Heidelberg where all the students are so clever with scars. Heidelberg—have you been there?No again, I expect . . . ' She sank back with a curious luxury, spread her hands over the vagrant letters in her lap and said in a tone of the purest regret, 'How much more there is to say—after one is sure, I mean, that one has said it all! But tell me; what was it that *you* thought you were reading?'

'*The Seven Pillars of Wisdom*,' he answered, rising and pushing his chair out of reach of the faintly sickening heat playing on his back.

Miss Bellingham's cheeks quavered with a flaccid, half-controlled mirth.

'In that *mood*,' she declared, 'I should plump for Leviticus. Pauly knew Colonel Lawrence, I believe. Not *well*, you understand. That was assumed impossible.'

Richard said that he thought there was something noble about the book as a whole.

'Noble?' she interrupted, pouncing on the word. 'Now there's a discountenanced adjective if ever there was! Tell me, Mr Brand, should you imagine that there will be a war?'

'Well . . . ' he began.

'No, don't,' she said. 'Don't let an old woman drive you into that sort of dullness. Anyway what are such prognostications worth—yours—mine—anybody's? If you will be good enough to open that cupboard you'll discover *my* skeleton in the guise of some poorish sherry-wine. Glasses are behind. Do you know that I have spent a lifetime filching drink from my own pantry? I couldn't enjoy it if I didn't gulp it down at the wrong hour in the wrong place and with a weather eye open for the cook. Oh, the remorse we get from our shoddy little sins! Remorse for me, Mr Brand, has been a deal more salutary for keeping my weaknesses within bounds than any threat of the common law. Yet when I was a girl it was reckoned —at some dinner tables at least—that there was no more direct proof of ill-breeding than a capacity for shame. My great-grandfather was a miller and a Methodist, and he left enough scruples behind when he went to keep the family in anxiety for a century. To think that without him I might have inherited the moral armour of a reasonable woman! As it is— But why complain! Who, what are any of us, but the latest link in a chain of accidents?' She nodded her great head sadly and her hair bobbed in the yellow gaslight like a petrified flower.

Richard poured the sherry slowly from its squat decanter into two beautiful engraved glasses and as the wine climbed to its placid ellipse, he noticed from the corner of his eye Miss Bellingham's hands go up and touch in turn her ear-rings and afterwards, her rings, twisting them round where the heavy stones had fallen to the fore.

'Steady!' she cried suddenly.

'My fault,' he acknowledged, 'they're much too full.'

'Much,' she scolded. And then, 'If Cadman knew I'd got hold of this . . . ' She stopped suddenly. 'What actually happened?' she asked in a measured, curious voice. The wine-glass glittered as she rolled its stem slowly between her trembling fingers. 'Did he go to bed?'

'When we came in,' began Richard uncertainly, 'we met Mr Winsley in the hall. He——'

'We?'

'Bates—Mr Bateson and myself.'

'Never mind Bateson,' she said tartly, lke someone talking to a servant, *'what was Cadman doing?'*

'Nothing. I mean he was just standing in the hall. He was wearing his dressing-gown and we thought that he was waiting for us to come in before he locked up. Then we could see that he was worried and the next moment I noticed Mr M'Tooley as well—he was over against the stairs . . . '

'Oh my God!' she interrupted in a despairing tone, 'don't go on. As if their names aren't suffocating enough! Stop! stop! He said that I was ill—so you went to bed. Is that it? No, don't answer. How sensible of you. He—Cadman this time—thought that I had a stroke? Those are the terms in which they think in relation to myself; a sharp turn of phrase that they imagine will adequately cover any of my poor little collapses! But I'm wonderfully well. Just look at me——' Just then the merest caprice of a tremor shook her, provoked, perhaps, by the sound of the greater destruction she could be so bold about. The sherry slopped all over her rings and ran in a golden lane across the mottled skin of her wrists. 'But go on,' she urged, drying herself with a scrap of rag. 'Cadman came in with my message and there you were, all tucked up and reading Colonel Lawrence's little book. What then?'

Richard watched her briefly before replying. She would set great store by this answer, he thought. Here was the hand of friendship being proffered; a twisted—even a fleeting hand, but still a hand possessing that kind of inner warmth which he found so peculiarly valuable. Her method of presenting it had been eccentric in the extreme, but that was because, rather than run the risk of a rebuff by stating her terms in clear-cut black and white, she had chosen to tempt him with this playful chiaroscuro of her talk. He realised her shrewdness at once. She had managed—in so short a time—to 'sum him up'. He would have resented this vigorously from most people, but not from her. Selfishly or not she was making great efforts to enthral him and he supposed by rights he ought to be horrified. Instead he discovered himself thinking of her with the most tender regard. She had found out what he loved most, which were words, not deeds, and from her huge repository of old talk and avid reminiscence, she had raked out a few outlandish samples for his wonder. If he accepted the conditions it might still be some time before they could be easy with each other. Her massive banter would have to die away gradually like thunder. But he fully understood this. She could take no risks—she hadn't the time. She was too old, as well as too clever, to lay herself open to mockery and hurts of that sort. Only one thing was certain—he felt this as he watched the slow, mandarin transitions of the wine-glass as it swayed from one knotted, yellow fist to the other—*hers* would be the only gift worth the taking amongst the rag-bag offerings of Copdock. Moreover it would be a kindness on his part and, who knows, he might even enjoy climbing up the choking, furry stairs now and then to listen to her shaking up the bizarre pourri of her experiences.

'I came,' he said simply.

It was her turn to reflect. It might be a trap. She found him tremendously polite. She faced him, staring at his extreme youthfulness, as he sprawled under the hissing gaslight jutting from the chimney which supplemented the blue glass table-lamp at her side. The stuttering yellow of both lights merged above his head in a smudge of dirty gold.

'Thank you, Mr Brand,' she replied very calmly.

After that he found it easy to visit her, but because he had read somewhere of the gusts of amusement caused by a young man's patience with old women, or because he didn't care to delve too deeply to seek the reasons for his own devotion, he was at first discreet about these visits. Even sly.

When he wrote to Mary he took care that she only got what she might expect to get from him in the way of descriptions and even affection. He was cautious, non-committal—life was opening up for him in too many directions all at once and it was essential that he should know exactly what new ground lay before him. He did not wish to race forward blindly, nor get lost and, most particularly, not to get submerged. In this way he had all Quentin's refinement of selfishness, yet not enough of Quentin's pride. A great deal of his spirit was expended in self-apology. So when, in his letter, he attempted to convey the broad effects of the school and his baffled respect for Miss Bellingham, the result was a mixture of hedonism and flatness which Mary interpreted, correctly, as a mere blind. Life, it seemed, was dreary enough at Copdock, but not so dreary that her company was actually longed for. There was a sharp old woman to listen to, not to mention the possibilities lurking at Sheldon, and the company of one of those matey young men with colourless hair and eyes which look as if they had torn themselves somewhat reluctantly from the contemplation of a peak in Darien, to drink Bass with.

Mary read the letter dully, two or three times, unwilling to concede that there was no more in it than what he had written.

'I wish you could meet her,' he had begun. 'She's amazing. A kind of half-amused oracle who will only tell you about the more trivial side of all the people she has met because she assumes naturally that you have read everything they have written. It's usually writers, but with an occasional politician thrown in for good weight. And she makes a colossal effort to *please* when she talks. I expect she would call it something like "the art of awakening a sense of privilege in others", except *she* wouldn't be so pompous. I'm afraid she's rather crazy and I suppose, rather wicked. But listening to her when she's really got going sends me into a trance of admiration. The most imaginative scraps that I can possibly write are like grocery-lists against what comes out of her fuddled wit. She drinks—or says she does. But I must tell you more about all this when we meet.

'What else—nothing much. The boys are appallingly well behaved, in fact really limp. You soon realize that most of them are conscious of some trivial sense of superiority by their being at Copdock. It's considered one-up from the "Grammar", though God knows why! Twenty live in and thirty-one are day-boys. They play games and call themselves by houses: "Bloomfield"—after the poet; "Tattingstall"—after an O.B. who did well at the Dardanelles; "Montessori"—after the method (which is also about the only creed Miss B has ever believed in); and "Abbott"—after you-know-who. But there's no proper division and it's all pretty futile.

'I saw old Yockers going down the High Street on Wednesday. Expect he was visiting his ancient sister, or working out an escapade for the Archaeological Society. "A transitional sedilia". Can't you just hear him!

'I go to Sheldon on Tuesday. Afraid the Belle's colourful obscurities about the place (and about Sir P.) have rather intimidated me . . .'

She skipped lightly over half a page more of this friendly stuff and then read with increasing irritation; 'Yes, *of course*, come over—but wouldn't it be better to wait until the weather clears up? That's all I meant by what you term my "casualness". It's freezing here. Nothing to do—nowhere to go. True, there is a terrible kind of visitors' room at the School, but you should just see it! Slippery sofas, bell shades and the very latest Dornford Yates on a Benares table. There is my room, of course, but you'd hate that even more, even if you were allowed into it. Let's make it Sunday then. I can do that. Meet you Sunday. Hmm? Bestest love, Richard.'

8

WRITE to him at once, common sense told her. Say, 'of course you wouldn't dream of arriving in Stourfriston on a terrible winter's day and that, anyway, it would be selfish to interrupt his settling in. Oh and yes, how glad she was that he liked Miss Bellingham. She sounded intriguing, fascinating . . . (revolting old woman) and . . . that she loved him—was he too far gone in his maze of doddering eccentrics to realize that? She loved him . . . *loved* him! But instincts are not necessarily actions, indeed they very rarely are. Perhaps on the whole they dare not be. Whatever the reason for her dilatoriness, Wednesday drifted by without the letter getting itself written and Thursday too. In fact Thursday hardly occurred to her at all until she looked back on it from Friday and was then appalled that a day could vanish like that, the entire featureless twenty-four hours of it! Hustled out of her vagueness by this merciless drifting of time, she scrawled a note to Richard to say that he was not to mind the weather, nor the visitors' room. She was coming. The drive would be nice, and she wanted to see him. So that was that. She also added that Mr Yockery was to lunch at Meridian on Sunday—as though that were anything unusual—so her mother wouldn't be left alone. Then, having posted the note, she immediately began to wonder how such a simple, harmless little jaunt was to be proposed to Mrs Crawford without it appearing absolutely outlandish in her eyes.

Mrs Crawford excelled in a ruthless ability to nip the illusions of others in the bud. She prided herself on having forestalled any amount of suffering by promptly applying her bleak methods to any situation 'bolstered up', as she called it, with emotion. Emotion in itself she found deplorable—'a pity'. She must have seen it as a balloon, something bulbous which fed on the too fertile imagination, since her way of destroying it was always sharp and cruel. If she were completely truthful she would say that emotion in those very near to her was an embarrassment and if it happened to be sexual emotion—and it frequently was—then it became unthinkable. Her witty pincers would suddenly lash out to make short shrift of any nonsense of that sort. She possessed two criteria for assessing level-headedness in her friends; their current reading and their attitude towards food. Her own taste in books was faultless. She read a great deal, mostly novels and biographies, and never came adrift when the ideas changed as so many of her friends did, so that some of them, particularly Edwina who liked to read absolute rubbish, were apt to regard her as an intellectual. She wasn't a bit. She read well, because she couldn't help it—any more than she could help the curious trundling dignity of her walk, or her rather declamatory voice. She had what one can only have without really knowing it—style. But even more than reading, she enjoyed her food. She ate with an interest and concentration which some people decided was repellent, but which was actually French. People who didn't *eat*—Mrs Crawford meant forage about the table in a certain way, accept the menu in restaurants with reverence or talk recipes—she found unrewarding. With Mary she used mealtimes as a barometer. If Mary ate, even if it was only in her usual rather thankless manner, then there was nothing to fear. Should she 'pick', then she had a cold or a notion and either must be nipped in the bud.

She was picking, Mrs Crawford noticed, this morning. It was Sunday. The church bells clashed goldenly across the paddock and for the first time since Christmas it was delightfully fine. The sun flooded its way into the tall, narrow windows of the dining-room and was splashed palely over the carpet and brought out the gold in the satinwood chairs.

'You're not eating,' accused Mrs Crawford. Sunday's was what she liked to describe as a 'good' breakfast; toast, fruit, bacon and eggs—everything. 'Mary—did you hear what I said? Why aren't you eating?'

'Me—not eating—Oh, aren't I——?'

'And you're not dressed——'

This meant that there wasn't that special tidiness about her which spelt church. She had put on a suit of plum-coloured corduroy which, modest in the good little shop in Upper Berkeley Street where she bought most of her clothes, had turned out to have far too much dash about it for Lafney. But she had remembered Richard's crinkle of distaste at the Shetland tweed she had hardly taken off since the cold snap began, and also his affection for colour.

'Not for church,' she said,' because I'm going to be wicked for once. I think it must be the sunshine—' She saw it suddenly as an alibi, as a vast, glittering excuse to ward off her mother's ready snub. 'I thought I'd have a little outing—take the car—

you didn't want it, did you, Mummy?' How easy it was. How simple! And when she came to think of it, how right. Why should her every action be scrutinized, catechised! A tiny ghost stole up out of the past, insubstantial even for a shadow. The fair young man at a hunt ball with his playful gallantries, the careless momentary happiness of it—and then the sensible strength with which Mrs Crawford severed the wispy link which had so briefly brought them together. 'What do you think,' Mary heard her croak in her rich, loud voice to old Lady Stowupland, 'Mary kept them buzzing at the East Anglian Harriers! *Quite* the belle, Gracie, I assure you. You should have seen them!' When they got home there had been a 'little talk'.

'You could have told me before. Why didn't you?'

Thinking of Wednesday, Thursday and Friday, Mary said, 'Oh I couldn't be certain,'—there was the dust of truth in this.

'I can only believe you to be most extraordinary, *most* extraordinary,' Mrs Crawford insisted in an aggrieved tone. 'When you knew Father Yockery was coming to lunch, you airily announce that you've taken it into your head to go off for the day in the motor! *Where?*'

Already she was bustling into that *flair* she possessed for indignation, the aptitude for which left her curiously undisturbed. Words would fly and her colour mount, but her knife and fork (these outbursts would invariably be co-ordinated with breakfast or dinner); would pursue an industrious policy of their own, so that a secondary battle of rancour versus nourishment would ensue. Then she would complain that her health was being ruined by the thoughtlessness of others and rise and ring the bell viciously for Hibble to present the next course. On the whole such scenes were scarce, if only for the reason that it took more than one to make them. If Mary got on with her meal in a flinching silence then Mrs Crawford's accusations would shuffle to an apologetic stop, and a terrible muffled hush would descend like a carpet, during which Hibble would respond to orders given her in a small, silly, fretful voice which was quite unrecognisable compared with her mother's normal tone. Hibble, revelling in the unjustness of the young and the righteousness of Mrs Crawford, would drag herself about the room like a gaunt Niobe, intent on showing by every mournful gesture the intense disapproval her tongue was prevented from giving expression to. But if Mary argued the meaningless bickering might be extended until bedtime, though never further. As Mrs Crawford once said, when Mary sought to justify her point of view from the evening before, 'But that was *yesterday*.' So their mild rows didn't go on and on.

However, Mary had no wish to say anything this morning. The clockwork protests would reach their zenith and then subside in small flung-away spurts of self-pity, but she would remain invulnerable. The brightness of the day protected her, the suggestion of warmth, the furled yellow buds of the potted daffodils, the pretty white room with its ornate lozenged ceiling, the rich shifting of her red velvet skirt and the comparative ease with which she had got away with her plans. So happy was she, in fact, that she felt she couldn't even bear her mother's irritation to run down in the usual way. She had to rise and go to her, bend lightly and kiss the top of her head. Hibble, who was staring at she manoeuvred the hatch, was horrified. That's a Judas trick if you like! she said to herself.

'Darling,' said Mary, 'what a fuss!'

This was daring because it at once reduced wrath to testiness and any grief that might come from it to an indulgence. 'Fuss' insinuated all that. There was also the unpleasant fact, which ever way Mrs Crawford looked at it, that Mary was, after all, independent. It was something she must never forget. She wheeled round slowly in her seat.

'You know Mummy never minds so long as she is *told*.'

'Oh' . . . said Mary, momentarily floored by this saccharine departure into nursery-land.

'And wrap up warm, dear.—Poor Father Yockery, he'll be so disappointed. He has a nephew coming to stay—the one who is hoping to be a scientist. John, isn't it? And the Faculty are going to let him have a new altar—isn't that nice! What about your lunch—what shall you do about food?' She stood up, pinching the heavy silk of her frock into place over her fat hips. Then, casting a searching look over the tablecloth all marked with toast-dust, she said, making it sound the most ordinary thing in the world, 'I'm told they do one awfully well at Stourfriston "Eagle" that is, should you find yourself that way . . .'

Why I don't say I'm lunching with Dick Brand and have done with it, Heaven only knows, Mary told herself. But she didn't say it.

★

'But I can't understand it,' he protested.

'No,' she agreed sadly, 'who could?'

Coming along in the car the first doubts had assailed her. The day was too majestically perfect. You could bite into it and taste clean, cold gold. The naked hedges fled by and new ploughing had tipped up the fields in long, wet, silvery slivers. Country people darted in and out of cottages that were like nests, and because she wasn't obliged to linger in them and suffer their crippling proprieties, the Sunday streets of sleepy villages had seemed to her unspeakably elegant in their self-conscious quiet. Once she stopped and walked to the tip of a little hill and the wind rushed against the back of her head and drove her hair forward in a fine drift against her cheeks. She could have stretched her arms out then. It was that kind of peace, that dancing realization of happiness.

'Well, I'm glad you've come,' Richard said. He hesitated, aware that she was searching for sincerity in his words and actions.

'—I am—honestly . . .'

'I'm glad as well,' she confessed. 'Where are we going to eat? I thought I was invited to lunch.'

'Soon. You were. But first I've got to exhibit you at Copdock —I was bound to promise that. It seems that *this* Sunday was a bit difficult. Not really you know. The Winner just likes to make it sound like that. He's waiting with sherry now, so we'll have to go.'

She found the school shocking, much worse than she had imagined. The staleness met her as she entered. The staircase was like a shute down which outdated instruction swept in a muddied eddy to the classrooms. One room was open and she caught a glimpse of a waxy yellow wall-map and a splintery floor with protuberant knots standing up out of its boards like bunions. An overgrown, loutish-looking boy crouched

in a little cast-iron desk with his back towards them.
'They write home on Sunday,' explained Richard.

Mary's charming velvet suit, which had started out with such a demure pleasurableness in the morning-room at Meridian, progressed to a delightful extravagance when she had unkindly compared it with the dumpy respectability of the farmers' wives bustling to church and had, in the vivid January sunshine flooding Stourfriston, returned full-circle to the joy she had felt when her eye discovered it in the Upper Berkeley Street shop, suddenly slumped in her regard. She was too got-up and they would stare. Richard, walking a step or so in front, she noticed, sharing this feeling, but in another way. He was also too got-up, not in clothes, but in the vitality of his body, in his hair shaking forward across his forehead, hair which looked so cloudy and fine, but which she remembered was rough and coarse. Humpson, their gardener, she recalled, used to have a refuse place, a compost heap, she supposed it must have been, from which she used to rescue the house-flowers that were not quite dead. No one ever knew the anguish it cost her as a child to find carelessly thrown-away blooms in that stagnant corner. She would snatch them from the top of the rotting mass and nurse them in jam-jars lined up in the stable windows until their very last petal had fallen. No need to go any further, she told herself: I know the kind of wastefulness which goes on here ...

'Richard—'

'Mmm?' He swung round and said, 'Sorry. I didn't mean to barge ahead like that, I was just trying to find out where they'd all got to.'

'Perhaps they aren't really expecting us,' she said hopefully.

'You mean perhaps you've got cold feet!'

'Perhaps I have.'

'Don't worry,' he said comfortably. 'They only want to be polite.'

Would 'politeness' extend to her having to meet that dreadful old woman upstairs, she wondered. Would she descend, like some fearful female prophet, a kind of transvestist Elisha with cats in her wake (they always had cats and tight little caps of hair like pot-scourers and infinite opinions on endless subjects. They were also atheistical; admirers of Beethoven,

Edward Carpenter, Nietzsche, Thomas Huxley and Alfred Munch, and they didn't bathe; at least, not much.) One thing was certain—and she couldn't but help feeling rather pleased with herself for knowing it—and that was the perilous fascination of their ambiguous natures. With absolute lack of justice she allotted Miss Bellingham two heads, not realizing that a more single-minded person had rarely existed. But she was right about the baths.

They passed two or three blank brown doors and then came to the visitors' room—it said so—VISITORS—in cracked black paint over the liver colour. The boy who was writing the letter, started up, thrust a blotchy face towards them and said, 'That's right, Sir; in there.'

'I still haven't got the hang of the place,' Richard said.

Mary smoothed her skirt nervously and unnecessarily and stepped into what at first appeared to be an enormous copy of one of those iron and stained-glass electric lanterns. The wallpaper was patterned in a frolicsome disorder of heroic chrysanthemums and grapes, and a stem of gas-piping, descending dizzily from a decoration the colour of soiled sugar-icing, flowered into six pink glass canterbury-bells. The carpet complemented the rash harvest of the walls with a perplexing exercise in dusty Turkey-work. She saw the slippery sofa and the Benares table and like odalisques, because of their frozen interest, the staff.

'Ha! Brand, come and have a drink.'

'This is Mr Winsley,' said Richard. 'Mr M'Tooley, Mrs Winsley, Canon Ribbs—' He stopped, brought to a halt by a fluffyheaded middle-aged woman clasping the Book of Common Prayer in one hand and a sherry glass in the other.

'Miss Ribbs—my niece,' explained the Canon.

'Miss Crawford,' Richard said. But the fluffy woman made not the slightest effort to further the introductions and stared at him with an intensity that by-passed the personal and entered the purely objective. Later he was to understand that that was 'her way'. She went out very rarely and when she did, she made the most of it.

'We *are* glad to see you here,' said Mr Winsley to Mary. He presented her with sherry as though she had won it. 'We don't—as I expect you can guess—have the pleasure of a great number of visitors nowadays. But it hasn't always been like this, oh no!' He looked round the chilly, cluttered room for some confirmation of its ancient glories and his eye fell upon Mrs Winsley. 'Tell Miss Crawford, my dear, how we used to do things!'

'Miss Crawford won't want to hear all about our old parties, I'm sure!' smiled Mrs Winsley, tilting her face towards Mary in a pretty gesture unconsciously borrowed from Zena Dare. Her huge eyes swam with a dogged girlishness and her cheeks were pushed out into two podgy little hillocks of pleasantry. She put up a hand and explored her springy curls. 'We *did* hope that Mr Bateson was going to be here to meet you,' she said in a puzzled voice, 'but it seems that he has gone out . . .'

'That reminds me of an anecdote I heard recently—or I may have read it,' began Mr M'Tooley. Then he stopped abruptly and peered down into his sherry. This action was perfectly understood by everybody except Richard, who imagined that the story had been quelled by some reminder of seemliness on Mr Winsley's part. As he thought this was bringing classroom ethics far too near their private lives, he urged,

'Well let's hear it,'

'Do,' beseeched Mrs Winsley.

'I forget it rather,' Mr M'Tooley said off-handedly. 'Apparently a friend enquired for André Gide at his Paris hotel and the porter said something like, "Ah, Monsieur Gide . . . he is always going out . . ."' There was a stifling silence and Mr M'Tooley added, 'We were talking about Bateson—he's not here and somehow it reminded me . . .'

A frond of ancient pampas grass rustled from its vase on the lofty chimmneypiece into the grate and was burnt up with unsuspected brilliance in the hot ashes.

'Is that all?' asked Mr Winsley complainingly.

'I think,' said Mary, 'I see the sadness of it.'

Mr M'Tooley shot her a look of gratitude mixed with apprehension.

'Paris hotels are dreadfully uncomfortable,' declared Mrs Winsley, dimly recalling the whole duty of hostesses. 'What was the name of that one we stayed in, Cadman—do you remember? The Pandore . . . the Panache—*Pan*-something, I know! It was behind the Jardin des Plantes and I always remember saying that *that* was where all those little insects must have come from. They were all over the place, my dear,' she went on, turning to Mary, '*absolutely* harmless, except it was like treading on spilt sugar when one went to bed.'

'Isn't it curious,' Mr Winsley observed to Richard, the smile on his thin lips laced with the merest ghost of his annoyance, 'how the female mind retains the husks of experience only. My wife, you see, has quite forgotten the Russian Ballet although a few Parisian earwigs would seem to have made an indelible impression. What about the Russian Ballet, Minna?' he demanded in a loud voice.

Mrs Winsley, who had just begun a conversation about Today's Young People with Mary, looked round in alarm.

'The Russian Ballet . . .?'

'Who was the little girl who adored Njinski?' enquired Mr Winsley with frightful playfulness.

Mrs Winsley arched her throat like Zena Dare again and said very softly, 'Oh, Caddie, I'd quite forgot.'

'A a ahh . . .' breathed Mr Winsley. His rigid finger waggled admonishment across the room. 'And the Pantheon *and* the Place du Tertre . . .'

Mrs Winsley gripped Mary's arm and laughed in her pretty, soft way. 'The *Pantheon*,' she said triumphantly. 'My dear, I remember now; our hotel was called Les Ambassadors . . . You know it? It's that one with the prickly roof immediately behind the Jardin des Plantes. What makes one forget things, do you suppose? What *causes* it, do you think?'

'Being busy, of course,' smiled Mary. 'I expect you help a good deal with running the school?'

'We all help in our way.' She let her eyes travel from one person to the next with a limpid, but rather fatuous regard.

'What I really meant,' insisted Mary, 'was, do you do any of the teaching? Or perhaps you help more with the administration?'

Mrs Winsley at once became deceitful. For forty years it had been drummed into her that what went on inside Copdock was a private affair. 'Don't let them question you,' Cadman had said. It was her single well-learnt lesson.

'My husband's the one you must ask about those things,' she retorted tartly.

'I'm sorry,' said Mary swiftly. This was the limit. So she was to be judged by their own prying little standards—unless the woman was an utter simpleton, but there she couldn't be sure. That girly-girly attitude might hide anything; tenacity, astuteness—some private world the path to which, though of roses, would certainly turn out to be of the thorniest kind. Looking around, she thought of Richard as a feckless, rather than a helpless victim thrown to a cluster of decrepit lions which, though too enfeebled to gobble him up, still had enough power left in them to impair his spirit. Somewhere on high, lodged in a wickerwork chair between the dormitory ceiling and the slates, she remembered, was Miss Bellingham. Not a lion in the ordinary Winsley sense, but something more fabulous, more mythical and so something to be more chary of—someone infinitely dangerous. As she took a discreet look at her watch—she just managed to flash a glance at her wrist and catch its reciprocal glitter of time and gold—the door opened and Bateson came in.

She knew it was Bateson. She had seen him many times. Straddled against the spinnaker of a coasting yacht, wind-raked in an unthrottled Bentley, as Leander diving off the pier, as Orlando returning with the West Suffolk Hunt, as Paris's performing wonders at the monthly hop at the Athenaeum and as a Burne-Jones archangel in church; kind, brave and mindless, there he was, the English paradigm—Bateson.

'Gosh—I'm sorry,' he said.

'Never mind, never mind!' boomed Mr Winsley. Sherry had nourished his normally diffident voice and his jocose remarks were bounding around the room in the most audible way.

'Oh Mr Bateson!' Mrs Winsley cried. She fluttered to the Indian table, raised up the lone bottle of Tio Pepe it supported and exclaimed, 'Oh goody! I think we shall just manage it.'

Mr M'Tooley at once placed his palm over his glass and said, meaningly, in what was very obviously a nudge to the rest of the company, 'Not for *me*, Mrs Winsley.'

'Not for you . . . she sighed. 'Really . . .'

'Really.'

Mrs Winsley said, 'Lovely sherry party' and returned the

bottle with such abruptness to the inlaid picture of a Peshawar court which made up the top of the table that its obvious emptiness reverberated sadly through their talk and caused Mr Winsley to spread his arms as though the awkward little group were a brood of fourth-formers which had to be hustled out to play.

But this was too precipitous for Mrs Winsley. There were questions she had still to ask: important ones. There was young Mr Brand lolling against the brown and grey marble fireplace which had always struck her as looking like cleverly arranged brawn. His glass swung upside down between his fingers and his eyes were two intensely dark lines because of the way he was watching the hearth-rug, an absorption accentuated by the way in which the Canon's niece watched him. Mr Brand, decided Mrs Winsley, was really nice. A clergyman's son. She had traced it all in an old Crockford; 'John Launcey Brand, M.A. Wilt. Coll. Ox., B.A. 1912; M.A. 1914. d. 1915 p. 1916. C. in charge S. Saviour, Owleaton, Salop. 1917–20. R. of Lafney, dio, Ipswich and S. Eds., Suffolk. Hon. Chap. R.N.L.I. Address: S. Prolixia's R. Lafney. Publications: *The Pauline Dilemma. What is the Matter with Our Missionaries?*' Those were the kind of antecedents which promoted confidence! She found it not difficult to imagine that dedicated home, with the gentle brothers (she had discovered that there were two of them), the wife—the mother—the widow ... Really Mrs Winsley could weep! Soon, quite soon, perhaps, there must be further privations. It was in the nature of things that there should be. No one could go on for ever—not even *her*— the name musn't be breathed in case Caddie should hear; because the very idea of *her* going drove him into a passion. Why? she wondered. It would be—what did they call it—a blessed release. And then Copdock, everything, would be his, Cadman's. That was why Mr Brand was so important. He might not have a degree, but he was the right *stuff*—wasn't that what her darling Daddy had called it! The right stuff— and *he* certainly was. Just then she became perturbed. Why was that old bitch Muriel Ribbs clutching at Mr Brand like that, and why did she have to *stare* so. And who did this tall, cool girl who was rather too much dressed-up for them, say she was? It really was awful the way she forgot things!

'Have you known—have you and Mr Brand been friends for long?'

'Ages,' smiled Mary.

'*Really* . . .'

This was giving more astonishment than Mary intended. 'We were children together,' she explained and then realised her error at once. Mrs Winsley's speedwell eyes dragged themselves away from the fireplace to run doubtfully over Mary's person. She's staring at my ears, Mary thought. Urgh! how terrible! And Mrs Winsley reflected, she's showing her ears because they're pretty, in which case she can't be so sure of her more ordinary features! She congratulated herself for being wise enough to observe this. The suit was lovely, although it wouldn't do for her; the colour was wrong. Strawberry, she supposed. *Who* did she say she was . . .? A childhood friend . . .? How *could* she be! She would have asked more questions, but Mary was moving away. Mrs Winsley could see that she longed to snap on her black suede gloves and leave—which was odd when you came to think of it, the girl not having been inside the house twenty minutes!

Just then Bateson began to make his way towards Mary. Like a Hatton Garden merchant confronted with a tray of miscellaneous stones, his eyes, too candid with what they required, too certain of their getting it, hardly noticed the rest of the company before they met her own. She attempted to withdraw, in fact did drag herself back a fraction from his downright stare, but even then, although not truly focussed, she held her own views in this wilful transaction until, rather furious with herself, she turned away. Even then she knew the wide, clear but almost colourless pupils were absorbing her and the barrenness of this attraction almost shocked her. All the men she had previously known had reserved for her the 'look-oblique'. The compliment, the interest—or whatever it was—was snuffed out immediately she was in moments of interpreting it. Being the creatures hand-picked by her mother for Meridian, there was little wonder in this. Their reasons for not taking her seriously were reflected in their gait, or in the way they brushed their hair, or in their subservience, or in their arrogance (which is often the same thing turned inside out). Every summer they arrived for tennis—'a little party, darling, won't that be nice!' as Mrs Crawford called these occasions in her special 'treat' voice—and every winter for bridge, or just a good dinner. 'I thought William Strangly, darling . . . He's home again and will be able to tell us exactly what the Government *is* doing in Lucknow.' So they came and went as winter furloughs succeeded summer leaves, and they were all polite and informative. And that was how her twenties had drifted by, without one of them ever having the gumption to realize that there is simply nothing more ageing than respect, and that there were times when she would have preferred their dislike to all their dreary considerateness. There were times too, in her mother's flimsy sitting-room, as between them they scrawled out these tedious invitations, with the stumpy hyacinths prinked waxily against the pink wallpaper and the whole atmosphere plaintive with so much feminity; when she could have shouted, *No!* Feed these bores yourself! But don't ask me to help you with what is rightfully mine—my youth, my imagination, my capacity for love! Why should it be rifled piecemeal by you to bolster up your own fading days? This, then, was what we meant by being 'filial'—pouring back one's own personal existence for the sake of its fountain-head; in her own case, accepting without cavil a vulgar Edwardianism with its spectrum of subtle snobberies! Fuming inwardly she would write, 'Dear Doctor Miller, If you are free on Wednesday 6th please come and have dinner with us. Bill Strangly will be here and Mr Yockery . . .' And they came and they talked and by their bloodless good manners they contrived to lessen the fact that she was young and she was a woman.

Now here, suddenly, in a room remarkable for its deadness, she had been made naked in a rapid, expert, coarse, maskless assessment. She might have been a tart. She could call it an insult, or she could imagine it a compliment, though neither would be true. It was merely Bateson's interest in a woman whom he could see had dressed herself with some intent to please. Bateson smiled and showed perfect teeth and Richard, dragging himself up from his lolling position against the brown marble fireplace, said hurriedly, 'Oh Mary, this is Mr Bateson—remember?'

They shook hands. Bateson's fingers, surrounding her own

like warm, pliant stone. There were no confusions in the contact; no obscurities; no tentative request that she should make allowances, no ambiguity and, of course, little understanding. Although this last did not cross her mind, fascinated as she was by so much maleness.

'If I'd known we were going to have company . . .' Bateson said. At 'company' his eyes, bright as pebbles in a brook, flickered in a way he would have liked her to believe was appreciation and which, normally, she would have flinched from in some kind of disgust: yet she didn't.

'None of us knew,' Richard grinned. 'Mary decided to run over from Lafney and we thought we'd meet somewhere quietly, when the Winn—Mr Winsley caught me up and said come and have a drink before luncheon.'

'Ah,' said Bateson, 'that's just to satisfy themselves. You should have known that! I remember when I first arrived at this dump, the little woman there—' he nodded gently in the direction of Mrs Winsley, 'said, "Oh, Mr Bateson, why don't you ask your sister over for the afternoon"—my sister's an obstetrician believe it or not—and the way they milled about her when she did finally come you'd have thought she specialised in delivering dragons.—Sorry,' he added, 'now I've spoilt everything haven't I? Perhaps you wanted to believe that they were nicer folk than that?'

'No,' she said hesitantly, 'no you haven't; why should you?'

'You might have taken it as more of a compliment—your being asked here, I mean.'

'My inquisitiveness matched their own, I'm afraid. My mother knew the school when it was known as 'Miss Bellingham's Experiment'. I often wondered what it was like inside.'

'So now you do,' said Bateson. 'Surprised?'

'Not really.'

At this point Canon Ribbs thrust a jolly hand between them and said, 'Good-bye! Good-bye! in an absurd partified voice and Miss Ribbs, following, half-backed from the room staring with all her might.

'We must go too,' said Mary.

'Go?' said Bateson. 'Where . . . ?'

'We've got to eat,' she answered, but in a jerky, unnatural

voice for her. 'No: we particularly want to see the castle and one or two other places.'

Bateson screwed his eyes up in exaggerated disgust at this, in a way which generally had the effect of making others agree with him—his was, after all, the bright and exemplary world of the norm, and he its brightest and most exemplary arbiter. Others were clever, no doubt; but he was *right*. Statistics proved it. *Their* world, so hesitant with subtleties, foxed him frequently with its shades and half-tones, accustomed as he was to a simpler realm of pure, blatant colour. Coming all the way to Stourfriston to see the castle! In January—and with that edgy look ... Old Brand's going to have a spot of trouble in that quarter if he doesn't look out, he was thinking to himself.

Richard, impressed at once by Bateson's attitude, was about to agree when Mary said surprisingly, 'I happen to enjoy sightseeing, Mr Bateson. I do it for no other reason.'

'When you've done all that, come back here and let me get you some tea.' He turned to Richard, 'Show Miss ... ?'

'Crawford,' she said hurriedly.

'Show the lady the way the dominies live, eh boy!'

'No—thanks, I shall have to get back.'

'I'm sorry.'

She watched as he seemed to be searching about his mind to discover some reason for her abruptness. 'I must,' she added. 'Good-bye, Mr Bateson.'

'Be seeing you,' added Richard briefly.

There was a gong and hurtling footsteps. Mr M'Tooley declared 'very nice and let them hope it wouldn't be the last time'—knowing full well that any further entertainment was more than unlikely. They had seen Miss Crawford and that was that. If they wanted to see her again she was sure to be in *Country Life*. *That* was the kind of girl Miss Crawford was, thought Mr M'Tooley. He hurried off to take 'tables', which meant supervising the loading of a stack of huge, chipped plates and shouting out things like, 'sit up! Sanders—Pratt—Wiggborough—that *lout* there! And, For what we are about to receive may the Lord make us truly thankful ...'

★

They trailed about the town in the golden coldness, had their luncheon in a snug hotel whose walls boasted its warming-pans like preposterous medals and, later, in the museum, read the yellow tickets glued to fossils, corroded weapons, little late Roman plates, pots of Samien ware and dirty Victorian toys. Memories of the peaceful luncheon still closed them in. There had been a small, red-faced waitress with fat, bare, white arms and a crisp linen frill high up on each of them biting into a pump, smooth bicep. And there had been the release, too, from the tension of the horrible little party which caused them to be touchingly grateful for just each other's company. The menu had said duck and nothing else, and this she decided was as it should be. It was right. There must be no choice. The day must take the course ordained for it, however trivial it might be. In the first place she had Bateson to forget, and as memorable as he was, she very soon forgot him. His upsetting downrightness faded under the many pleasant nuances of her present situation, and when she saw the expression in Richard's eyes as he gazed at the Roman ornaments, a kind of eager attention begging to know more of their strangeness, she knew that she was right in loving him, and the disturbing image of Bateson melted away. They drank gaspingly over-chilled hock, which routed the Winsley's sherry, ate the duck, smiled kindly at the waitress and were glad.

The castle had exchanged its cruelty for some more furtive quality of casual meetings and shuffling assignations. Eros, who's warm amatory delight figured so exactingly on both sides of a large twin-handled cup retrieved from beneath the local football field—lying there all that time, thought Richard lovingly, with the phantom of its wine still inhabiting it and the clownish game going on above—Eros, though debased, Romanised, possibly even Britainised, still showed the haunting perfections of that earlier joy which was in such direct contrast to the sniggering impropriety of these Sunday-suited youths seeking to kill a winter's afternoon in the municipal museum. From looking at this, Mary had turned to slender phials of azure and virescent glass, each of them splintered finely with the gossamer cracklature of nearly two thousand years. There were trinkets taken from the graves of girls; pins and brooches and clips that had once held tunics tight on warm limbs, fillets and combs with no hint left of the bright heads they had nestled in; a boy's sandal, dice, seals; the bibelots of the strong, the rich and the beautiful, whose trivial worth had proved itself more lasting than any of these; for the dead had lost all identity and their personalities had contracted until nothing remained but that which was heaped up so dully before them—a few calcined knuckles in a showcase. The central heating belched luxuriously on the ratepayers' money. The attendant snatched clandestine delight from the *News of the World*. Two girls passed and then two sailors. A small boy wept and the woman dragging him went doggedly from case to case as if she were searching for the hardware counter in Woolworths. 'Look, Kevin,' she cried, 'a gee-gee—a dolly! Oh, *look!*—a pretty picture . . .' And the tears slid drearily from the child's wet cheeks as he stared in hatred at Plantagenet playthings. After this they peered from narrow window slits down into the dry moat, which looked like a rough setting from which a jewel had been prised—a long bar of turquoise it should have been in this instance, flecked with swans, perhaps, and dragging down into dark rushes the reflected geometry of the keep. Instead there were terrible little flowerbeds, so neat they might have been perpetrated with a pastrycutter. But to see these they had to climb a sill of herring-bone bricks which at once had the effect of isolating them from the prim rôle of individuals in a museum. The short step up from the level of the showcases carried them straightway from being woolly interpreters of history into history itself. Vaguely aware of this, they continued to stare from the slit, and the crouching masonry, like a grim *souteneur*, urged them together. They were quite hidden. Far away, they heard the rustling interest of those who, in an eventless present, were condemned to peer at the habiliments of the happiness of others; a wedding dress, the uniform a little captain had worn during the Peninsular victories, a sandal . . . a ridiculous helmet; a glove or two. The passage which led to these things skirted the deep aperture. But they were alone. Richard's hand rested nervously and lightly on her arm. She felt a reeling, precarious joy. It was like the coming-down motion of a swing, exquisite, but sickening. Go on . . . don't stop . . . a part of her begged, so she was astonished to hear herself saying, levelly enough,

'Richard . . . do you really want to go on with this?'

'Go on . . . ?' He was mystified.

She repeated his words without expression. "Go on. Don't force me to explain."

"So *that's* what has been keeping you so quiet!'

She let him believe this, although the thought had only just moment entered her head.

'You know I have been happy today and if there was the least guarantee of any more days like it, I wouldn't ask such a question. But there won't be; you know there won't be. It's because, I suppose, most people meet, kiss and come to an understanding of each other in some progressive way. It's an adventure. What is there adventurous about two people like ourselves trying to find something new to say—when we have known each other all our lives?

Richard, leaning forward now as the bowmen had once said, 'Surely that *is* the adventure. Anybody can find something to entrance them in a brand-new relationship—what is there in that? It's us, ourselves and . . . and . . . '

'Yes . . . ?' she insisted anxiously.

He turned to face her. She saw the cool, fine line of his cheek in semi-profile and his neck, thicker than she had remembered it, aggressive even, the white skin vanishing abruptly into a dark poll of hair. His words could be tactful, but nothing could lessen the insolence of his being so much younger than herself, so that when she heard him add, "and because you are beautiful," in the rather unsteady voice of a person unused to expressing compliments, she reacted with a faint, but apparent fretfulness. He drew back at once. If she only enjoyed practical things, then he would *be* practical!

'There's only one thing that will make it fail,' he said quietly; "your evasiveness—that and the way you exaggerate everything—you know, Lafney and Mrs Craw—your mother and . . . and . . . about my getting this new job. It's only a bit of schoolmastering after all. You thought the people in the bank pretty awful——'

'I never said so.'

'Not to me, but you did to Quentin. He told me.'

'It's only because I thought you were wasted there.'
'And now I'm 'wasted' at Copdock?'
'Of course you aren't! I never said that.'
'Not in as many words, but I could *see* you hated them.'

She was bound to protest at this, it was so entirely untrue. They had astonished her, appalled her even; but that wasn't hate. She saw how easily he was taken in; how easily he could accept the fifth-rate—something Quentin would never do. It wasn't tolerance, it was licence. Tolerance implied broad limits, the other thing, none. Five years in such a place and Richard might soon become a fuddy-duddy like all the rest of them. He brought this trail of surmise sharply to a head by saying,

'Except Bateson, of course. You liked him.'

She felt the blood rushing to her face and hardly knew what to answer. This suppressed rancour—in a museum of all places —had to end in vulgarity—if it was to end at all; she realised that. But such an ending! She was about to reply when she noticed the expression on his face as he studied the passersby on the gravel paths below. What he had said was intended to be clear and unambiguous. She *had* liked Bateson. He had seemed to her wonderfully wholesome, coming in like that after all those other masters and their wives had been pecking away at her.

'Of course!' she said lightly. 'And I expect the others are quite nice. I hardly spoke to anybody except Mrs Winsley, so how can I tell?'

'Never mind about *them*,' said Richard. Her hands, hot from their clinging suede gloves, lay crumpled in his. He was kissing her and doing so with a kind of consolation, like somebody making amends to a cheated child. She might have been a shop-girl and he one of those tittering louts! If only she could explain—*now*! But when she half-raised her arms in a little desiring movement, he took her by the waist and for a nervous moment she was trapped helplessly by her own shudderingly exquisite fear which made her feel that she might collapse abjectly against the harsh Norman stones. She pulled herself away and struggling to sound normal and at ease, said, 'Darling, we're terrible fools—both of us. We get so *cross*. You go to Sheldon Tuesday I suppose?'

'Sugar . . . Milk . . . ?' he mocked gently. 'You don't have to be so polite you know. Yes, Tuesday it is.'
'And you really want to do this?'
'*This?*—or that?'
'That,' she replied slowly. 'Go to Sheldon and have all that is left of your spare time absorbed. Because it will be; those kind of jobs take up every minute.'
He frowned. 'I don't quite understand what you mean. In fact I don't quite understand what anybody means. I'm invited —or rather it is suggested, that I help a writer get a few books and papers straight. Why should this strike everybody as being so curious? Perhaps you can tell me because I'm afraid *I* don't see it.
'No,' she said rather wearily, 'no, you don't. Why should you? And it isn't curious anyway.'
'What is it then?'
She hesitated before she said, 'It's a kind of death which touches everything—dead causes, dead manners, dead affections—just deadness. That is all! And because these things can no longer go on under their strength, they batten on to the living.'
'Then you think that Sir Paul is likely to 'batten' on to me?'
He grinned to think of so brilliant a figure doing anything of the kind. Sir Paul Abbott's detachment in a ganging-up world was too notorious for anybody to successfully accuse him of any limpet quality. If ever a man had described self-sufficiency, he had. He reached down from the Olympian loneliness of his prose to revive pleasures that had dropped into abeyance, restore the unfairly neglected and add each year, with unwearying constancy, some new and lively tribute of his own, splendidly bound and respectfully received by the current arbiters of style, since in this at least he outdid them all, scribbling them well under the table. Richard reckoned that he would be lucky if he saw Sir Paul at all. Sheldon was large and the click of a vintage typewriter coupled with bulky envelopes on the hall table at tea-time might be the only hint of that dedicated existence. He was beginning to dread the whole idea, not because of anything Mary or Quentin or anybody else, if it came to that, might have supposed, but because of his own feeling of inadequacy. This convinced him that

Sheldon could only mean a short period of box-lifting, stamp-licking drudgery. Not that he minded. It was rather a relief.

But she quenched these day-dreams by saying, 'I didn't mention names and I wasn't thinking about Sir Paul.'

'Who then?'

Me, she ought to have said; herself. He was forcing her into competition with things and people beyond her powers and when she lost—as she was bound to do—would only despise her for it. Those witty old women! That famous old man! (Sir Paul was fifty-four, but that seemed immaterial to her present way of judging things.) They were gleaming, many-faceted quartz, heavy with subtleties. And she was crystal—which is really very dull stuff because of its apparency. She could not conceal, nor trap, nor intrigue and so she would bore him as she knew she bored Quentin.

'I was just being selfish, Richard,' she explained humbly. If so much of her nature was on view, why attempt to hide this?

'You force things along, don't you . . . ?' he answered more kindly. 'And you're always raising doubts. Don't think I'm criticising you,' he added hurriedly, 'I'm not—honestly. But why not let things come to us slowly and naturally—instead of us racing towards them? Don't you think that's best?'

'I suppose so . . .'

'Suppose?'

'Don't pick me up,' she said sharply. Glancing down she noticed a chevron of dust streaking across her skirt. For a moment she gazed at it, surprised that she had managed to get so messed-up. Her shoes were dusty too, and, she suspected, her hair. It would fall all the time in a place like this, she thought; dust, that final evidence that something had been; and even dust itself would eventually disappear, must filter from history into the void. It came off the fake Norman stairs the Council had erected, she supposed. She must have brushed against them as they came up. Somehow this inevitable disintegration of all things soothed her. It brought her back to her habitual commonsense. 'Oh, how silly we're being!'

'Has that only just occurred to you?'

'Just. Look at me—I'm smothered in dust—and my Murea suit too . . .'

'Is that something special?'

'*Frightfully* special!'
'Here—let me . . .'
'When we get out will do.'
'No. Stand still. It's off the wall.'
'I thought the stairs. Do you like it?'
'Love it!'
'You haven't said so before.'
'But I knew all the same—even before you got here. Mary will look wonderful today, I said. And then you arrived and you did. You're beautiful.'
'Not 'beautiful', Richard.
'I won't have my judgments amended. Beautiful.'

She laughed and stroked the ends of her gloves up under her sleeves, pretending to overlook the intent stare of his eyes and said, 'Am I?'

'Very . . . ' he replied gravely.

When I look back on this, she thought, I shall see that the danger began at this point. Not at Meridian years ago, not during the walk to the Martello tower, not even at Dunwich —although there the hazards were ominous enough! But here, in a thousand-year-old window, and in a rather common way. But that won't matter. Not then. She made a final effort to pull herself out of all this dolorousness. After all, she had still the power to refuse. Mightn't that be the highest power of all, she wondered? To say no? To be able to reject? 'Don't take it if you don't want it', she recalled Edwina saying dozens of times to her children—Not that that ever made the slightest difference. Their plates always ended up by being crowded with crumpled bits of this and that which they hadn't quite enjoyed. Thoughts of Edwina turned easily by a natural process to thoughts of her own mother. Wasn't it time she should be getting back? A rather maudlin affection took over from the irritation she normally felt where her mother was concerned. Distance had done it. Twenty short miles had turned Mrs Crawford into a dear, pathetic parent. Mary could really despise herself. Yet all the pull-yourself-together, stop-worrying, be-sensible, self-advice churning around in her brain could not put a stop to what must surely be a groundless apprehension that something at Meridian would take this opportunity afforded by her absence to go amiss. It was rubbish—baseless, she knew and yet was now eager to get back to Lafney.

'Dear, dear Richard . . . '

'Don't go. Stay and have some tea.—Stay and have some supper?'

'Silly. You know I can't. Next Sunday—how about that?'

She knew this was a mistake the minute she said it and was relieved when he said, 'Hopeless, I'm afraid. Sheldon.'

'Oh, of course. Stupid of me. Well, soon anyway.'

'Soon' he repeated but, she thought, so complacently, that her simmering hurts bubbled up afresh in an uncontrollable wash of pain.

'Well we can't stay here,' she murmured, feeling quite sorry for herself. To support this there was a solemn gonging from below-stairs, an expanding glory of noise which sounded wildly oriental in its progress through the stocky arches; it declared the museum closed.

'One day,' said Richard in a taut I-told-you-so voice, 'you'll believe what I say . . .'

She gazed at him with amazement. 'But I *do*.'

'You do?—No you don't; not quite.'

'What?'

The splendid Chinese noise repeated itself and if Richard answered her, then she did not hear him. He helped her climb down from the window and with its dust still smirched faintly down the side of her skirt, they left the museum and all its accurately docketted odds and ends to darkness, trailing out with the other visitors past the cold armour, under the jammed portcullis and so into the smoky gold of late January and a lane of dripping-wet chestnuts. He settled her in the Alvis, but too solicitously, so that when he thanked her—just 'Thank you' said very simply—she flared up. She couldn't prevent herself.

'For God's sake, Richard, do you have to be so formal . . .!'

'You've been irritable from the minute you got here,' he accused her unjustly. His easy, immediate anger shone in every syllable.

'Irritable . . .? Have I . . .?' She weighed this up with aggravating detachment as she fixed the driving-mirror and then a scarf over her head. Her poise grew and grew until she knew it must seem to him absolutely outrageous. So did her misery, but he didn't suspect that. If she were nineteen she would cry. At thirty-two one might only be sick. She would do that—be sick, perhaps in the crackling darkness of the Forestry Commission's firs where the spindly aisles reeled on and on like a remorseless exercise in perspective. The last thing she wanted to do was think. The starter, the wheel, the smeary mirror reacted confidentially to her touch. She saw him standing there, but these things assumed precedence. *They* mattered; they would get her home.

'Good-bye,' she smiled through the glass. She heard the sound but he didn't. Only the desperate sweetness of her mouth travelled beyond the window. She saw his hand flutter up to about the level of his lapel, then fall uselessly as he automatically returned the smile. Then off she went, not fast, if anything she rather jogged out of sight.

9

HIBBLE, on edge for hours for the front door's click, let her in. 'Oh, Miss . . . Oh, Miss . . .' was all she managed to get out at first. Then she said, 'Thank the Lord!' which was a genuine prayer since she at no time used the sacred titles casually. 'Oh you poor dear,' she fussed. Her concern was mountainous, although hardly outdoing her very obvious delight that there was something to be so concerned about. The responsibility which had been hers (for how long? Mary wondered miserably) had puffed Hibble up into a threatening pregnancy of self-importance.

'Better tell me in here, Hibble.' She pushed open the door of the morning room and saw with wistful astonishment its sameness, how the polished buds of the daffodils gangled at the tips of their over-forced stalks, and how the cushions were all wragged together at one end of the sofa for what Hibble termed, 'Madam's lay-down'. The *Sunday Times* had drifted into a crisp ruin across the carpet. A book she had been reading the evening before lay face-downwards on the windowseat. A misaddressed envelope curled in the fender—she had cast it there a minute—an age ago—who could tell? Still there it was, slovenly and chiding. She stooped and picked it up and said to Hibble.

'Sit down please, Hibble. Tell me what happened.'

'It was after luncheon . . .'

'After luncheon—when Mr Yockery was here?'

'No, Miss, he didn't come. He sent a message to say he had the headache.'

'Did he?' she asked, flopping wearily into a stiffly buttoned chair, 'I am sorry. Now just tell me quickly what happened to Mummy. Was it long after I had gone? Where is she—is anybody with her?'

'She's in her bed which is the best place for her, poor lady. She fell off her chair and when I found her she was moaning against the carpet'

'That's how she was lying, Miss—Oh, she wasn't hurt—least not by that—the tumble, you might say. But her poor face was wet and you could see the weeping.'

'You say you telephoned Doctor Fitzsimmons as soon as it happened?'

'I didn't say, but I did, of course. I'm not the one for using things like the telephone on the Lord's Day out of idleness.'

'Then what is it—what did he say it was?'

Hibble waited. There was something consummate in her power to protract. Something merciless, too. On no account would she be deprived of what was rightfully hers—the joy in the telling. She sagged forward, causing her thin, polished body to slip remotely inside its cocoon of Sunday silk. Her hands were clapped against her cheeks, her head niddered in a kind of disbelief that what had happened could have happened.

'She had a stroke,' she said.

'When?'

'I don't know *when*, Miss. She was well enough for her lunch, because she ate it all. I came in later to see to the fire—and there she was, the dear soul, with the cards all round her.'

'The cards—but you said she was alone? Oh, Patience, yes, of course . . .'

'I don't know about *that*,' declared Hibble, rubbing her handkerchief up and down one shining nostril—she fostered an implacable ignorance where some things were concerned;

cards, drinking and what she called 'common songs'—though where she expected to encounter the last in the neighbourhood of Meridian, had always been a mystery to Mary. 'But there was cards all over the place, you might say. Cards in the grate, on the floor . . .'

'Never mind about the cards. Who is with her now?'

'She's sound. The best thing too—that's what Doctor Panton said; "sleep", he says, "nothing better"—those were his words. Although why these doctors always have to tell a person things any fool would know . . .'

'Doctor Panton? You said Doctor Fitzsimmons.'

'I know I did, my lamb—and he sent Doctor Panton.'

Then Hibble began to cry, a thing she had been longing to do for some time. Her tears were messy and had less in common with grief than with a severe cold. Usually they had the effect of making Mary search for her own handkerchief to ward off such a virulent drizzle. This time, however, she placed an arm round Hibble's knotted shoulders and said, 'There, Hibble dear; you've been very kind. You've done everything you should have. I'll telephone Doctor Panton now and then I'll go up and see her.

'She called out, Miss. She kept *on* calling out . . .'

'Well that was quite natural, wasn't it? You go and get some tea now—get us both some and I'll have a word with Doctor Panton.'

At the door, Hibble paused. 'In here?' she enquired with a formidable melancholy.

'If you like, Hibble. Yes, in here; there's a fire here.'

Waiting for the operator to answer she heard Hibble singing with tremulous refinement, . . . 'And nightly shift my earthly tent a day's march nearer Home . . .'

Doctor Panton treated her qualms with flighty cheerfulness. They hadn't met; he was old Doctor Fitzsimmons's new partner, a youngish G.P. whose uncrushable conviction it was that anxiety outdid every other failing of the flesh. Root *that* out and then see how little there was to fear amongst the more easily-classified plagues!

'Don't worry—not a bit,' he told Mary. She hadn't the faintest doubt of the kind of female he was imagining at the other end of the line, one of those oddly-dumbfounded creatures, virginal and frightened, who packed towns like Lafney.

She hardened her voice and said with absolute politeness, No, she would try not to and perhaps the best plan would be for him to call round and see her that evening since she had to know exactly what had happened and the telephone was hardly the thing for that. The telephone system belonging to Lafney possessed its own ethics where the really confidential was concerned. Gossip might be helped on its way lightly enough, but tragedy froze the service-end of the line. Between the two speakers there existed an elephantine ear, an inescapable confessor into which sank, as inevitably as pebbles in a marsh, all the hard news of the place. Mary sensed the ear new fixed expectantly between the doctor and herself like a listening fungus. 'At six,' she repeated. 'Yes, that would do very well.' Before ringing off, she thanked him for all he had done, then hurried up to Mrs Crawford's room. Before she went in she snatched the silver clip from her collar and put it in her pocket and pressed her hair flat, sensing that some of her 'special' look might still remain and give offence. Then she entered.

Her mother was propped up in a half-sitting position against a heap of pillows, a pink mountain against a white.

'So you've returned!' she said in a frighteningly strong voice. The sound of it was like somebody declaiming in an empty room. There was an unnecessary wealth of vowels floating on for ever and ever. The inflexions were the same; it was her mother who was speaking, but in an entirely new register. It was like a terrible impersonation of herself by a guardsman.

'Poor Mummy . . .' Mary went forward quickly and grasped the fat white hand, winking with rings, which twitched above the sheet. The sour, rather indecent smell she had noticed when she first opened the door, increased. A glance was enough to tell her that every window was tightly fastened. 'Let's have a little air—shall we, darling!'

There was a catch in the cumbersome breathing and then Mrs Crawford said, 'No.'—so abruptly in her new deep voice, that there was nothing for it but to put up with the foetid warmth. Then she asked, 'Did you have a good time?' There was anger in this but Mary, vaguely conscious of sick-room ethics, brushed her way past it and answered simply,

'A nice time, darling . . . Can you . . . can you tell me about it?—Or shall we do all that later?'

She bent over as she spoke and tugged the oyster-coloured eiderdown straight and picked up a scratchy lace handkerchief from the floor. Mrs Crawford twisted suddenly, the bed made a sad wiry noise and a glossy sheen ran vulgarly from hummock to hummock over the eiderdown. This time it was a biscuity-looking quilted thing which began to slither floorwards. It was when she was putting this straight that the real cause of all this disorder became obvious to Mary. Her mother was not so much lying, as floundering in her bed. Her body was drifting helplessly, shapelessly in a too-snug welter of sheets and counterpane. It was uncontrolled and enormous. Only her nose and her brow, the last smooth and tallowy, escaped this anarchy of the flesh. They stood out, thin and handsome above the soft ruin of the throat. As well as her rings, Mrs Crawford still wore her gold chain. In the scrunched-up frill of her nightdress its links glimmered and fled like beetles.

'I went to Stourfriston—to see Richard—Richard Brand. We just had luncheon, then afterwards we went to the Castle Museum and walked about a bit. Darling, if only I'd had the faintest idea . . .'

'Why are you explaining? Nobody has asked you to.'

'You were so well when I left. So absolutely right . . .'

'What has that got to do with it?' persisted the peculiar mannish voice from the pillows.

'Only that if there had been the slightest hint, the merest suspicion, do you think I would have gone?'

Mrs Crawford, cruelly adroit in her new rôle, turned her face to the sea and said, 'You might.'

I might—but I wouldn't have, Mary was about to retort in her old way, then she sensibly switched her mind to the real situation. Her mother had collapsed. She was ill to some curious degree. But what strength had raced from her ponderous physique, had not raced from her altogether. It had left her body to sink so that it might add to the soaring capacity of her will. In that way she had never been so robust. So Mary just said, with a kind of cosy playfulness she hoped would mask her distress,

'Well *you* know I didn't know!' Anyone else, she implied, Hibble, the doctor—the local gossips when they found out; they could say what they liked!

Mrs Crawford's head rolled slowly down the pillow until her eyes met Mary's a second only—no more. 'Pray don't explain,' she said.

'But, darling Mummy, I want to know.' Surprisingly at that moment she did. If it had been possible she would have said everything. It would have all run away from her like a freed stream leaving her with gentle, tolerable shallows in which she could reflect occasionally and regret nothing. But the moment passed and from then on she knew the depths would always remain to bewilder her.

'Know what?'

It was too much. How was she ever to compete with this fierce, new-found sagacity? The weakness had previously exploited the flesh and had been present for all to see. Now the body could be dismissed. No one would ever refer to Mrs Crawford as a big dominating old woman again, perhaps. She would be Mary's 'poor mother' and as such would enjoy a far greater calculating power than all her earlier ability to trundle heavily from room to room had allowed. It was a sardonic apotheosis. Comprehending it suddenly, and with desolating clarity, Mary could only stare down on the bed, fascinated and appalled.

'Nothing . . . nothing,' she answered.

In the hall she faced Doctor Panton.

'Ah—Miss Crawford,' he said, unnecessarily merry.

'The thing is,' she told him, 'I am *never* away—that's the really amazing thing! Then just this afternoon . . .'

'Always the way.'

'Always,' she replied, finding it pleasant to play this polite game after the barbed talk upstairs. She wondered if it might be the moment to say something about wishing him well in Lafney—he had been there just a month and neither her mother nor herself had so far called—then decided it to be the absolutely wrong thing to do. For one thing, she had never seen a pair of eyes manifesting such a brilliant, bird-like interest. So she just asked, 'Ought we to have a nurse?'

'A nurse? Goodness me, no! Mrs Crawford should be up and about in a month. You can, if you feel like being extravagant, of course.'

'In a month?' She could hardly conceal her astonishment. 'I understand that there has never been anything like this before?'

'Oh no, never.'

'Well then a month should see her right again. And that's only a precautionary measure, added to which, you might say, a rest never hurt anybody. I should put it down to her being a bit upset over something.'

Mary began to lead the way to the stairs but Doctor Panton seized his hat, flung out an arm to see the time and said,

'No need! No need! Much better if I didn't, if you know what I mean. It might alarm her. Just keep her happy and later on we might do something about her weight. That should help a bit.'

So she let him out after he had conveyed Doctor Fitzsimmons' regrets. There was nothing else for it. How wrong he was soon proved itself.

Mrs Crawford, expertly wise to her new dichotomy—this complete severance from the handicap of her lumbering person, which now lay screened from herself and from the world between a pair of the best Irish linen hand-stitched sheets and a jumble of new novels from the local branch of Smith's Library, refused to get up. She couldn't, she said, and in her new tough mental renaissance she was hardly to be argued with. An invalid soon discovers the way to words no healthy tongue would dream of uttering. Mrs Crawford tried her new demands out on Hibble first and was amused at her flinching. Then on Mary. But she took good care not to alienate Hibble in the process, determined as she was never to sink to being the misled recipient of the kind of confidences deliberately diluted to suit the sickroom. And Hibble, leaping like a flame to even this calculated warmth, industriously filled-in all that Mary had thought best to leave out. The tangible evidence of all this appeared in the form of a brooch which suddenly adorned the stern neckline of Hibble's dress. It was not valuable, but it had been Mrs Crawford's, and she had never been known to give jewellery away before, at least not to Hibble. Mary accepted this fact as a warning.

Another sign of her mother's intention to go all-out in her new career—for it was easily becoming that—was her insistence that her bedroom should be what she termed 'more comfortable'. Actually it was a plea for elaboration. She came of an age set between the heavy confidence of the Seventies and the post Nineteen-nineteen experiments, a period which equated simplicity with poverty. She wanted things dragged in from other roms. They used to be in her own, she complained fretfully, although Mary could not recall when. She kept the shutters closed against the sea. She couldn't bear it. It was so bright and lively, so *actual*. All day, dull or fine, she lay in the slatted light, only interrupting her reading to ring for Hibble. From the rosewood tallboy her early self looked down on her, a generous beauty in Court feathers and a fulsome train, sealed in an embossed silver frame. When visitors arrived—they were frequent, to Mary's never-ending surprise—they, too, were forced to put up with the reduced light. Mr Yockery came most of all, wholeheartedly delighted that she should be so available and deriving from these visits the double joy that in certain instances it was actually an act of charity to *receive* pleasure.

*

For the next few weeks Mary was taken up with the essential differences of life at Meridian. The rooms, with only herself in them, began to tempt her with daring new arrangements. That over here, she began to think and the curtains kept right back to let every streak of light in, and not massed half-way across the pane as they were at the moment. A reassessment of the pictures? She rather hesitated to shift these around and excused her cowardice by telling herself that she hadn't the time, although this was ridiculous since it became more and more apparent that it was Hibble and not she who carried the house; Hibble, who was beside herself with importance and tremulous with duties, and not only that, but able to *be* important. It showed mostly in her walk. She used to trot and now she loped. There was a fearful authority in that dragging stride which carried Hibble from floor to floor—usually with a large, round paper-mâché tray crammed with tea or cosmetics or just the latest letters for Mrs Crawford. The house became more and more ship-like, only this time a Homeric galley of which Mrs Crawford was the guiding, unwinking, all-seeing eye painted on the prow which, although excluded from any normal vision, could sense in an occult fashion the life flowing past it.

Gradually a pattern was decreed and kept to. The mornings were Mary's own. Luncheon was regular but seemed less so by the faintly derogatory way in which Hibble scattered it across the shiny table at the last possible moment, which compared badly with the hours she spent turning fresh napkins into fans and rabbits for Mrs Crawford's tray and prettifying the food to go on it out of all recognition. Between tea and dinner, seated upon a pale cane nursing-chair, Mary read to her mother, at first self-consciously and then with relief and ease. A novel had ceased to be a mere entertainment and was now an uncommitted country in which they could meet, speak and yet not take sides. Difficult conversations were smothered at birth as fictitiously as possible. Mrs Crawford's taste in such matters became quite bizarre and, Mary noticed, mildly salacious. Her library list, combed from the Sunday papers, puzzled the young lady at Smith's. Father Yockery, who took broadmindedness to be a duty, concurred a little too wholeheartedly in all this. Their arid discussions could be heard like a rather bitter litany going on behind Mrs Crawford's bedroom door. Sometimes Mrs Crawford laughed with unbelievable gusto and Hibble, setting down what she was engaged upon, would mutter, "Poor soul, it ought to make us count our blessings . . .'

Edwina came and said innocently enough, 'The boys send their love.' She said it every time she called, totally untrue though it was. She played cards with Mrs Crawford and Mary, passing by to her own room, would hear them plonking them down with suppressed delight, like two naughty monitresses in a prep school cupboard.

One day a man came to count the rooms. He was quite incredibly thorough. By a single glance from his scuttling, porcine little eyes, Meridian and all that pertained to it was snatched away from her and made an annexe of the State.

'Eleven bedrooms,' he said—greatly to Mary's surprise. Described flatly like that the place became barn-like. 'And downstairs?'

'But you wouldn't sleep them downstairs?'

'All depends how bad it gets,' said the man. 'That's what you might call the best of these big old places—sleep them anywhere.'

'But . . .' she began.

The man tapped the bitten metal end of his pencil against his front teeth. 'Oh, you get an allowance,' he said. 'Yes, yes, you get an allowance . . .' But if she asked him they wouldn't be billeting along the coast anyway. So it was just a waste of time his coming here, wasn't it? But *they* knew best, he supposed. 'Or they think they do!' he shouted familiarly from the front door.

He left her with a Goyaesque impression of the drawing-room floor like a kind of camp, with maternal figures squatting in each corner of it and sheltering their young beneath capacious shawls with stoic dignity. In the centre, with steam rising up from it and dimming the lustres, was a soup copper with Hibble serving from it. But when the man came again, this time to leave her some forms, she almost welcomed him. When one's own affairs have slurred to a standstill there is always a sort of relief to be found in the topsy-turvy possibilities of the world at large.

Then the very day she wrote to Helen Gascoigne begging her, rather than inviting her, to come over for a few days, by the second post and somewhat ostentatiously as it happened since it was the only one in the postman's hand, she had a letter from Richard. Hibble came in like clockwork and said, 'I'll take it up.'

'There's only one, Hibble, and it's for me.'

'Will that young lady be coming here, then?' Hibble stared greedily at the envelope.

'Mrs Gascoigne?—Oh, I have no idea. This isn't from her. I've only just invited her as a matter of fact—this morning. The postman took it away with him.'

Hibble looked down and rubbed her palms together with a rustling sound. 'About a week, I suppose—she wouldn't want to stay much longer than that, would she?' she said cautiously.

'I said a week, but it all depends. We shall have to wait until she arrives. After all, she hasn't said she will come yet, has she!'

'She'll find it cold after Africa.'

'Anywhere would be cold after Africa.'

'The Mistress says she can't remember her.'

'Oh, what nonsense, Hibble—she often stayed here for *weeks*.'

'Weeks once,' said Hibble. 'Weeks in years gone by.'

'Well Helen remembers Mummy all right.'

'She's sorry she's been taken so bad, I suppose . . . ?'

'Of course she is. What a silly question.'

Hibble sighed deeply, made a profound noise that is, since there was only the vaguest movement of her long thin chest. Then she loped out into the garden to search for snowdrops to put in the weighted vase on Mrs Crawford's tray. Mary jagged her letter open thinking all the time as she did so, I could burn it—there's the fire—it could float right into it and be nothing in a second. Helen's coming. So is the war. I don't *have* to have this kind of misery. I am not committed to it. Anyway, he would only be writing to her out of some kind of politeness. His writing, rather bold, made a dark oblong down the page.

'Dearest Mary; Don't say you're surprised. Indeed, don't say anything but I like it here—news that will shake Quenny more than it will you. I suppose I ought to say something apologetic about not writing and *will*—if you will say it too. Hardly any news from Lafney. You know Mummy only writes letters to Stella—whom she sees every week. I think Mrs Crawford wasn't very well when she last wrote, but that was ages ago and I expect she must be better now.

I have had a few good long talks with old Winsley and, do you know, he's right! Copdock *could* be quite a school again. His idea is to make the four houses into two—Bloomfield and Montessori—I think I told you; put a youngish master in charge of each of them and then he says we'd see the difference at once. Except of course, it can't be at once. It's something to do with Miss Bellingham.

Do you remember the skull? Well Bateson's got it now—on

a mantelpiece with two clocks, a letter-rack, a china dog, a glass fish and all his cups. You'd hardly notice it. I'm afraid that this isn't the kind of letter I intended to write at all, but why tell you that, since nothing could be more obvious. The *other* letter would most likely have ended,

Bestest love, R.'

She wrote back and told him about her mother and about Helen Gascoigne's possible visit, then noted with satisfaction how busy these facts made her single page look. She didn't trouble to ask, 'what about Sheldon? What about so many other things . . .' The unexpected joy she experienced from his handwriting made her forget how skilfully off-hand he could be. When Helen came she made no pretence of screening from her a shadowy but definite happiness.

Helen had been at school with her. Then, with dazzling rapidity, had married and held elegant sway in an impressive number of equatorial consulates. She was a lively, cheerful creature, quite maskless and so free of complexity that she could concentrate all her energies on being entirely selfless. There was nothing simple about her in the sense in which simplicity is generally admired. Her genius existed in her power to salute each day as it dawned, and an ability to get really worried about such things as hats, and yet never to appear trivial. When she did so there was a sameness about her which made her reliable, and yet this sameness, which, for all her poise, could have carried with it a very humdrum outlook, was more like that of a fine clock who shares its basic principles with any little time-keeper, yet contrives by means of a certain indefinable air to do so much more than merely giving off a dull and dutiful tick. Mary never saw Helen without noting this effortless perfection. Perhaps that was why they met so seldom. Such equability could only reflect her own hesitant inadequacies. One didn't really go to people like Helen Gascoigne for advice, since ordinary distresses must seem to them not so much sad, as incredible. How on earth could such a thing have ever *begun*? they were more likely to wonder. How simply fantastic to let yourself in for it!

Yet Helen must be told, of course. Mary steered her out into the garden for this. It was bright, but alarmingly cold—particularly after Tanganyika. But there had been a month or two in Cheyne Row in between and that was enough to cause Helen to stretch out her neat little arms in the dizzy bright air and cry against the faintly herring-smelling wind, 'All this, darling. Divine!' They picked their way across the wet grass and round each promontory of shadow which the cedar spread like a black map over the garden. The sun licked their cheeks with an elfin warmth and the sky was like very fine old blue glass. Gulls ravaged it with their petulance and the cedar groaned dismally. Helen was enchanted. It was a habit of hers to be so. She fluttered her hand appreciatively.

'*When* was I last here?' she demanded.

'When you came back from Zurich.'

'When I was eighteen—so long ago?'

'Does it seem so long ago?'

'Billions of years, darling. Now tell me why I'm here. Exactly why, mind you.'

'I . . . I . . .'

'Shush!' said Helen. 'Can't you hear it?'

'The town crier?'

Helen shook her head, although it was true, there was a bell and some shouting going on down there in the main street. She stood still and listened again. Under the muffled ululation of voices and traffic the drag and fall of the waves could be heard as they laved against the beach, building up glistening cairns of shingle and destroying them again with a softly purling grief. Lower than this retained note of stones fretting and falling there was another sound, urgently repeated, shuddering and strong. Just *boom*, but *boom* with inexhaustible majesty.

'That,' said Helen.

'That——? It's only the sea.'

'But does it always . . . ?'

'Always and always. I suppose it is rather dreadful when you come to think of it. It's the sea eating up Lafney—at least that's what the coastal-erosion people say.'

'Heavens!' murmured Helen. 'No wonder you're depressed. I should feel the same if my house was like the ornament on a piece of cake that was being nibbled at all the time.'

'Oh Meridian's quite safe. Absolutely. But surely you remember the outlines of old cottages we used to find when the tide went out and how they were once streets—up by the Martello? Oh you must, Helen. We bathed there dozens of times.'

'I forget.'

'Do you—much?'

'No, darling, of course not. Only 'boom—boom' and things like that. Nothing else. Why only in the train this morning I stared out of the window at a meadow, just a meadow, mind you, and said, hullo, I know you. You were where we bull-rushed!'

'At Snape—at the edge of the marsh, but that was years ago!'

'I was twelve,' said Helen. 'Exactly. You were twelve, too, and Stella was either eleven or thirteen, but whatever it was, she was sure to have thought it better.'

'Stella—was she there?'

'She was,' said Helen. And then, taking hold of the soft, lustrous bulb of her chignon between her long white fingers, 'I'll tell you something, darling, Stella always scared me stiff!'

'Rubbish, you weren't ever scared!'

'I was of Stella. Do you know, she once tried to convert me —that was when I was fourteen and she was thirteen or fifteen. We were on our way to see you—the long way round and she ran through my sins like wildfire. She knew them all, everyone.'

'Well she's quite changed now. You'd hardly know her.'

'Oh I'd *know* her all right,' said Helen. 'You see I buy all her books—for old acquaintance, you know. But I shall have to stop soon. She's so prolific. Not to mention the queer looks I get from people when they find dozens of dormitory epics in every bookcase.'

There was a pause during which two or three booms shuddered against the sea-wall and a gull fell down the glassy sky with lackadaisical grace and then Mary said heavily, 'I believe she's doing very well . . .' She had patted away at this lissome shuttlecock of a conversation long enough and now that they were approaching the real reason for Helen's visit, she felt she had to get to the point at once. The talk had been liturgical anyhow. Both suspected its general direction. Its answers were foresworn.

'Mr Brand died, didn't he?' Helen watched a ship with steady eyes. She had settled for the rôle of fundamentalist.
'Oh a long time ago.'
'I remember something. Tony may have read it out from *The Times*. Who is rector now?'
'A Mr Yockery.'
'Nice?'
'Oh, Helen, "nice"!'
'Well is he?' demanded Helen, hanging on to cheerfulness for a hairsbreadth more.
'No, nasty. He's a friend of Mummy's and I expect you'll meet him.'
They leant forward against the sudden flaring, tearing wind. Helen hankered a little for the snug beaver coat she had recklessly flung down across her bed. Now and again she toppled a worm-cast with the toe of her very expensive shoe. The hush then the rush of the sea seemed to be pressing itself physically against her temples. She felt remote, like a somnambulist on a headland. In a minute she might tumble down . . . down . . . And yet she was not afraid. Mary's fecklessness worried her a little—she didn't care to call it anything other than this—but *surely* . . . at her age. No? That was cruelty. What had age to do with it? When she met Tony she was seventeen—just. And all they could find to say were things about her age, as though that in itself could alter what she felt in her heart, or at her very finger-tips even when he happened to be near. She had been lucky as it turned out. She had married Tony and from that moment the years had been as limpid and as certain and as fresh as a mountain river without even the slightest effort on either of their part to make them so. They were in the grip of circumstance from the moment they met. That the circumstance was happiness had been nothing but the merest chance. But she could truthfully declare that neither Tony nor herself was smug. Incredulous, yes—and often; as people must be who have woken up to find the fruits of the earth plopping down at their feet, but not blinded nor oblivious to the misery of others. When their friends were miserable they felt they could shake them. Helen, for instance, could not but help remarking to herself ever since she got off the train, the unforgiving and rigid quality

of Lafney. Its stiff ways had pounced upon her the moment she had struggled out with her luggage on to the platform. The porter looked, the other passengers looked, the girl in the bookstall, the taximan—they all looked. And just when she thought she was free of this remorseless scrutiny, when the taxi had ground its way past the rattling rhododendrons, Meridian itself took up the stare. She felt it eyeing her from the second she set foot on the front steps. Commonsense told her that it must be because of poor Mrs Crawford lying up there on the first floor with so little to do except peek between her shutters, but this didn't make the situation any more palatable. The fact was, she hadn't been in the house five minutes before she had made up her mind to take Mary out of it. Only for a holiday, of course. She'd take her back to Cheyne Row. Then she wondered about the man. Who could it be? Someone not eligible for the rusty gates of Meridian evidently. Else why all the fuss? Perhaps one of the fishermen, something foolish and romantic—although she hoped not. That sort of thing never did work out. But whoever it was, he would be strange and extraordinary. Mary would be sure to make that mistake. She looked round at Mary following her along the narrow, sluggy path which would lead them out on to the cliff.

'Are we to go right on?'

'With the talk—or with the walk?'

Helen grew deliberately playful. 'They don't appear to be separate, darling.'

Mary just said, 'I can see you're freezing. I'm awfully sorry. Living here I forget all about it. You should have said. We'll walk back.' Walking back and scratching her hands deliberately against the shaggy rosemary hedge she said lightly, 'Stella's brother is now at Copdock—you know, that funny school at Stourfriston.'

'Those babies!'

'Richard . . . is the particular baby . . .'

'Yes—?' said Helen distantly.

'He—I . . .'

'Ohhhh?' said Helen. The utter formality of it! She longed to give one of her high, gay, kind laughs which were her expression of 'Amen' to every smoothed-out predicament, because already she saw it as that; ordered, healed or whatever it was that was necessary to view it unconditionally. But she was cautious. Tanganyika, Benin, Freetown, Leopoldville, these torrid places had taught her a thing or two. There one had to be wise or mad. There weren't all these subtle variations which an old civilization allowed. There you had to grow up— or be a great big baby hankering for the gin bottle. Helen had plumped for wisdom. She and Tony had been so brilliant in the management of their own lives that they had soon become the most sensible people their friends knew. Unfortunately, being so sensible was bound to take its toll of other virtues, and Helen in particular lacked the essential refinement of the rough grace for which she was celebrated. She had a wonderful amount of busy, active kindliness and there was nobody like her when it came to pulling some poor floundering creature out of the mire of his own fecklessness; but beyond this she could not go. She had little sensitivity. This present situation, for instance, the simplicity of it dazzled her. And she could not understand why it didn't dazzle Mary.

'I take it he means so much to you, darling?' she enquired comfortably. And then even her well-meaning insouciance sank under the amount of truth swelling Mary's brief answers.

'To me, yes. I wasn't quite certain at first, but I'm sure of it now.'

Not caring to say another word they walked slowly back to the house.

'She's been ringing,' announced Hibble in a rather satisfied voice when they entered the sitting-room, and to Helen, 'She thinks that she remembers you, Madam.'

'I should think so indeed,' Helen laughed in her best happy-scolding tone. '*You* remember me, don't you, Hibble?'

'I never forget no one, Madam.'

'Good. It's fifteen years anyway,' she added reflectively, thinking of Mrs Crawford. 'Your mother may not like what she remembers, nor care for what she sees.'

'The room is rather dark,' Mary said vaguely. She felt apologetic. Helen could be one of those people who go to pieces at the idea of sickrooms. Perhaps she couldn't face it. She had hoped that her mother would not have insisted, a rash hope, she had to admit. Mrs Crawford's greed for what was going on at Meridian was on a par with her interest in its kitchen. Mary thought she ought to explain the general outline of her mother's present ways. They might be rather daunting if she didn't. 'The room has shutters—they all have, but Mummy keeps hers closed.' She waited until Hibble had left and then added, 'There's a wine smell: I'll tell you, because you're sure to notice it. The shutters make it worse, of course, but being there all the time Mummy doesn't seem to notice . . .'

'I am sorry,' said Helen. 'I hadn't realised how ill she was, to be absolutely candid.'

A dull contradictory expression came over Mary's face. 'She's not ill,' she said, flat and matter-of-fact. 'She was. She had a stroke.'

Helen waited. She put out a little feeler of silence before she said, 'Let me go up now—before we have our tea. That's obviously the best thing to do, isn't it? Hibble!', she called, 'Oh, there you are. We'll take Mrs Crawford's tray up when you've got it ready.'

Climbing the staircase behind Mary gave Helen a chance to reflect. This was supposed to be a nice white, airy house, she thought. And just look at it! Everything as brown as toast in the passages, doors, papers, floors, curtains; all of them rich and still in the dark. She admitted that they were good, in fact rather splendid. But so morose! Odds and ends of things told her that this was a passage she had walked down before; that, a door she had stepped through; this, a window in which she had sat and waited—for Mary? For Stella? Stella had half-lived at Meridian in those days, she remembered. Helen saw them all bouncing up and down in this long corridor, dressed in prickly gym slips and heard Mrs Crawford calling out in her big, jolly way, 'Come o-o-on!' This memory comforted her particularly. People did not alter to that degree. But Meridian had. She must admit that. Meanness had set in, not smallness. The spaces, especially after Cheyne Row, were enormous. These great shiny doors, and the giddy cornices which should have been all very sweet and Pompeian if they didn't rather remind her of an ambitious railway restaurant. Mary went on in front, the tray tinkling pleasantly. Faintly ashamed of herself, Helen was thinking, too many chairs, too many pictures, books, rugs, ornaments; too many walking sticks in the tea-jars on the landing. And drawers everywhere. Full of knives and forks and spoons, she supposed. Even napkin-rings with dead people's initials on them, she shouldn't wonder. Nothing ever got rid of. Nothing ever given away. But to whom could you give a chalk and charcoal Crawford to—or a greatly inflated Crawford described in a billion photographic dots? There were dozens of these. They watched from every wall in pale maple frames the colour of speckled honey.

Suddenly Mary disappeared and Helen heard Mrs Crawford say in her surprisingly vibrant voice.

'Come in, my dear. Of course I remember you.'

She has the advantage! thought Helen recklessly as she followed Mary. She traced in front of her something long and white and billowy which grew faintly animated as Mrs Crawford talked.

'I *loathe* a hard light,' she was saying. 'I expect you can remember that from the old days. Why, there's only one cup. There's only one cup, Mary. Tell Hibble will you?'

'Our tea is already by the fire downstairs, Mummy. Helen has just come to say how-do-you-do now and will come and have a longer chat a bit later on.'

'Oh . . .' said the voice from the snowdrift of pillows, sheets and sprawling novels, 'if that's the case, don't let it get cold on my account . . .'

'Just a few minutes,' said Helen soothingly. Things were introducing themselves from the shadows, a cluttered dressing-table topped with an oval, smeary, powdery looking-glass. A tallboy festooned with gilded drop-handles and on top of this, yet another prodigious photograph which turned out to be of Mrs Crawford herself heightened by feathers and fettered to a studio palm by yards of velvety train.

'Delhi,' explained the richly clotted voice.—'I came out in India.'

Helen could see her now. She lay massively on her back in an attitude of stranded luxury. Her head was a little twisted to see the chair for visitors set towards the right of the bed. Her plump, strong hands nestled on the eiderdown like contented rabbits.

'You are a tiny little thing,' Mrs Crawford said, reaching

out for her spectacles and holding them briefly against the spritely bridge of her nose.

'I must have grown a bit since I was last here!'

'I suppose you must have.'

'Well sit down for a second, anyhow,' said Mary. She tugged the chair and there was a muffled squeal of castors.

'I can't begin to tell you how much this house has always meant to me. It was part of my childhood for one thing and that's always frightfully precious, isn't it? All the scraps one has saved up from it I mean. I always did adore Meridian.' Nerves always had a yeastlike effect on Helen's superlatives. In a social quandary she stressed and strained. The nervousness was rarely on her own account, but because of her desire to please.

'That must be why you come here so frequently,' Mrs Crawford said.

'Fifteen years,' Helen lamented, 'isn't it ghastly!'

'But you do write—? At least that's what I'm told.'

'Mary has always been the more consistent about that, I'm afraid. She writes wonderful letters. I read them, Tony read them—in fact nearly everybody in the bungalow used to read them. They became our despatches from Suffolk . . .' She chattered on. Mary, pressing her hair back from her forehead, rather confusedly interrupted with, 'Helen!' and 'No!' and little uncertain laughs. Now and again Mrs Crawford interposed with a loud sound that was not quite a word and for a minute or two the trio of talk drove out some of the room's darkness. Too confident by far—wasn't she breathing new life into this ridiculous situation?—Helen cried, 'But everything is *just* as I remember it . . . !' and then she stopped, appalled that she had left out Mrs Crawford's normally abundant health.

There was a pause and then Mrs Crawford said, speaking in a rough, half-smothered voice, 'Including Mary? Don't you find a difference there?'

'Mary? No—how? Of course not.'

'Well she's thirty-two for one thing.'

'*I'm* thirty-two, Mrs Crawford.'

'You must be, of course, only I can see you are being sensible about it.' She heaved herself up suddenly to a sitting position and said loudly, like somebody correcting a child, 'Do keep still!'

Mary shrank away from the tallboy in agony. Her face and throat were ruled with reflections cast by the locked shutters.

'Hibble left your handkerchief drawer open, darling.'

'Then Hibble can close it. I hope Mary's behaviour won't irritate you as it does me, Mrs . . . er, Mrs Gaskell. If it does you must make allowances.' The fat, bunny-like hands trotted up her steep bosom and played a game with her necklace. 'It's love,' she said. 'But I expect you've been told all about that with all the rest of the gossip from this part of the world!'

Helen felt misery pressing against the back of her eyes. And compassion. Where was funny, nice Mrs Crawford who taught them croquet? Where was the Mrs Crawford who took so many things away for a picnic the car would hardly start? And the Mrs Crawford who sat at the head of her own dinner-table like a rather splendid bird and enjoying everything so? Where was she? Where had she disappeared? Even the furniture at Meridian had changed and grown malicious. The chair she sat on nipped her cruelly, and a hidden clock ticked away as maddeningly as it could.

But Mrs Crawford was still enjoying herself. In a different way, that was all. 'No scones? I thought Hibble said scones?'

'I—I'll get them, Mummy.'

'*Hibble* can get them.'

But Mary insisted and after she had left the room, Mrs Crawford said, 'She will try and do everything herself! One of the first rules the Admiral instilled into me was 'give every person a job and let them get on with it.' She just won't— Mary, I mean. I think that must be half her trouble. You know she's most frightfully anxious about something or other? Well she is. I *know*, of course. Mothers always do. How long are you staying—I might be able to tell you about it and when I do, you will see that I am absolutely right.' Then she switched the conversation adroitly as Mary returned with the scones. 'And then we thought we'd get all the Virginia creeper off this side of the house; it must be that which is making it damp shouldn't you imagine . . .?'

'I think Mummy must be getting tired,' Mary was saying from the door, it might be almost satirically. She had brought up another cup and saucer for Helen and some more cake, but nothing for herself. The door, caught against the thick rug behind it, had to be pushed and leaned against before she could get through with this second tray.

'There—you see!' insisted Mrs Crawford triumphantly. Hibble can get through that door without your knowing it but Mary heaves herself against it . . . Oh, but what is the use of talking!'

Sense, sense, Helen told herself. Do what you can. Stay a few minutes and see it out. That would be a real kindness. 'How nice,' she said. 'I can pour out and I'll join you downstairs in a few minutes, shall I, Mary?' She divided her comforting look between them and refused to see the apology in Mary's own eyes.

But Mrs Crawford shouted, 'The door! the door!' in what seemed a deliberately uncontrolled way and fell back on her pillows slack and puffy with self-pity. When they were quite alone she added, 'That's nothing to what she's like sometimes,' in a quiet, pleased voice. And then she began to cry.

'Don't . . . you musn't. Here let me . . .' What should she do? Ring for Hibble? Punch the pillows, but that was hardly necessary. They were enormous and ebullient. There was a bitterly stale cobwebby substance pressing against her teeth. 'I know,' she said in a cheerful voice which she knew must sound despicable, 'we'll have a window open, shall we! Just one and only for a minute or two.'

She waited and heard a sound from the hunched-up bedclothes, a sort of rustling grunt. It might have meant yes, no—approval, resentment—anything. That decided her. She clacked the shutter back against the mesh of naked stalks where the leafless creeper sagged against the plaster and colour. A warm river of brightest yellow and heady blues poured in. 'Is it too much?' she asked anxiously. The transformation of the room was drastic.

'She wants to leave me,' said Mrs Crawford. Her eyes were closed tight.

'No,' answered Helen, slowly, but with certainty. 'You must understand that I know few of the facts as yet, but I do know —I *feel*—that Mary would never leave you.'

'Then what?' The eyes opened and conducted a sort of

haggling bargaining from the stillness of their surrounding flesh. They winked and flickered, partly with tears and partly with the unaccustomed light.

'I'm still supposing, but I should say she just wants to marry.'

'And go off, of course?'

' "Go off" isn't the right term, is it? She wouldn't leave you if you needed her.'

Mrs Crawford pounded the bed to demonstrate her position. 'But she did—she does; she's always going off, my dear! Using polite sentences won't make it sound any better. She'd gone off when I was taken ill, for example. Did you know that? And lots of times since—afternoons, evenings. I hear the motor turning out of the drive and that's about all. Isn't that worrying enough? If it isn't, what is?'

Helen filled the cups. A dozen sensible district-visitor things occurred to her, things she realized that might give comfort to most situations, yet curiously not this one. Meridian might be sawn in half, for example. Why not? It was big enough. Mary, single or befriended (somehow Helen could not think of her as married), could have one bit and Mrs Crawford the other. There would be independence and interdependence; the isolation and the nearness. Why on earth did people think it was in the sphere of loving to be on each other's toes all the time! Mary might have a job—like Stella—and be home for weekends. Would not that lessen this fretful tension? Or ! and how to begin this Heaven alone knew—Mrs Crawford might be cold-shouldered out of her invalidism. If so many little comforts did not come up to her, might she not begin to creep down to *them*? The spring was coming and there were few places which knew how to be as dazzling as Lafney in May. All these ghastly magazines with their sleek pages upon which the mind slipped, the sedatives in their various guises on the bedside-table which so soon took on the role of sacraments; the apologetic narcissi, three feet tall in their shallow grey pots; the past distorted by a camera-flash and the present shut out by Venetian blinds; *they* were the sickness. It was all as simple as that. And as difficult. Very much despising herself, Helen listened to her own voice saying, 'Of course it is, but worrying won't help, will it?'

'It's her not confiding, her not telling me anything,' Mrs Crawford complained.

'Isn't that a natural thing—when a person's still a little unsure herself, I mean?'

'Are you taking her part?'

'I told you, I don't know her part—not all of it.'

Mrs Crawford grew sprightly. 'It's hardly necessary to be word-perfect to have the gist of it.'

'Well I know she's in love, if that's what you are implying.'

'That must strike you—as a woman of the world, I mean—as pathetic.'

Helen did wince at this. The pure, unadulterated selfishness of Mrs Crawford's intention grew plain. It was so basic that it was almost admirable. She had even dispensed with guile. Mary was as much a part of her life as that Boule chest, for example, which had come to Mrs Crawford so properly through aunts and cousins. It was *hers*. Her argument was as simple as that. Why go in for niceties to prove what was so indisputedly one's own? Why be tricked out of possession—particularly when you knew that the other person had no real interest in the article in the first place? Here you became more than the owner. You were the guardian, the cherisher, Love came into it. You were more than the proprietor, you were the protector. Therefore it could only seem pathetic that Mary should not only want to haunt the brink of this unknown, but to plunge herself into it! Sincerely shocked by all this, Mrs Crawford had searched about her for means to stay such an action and had discovered it, fortuitously at first, in the guise of her bed. But in a very short time she realised that there is nothing easier to get into than the routine of other people's illnesses. That, after all, is half the secret of a successful hospital. Mary, Mr Yockery, Edwina—in fact most of Lafney fell in with her new ways. They called when they knew they should, and left when they felt they ought. They knew when she ate and when she slept and when she would want her library books changed and that she couldn't stand the light and that Hibble was a darling, and that by being this she was promoted in some way. Hibble, at any rate, enjoyed her extra circumspection. She inflated the sense of sadness by a word, or by her head-shaking lope. Entering Mrs

Crawford's room made people lower their voices as a matter of course. All this was perfectly splendid—she would be a hypocrite not to get some kind of pleasure from it—except for Mary. And she, who should have had her hands full enough with all this, had contrived to possess, and indeed did possess, a greater freedom than ever. When Mrs Crawford heard the Alvis grind and turn at the gate her desperate affection for Mary soured to a wild determination. She wouldn't be robbed! Blast those Brand boys with their quirks and graces! Blast Mary's secure six hundred pounds a year ... And now blast this pretty little creature with her burnt face and not quite considerate ways. If she didn't know everything, Mrs Crawford felt certain that she soon would. She was so patently the confidence-receiving kind.

The sun, soaking through the window, drew out the warm, winey heart of the room, exchanging the cosiness for its own cold March brilliance.

'You must realise,' said Helen slowly, 'that I cannot discuss things I don't know about and even if I did know about them, that I couldn't be disloyal in any way to Mary.'

'I'm not asking you to be disloyal, as you call it. I wouldn't ask anybody to be that. No, not a cake, thank you. You mustn't take me up, as they say.'

'No, of course not. I'm dreadfully sorry.'

'That's all right.'

'All I meant was that Mary does as she likes, she's—'

'She doesn't,' interrupted Mrs Crawford fiercely; 'none of us does. Do you believe that we are here to "do as we like"?'

'We have certain freedoms, freedoms that are ours alone.'

Mrs Crawford's bed scrunched heavily. For an anxious moment Helen thought she was going to get out of it. But she was only raising herself up to say what she had to say. Her mouth was pursed in its old 'organising' line.

'That is not what I was told, Mrs Gascoigne,' she declared rudely, 'long ago, you understand ...?' Her angry head nodded to the Court lady on the tallboy. 'There were other things.'

Helen, sounding braver than she felt, said, 'I suppose you mean the conventions?'

'You don't lessen a thing by giving it a stuffy name. Why not say "duty"?'

'I can't go on from here,' replied Helen with more calm than she could possibly have believed herself to possess. 'Perhaps I do mean duty. I don't know. I haven't been told. If Mary goes out, it's just because she must. To me it doesn't appear unreasonable. The real pity is that you are ill.'

'But she lies to me.'

'She doesn't mean to. It is not her intention. It is part of her escape.' She said this too hurriedly and realised her mistake at once. Mrs Crawford pounced.

'Then you *do* know!'

'I only feel that it is like this.'

'In that case you might like me to fill in a few gaps for you.' As Mrs Crawford sank into her bed it was like watching her sink into herself. Her warm bulk became quite divorced from the cold liveliness of her eyes. 'Mary is making a fool of herself over young Dick Brand who has two hundred a year and an increasingly good opinion of himself.'

Helen, toying with tea-cups and with the idea of leaving, thought, Stella's brother! What was so terrible about that? He would be a bit young, perhaps. People were no more than this to her; a bit young, a scrap older—what possible difference could it make? Very much relieved at the ordinariness of the situation and allowing for the fact that Mrs Crawford, having had a daughter on her hands, for so long, so to speak, would naturally feel deprived of some of her contentment if Mary placed herself in another's grasp, she still couldn't help but say, 'But the Brands are nice. Two hundred a year isn't much, I know; but Dick—isn't he the clever one? He's bound to do better. Anyway I must say I always liked them.'

'Them or him?'

'Oh, Stella, Dick—the tall thin boy, what was his name? And, of course, darling Mrs Brand. How is she, incidentally?'

'Edwina? Very well indeed I should think. But what was it that you liked about them? What is it that you remember them by?'

Still a trifle nonplussed, but suspecting it to be a time of returning benevolence, Helen confessed to a cosy regard for the past. Like Meridian, like Mrs Crawford even, the Brands were part and parcel of her childhood and of those singularly memorable years of it which verge on puberty. The purest, most heart-breaking degree of childhood occurs then. Whoever recalls being eight? Whoever forgets being twelve . . . Stella's the only one I really remember. The boys were babies.'

'They haven't changed!'

'Oh!' Was this mirth? Was light coming through? Was she to laugh . . .? She looked ahead, out from the confusions to where the elms, faintly green, bent inland from the sea; a sea forgetting to be sinister and glinting with gaieties. A windlass cracked. She was just about to believe in this suspected transformation, when Mrs Crawford, in a stifled voice as if what she was saying and what she was thinking bore no relationship, said, 'And now, when you've seen what you want, be good enough to close my window.'

Helen, when she remembered this later, was more shocked by her own immediate anger than by the cause of it. To be spoken to like that! What right had Mrs Crawford—anybody —to such behaviour! Here she was at Lafney, a nowhere if you like, being bludgeoned into its ways! Lafney, with its gossip that was like bubbles from a puddle, and its cramped little acts. She saw at once how different was her own life. Utterly, utterly, utterly. Perhaps one shouldn't return—to do so, or not to do so, was a threadbare problem. Yet how the heart insisted upon it! Go *on*, murmurs that pleasantly civilized thing, the mind. Go back! urges the darkling heart: remember what fun it was when you were twelve! How the trees were a thousand feet high, how beautiful the friends, how the sea used to sing as it raced up the beach, how you ate banana sandwiches on a prairie-wide lawn under a goldenguinea sun, with Meridian *Palace* behind you and Mary's mother, that nicest lady in the world, showing you how to play diabolo! Go back; return and find it all again! And so she had, and here she was—to find the glory gone. The kindness too. Yet not all of that. She would not include Mary. Mary's change had been the less surprising because it had been conditioned by their mutal letters. And this disregarding the fact that letters can be almost the most misinforming things one can receive from another person. But Mary's letters had been honest enough. Mary had read this and that, and Helen must too. (Could she get the latest Aldous Huxley in Freetown?) The Headlams had come and the Watson-Walkers had left. And very year they were going to get rid of the Alvis and have a Morris. That was one side of the letters. They had given Helen little grounding as to what she might expect when she returned to Lafney. The other aspect was a skilfully recollective campaign in which both she and Mary had each extended every particle of the experiences common to both of them. The things that were the bedrock of their friendship; their local 'coming-out', their long, talkative walks; their silly mistakes over boys; their mutal fear of Stella; these facts were tediously reiterated and enlarged upon and became the credo on which their entire companionship rested. All the rest of her schoolgirl friends had shrunk to a few accusing Christmas cards. But Mary remained. In her direction Helen was scrupulous and would always be so.

Helen was not simple, nor did she pretend to be. She enjoyed without apology the bright trappings of life. But she wasn't brittle either. Beyond the limits of its formal contentment and candid worldliness, she had always recognised the need for a confessor in her existence. Strangely enough, it was in the letters arriving so regularly from Meridian House, letters which she was bound to acknowledge were mainly dull and concerned with things she had grown away from, that she found the perfect outlet for what, although she was bound to laugh when it occurred to her as such, was a certain spiritual side to her personality. They struck her as sane and accomplished and right. She couldn't help feeling aggrieved when she found that things were likely to be just about as opposite to these states as it was possible to imagine. Mary of all people —and in this predicament! Helen felt she must do all she could to put things right. Her idol had not quite collapsed, but she could see it rocking precariously. She turned and fastened the window and then heard a clinking sound.

Mrs Crawford was busy at her medicine table.

'May I . . . ?'

'I can manage, thank you.'

She drank the stuff, then drew back to her pillows in contentment, pleased with her self-created gloom, enjoying the swags of shadow and the swampy paleness of the bed and the warm tentative luxury she had produced by the careful placing of a few pieces of furniture and the dismissal of the sun. Here she could hoard her strength. There was now no longer the need to compete with the hackneyed tasks of everyday existence. Edwina, occasionally catching her in this mood, began to wonder if her friend wasn't growing insensible, torpid—until the liveliness of Mrs Crawford's eyes convinced her of how unlikely that was. In fact she was alive in a way that she had never been before. She could be unkind without too much apology afterwards, because cruelty was what other people expected of invalids and she had no doubt that she was wonderful because she heard people saying so all the time. They meant, of course, that she was formidable. Only Stella hadn't been intimidated—but then Stella hardly ever came to see her. Sickrooms were Stella's Achilles' heel. They reduced her to a kind of helpless misery, so she took care to keep away from them. She wrote instead, rather nice, gossipy letters which Mrs Crawford soon scrunched up and tossed into the brass scuttle, which was the same shape as a Roman helmet and which she kept for waste-paper. Like so much else, she liked to think that she had done with letters.

Helen collected the tea-things and asked if there was anything else she should do.

'You could tell Mary about Sir Paul Abbott,' said Mrs Crawford surprisingly.

'But—won't she know——?' Perhaps it was something to do with Sir Paul's latest book. Helen was entirely at a loss.

The bell from Lafney parish church began to toll agreeably in the distance for week-day Evensong. Mrs Crawford heaved herself back into the centre of the bed and said in a panting voice, 'No she won't and this might be quite a good time to tell her.' She would say no more than this, so, mystified, though not particularly perturbed, Helen tiptoed out with the tray.

10

BUT to go back. Late in January Richard bicycled to Sheldon. He did so cautiously. The roads were onyx with the snow all crushed and darkened and laquered down into a frigid veneer across which the bicycle-lamp flung a petulant beam. The moon, which had stuck motionless outside the classroom window all the afternoon, as timid as damp tissue, now shone brilliantly as it swung free from flurries of snow. The snow, pitted against the moon was as black as that ground into the tarmac. In Stourfriston the green copper spire of the parish church, a slender, greaved, octagonal cone, shone like powdered jade. All the rest of the town grew perversely darker under the journeying cold. Streets spoked away crookedly from the market-place towards a forlorn periphery of allotments, bungalows and ice-thickened telegraph wires. The air against Richard's face alternated between a humbling rawness, so stationary, he felt as though he was forcing his way through frozen blankets, and a jaunty, rakish wind which sprang up in a minute and died down as soon. The sudden gust would set the shop-signs screeching and the nervous flame in the gas-lamps would drag itself up in apprehension and, as this fear was commuted from lamp to lamp, a whole street would blanch and tremble. The bicycle, chose these moments to slither a little down the camber of the road. Richard hung on fatalistically, knowing that when the wheel should really slip he must fall. Under his tweed overcoat he was wearing his one really decent suit, and he was already regretting the fact. The tyres sang against the ice. His hands twisted against the pudgy rubber grips. The saddle plagued him in some way; it was Mr Winsley's bicycle and there was a rectitude about it which somehow forbade any pleasure in riding it. It seemed to have been ordained. The reek of carbide from its bouncing lamp lent a certain credence to the general theological feeling.

He passed the Masonic Hall, which loomed out of the night like a wedge of pink cake, and then skirted the War Memorial. If the bronze woman who reached out with her laurels had been of feasible dimensions, her round limbs and naked breasts might have gathered a glance or two during all the years she had stood there balancing on one splendid foot. But she was immense, the town council of nineteen-twenty-four ostensibly believing that only the heroic was fit for heroes. Was she Demeter? Richard wondered, pedalling slowly by. Was she Maia, that luminous creature? Her head was bent. Sparse snow hung in the fillet wired bleakly across her brow. Snow, too, clung to her breasts. Whether the dying soldier at her feet reached out for these, or for the iron chaplet in her hand, it was difficult to tell. But there he was, dying certainly; a square-faced young man whose puttied legs sprawled across the Caen plinth. His cheese-cutter was rolling away, his rifle toppled; one hand lay limply across his Sam Browne, the other scrabbled up past the engraved names to the tantalising rewards so entirely beyond his reach. Was she mother or lover to him? Neither, perhaps. Just the dutiful female who awarded the prizes. It was hard to say. The soldier's hat, Richard noticed, was neatly filling with snow and all the names on the north side of the memorial, the side he was passing, were whitened out.

After the War Memorial there was a suspicion of suburbs and then began the long valance of higgledy-piggledy fencing put up by an earlier Sir Paul to signify the nearness of Sheldon. The park proper, however, was still a mile or two away and after this there was the lengthy approach to the house itself. Behind the fence hummocks of rabbity blackberry bushes heaved the filched common-land up under its even sheet of snow like a flocky bed. Staring at it Richard thought that only sheer greed could have made a man enclose such a waste. A mile further the lane grew processional with oaks. The bicycle lamp fell across each tree like a knife. A gothic octagon popped up, too pretty for words. Then an arch. Richard grew vaguely fearful. That was how things always seemed to happen so far as he was concerned. One minute they were miles, months, whole situations away; the next they were upon him. Until the first lodge had come into view his journey still seemed to contain all the leisure in the world, now he was *there*. He bicycled under the arch into thick, soft delicate snow. A huge S stretched itself through shrubberies and lawns up to Sheldon itself. The bicycle ceased being clerical and just became *louche* and swung its beam inquisitively from end to end of the big blunt house. Richard, who had sustained a little fantasy of Sir Paul tucked away towards the rear of his inheritance writing in a lamp-lit library, was further troubled to see an entire row of glowing windows on the ground floor, fretted lanterns winking in the portico and, upstairs, figures passing and repassing against pale yellow blinds. This was decidedly unlike a house that had been shut up for ten or more years. Where were the tea-chests stuffed with papers which he and Sir Paul had to sort?—because that was how he had seen it—a modest room crammed with letters and odd volumes, and with a make-do table at which Sir Paul would occasionally sit when what had occurred to him had to be written down. 'Those letters from James,' he would say to Richard, 'you'd better leave those out if you don't mind.' Sir Paul would then turn his big ugly face aside (he was very like Miss Bellingham in the fantasy), and between them they would put the Rye correspondence in one heap and the Venetian letters in another. Suddenly the shrubbery ended and, rather than be seen trundling the bicycle up to the front door, he turned to the right, where there was a stone summer-house, into which the moon, the snow and the night simultaneously poured. Five of its eight walls had stucco medallions of Roman worthies fixed to them inside. Bays and lyres blistered up from the plaster with delicate aplomb. There was a strong, unpleasant smell of soot and decay and rotting plants. Mr Winsley's bicycle sank gratefully against the wall below the deified Augustus and Richard hurried up to the house. Penchant, Sir Paul's caretaker-cum-butler, gravely admitted him.

'Sir Paul,' said Penchant, opening the door again and shaking Richard's damp coat against the night, 'will be down directly, sir. He is finishing a letter.'

He lead the way across a rather gritty slate and marble floor. Over their heads, dust-sheets hung forward from tilted paintings. A suit of armour wore a bowler hat. There was a delicious warmth, which Richard realised would soon be for him, too warm; an almost blatant smell of food—pheasant, he thought it might be—and a more submerged pourri from which he managed to extract the individual breath of furniture oil, apple-lofts and hoarded linen. From an open door he heard the immoderate joy of caged birds. Quite near, but hidden, someone was typing with great efficiency. They entered the drawing-room and then it became plain at once why the house from outside had looked like the Duchess of Richmond's ball. It was a high white room pierced on the garden side with a whole row of orangery-like windows. The park, seen through so many frames and sub-divided by so many bars, was like a painting by Winterhalter or Van der Meer in its various stages of completion, tentative and sketchy in the far window, where the bars were as thin and corrective as pencil lines; dreamily finished in the window nearest to him, as a broad oblong of light fell across the garden and lead the eye on to skeleton trees and a small bluish lake. A fire burnt at either end of the room. From a sugary wreath in the centre of the ceiling hung a huge grey cotton bag. A smaller chandelier at each side had been uncovered and lit. The fires spat and the flaring wood, still damp and muddy, as though it had just been dragged in from the park, gave out a smell of rough comfort curiously at odds with the insistent elegance of the surroundings.

Forsaken by Penchant, Richard began to look around him, tentatively at first and then deliberately, as if he were in a museum. As he passed from cabinet to cabinet, from picture to picture he saw that disorder had invaded the ledges and shelves and table tops with an almost locust thoroughness. A dusty avalanche of china, framed photographs, ebony and ivory animals, silver knick-knacks of all kinds, dirty tea-cups, gramophone needles, envelopes in jagged caches, ashtrays as bitter and sour as charnels, press-cuttings in crisply curling lengths of jaundiced newsprint, telegrams and bills impaled like Buddhist prayers on wiry spikes, a scattered packet of Terry's chocolates and everywhere, books opened and turned face-downwards to keep the place. All this Richard took to be yet even greater proof that Sir Paul must be very much like his aunt, Miss Bellingham. He was thinking of this as he looked at a portrait of a prim, dark man not over-comfortably seated in a Georgian chair. The man, however, was modern and if a date might be guessed at, Richard thought about early nineteen-twenty-something. The artist, whoever it was, had evidently striven hard for distinction and had got it, but only distinction of a sartorial kind. Except for the rather livid fingers pressed together to make a pensive bridge and suggesting an extraordinary ability of some kind or other, the rest of the figure was formalised and remote. He stood back to get a better view and saw the sitter again at the far end of the room and framed this time by the moulding of a door.

'Myself when young-ish by de Laszlo, I fear! Good evening —How do you do?' Sir Paul began to cross the room. 'What an awful night, really awful! I wouldn't have been a bit surprised if you had decided not to come and now that you have come I've kept you waiting unforgivably . . .'

This Richard found somehow crushing.

'But how did you get here?' demanded Sir Paul, making the two or three mile journey sound quite a feat. 'But a taxi, of course. You must allow me to include that in my duty as a host. Such a simply shocking night!' He stooped forward. One hand advanced a little before his drooping, weary suit, its greeting delicate and full of considerations, in fact hardly a greeting at all. It was then that Richard saw in Sir Paul's other hand, the pen with its cheap holder and wet glistening nib. Could it be that this almost fabulous literary creature still wished to impress? For a moment the pen absorbed and then emanated for him all the vulgarity of a barber's pole. He just couldn't believe Sir Paul had just left his writing-table—although the butler had so clearly stated that was where he was when Richard had arrived. It was so utterly incredible, like waiting for Marlowe—no, not Marlowe—like waiting for Henry James to settle the last tenuous thread upon the page before he emerged from his den at the top of the stairs to say, 'Ah, my dear fellow . . . My dear fellow . . .' Richard's father had spoken like that, always careful to see that his affection was well and truly weighed down with the ballast of such phrases. But, Sir Paul . . . He must shut ears against the gate-crashing ghost of the Reverend John and his eyes against that blatant pen. He shook hands.

'I bicycled.'

He had expected some sort of amazement at this, but Sir Paul merely said, 'How sensible of you. I shall bicycle in the spring. Doing it in the cold weather always brings on the most frightful neuralgia. Tell me, is your bicycle a B.S.A.?'

'I really don't know—I mean I didn't notice. It isn't my bicycle, it's Mr Winsley's.'

But Sir Paul wasn't listening. He was inserting his pen, nib uppermost, in a china vase with much the same care he might have brought to the operation had it concerned a flower. 'There,' he said, 'and now for a drink.' He paused at a well-endowed wine table and touched corks and glasses thoughtfully. 'I'm giving you a gin—a gin and vermouth. That all right?'

'Lovely—thanks.'

'To happy days at Sheldon,' said Sir Paul, privately satirical. 'Sheldon.'

'Now I must ask you to forgive me—only for a few minutes. I must tidy myself up. Suffolk hasn't managed to enforce its routine as yet and I find myself constantly at odds with the hour. You will forgive me . . . ? Help yourself you know.' He waved his hand in a backwards motion towards the drinks and Richard noticed for the first time the narrow lozenge of ingrained ink all down the side of his second finger. There was also a glint of stubble on the pouching flesh which did not yet conceal the fine line of the jaw and the broad lapels of Sir Paul's double-breasted suit sagged forward wearily and hinted at a long, unmuscular chest.

He returned remarkably soon and remarkably changed like the advertisement for bath salts which says, 'Aunt Gussie goes in, but the Lady Augusta Tantivy comes out.' Richard had gone back to the portrait and, as one pores over a photograph in private with a shameless insistence that it gives up every fleshly secret, was bent forward to take in the competently sketched-in features, seeing them one at a time mercilessly, even clinically.

'Titian,' remarked Sir Paul, 'could hardly have deserved greater homage . . .'

Richard blushed and started back. He couldn't have been more embarrassed if he had been discovered at a key-hole. Sir Paul had changed. Not his suit, although even the wrinkles in that had somehow reduced themselves. He was straighter, more lively. His eyes, made the smallest bit oblique by a listless crumpling of their lids, darted about with unapologetic amusement. Richard noticed the mouth. As in the portrait it betrayed the essential weakness in the face. There was a hint of feminine sweetness about it which in youth must have presented a somewhat equivocal attraction, but which now marked the calm of the fine sallow face like an indiscretion. Aware, as so many are, of a feature they would wish to be other than it is—not from any actual vanity, nor even because experience has long shown them its handicap—Sir Paul unconsciously and continually pressed and straightened his lips in a useless attempt to have them in a less perfect line.

'Sorry. I didn't mean to behave like a tourist.'

'Why ever not? Surely there's nobody worse than a person pretending not to see what they're simply dying to see?'

'It's such a beautiful room . . .'

'Then more's the reason for looking at it. There's . . . there's a little Gainsborough. It's over here . . .'

'Oh yes. A friend of mine described it once.'

'Really! How did he manage to see it?'

'It was Miss Crawford—from Lafney, you know. She came here once and the housekeeper let her see this room. She——'

'Crawford—I know the Crawfords, don't I? From Lafney, did you say?'

'Yes. He was Rear-Admiral Crawford.'

'Dead?' enquired Sir Paul bleakly.

Richard nodded. 'Ages ago. But Mrs Crawford and her daughter still live there and they have always been special friends of my family's.'

'At—at Lafney?'

'My home is at Lafney.'

Sir Paul lowered his head suddenly. He had been staring at the Gainsborough with a convulsed attention, yet with eyes which refused to assimilate the swirls of silvery white paint and record them coherently to his brain.

'Of course it is,' he said. 'What am I thinking about! Here, let me give you a drink—let's both have one—and then we must eat. You must be starving.'

'It's a splendid painting,' said Richard as they moved away.

'Yes it is. Splendid. Gainsborough probably charged a hundred and fifty for it, which is pretty reasonable when you come to think of it.'

'For immortality——?'

'Heavens no. For some sort of assurance; for certainty itself. There could be no doubt that you had your place in the scheme of things if you could see yourself like that. That's what Gainsborough did. That was his power and his secret. He proved to the sitter himself that he existed—and all for a hundred and fifty pounds! What did your friend think of it?'

'Oh she liked it immensely.'

'She is an authority on the artist, perhaps?'

'Lord, no!'

'Well people do set themselves up as such . . .'

'Mary's faults lie rather at the other extreme. She's inclined not to be authoritative enough—about anything, I mean—and when she has a perfect right to be.'

Sir Paul smiled; a wintry, fleeting ghost of a smile. 'You must let me decide that when we meet,' he said. 'Come, didn't I hear dinner!'

Somewhere, in the garden it seemed. a bell was making a low, sodden noise, as though its clapper was made from a turnip. *Dunk-dunk, dunkle-dunk.* While they were proceeding from the big white drawing-room, leaving it, as it happened, just as Penchant was about to enter, thinking that they had not heard the bell, Richard made a hasty effort to map out a plan of what his attitude should be during the meal. In spite of the Gainsborough conversation his own uncertainty was increasing by leaps and bounds. In the first place, why was he at Sheldon at all? Wasn't it likely to prove the finest trap that he had tumbled into so far? Copdock was a trap, but he had an eye on its workings and he wouldn't be held down for long in that direction. But Sheldon . . . where would that lead . . .?

At the dining-room door, Sir Paul stretched past him and turned the oval doorknob himself, but underlining the act with a pointed graciousness which suggested that such kindness might be for this occasion only. They sat at a large square old-fashioned table like the *table d'hôte* in a superior boarding house. The cloth hung down its sides like a pall. The silver glinted warily in the dull brown light.

As they ate different aspects of the room began to interpret themselves. Now and then, Penchant, coming in by the far door which appeared to lead straight into the kitchen, would admit a long bar of harsh yellow light which would destroy all the warm subtleties of the endlessly carved Victorian furniture. Sir Paul ate nervously and without enthusiasm.

'I was thinking,' he said, 'Miss Crawford—she must be about thirty now?'

It was on the tip of Richard's tongue to give Mary's age

when the placing of the question struck him as curious. 'Something like that,' he admitted cautiously.

Sir Paul said, 'Of course I remember them quite well. Mrs Crawford dined here quite a bit when she was a girl. She married very young, you know. Crawford was away a good deal at first. She could have gone too, I suppose, if she had wanted. But she seemed to prefer England—they were never what you might call "devoted".'

'Mrs Crawford has mentioned that she used to come here.'

Sir Paul ruminated. 'There's not much sense in your giving her my respects,' he said after some consideration; 'I don't really know her. It was my father she came to see. In those days to inherit a house like this was like having to run a country club. Everybody used it to eat in and stay in it when they felt like it.'

Penchant entered for about the dozenth time and lit a spirit stove in a silver dish and set it down on an elephantine sideboard. Its blue flame played coldly over three large tea-chests set one upon another in the corner, played too, as it happened, on part of Sir Paul's history. These had not come from Sicily. They contained the evidence of what had preceded all that, thousands of press cuttings, six letters from Ronald Firbank and hundreds from practically everybody else. But most of all, photographs. There was the one, reading left to right, of Logan Pearsall Smith, Mr Paul Abbott and Diaghilev at Venice, a quite changed Sir Paul, with hair like paint and in tennis clothes, but with black socks. Diaghilev stood near, portentous, claiming, absurd. An ageing sugar-plum. There were simply hundreds of photographs. The most evocative always depicted people in trains all ready to move, usually leaning out and saying goodbye to Isadora Duncan at the Gare du Nord, to Michael Arlen at the Grand Central and to Lytton Strachey at Liverpool Street. Flicked over cinematically these faded, frozen attitudes might jerk into a record of those wild enjoyments which followed so hard on the heels of the Armistice. *Flick*—and there they would go—that merry jigging horde of young men miraculously left over from the holocaust; dancing, rushing for cabs or to the skeletal embraces of their broomstick women, making their ways up still well-swept steps and into still parlourmaided halls, tipping their boaters up and down like lids of neatly fitted mustard-pots and waving, waving, waving before they all disappeared with voiceless shrieks under the satanic Doric of Euston. Because the age had always insisted that they should be going somewhere. There was no time to rest. Whole novels seemed to have been written on these trains and quite amazing pictures painted in the waiting-room at Arles. This was what would confront Sir Paul when the tea-chests were opened, these lively ghosts of dinners eaten and lovers forgotten and journeys beginning and ending. Sir Paul had discovered the chests on his first day home—made a point of doing so. They were labelled, 'Personal, 1921–26'. They were in what had been his mother's bedroom and he had got Penchant to drag them downstairs.

Richard, like most people attempting to understand a decade they were too young to have experienced could only see Sir Paul in his early days by what he had actually accomplished. To him the twenties were just a long line of book-titles which anecdotal interruptions from other people's memoirs. He found it all vaguely intimidating. Behind all that, shielded from the beady-eyed biographer and the scholar's scalpel, was the quintessential truth. He glanced across to his host to see if he might discover a fraction of it. Sir Paul was spooning away inside the near-hollow drum of Stilton on its blue, pedestalled dish.

'There's not much of it, but what there is is absolutely right. If you'll pass your plate . . .'

How hard he must have worked, thought Richard. How *constantly*. And yet never alone. He and his age had never claimed solitude, never seemed to need it. Their books and their paintings were interdependent, relying on some corporate strength in their efforts to create something fine among the ruin left by the generals. Their artistic manners may have been individual, but taken altogether they made a sturdy movement. The new faith had dated in almost less time than it had taken to create it. Here and there this colourful literary and artistic edifice, like a concrete cathedral, showed signs of questionable taste, though never in Sir Paul's contributions to it. He alone, it seemed, had kept up the pace, expanding essay after essay, deploying his eccentric characters through novel after novel until his output was enormous and he succeeded in being in the literary world a very old-fashioned member of the *avant-garde* of two continents. The critics who had screamed with what they now insisted had been approval of what Sir Paul had written in the twenties, but which had then sounded very much like rage; now announced each new Abbott with grovelling care. It had been a near thing—almost as bad as the day Gide had turned down *A la Recherche du Temps Perdu* . . . It was Sir Paul's fault, *le style* being so emphatically *l'homme*, that they had made the mistake of not taking him seriously. Winners weren't generally such fancy beasts.

'Now, about the work,' Sir Paul said suddenly.

'Yes?'

'I fancy it isn't going to be as interesting as you seem to imagine. A matter of sorting and that kind of thing. Do you feel that you would like to do this?'

'It's awfully decent of you to ask me.'

'Well would you——?'

'I think I would—very much.'

'You're sure?'

Richard smiled uneasily. 'Quite sure.'

'And when could you come. When would be the best time?'

'Sundays?' hazarded Richard.

'Sundays would do beautifully. Does that mean that you could manage every Sunday?'

'I expect only every other one. We have a duty roster—church and meals and that sort of thing—which the masters have to share.'

'Well never mind; every other Sunday then. You'd better come early and make a day of it—if you will be so kind, of course.'

'Of course. I mean I should love to spend the whole day.'

'Then that's settled.'

'Yes.'

'You've been at Copdock some time I expect?'

Richard shook his head. 'No, I thought you knew all about that. I've only just arrived, as a matter of fact. This is my first term.'

Sir Paul drew in his lower lip and bit down on it. 'I see, I see,' he nodded judiciously; 'I expect Aunt Fred forgot to mention it. I hope you like Aunt Fred?'

'Miss Bellingham? Oh she's been awfully kind. I like her very much.'

'I bet she adores you.'

Startled, Richard looked up thinking to find Sir Paul either regarding him with amusement, or indicating that the remark possessed inverted commas of some kind. But he was pursuing Stilton crumbs across his plate with a fruit knife.

'You have always wanted to be a schoolmaster I suppose?'

Unwilling to go into 'all that' at the moment Richard just said, 'I suppose I have.'

'It seems to me a very unhealthy life, if you don't mind my saying so. All that blackboard dust, who is to say that it doesn't produce some academic kind of silicosis?'

Richard laughed. 'Oh really! I hadn't thought of that. No, if there are what they call 'occupational risks' they are far more likely to lie in some maintained kind of mental immaturity.'

'So Aunt Fred's mentally immature!' Sir Paul scrunched his napkin together and dabbed it at the corners of his mouth.

'You wouldn't tell her?'

'I can't be sure that I won't—I gave up those sort of promises ages ago.'

'Oh, please—but you wouldn't? Anyway, I wasn't thinking of Miss Bellingham.'

'Old Winsley, perhaps?' asked Sir Paul.

'Well . . . perhaps . . .'

'Aunt Fred won't love you any more for fastening such limitations on *him*.'

'I did know—I'd gathered that they were once great friends.'

Sir Paul stood up letting his napkin slide slowly down the length of his suit, 'Great friends! God God, they were lovers, my dear. Indecency wasn't in it! They were the Abelard and Heloise of East Suffolk. You'll never believe it, but old Winsley used to look exactly like the Prince of Wales when he was—let me see—about your age, I suppose. How old are you—twenty-two—three? Well, about that. And he'd really done most awfully well at Oxford. It was an absolute foxer why he'd ever *dreamt* of going to Copdock in the first place. I mean it was just another of those high-principled, low-geared establishments which were springing up everywhere at the time to—to cash in on the current snobberies. Winsley should have taken orders and then tried a place like Repton. He might have been a bishop by now—who knows!'

'He applied for the position in the normal way?'

'What—?'

'I mean he didn't meet Miss Bellingham in some social capacity and come to the school in that way?'

Sir Paul let Richard open the door for him and said in a chilly voice without turning round, 'Really, you can hardly expect me to be word-perfect on these legends when I was only a child at the time . . .'

Ghastly old gossip! thought Richard furiously. Who had started it anyway!

Leading the way, Sir Paul passed to the opposite side of the staircase and pushed against two tall rosewood doors which parted with a small click. They led into the library. It was icy. The tumbled, half-dismantled dust-sheets showing a fat table-leg here, a gaping bookcase there, made it look like the setting of some recent rape. The bookcases were at right-angles with the wall and each one terminated in a small marble bust. The windows were filled with late Victorian library glass which made gloomy jig-saw patterns against the night. There was a smell of damp stationery.

'I thought we might work in here,' said Sir Paul more equably and, sensing Richard's involuntary shudder, added, 'We'll warm it up, of course.'

After this they returned to the drawing-room. It was half-past nine. There was a dogged feeling of conclusiveness. When Richard mentioned going, Sir Paul didn't say, 'not yet' or any of those polite things. Merely that so far as he was concerned, the arrangements they had come to appeared perfect. He hoped that they appeared the same to Richard. He became so kind that Richard regretted his own recent ill-humour and began to search around in his mind for something to redeem it. The opportunity came in the guise of *The Times Literary Supplement* spread open at an article entitled, 'Abbottiana: Some further incursions into the Kingdom of Wonder.' It could only be about Sir Paul's last book of essays. He said, hoping it would not seem too apparently respectful, 'I'm longing to get hold of a copy of *The Peach Orchards of Iken.*' It was a mistake. He knew it the moment he had said it. Sir Paul turned swiftly and stared at him with undisguised irritation. Richard thought, Oh God: I've as good as asked him to present me with a copy . . . Why couldn't he have said that he had just ordered it from the library or from Smith's? It wouldn't have been exactly truthful, of course. But neither was his saying that he 'longed' to read the thing. He wouldn't *mind* reading it. But that was a very different matter. Well, he'd said it and that was that. He returned Sir Paul's stare helplessly.

Sir Paul's reaction was curious. He appeared to be gathering himself for a leap or a drill movement. His hands fell to his sides and swung there awkwardly and a film like a secondary lid slid warily across his eyes like a transparent protection through which he might take the measure of an enemy without injuring his own percipience. It was a famous glance, though Richard wasn't to know that. It had put Frank Harris in his place and toppled Arnold Bennett, on occasion, from his. Above all, it wasn't an act. The chameleon, the stick-insect, the hedgehog, the zebra and the electric eel each have their own barricade of one sort or another against the critics of their existence and Sir Paul had his. Life had not needed to prove to him that he was to be included among the pursued, he had accepted such a fate from the very start. The difference between his mind and most men's was the difference between a seismometer and a weathervane. He was alerted to the least lasting, most evanescent hint of trouble, whereas the majority of the human race never give it a thought until it twizzles them round. In society generally he had always preferred, and himself maintained, a mannered approach towards the naturally gregarious, and grew instantly wretched and apprehensive at smart parties if the formalised farce broke down under drink or horseplay. When the screaming began, Sir Paul was among the first to hurry away. This had increased the legend of his politeness—small compensation, as it happened, since he would frequently have given his soul (had his nerves only allowed it) to have heard what was being screamed. Was it just his fancy, or was there some kind of mockery in the air now? Could he detect its buttery smell? Richard's bewilderment reassured him. It had only been clumsiness. Sir Paul had never been slow to forgive that, indeed, in the young he found it a somewhat endearing trait. Being as suave as muscat himself he had always envied a little awkwardness in others.

'How kind of you to say so,' he replied. 'You must let me get you the book. No, no—*please* . . .' He retired from the room with all the dignity of a reinstated dean.

Richard at once began to walk about and seize upon various objects as though these contacts, by their reality, could obliterate for him the memory of his hazy *faux pas*. Put my bloody foot right into it, he admitted to the diaphanous Gainsborough lady. She returned his living gaze with one of sloe-eyed detachment. Unhelped by utter indifference, which is the prerogative of the inanimate, Richard returned to the sofa and picked up *The Times*. He found the personal column. Nothing like other people's discomfiture to make you forget your own. 'Lady of title wishes to dispose of beautiful Manchurian squirrel coat,' he read and 'Grateful thanks to St Juan of Redondela for favours received.' And then, set between these two and with the perfect urbanity of the terrified, 'Viennese lady, excellent cook . . . housemaid . . . anything—seeks position in England. Apply 177, Strasbourgstrasse, 2, Wien.' Further down, set between a cigarette advertisement and a plea for individual chalices at Holy Communion, was another similar cry for help. 'Young Austrian Jew, 24, Graduate; can drive, can garden . . . apply at once 134. Hoffmannplatz, Salzburg . . .' Suddenly nothing seemed to matter. Sir Paul, who had arrived at the same conclusion, but by other methods and a good many years before, returned to discover Richard kicking abstractedly against a firedog with yesterday's edition of *The Times* straggling limply from one hand. Not associating the newspaper with the attitude he was touched by this downcast state and blamed himself for being so quick to take offence. He held out *The Peach Orchards of Iken*. Then with hasty second thoughts, he hurried to one of the muddly Pembroke tables and wrote, standing up. 'Richard Brand. With kind wishes, Paul Abbott, 30th January, 1939.'

'There. Well it's next Sunday then?'

'It really is most terribly kind of you . . .'

'Rubbish. Ten o'clock—did we fix the time?'
'Yes, ten.'

In the park the fine, though persistent snow had brought about the acute forlornness of deep winter. It had filled up the classical amphorae on the terrace and was spattered primly across the loins of a much-weathered muse. It melted against Sir Paul's face as he watched the bicycle lamp nidder-nodder from tree to tree the whole length of the drive. It would be snowing in London, he thought, and in Warsaw (he had never really *enjoyed* Warsaw), in beautiful Berchtesgaden and in the Place Vendôme. Or so the London Regional announcer had implied at six. He found it moving to think of Europe's passive whiteness, all the capitals and streets and squares mutely enduring the glacial cold. He walked slowly along the whole front of Sheldon. The snow drifting against the back of his head felt like an approaching helmet. I'm getting on, he decided, not without satisfaction. They had better start with getting all that Tullingham stuff in order. He might give it to the FitzWilliam. A sudden wind whirled the landscape up into a blinding chiaroscuro. Sir Paul hurried in.

11

BUT instead of sorting the Tullingham papers on the first Sunday, they put the library straight. This, it soon proved, was essential if they wanted to work to any system. Daunting to begin with, both Richard and Sir Paul found the clearing and dusting and then re-establishing of each smooth shelf wonderfully satisfying. The middle of the floor grew mountainous with odd volumes. Sir Paul wore for his task a baize apron borrowed from Penchant and a lemon-coloured scarf tucked inside a cricket shirt. His hands trembled under the wobbling piles of books which Richard handed down to him. For the first hour or so, neither of them spoke, except about the job itself. Richard, who had removed his jacket, toiled too precisely to be really at ease.

'I still haven't come across volume three of the little Hudibras, Brand. Let me know if you see it.'

'Oh I have—I mean it's here with the others. I found it a few minutes ago.' And then, because he suspected that it was this paucity of conversation which was to blame for the slightly congealed atmosphere, he added, 'Miss Bellingham reads Hudibras—or so she said.

'That's about the most unlikely thing I ever heard!—But what odd subjects you go in for—you and she!'

'Books, are they odd?'

But Sir Paul had made up his mind to be amused. 'This *is* a new light on Aunt Fred! She reads Hudibras in her antiquity. And what's more, she chooses to talk about it with charming young men. I'm afraid we've all—the family, that is —have always thought of her as rather a wicked old darling.'

Richard stayed silent.

'Well?' demanded Sir Paul. 'Haven't you at times?'

'I feel I shouldn't talk about her.'

'That is polite, certainly. It might even be kind. But *I* shall talk about her and unless you enjoy monologues you had better join in. You are a bit too polite, you know.'

Polite . . . is that what it is? Richard wondered.

'I am——?'

'Oh, you mustn't apologise for it. It's just the least bit indefinite, that's all' Richard felt a glance from the heavy-lidded eyes somewhere about his turn-ups. He shuffled uneasily on the library steps and Sir Paul continued; 'What I really meant is that your sort of politeness can let one out of all kinds of commitments, and in the long run one is bound to be committed to something, don't you think?—You don't. I can see that. Never mind; you will.'

At that moment a shower of odds and ends fell from a book Richard was holding and Sir Paul said eagerly,

'Is that *Praeterita*? Yes, it is—the one Eddie gave me.' He was all at once in the very highest spirits. 'I almost took the house to pieces to find this once. It's been lost for years. What a find! And all his poor letters all over the floor . . . My dear boy, *what* a mess! I shan't feel any dustier when they scatter my ashes on the front steps of Baalbec . . . But it was worth it!'

Encouraged by such cheerfulness Richard asked, 'Are your books in this room? . . . I suppose not . . .' And Sir Paul said, straightening himself up for a moment, so that Penchant's apron slipped sideways on his narrow body, 'No,' quite sharply, but supplemented this by adding, 'Does Aunt Fred still buy me, do you know? She used to be frightfully loyal.'

'I don't know, it's difficult to tell. Her room is so filled with books. She's got the one about Assam. It's on the telephone shelf along with all the directories and timetables and things.'

'Really? How splendidly ridiculous she is! I haven't been to see her yet, which is rather awful. You'd better say that I am on my way should she say anything. I'm afraid she's bound to if I don't manage a call during the next week or so.'

They moved over to the central bookcase. Each shelf of it had a little scalloped fringe of gold-embossed leather. Richard climbed the steps again and took down the books, handing them in twos and threes to Sir Paul, who in turn stacked them in precarious stalagmites on the floor. The contents of this case were made intriguing by the number of errant slips and sheets of august looking writing paper with which they appeared to be crammed. He longed to investigate some of the letters. Aware of this temptation, Sir Paul said,

'They do look rather fun, don't they? But they're not, unfortunately—unless you find people like Round and Clodd and Thomas Huxley up your particular street. I've been through them all most carefully hoping against hope to discover a scrap of something or other headed 'Brasenose, 1880', but it would seem . . .' a small lurching laugh heralded a pun, 'that —that father had never heard of P-Pater . . .' Then he put down his duster, smoothed the sides of his head in a slow gesture of weariness from two stiffly-spread palms and gazing fixedly out into the frigid morning, said,

'I was conceived when my father was seventy—I state the fact, no more. But the result remains that I have never been able to consider myself as anything more than a defiant gesture in the face of Time. It is most extraordinarily interesting when you came to think of it, because what is there to be hoped of a man whose grandfather once dined with Talleyrand? Or if you like, what *not* hoped of him . . . ?'

The extraordinary fact took possession of him as it had done so often in the past. He forgot Richard, forgot the very existence of speech itself and when he continued it was as if he was engaged upon one of his celebratedly tenuous essays.

'I mean the staggering fantasy existing in the reality must —must make p-puny all subsequent invention—you agree with me, surely . . . yes?'

'You mean that a fact from the past can have determined what you—what a man is?'

'That's a nasty text-booky way of putting it,' said Sir Paul irritably. 'No, I don't mean that at all. Not the *fact*—if you understand me—but the *knowing* of it! Look at Montesquieu; if he hadn't been told of his being descended from the earliest kings of France he would have been a—I was going to say, a dear—but he would have been something more than that. He might have been a real poet. As it was, and as we know, he ended up by being just good copy. I'm always terribly amused, aren't you, when biographers let themselves go on what they call the 'original' of some fictitious person and speak of them as being 'immortalised', when, in fact, their mortality is only too miserably stressed—as indeed it must be when it's imprisoned forever in a g-ghastly galantine of paragraphs!'

With his own head on a level with a very dusty one of Seneca, Richard peered down at Sir Paul as he talked and stalked. Montesquieu . . . Eddie . . . Who the hell were they? It was no use pretending. Now if Quentin were here . . . But Sir Paul was explaining, courteously, if relentlessly. It appeared to be part of his rôle in life to interpret the world to the young. The clock chimed one before he had finished and like an extension of its accuracy, Penchant entered with drinks on a tray, and following the drinks, with luncheon on a trolley.

The meal was distinctly disappointing for such a cheerless day. Some soup in a silver tureen, rolls, fruit—apples, pears and a partly despatched melon—cold meat and a sort of tepid salad comprising a confusion of beetroot and diced potato; not any of it very attractive. Penchant served it with detachment. He had left the door open and it was no secret that he and Mrs Penchant were having a roast and possibly treacle tart.

Sir Paul dragged his palms against his temples and said, 'I thought that if we had our meal in here we would find it easier to go straight on with the work.' But he had lived in Sicily too long to rough it absolutely. 'Penchant!' he called out to the butler, who was gently beetling away, 'Penchant, there's bread, that's right; fruit, meat, which is what I said, but that isn't all is it? What else would occur to *you*, Penchant . . . ? Your mouth being as full of dust as mine and, er, Mr Brand's are?'

'You could have a hock, Sir Paul, a nice decent hock. Or there's a burgundy, only that will mean waiting a few minutes while it goes in the kitchen fender . . .'

Penchant lacked enthusiasm. A meal like this threw him out more than an elaborately arranged table. He stood waiting at the door, too waxen and particular by far. He had lost all his hair at a very early age and the effect was noble in the extreme. This patrician accident was ruined rather by his voice, which was thin and whiney and E.C.4. Sir Paul's long absence abroad had been the ruin of Penchant. He had found himself the master of Sheldon for twelve whole years and during all that long time he had never left it. He had reigned supreme over his dust-sheeted empire, forwarding letters, polishing things and then covering them up, bossing the two other servants and his wife. He had grown to believe that it would never be otherwise and had had ample excuse for doing so. Sir Paul's homecoming had affected him like a sort of millennium—something which presumably *had* to happen, yet could not be credited until it had.

'Burgundy, Penchant, that's the very thing.'

'Very good, Sir Paul.'

When it came and Penchant had managed to inject some note of finality in the way in which he closed the door, Sir Paul said very quietly, 'To this meeting, Richard.' He was flung back across, rather than sitting in, a revolving chair, with his long legs splayed out over the dirty carpet. The wine shook a little in his hand. 'I have a certainty that all this has been done before.' He indicated the library with a wave of his crested fork. 'It's the putting of one's house in order before the barbarians arrive. I can imagine similar scenes at Uriconium, at Camulodunum, at Rome itself and at Carthage; men touching their books for the last time . . . It's too, too terribly sad . . .' He sighed heavily. 'You must tell me if you feel it otherwise than this. You are young and you hope to be a writer, do you not? But there are some—and you may be among them—to whom even a war is preferable to their own particular kind of boredom.'

'Oh I'm not bored—not enough to want the balloon to go up, if that is what you mean. I think Bateson is—he's the coach at Copdock—I may have told you. Bateson feels that he has to make some kind of gesture . . .'

'Not a rude one, I hope,' interrupted Sir Paul surprisingly. 'No, go on. I'm interested in this.'

'There's really not much point. I was only going to say something about the need of the male for the kind of glory which wars provide. It's not a very original remark, I'm afraid . . .'

'No,' said Sir Paul, 'it isn't. But it won't lose its truth because of that. Well, I can take it that you're not a Bateson?'

'Oh we get on pretty well.'

'You wouldn't if you were as consistent to your nature as he is to his,' Sir Paul said flatly. Then he tugged himself up to a happier position and added hurriedly, 'But there, I don't know this knightly young man, so we'll retreat to more common ground shall we? Tell me about Aunt Fred.'

That was quite in order, Richard decided. It was, after all, through Miss Bellingham that they had met and for the next little while she would have to be the unseen presence in their midst through whom their remarks would have to pass if they were to gain in roundness and substance. Without such a mutual personality about which to loop the haphazard strands of their opinion, they would have to make do with a system of questions and answers which would, in a very short time, play themselves out as the more readily given facts about one another were exhausted. It was Sir Paul who first saw the considerable advantage of retaining his aunt for such a purpose. He had had some difficulty in hiding his relief when it became apparent how far this cautious young schoolmaster was in her confidence. He added, 'When I was twelve she absolutely fascinated me.'

'Why 'twelve'? What happened after that—did she let you down in some way?'

'She let herself down,' said Sir Paul carelessly. '—and that's the worst thing of all! When people do that they are apt to give their whole acquaintanceship a bump. Don't you agree?'

'They might,' said Richard slowly, 'It all depends . . .' On the acquaintanceship, he was going to say, but Sir Paul, interrupting, said,

'Of course they do. That's been proved enough times, God knows!—Here, help yourself; you seem to be getting behind. Some more of the meat? Well, take it. Have some more wine as well. No. Aunt Fred was well and truly—I was going to say *massively*—endowed at birth with everything you can think of, brains, money, most frightfully good health—everything, as I say. Not beauty, though. Poor dear, she's always been more than plain, not to say hideous. But even there she was blessed in some way because she quite truthfully didn't care. So one can never say that being behind the door when looks were given out has spoilt her life, or anything like that. If anything has ruined her life, it's greed. Well don't look at me like that! I don't mean that the poor old creature has been going in for robbing or hankering or that sort of thing. Greed, after all, is mostly insisting on having what nature has ruled out so far as one's self is concerned. Marriage for me would be the most ghastly gluttony, if you see what I mean. Aunt Fred was a born don. Remembering my grandfather Bellingham—though ever so slightly, you realise—I can only believe that her very conception was an academic act. She has always been one of those people who get things right the first time. She was never lead astray by some gallivanting hypothesis, or anything of that sort. She just knew what she was doing all the time. Her answers were always the same as those in the book—just imagine how much simpler life would be for all of us if we were only drawn to the correct solution every time! Well, being so brainy she decided on Oxford and one of the new women's colleges of that time, and became so brilliant that her name was always quoted as a justification for them— the women's colleges, I mean, of course. Then she became an educational experimentalist—there were dozens of them cropping up everywhere in the eighties. None of the teaching systems would do for her, so she invented one of her own. And when her father died she turned that horrible house at Stourfriston into a school. Mama, I know, was appalled. And when they heard that no one was ever whacked there, so were all the boarding-schools in the county. I fancy they must have believed in the dictum of every following having its compensations and that Aunt Fred's doing without the cane was pretty ominous, to put it mildly. But she prospered. How, I can't say. Mama and I never went near the place. If it comes to that, we never went near *any* school. We had governesses and things.'

'Miss Bellingham has sometimes spoken of the Montessori method in teaching,' said Richard, faintly bored.

'Maria? She was only *one* of them. There were literally dozens. And all with the very best intentions. So were Aunt Fred's, of course—simply marvellous intentions. And so have we all! The agony of biography is that it harps entirely on what one has done, without taking into consideration what one set out to do. When Aunt Fred goes they will say that for fifty-something years the poor dear ran a prep-school in Suffolk. No one will have the bad taste to say that her intention was to turn the whole idea of instructing the young upside-down. She could have, you know! But not from the turnip fields. She should have stayed at Oxford with all the port and talk! Too late now! Well that was mistake one—Aunt Fred's first essay into acrimony, so to speak . . . Whether I divulge the second . . . will depend upon how our dusting goes—not to mention the results of my assessment of your discretion!'

Sir Paul then stood up and undid a packet of Sobranies and shuffled the cigarettes into a curved gold case. 'Tales out of school—that's fitting enough, don't you think?' He smiled and the too-ready sweetness in the curve of the lips showed, like an archaic Apollo, not so much a discarded morality, as an innocence of the ethical law altogether. The smile was brief. Sensing indiscretion, Sir Paul speedily clamped his strong, faintly stained teeth down on his lower lip.

Penchant arrived and, seeing they were smoking, said, 'There was the cheese, Sir Paul, the *Pont l'Évêque*, Sir Paul, if you remember . . . ?' And Sir Paul said, 'Cheese? We're past cheese, aren't we? No, thank you, Penchant, so you might clear.' When Penchant had gone, the wagon crashing fretfully over the marble diamonds, Sir Paul asked, 'How much burgundy was there left, did you see?' And when Richard shook his head, 'Well there was about half a bottle if I remember rightly, and old Penchant won't touch a drop of it. Not that he's an abstainer; he's not even abstemious; but he's as straight as a die—and they're awfully straight things if all the rumours about them are true. Penchant's honesty is nearly driving me mad. Or it was until I realised that it was his 'thing'. Some people are funny over animals, or gardening or b-bus-conductors. And Penchant is thrilled to bits by his own integrity. *Sickening*, don't you think!'

'It might be even more sickening if you couldn't trust him,' Richard laughed.

'Oh I don't agree. Whatever you say about pilfering, you can never call it an ostentatious defect. If only he *would* pinch a drop of the wine! If only somebody would prick him and let the Seventh Commandment out! Do you know, the first day I was home he followed me from room to room as much as to say, "look under the rugs if you like, you won't find a tack missing." I never saw anybody so eaten up with pride . . . But we ought to be getting back to work if we hope to get this plan of ours really going.'

The plan was to squeeze all the books into three sides of the library, leaving one wall of shelves as a sorting space for the various boxes of papers. Once Richard tried out a remark.

'I expect you have brought most of the books from Sicily home?'

'What——? No. No, how could I? And what would have been the point anyway? They belong where they are, just as these belong here. It bears out what we were talking about before luncheon, doesn't it. Look your last on all things lovely . . .'

Richard was touched by this. Like most people who have never possessed very much, he over-valued possessions greatly. To have to forsake them seemed to him tragic. 'Did you leave everything then?' he asked.

'Not all, but most. Alessandro and I went through them, just as you and I are going through this lot, the only difference being that your composure makes it seem a less mournful task.'

'Alessandro—he—he wept?'

'Alessandro he howled! Poor Alessandro! He won't like working in the factory in Syracuse a bit. I can't help thinking though, that even he wouldn't have been very upset by our present job. All these endless commentaries . . . You would have liked Papa. He was more your sort.'

This was unexpected as it was unflattering. This was what one got for not having heard of Mont-what's-his-name and Eddie. Well, if that was the kind of help he'd better get in touch with Quentin—except, of course, there *was* one drawback; Quentin didn't dust. A little vellum volume dropped into his hand. 'Three Shrieks against Perdition' he read, 'The Pope, Satan's Catamite' by Master Prynne; 'Containing also 'The Naughty Priesthood of England's Tears'. He handed it down to Sir Paul who put it with Biglow on Heffers as an odd book. Then, from his advantageous position on the shiny yellow steps, he looked down on the tall, unhurrying figure with a sudden dislike. All unknowing, Sir Paul worked on, dragging books from heap to heap; mountains of *Who's Who*, blood-coloured as they should be; a wall of Crockford's Clerical Directories, sable as the Cloth itself; all the Early Fathers, the prolific findings of the Early English Text Society, Archaeologia, the Seldon Society, and the transactions of a score of other such institutions; banging the volumes fitfully against each other to exclude a little choking dust and, now and then, pulling himself upright and gripping the small of his back. His hair made a short arabesque above the white, tight skin of his forehead. His ears, too, were strangely plastic and colourless in shape and texture. They were neat and slightly convex and bent back against his head and their tips were hidden by the coarse, bunchy hair springing away from his temples. The interiors of his ears were taut, glistening and shelly. Richard could not help comparing them with Miss Bellingham's ears and the terrible interest with which they often appeared electrified as they hung away from her head like listening toadstools. And nothing could be less 'Bellingham', he decided, than Sir Paul's jaw; hers so ruminative, so ceaselessly concerned; his set and white and stark with a stillness that could not have been more still had it pertained to the dead. Across this refrigeration of the rest of his expression, Sir Paul's eyes drifted endlessly. They were gold, rather than brown, and their habit of seeing all they could made them seem just the least but untrustworthy—particularly in England, where such personal integrity a man is presumed to possess is judged by the blankness of his stare. About the whole of Sir Paul's person generally, there was something fruit-like, a glowing ripeness in the unathletic flesh which once may have had its attraction, but now made him look suspiciously well preserved. He moved about with a constant air of expectancy. Life, for him, was never on the level. It was the heights and the depths. Any moment, one felt, that for him the door might open and a glorious reunion take place, or he might look out of the window to see a cardinal's procession crossing the park, or the telephone might ring, or a trumpet sound and that Penchant would summon him to the first and some more awful authority to the other. His hands fidgetted helplessly. They alone of all his person seemed utterly overcome by the sheer uncertainty of life.

'I suppose one could say 'show me your books and I can tell you what you are'. Would you say there was any truth in that?' asked Richard.

'I'd certainly say it.'

'Well then, I can quite honestly say that I'm not like Sir Eric!'

'Why? Because of this?' He waved his hand round the room. I can assure you Papa wasn't the least bit like this! Good Lord! He would have been surprised! No, these are only the public shelves. A house of this size always has two libraries and this just happens to be the one people were shown into...' Sir Paul gave a short laugh and Richard wondered whether he had imagined the note of regret in it. 'No...' he continued slowly, 'Papa had his subtle side, although there's precious little left to prove it.'

'They were lost then—the other books?'

'Burnt. Mama burned them.'

Richard was shocked. Lady Abbot—the Belle's sister capable of that sort of thing! Didn't that rather alter everything?

As though conscious that it might, Sir Paul said, 'Tolerance doesn't run in families, you know, like a Roman nose.'

'I was just thinking that Miss Bellingham would be the first person to be upset by that kind of behaviour.'

'You're quite right. She was. But she put it all down to what she called the 'fearful alliance'—She meant the marriage itself. Although they were sisters, Mama and Aunt Fred were never the adoring kind, you know. How could they be, with one of them trying to live up to Sheldon and the other just on the fringe of being great most of her life? I'm afraid that to Aunt Fred, Mama was just another baronet's wife and to Mama, Aunt Fred was just another crank. They had forgot to be sisters quite early on. I did rather wonder if I should be telling you all this . . .'

Richard wondered as well. But he was soon to learn that there was little, if any, difference between Sir Paul's scarcely noticing a person and his entirely befriending them. The elaborate etiquette got up by society for its protection against human warmth was quickly swept aside when Sir Paul wished to advance, and remained impenetrable when he did not. Quite often a victim of this extreme friendliness, feeling himself committed to a greater intimacy than he had at first intended, would attempt to go back on his first reaction to Sir Paul's embrasive smile and would seek refuge in the safe old social abracadabra of 'how-do-you-do' and 'what will you have' and 'how do you like Naples, Funchal, Inverness, Paris . . . San Francisco . . . ?' Either this, or they were flattered into a rapid exchange of Christian names and confidences of the sort they would have thought twice about before telling them to a priest. Richard floundered between either course. Sir Paul's charm was remorseless. Like the headlamps of an approaching car, when it was turned on it blinded one helplessly. One either had to turn one's back on it or succumb. Sir Paul looked up suddenly. The Adam's apple under the stretched skin of his throat rose and fell, tender, nervous and sad.

'Let's call it a day,' he said.

He tugged a frayed bell-pull and Mrs Penchant came this time, a short, fat, happy little woman, as contented as a tea-cosy. When she began to thrust books and things about to make a space for tea-cups Sir Paul said, 'Oh not in here, Mrs Penchant. The dust is killing us.'

'There's a fire in the gunroom, Sir Paul.'

He hesitated. 'In there then.'

Later, when they were settled in a funny, too tall room, which had certainly once been a gunroom, but was now a mere apology for one, with streamers of flame unwinding themselves from a fire of hornbeam stumps and terrible portraits of Regency stallions all round them and the dull blue perpendicular guns glinting in their glazed rosewood cases and the floor covered with nursery rugs and the ledges crowded with photographic groups of apoplectic shooting parties of the eighties and nineties; Sir Paul continued his earlier remarks. He pointed to one of the yellowish-brown photographs and said, 'There's Papa.' His finger rested on a gangling young man in a billycock hat hemmed in on both sides by serge-skirted, grim faced women. Richard saw a good-looking face as blank as a mask. He could see no resemblance. 'That's a most remarkable photograph,' said Sir Paul defensively, 'It's Papa when he was thirty and it was taken in eighteen-fifty-one.'

'He would be amazed if he could see what had happened to his nice secure world.'

'He never even felt the beginning of the going of it. He died in nineteen-nine. Wasn't he lucky!' Sir Paul turned away from the photograph. 'Suppose it doesn't happen,' he said. 'Supposing the Prime Minister's right and we have plucked something called safety, well, then what?'

'For ourselves I suppose you mean. Well I quite truthfully hadn't thought of my new appointment as anything the least bit temporary, but now that I come to think of it, it's pretty obvious that I should have thought twice about Copdock if it had seemed likely that I might be spending half my life there.'

'You're just filling in time—like our friend Bateson?'

'Perhaps, though not in quite the same way.'

'No, you'll always lack Bateson's directness.'

Richard objected to this. He still found it pleasant to indulge in little dreams of various ways to improve himself. He hated the idea that his personality had been poured into its mould years ago and had already taken shape. Quentin was disarmingly clever, so he would eventually be the same—there was always heaps of time in these fantasies—Bateson had this enviable sunny quality and he had already decided that he would take steps to develop in that direction, when here was Sir Know-all telling him that it was impossible. It was even worse than that, because it meant that Sir Paul had been busily thinking about him all the while they had been in the library.

Far from making feel him complimented, it reduced him to a cautious shyness.

'I expect you're right,' he said abruptly. 'Old Bateson's a pretty straightforward type.'

'You must forgive me if I occasionally make these personal assessments,' Sir Paul said in a vague, absent voice. 'Habit can be very tiresome at times. After a while one's mind seems to become entirely wax and the senses, helplessly impressionable. The difference between yourself and our friend Bateson is that you can fully understand what I mean and he won't ever!'

It was a compliment and Richard accepted it rather gratefully. His being denied Bateson's peculiar kind of honesty had made it seem for the moment that he must be quite pathetically unlike Bateson. Now it was plain that Bateson was pathetically unlike himself. He would not have been able to follow this obscure talk, for example. It would have irritated him profoundly. Richard wasn't absolutely certain that it didn't irritate *him*, but at least he didn't go about expecting the world to be black and white and becoming baffled and angry when it became obvious that it wasn't.

'Yet one envies Bateson,' he heard himself saying, '—all the Batesons.'

'One does at first, but one ceases to.'

'I still do I'm afraid.'

'Of course. At your age it would be strange if you didn't. Don't worry, it's one of the more circumspect jealousies. A more intelligent society than our own used openly to encourage it, though never at the expense of the so-called intellectual. That is where we go wrong, of course. We divide our society into two sneering camps, the one all bombast, and other all barbs. There, why should I lecture you! You know all this as well as I do!'

'There's always my proper work,' said Richard incautiously.

'Your proper work?'

He plunged. 'My writing——'

'Oh,' said Sir Paul with fearful tolerance, 'your book. Of course, I should have asked you about that before.'

'But . . . but I've never even mentioned it.'

'You didn't have to, did you?'

'I'm as transparent as all that?'

'Not transparent—wherever did you get that idea! I don't see through you, but into you. It's a small privilege one's allowed after sitting thirty years at a desk in front of reams of achingly empty paper. I can see, like all young men, you fancy yourself a brand-new contribution to the world's types. Well, just thank God you're not. Believe me, it's always a comfort to know that there are a few more about like oneself—however odd. Call it cowardly if you like.'

'I don't call it cowardly and as a matter of fact I had never thought of myself as exceptional; not in *that* way at least.' The spirit of truthfulness, having descended that far, he felt obliged to say that he hadn't even begun his book, not one single sentence of it. 'But I expect you know that, too.'

'Don't make me clairvoyant, my dear. I do suspect that you haven't, as I only suspect you to be a writer. Being the type and being the thing are very different matters. Besides, there's something else I suspect'—he permitted a mothlike malice to flutter across the tea-things—'You mayn't have the energy.'

'That's possible,' Richard agreed humbly.

'It's a matter of habit like everything else,' said Sir Paul, immediately regretting his tartness. 'You do that instead of something else each day and it adds up. A novel is three hours in the morning from September till March. Or from April till October. It all depends on whether you swim.'

'You're certainly making it sound ridiculously easy.'

Sir Paul, who was expecting a compliment and had automatically decided upon his answer to it, looked put-out for a second or two. Richard was making him faintly anxious. He veered so. He had been positively deferential in the library, well he didn't want *that*, but he found its reverse—this defensive abruptness—equally expendable. 'Am I . . . ?' he murmured in a complaining, abstract voice, '—the easiest thing in the world . . .'

In the stonelike silence which followed, Sir Paul munched away nimbly at the bread and butter. Mrs Penchant came in and filled up the teapot. Her bulging, seemingly impossible roundness made her look like Mrs Noah. She was propelled across the floor in her flat, single-strap shoes so professionally smiling and pleasant one could tell it didn't mean a thing.

'I think perhaps I ought to be going.' Richard confessed.

Mrs Penchant, carrying the kettle, went out.

At once Sir Paul leapt up and said, 'Did you notice surely you must have; she's as pleased as punch. *Why?*'

'I don't suppose she has much to worry about.'

'But to be as deliriously joyful as that, day in and day out! Honestly, between the two of them it's like living in a bin.'

Privately Richard couldn't agree. In fact he had felt positively grateful for Mrs Penchant's tabby-cat presence at that moment.

'The trouble with all English servants,' Sir Paul was saying, 'is that they have no style. Oh, they *had*—I'm not saying against what things *used* to be like. But now they try and impose their own kind of horrible cosiness on everything. Do you know what I heard that woman saying to her husband the other day? She was doing the drawing-room and she said, 'I don't think I shall ever get this room snug'. *Snug!* You should see the Sicilians when you employ them. Why they behave as if they had inherited the rooms. and in a way they have. They'd never refer to one's possessions as 'his old things' —as the Penchant woman did the other day.'

Richard laughed. 'Some people might think you blest, being surrounded by honesty and cheerfulness.'

'You're very critical of me, aren't you, Richard?'

This was so alarming—his appearing critical and of Sir Paul Abbott of all people—that Richard got up and declared, 'Believe me, I'm not; I'm . . . anything but that. If I'm anything at the moment, I'm bewildered. Oh, not by you,' he added hurriedly. This situation lurched dangerously and then recovered itself. Just then, thin. ravaged, un-gay and etiolated, a forlorn strand of dance music made its surprising entry. Somewhere in the heart of Sheldon a gramophone was playing. They both laughed, it was so entirely unexpected and Sir Paul shook an amused head.

'Snake-hips Johnson,' he said. 'How do I know? Mrs Penchant has a passion for him, believe it or not, and—well, there you are?'

So it was to saxophones that they parted and Richard pedalled wearily back to the school along the rime-dark road.

12

THAT should have been the end of the day. It was past seven when Richard wheeled his bicycle into the gardener's shed and impaled it on a stack of other decrepit machines. He thought vaguely of spreading the eiderdown from his bed on the rug in front of the gasfire and himself on top of it. He thought, I could write a story; a poem. The uncommitted evening sprawled in front of him comfortingly, soothingly; he was excited by its sheer vacuity. It seemed ages since he had had a few hours entirely to himself. He ought to write letters, not poems. He owed Mary one, perhaps two. He couldn't be sure she herself wrote with less duty and more affection. He could, and ought, to write to his mother. She had a day for letters herself and it was the regularity of her cosy little descriptions which gave more pleasure to Richard and Quentin than the descriptions themselves. But then he wouldn't write letters. He wouldn't do anything. He'd actually spread the eiderdown over the skimpy hearthrug and was seated on it, taking off his shoes, when Bateson burst in.

'Don't tell me,' he said, 'you're licking your wounds? High society's been too much for you?'

'I suppose you never do this. You wouldn't have to, anyway. Your armchair happens to have springs.'

'I came to drag you out.'

'*What*——?'

'Only for an hour or so.'

'But I've just decided to be *in*—very much in as a matter of fact. Sorry and all that.'

'You couldn't have,' Bateson declared dubiously. 'You know you won't be setting a foot outside this dump till Friday at the very least. It's your tables week—or perhaps you didn't know? Actually the Winner only plastered up his little notice about an hour ago.'

'He did ask me,' Richard said. 'Awfully sorry Bateson old boy and all that, but honestly, insane as it might seem to you, I'd sooner stay where I am.'

'You won't get a drink till Friday,' said Bateson warningly.

'I don't want a drink till Friday.'

'Oh my God,' Bateson sighed. He then assumed an attitude of classical despair; his eyes and his eyebrows drooped at their ends and he wagged his head from side to side. 'Do you know what you are, boy? You're a Winner, a little budding, embryo Winner.' He shrugged. 'Well, I'll leave you to it. I did,' he added rather forlornly, 'rather look forward to a can in your esteemed company.'

'Blast,' Richard searched around for his discarded shoes. Dulled and sodden with slush, they were an added and most eloquent reason for his not turning out again. 'Where was it you thought of going?'

'Have you ever heard of "The Case is Altered"?' Bateson enquired with great casualness.

'A pub?'

Bateson groaned. 'A pub—Oh, my God! If you go on like that you'll be having the law on them for serving you. Of course it's a pub.'

'Not—not at Stokely?'

'Yes, at Stokely.'

'But it's miles——'

'It's just two miles. How did you know it was at Stokely anyway? Have you been there before?'

'Never.'

'Then how did you know?' Bateson was oddly persistent.

'I suppose it's a trick of remembering villages by their pubs and churches. Quenny, my elder brother and I used to spend most of the summer holidays on brass-rubbing expeditions when we were so high.'

'That explains it,' said Bateson. 'Poor fellow, you've had the most ghastly childhood. Buck up with those shoes. I tell you, you're going to be bloody grateful to me one day. Now your coat!' He began to hum a little tune. Now and then he stopped to say, '*Poor* old fellow . . . Poor old Dicky Brand . . . !' and, '*Brass*-rubbings—did you ever hear the bloody like . . . *Christmas!*'

'There's no need to be *that* pleased with yourself.' Struggling back into his coat and scarf, which still had an unpleasant warm dampness about them, reminded Richard that it was barely twenty minutes since he had taken them off. But he was pleased all the same. Pleased like a fifth-former with having pleased Bateson. Now that he had made the effort he was bound to admit that curling up in front of a row of gargling gas-mantels was a particularly feeble way to spend the evening, all the more since, as Bateson had reminded him, it would be quite a long time before he was free to go out again as he liked. Mr Winsley preferred to arrange people's duties in large slabs, rather like the nursing shifts in hospitals or guards in the Army. 'Tables' meant one could say goodbye to any social activity for a week at least. Only Bateson contrived to remain unencumbered with such fetters. His position as coach made it difficult to nail him down to a rigorous timetable. It also placed him outside the actual surveillance of Mr Winsley who had learnt, over forty years, to take it on trust that the robust sequence of puzzlingly slangy, square-shouldered, stiff-chinned young men he had engaged in this capacity, did really instruct in the philosophy and technique of cricket and rugby football. Bateson, as it happened, was not only conscientious in his teaching, but successful in the result. He did it all effortlessly and squandered his very considerable energies in oddly futile pursuits, in loveless encounters and far-from-merry binges, from both of which he returned childishly unscathed both in appearance and mind.

'And there's something else you ought to know—I'm broke —or pretty nearly.'

'It's not a night club we're going to,'

'It'll be an extravagance for me if it's just beer and biscuits.'

'Well then, don't come,' Bateson said though not before making sure that he wasn't taking any risks by appearing so casual.

'How you can expect me to disappoint you when you're looking as about as pathetic as a St Bernard that hasn't been let out for a week, I don't know.'

But Bateson was dancing lightly round the skimpy furniture. His arms sheltered and guided an invisible girl. He sang:

> *'When a Broadway baby says, "Goodnight",*
> *It's early in the morning.*
> *Manhattan babies don't sleep tight*
> *Till day is daw-aw-ning . . .'*

'If we're like this before we even get to Stokely . . .'

Bateson swooped to a standstill. His hand remained outstretched cupping the small of a phantom back. 'The trouble with you—Dick—Don't mind me calling you that, do you?— No, what was I saying; the trouble with you . . .'

'No,' insisted Richard loudly. 'Don't say it. Just shut up, there's a good chap. Why the hell I'm so obvious a supplicant for this world's good advice, God only knows. But I am. *Everybody* turns to me when they want to get rid of a little— why?'

'I could tell you,' said Bateson flatly.

'After Stokely?'

'Perhaps you won't be in so great need of it then.'

'How sibylline you're being tonight, Bateson.'

Bateson was about to defend himself from any accusation of profundity when his eye happened to see the Reverend John Brand's half-hunter lying on the dressing-table among a welter of soiled collars, loose change and curling, unframed photographs.

'That's not the time—?'

'It is; to the second.'

'Well hurry, man. You do want to go, don't you? only we musn't expect too much,' he added. 'Then we shan't be disappointed—isn't that what they say?'

'I'm not expecting anything, unless it's cold feet.'

Bateson, who had reached the door and was holding it open looked round suddenly. He didn't speak. but as Richard stuffed a scarf inside his coat and kicked the gas-tap off, an unusual percipience took the place of the customary aggressive charm in his face. Then the percipience died, lacking, perhaps, the kind of energy needed to keep such a thing viable. He was Bateson once more. But for a single moment he had been about to interpret a quality (or defect) in the character of another person which, had such visions become a habit, could have put some very substantial thought in the too-airy spaces of his understanding. The moment passed. The gas fire went out like a lion. Richard started; it was a noise he found particularly detestable. Then they walked slowly out of the School into the Sunday streets. High above their heads Miss Bellingham's room watched the night, its gaze wily, oily and yellow. With maddening regularity, a shutter whacked the wall. It was freezing fast. Each step they took broke through a layer of soiled, crisp snow, the colour of damp brown sugar. Flakes still fell thinly, but so vacant and sparse in effect that they were less like winter than like smuts blowing up from a half-dowsed wood fire. Breath unfurled from between their teeth in ectoplasm strips. Bateson continued to hum when he wasn't cursing the fact that his foot had once again sunk more deeply and damply into the meringue-like gutter and discovered water.

'Did you take Church Duty?' Richard asked.—'I expect so.'

'Everybody went, everybody, that is, except the Winner. Incidentally, have you seen what they're doing to the old place?'

'What, the church?'

'They're sandbagging it.'

Richard recalled later the extraordinarily momentous effect this simple scrap of information had had on him. The knell of an age which is slipping away sounded so subtly and so variously that most people never hear it. It isn't until they are well on into the later experience that they can see part of their own endurance walled-off by time and events and never again to be approached except through history itself. When Bateson said, 'They're sandbagging it' Richard felt that the foundations of a barrier were being laid which was to keep him out forever from the life that had been his until that moment. It was tragic and yet it was exhilarating. He was appalled and yet made gay at the same instant. He supposed that even the most slavish traditionalist has his moments of perverse joy when all the vestiges of what he has spent a lifetime believing in are obliterated by some mighty leap in the world's progression (or retrogression). The thrill that something has 'gone' sometimes comes before the misery of knowing that one will never see it again. There is nothing so dazzling as the idea of revolution, nor any happiness so brief and questionable as that which follows one.

'Think of it,' went on Bateson complacently, 'all those trimmings from the good old horse-and-cart days being tidied away before the showdown! I wonder what the poor old Belle makes of it all. Not much I shouldn't wonder. They're going to take most of the stained-glass out of those narrow windows in the choir—it appears it's pretty classy stuff, though I must say I've never seen anyone looking at it. Old Lord Stick-in-the-mud too—the johnny with the toga—well they're making him nice and cosy too.'

'The Debenham memorial?'

'Uh-huh.'

'You've not heard anything more about joining-up I suppose?'

'Nope.'

As they walked, the swift, sweet and undeniable fact occurred to Richard that he would like to get drunk. What had been farthest from his thoughts an hour ago, now overpowered them to the reckless exclusion of everything else. Was it the same with Bateson, he wondered? But Bateson was jogging on quietly with nothing to show how he felt, one way or the other. Also, like so many sportsmen, he was finding a long walk curiously fatiguing. The magnificent resilience which made him a legend on the playing-field deserted him on a longish stretch of road.

'Roll on "The Case",' he complained.

It was rather a snivelling little place set a few feet back from the slushy road when they did at last get to it. Two trestles and four sagging forms left outside in the night were covered with fat white bolsters of snow. The bar was packed and seemed the more amazingly so because no hint of its raucous gaiety leaked out into the surrounding no-man's-land of beet fields and shivering sloe thickets. They pressed their way through the fudge of dubious jollity. The noise was incessant. Men were laughing and boasting and shouting and every now and then, like the cheer-leader of a Sapphic contingent, the enormous landlady would drag her brown satin bosom up from where it appeared to be resting on the brightly polished counter, and bring up a whole supporting passion of shrill female mirth by letting out a great whoop of her own unfettered enjoyment. Behind the fat woman a little thin man leapt about doing all the work. Four barrels lay on their sides on a hearse-like structure and he fled from one to the other of these with pots and glasses and imprecations. He worked against a background of fairylights, silver doilies and fretted mahogany. It seemed quite pointless to try and get a drink. In the uproar they'd never be able to speak to each other. Something told Richard that he'd never want to drink enough of the contents of the seeping, lachrymose barrels to get the effect he had earlier longed for. He even doubted if beer could produce such an effect anyway. In fact he was all for getting out of the place.

'What's wrong?' asked Bateson ineptly. Everybody laughed again with fearfully good-natured exuberance. Bateson's handsome head was bowed to the level of the landlady's. In a jolly, half-mesmerised way, lifting and letting drop her huge pink hands, she was advising him. She stared at him steadily, her eyelids falling and opening and her breasts rollicking under the generous satin. 'Back room,' bawled Bateson. 'Hang on.' The landlady swung a leaf up from the counter and led the way. Bateson followed holding two pints of beer high in the air like libations. 'She says it's quieter,' he was shouting. '*Quieter*—did you hear what I said?'

And indeed it was so. The back bar was a cell of quiet. Again, in some miraculous fashion, the Breughel uproar was sealed away and they found themselves in a hot, dismal little room where the fire blazed under a black-leaded Norman arch. The landlady, jelly-like yet agile, mounted a sofa and put a match to a swinging paraffin lamp. When she had gone they were left self-consciously with their backs to the fire facing a photograph of a bun-faced sergeant in labyrinthine puttees standing in front of a cardboard view of the Pyramids. On the opposite wall was a framed and glazed poster which said, 'Save the Women from the Hun.' It showed a lady in a lozenge-shaped hat criss-crossed with ospreys being chased by a gorilla. There were two dark pleasant buttony seats of worn leather, two highly-shone shell-cases filled with spills on the mantelpiece, a spittoon filled with fibre and planted with unwholesome looking bulbs of some kind or another, an upright piano, vaguely Parthenonian in design, its front filled in with dirty silk stretched across fretwork lyres and one small window absolutely crammed with frost-nipped geraniums. There was also a close, cupboardy, nudging smell, not wholly objectionable.

The landlady returned to put a log on the fire. When she

had gone, slamming the door behind her and cutting out the neighbouring hubbub as neatly and completely as though she had switched off a wireless set, their privacy was so intense as to be almost sensual. Bateson swigged his beer at an alarming rate so that Richard had to follow suit and say, 'the same again?' long before he was ready.

The bar was at the other end of a long passage. Feeling slightly amazed at the turn his polite day at Sheldon had taken, he walked down it hardly comprehending the boisterous uproar getting louder and louder at every step, and certainly not comprehending that in the minute or two since he and Bateson had passed to the snug, two girls had taken up their position in the passage and were regarding him with predatory interest as he edged his way by them. The landlady's warmth as she spilt his change all over the counter had to be answered and he was still smiling vaguely when he passed the girls for the second time. They smiled back narrowly. Richard's smile extended itself into a hard, meaningless grin. At once the girls' faces froze into immobility. One of them gave a short, rough little laugh, over almost before it began. Richard didn't look back but he couldn't help being faintly entranced by this. So that was the kind of evening it might possibly turn out to be! He continued to grin as he plonked Bateson's beer down in front of him.

'Still awful?' Bateson asked.

'Packed.'

'You soon got served.'

'It's the landlady—she seems to like you.'

Bateson pressed his lips together in a pleased smirk.

'All you have to do,' he declared, 'is to find out in what capacity a woman has decided to show herself in the eyes of a man—mummy, auntie or baby.'

'Oh—? What is it in this case then?'

'Mum,' said Bateson. 'Mum every time, old boy. Didn't you notice that matriarchal leer? Why it was all she could do to stop herself from turning me over and tanning my behind!' Then he lolled against the fireplace, his eyes half-closed, as though he was divesting himself of certain small graces. There was an edge to the most trivial of his movements, even in the way one leg rocked on the slippery brass fender. It was like a dress-rehearsal for the sort of person he wished to be known as during the next few years. And if you're sensible, he implied, you'll damn well be the same! Forget that potty little school, forget that odd fish, Sir Paul, forget all you've ever known—because, boy, it's going to be easier that way! A bright streak dramatised the wilting geraniums for a second or so and then travelled on.

'You on the searchlights?' the chalky-faced girl was enquiring.

'We're . . .' Richard began.

But Bateson was more alert. 'Not this lot,' he said with careless ease. The beam returned to the window, pierced the barrier of dusty stalks and entered the half-lit room like a waggish pointer.

'They're from Wintlesham I reckon,' said the chalky-faced girl. 'But there, we don't want to be nosy, do we!'

'You got wet,' stated the other girl. Looking down he saw the steam gently rising from the bottom of his trousers. The girl laughed her rough little laugh of silly concern.

'You didn't though,' said Bateson. He stared at her ankles with enormous deliberation, though hardly with interest.

Both girls at once began to shift, carefully, because of their platform-soled shoes, which were surgical in thickness.

'They had them in white, Rube—do you remember?' said the chalky-faced one. 'Fancy white, Rube! I wouldn't want white would you, Rube?'

'Are you at Wintlesham then?' asked Rube, ignoring her friend.

'Hush,' said Bateson. 'You heard what the lady said, didn't you—you musn't be nosy!'

'Rube!' cried the other girl. 'Oh isn't she awful!' She gave her friend a violent push.

'Well are you—?' persisted Rube. She obviously relished her role of *terrible* and knew it was her duty to lead the way in such encounters and to gain ground with her mock-childish daring that might later be consolidated with the other's more formal approach.

Bateson gave her a sample of his most splendid indifference, then turned to her friend. 'And what did you say your name is?' he asked.

'Miss Lilley,' said chalky-face. 'And I didn't say.'

'Lily's your Christian name?'

The girls shrieked suddenly and fell on each other. Then Rube cried, 'No. Her name's Daphne.'

'Miss Daphne Lilley,' said Bateson in a very proper voice, 'it's a beautiful name.'

'That's right.' They were at once composed. How lovely he talked!

A hiatus followed in which Richard struggled desperately to think of something to say. He felt as though he had been smiling for days on end. Seeing Daphne looking at the framed sergeant—she was actually looking through the sergeant at herself to see what her mouth was like—he said 'Was he the landlady's husband?'

Daphne wheeled round at once. ' 'Ow should I know?' she demanded indignantly.

'How indeed,' Bateson mocked, very sure of himself, and enjoying these brash preliminaries. He stared past Daphne at Rube. Rube stared back. Their wordless arrangements concluded, he said, 'Come on, what about a little drink?' His fist full of glasses, he disappeared down the passage.

'I just thought you might happen to know,' said Richard apologetically, '—as you live about here,' he added.

'You know a lot, don't you?' Daphne said rudely and then, in a surprisingly refined and solicitous voice, 'I expect you find it very cold working on the searchlights?' In the fraction of a second between her first statement and the remark she was about to follow it with, the significance of the wordless *rapprochement* that had taken place between Rube and Bateson had worked itself up in her mind like yeast. So that was the way it was, she thought. Winner take all—or first pick—which was about the same. No flies on old Rube. She was lucky. That big feller ought to go on the pictures. She resigned herself philosophically to Richard. He looked a bit artistic, she considered doubtfully. Though nice; ever so nice when you came to think of it. Rube was lucky though. Trust old Rube!

'Freezing,' Richard answered shortly. '—Does he know what to get for you?'

'Gin,' she said; 'gin and orange.'

But Bateson had got it right and was soon back and the

bantering, two-edged conversation was continued. After quite a number more rounds of drinks, Bateson and Rube, who had been sitting with superb detachment on one of the buttony sofas carrying on a laconic conversation, the gist of which could only be guessed at either by Bateson's snuffly laugh or Rube's sudden short scream, over almost before it began, were rapidly becoming much less detached.

'Well, really,' Daphne remonstrated, observing this.

'Aren't we awful!' said Rube happily. 'Go on, say it, Daph; you were just about to!'

'I'm not saying anything,' Daphne retorted primly. She held her dusty, dead-white face high and sniffed. Rube lolled against Bateson, sipped her gin like a bird and made no attempt to conceal her huge satisfaction at the way things had turned out.

Bateson hummed, 'When a Broadway baby says goodnight' under his breath, equally contented it seemed. Rube wriggled and said that's an old one and didn't he know 'Room 504'—it was ever so nice and her favourite. Richard, glancing round in search of the clock, discovered only the maroon timelessness of the wallpaper and the threadbare carpet and the Hun and the lady rushing helter-skelter through the dun confines of their mount.

' "Fleeter of foot than the fleet-foot kid,

Follows with dancing and fills with delight

The Maenad and the Bassarid . . ." ' Richard couldn't remember any more. But that's what the poster outlandishly brought to mind.

'What on earth is he jabbering about?' Daphne beseeched the company.

'It's just a poem,' he was about to explain, when Bateson, with uncharacteristic humour declared, 'Now *don't* tell me you've never heard of the Fleet-Foot Kid! Better than Tom Mix any day!'

'Go on . . .!' Rube said, pushing free of his grasp.

'Go on yourself,' retorted Bateson, pulling her back. He was expert at all this and enjoyed every minute of what might be termed his pre-conquest hour.

'He's a lad, isn't he!' Daphne declared admiringly and, Richard couldn't help feeling, critically so far as he was concerned. He defended himself by saying, 'He's always like that when he's had a few.'

'What's your name?' Daphne enquired.

'Di—Richard.'

'I thought it might be Arthur.'

'*Arthur*—why?'

'I don't know. I just thought.'

Something in the way she said this made him suspect that 'Arthur' carried with it some subtle insufficiency. Arthur wasn't a good name—it was déclassé in Hollywood perhaps—and Richard wasn't over-good either it seemed. '*He's* Arthur,' he asserted treacherously, waving the hand with his glass in it at Bateson.

'That's right,' Bateson agreed. Names meant absolutely nothing to him. 'I'm Arthur—he's Dick—Richard.'

'I think you're both soppy,' Rube said.

'Oh we are, are we,' Bateson muttered.

There was a slight scuffle, a loudish squeal and an ear-piercing, '*No.*' Richard waited in agony for the fat landlady to come bustling in and was surprised to hear Rube asking in a very politely moderated voice, 'What time did you say you have to be in by?' And Bateson answering her with, 'I didn't say—what time do *you*?'

'Really!' said Rube, outraged.

'Tut-tut-tut!' admonished Bateson. There was a further romp, a fainter, more rabbity squeak, then Rube shook herself free, reached for her gin and said:

'Those two standing up there—just look at them! Who do they think they are anyway—God or book-ends?'

Bateson considered this exquisitely funny. He rocked with spluttery laughter and in the process, rocked Rube as well.

'Do you want me to be sick?'

This must have reminded Bateson of some primordial disaster in his career as a lover, because he stopped clowning at once and gave Rube the full benefit of his two-thirds profile smile. 'You're not really going to be sick, are you?' he asked in a worried voice.

'Of course not, daft,' she said. 'But larking can make me sick.'

'Larking always makes her sick,' corroborated Daphne, who

was, if anything, managing to hold her head even higher on her pale thin neck. Most of the time she was smoking inexpertly; making little pup-pupping sounds and letting her weight fall first on one foot and then on the other.

'Come on, we'll take our ease too, shall we?' Richard said, aware that they must look pretty ridiculous standing one either side of the fireplace. Besides, although it hadn't seemed much at the time, the five or six hours he had spent perched on Sir Paul's library steps were making themselves felt. The backs of his legs didn't ache; they had atrophied into a kind of stony discomfort. I suppose it's all right . . . he was wondering. Any movement towards the buttony sofas at once implied so much more than sitting.

'They ring a bell when it's closing-time,' Daphne said, settling herself on the sofa with about as much enthusiasm as if she were going to have a tooth extracted. 'Mrs Rook's a good sort,' she added. 'One of the best.'

'Well it only wants the Winner to see us now . . .' Bateson said. Rube was sitting at right-angles to him with her head on his shoulder and her legs across his lap. A wordless debate made up of squirmings and little shoves went on between them in a struggle to decide where, exactly, Bateson's hands should be. As in most debates, there was a foregone conclusion and Rube's defence was rhetorical more than anything else.

'The Winner . . . ?' Daphne asked.

'Their officer, daft,' said Rube.

'I was talking to the butcher not the block. Is he?' She turned to Richard.

'I suppose he is . . .'

'Major Winner,' elaborated Bateson, for whom the fantasy possessed a singular piquancy.

'That's a crown, isn't it?' Daphne allowed Richard to squeeze her hand into his and knead the back of her knuckles with his thumb.

'Yup.'

'We thought you were pippers.'

'Oh——?'

Bateson's eyes shone with anticipated delight. He felt like the footman in an eighteenth century farce approaching the cue when he must go off-stage and return gloriously as the earl's son to the acclamation of the entire theatre.

'You're not though?' persisted Daphne.

'Er—no,' said Bateson regretfully.

'Must be chilly in them searchlight huts . . .'

'Must be,' Richard answered shortly. 'Here, isn't it time we all had a drink!' Feeling decidedly odd and unnaturally facetious, he said, 'How about you—Arthur?' and got a you-wait-till-later glower from Bateson.

'He's had enough,' Rube said repressively. 'Honestly, he's worse than my dad—I told him he's worse than my dad, Daph.'

Daphne confirmed this. 'Her dad's a one! You ought to see him.'

'I'd sooner see you,' Richard said promptly and was just as promptly appalled by his own unsuspected gift for banality.

Daphne was enchanted with this answer. 'I don't really want no more to drink,' she said, 'and I'm sure your friend doesn't. Just look at him!'

'Look at yourselves,' Rube said in a half-smothered voice. After which recriminations were ended by Bateson rising suddenly and declaring, 'This thing's smoking'—when it was doing nothing of the kind—and turning the lamp down until they were all but plunged into darkness and the dying fire tinkled into cinders and became a dull yellow puddle amongst all the brass pokers, tongs, shovels, scuttles and things which loaded the fender. Bateson and Rube remained reflected monolithically against the blind for a minute or so, then sank down and became united with the slab of horizontal gloom which was their buttony sofa. Rube chattered amiably the whole time, like a hostess whose party contains an unavoidably embarrassing element. 'Honest,' she was saying, 'you *ought* to see it. They're having it the whole week because it's so good. It's at the Palace, you know, the Palace in 'Friston. 'Friston's a lousy hole, isn't it Daph? We always go to Ipswich weekends, don't we Daph? You know Ipswich? You know the 'Bell and Book'? Well that's where Daph and me go. It's a Tolly house . . .' There was a clock-racked silence and the landlady bounded in and bounded out again saying, 'Whoops—*sorry*' quite abjectly. Richard kissed Daph but she didn't kiss him.

Dutifully she turned cheek or mouth or chin in his direction when she felt it obligatory to do so. Apart from these parroty considerations she maintained the equanimity of a well-powered clothes-peg.

It wasn't long before he concluded that she didn't like him and so was the more greatly surprised when, after he had sat up to have a drink, merely retaining her contracted little claw of a hand for the look of the thing, she made a small cheated-baby sound and tugged him towards her. He was then further troubled by the fact that, now his eyes had got used to the firelight, the room was just as visible as it had been before Bateson had turned the lamp low, in fact more visible, since their four bodies seemed to have absorbed the darkness and swollen up to twice their proper size. Richard had never been more aware of two other people in the same room as himself in his life before. Rube and Bateson had hogged so much of its privacy and its ordinary amenities that he felt like a gold-fish pushed up to the lip of its bowl and gasping for its very existence. Being so drained of action himself he was willing to forgive Daphne her *res infecta*. It was in the spirit of a solicitous understanding that he planted a last kiss or two on her fat red mouth. For most of the time she stared up at him unblinkingly with glassy grey pupils and once she smiled and showed two rows of exceedingly small teeth. And once she said, 'You're nice,' which in the circumstances sounded less inflamatory than it might had they been alone. It was a proof of the non-participatory state of his senses that all this time—in fact almost from the moment Bateson had arrived to drag him out—Richard was still going over in his mind all the earlier events of the day.

Then Bateson and Rube stood up suddenly, gave each other one or two playful punches, Bateson spread an arm in Richard's direction, a movement that was half-way between a yawn and a valediction, and they went out.

'She's left her bag,' Daphne said at once.

Mildly alarmed, Richard said, 'Where are they off to?'

The clothes-peg grew sprightly. 'That's telling! What have you been thinking about?'

'You,' he lied automatically.

'Really!' She was immensely pleased. 'I expect you're wondering about me aren't you? Well I'll tell you; I'm waiting for Mr Right.' She caught her breath suddenly and said, 'Pardon.' Her eyes lost their glassiness and assumed a rapt, almost ethereal longing. 'Fellers are all the same. They only want loving . . .'

'But won't Mr Right want that too?'

' 'E'll want me,' Daphne replied indignantly. She hiccupped. 'Ooh-er, pardon again.'

'I'll get you some water, shall I?'

'Ask Mrs R. for water?—Rather you than me.'

'Well I'll get something. Here, hang on a tick . . .' He made his way to the proliferating bar and ordered two beers.

'Your friend's a nice boy,' Mrs Rooke said. '*Beer*, dear? If that's for Daph you'd better go back and make sure. She usually likes her little drop of poison——'

But Richard insisted on something long and Mrs Rooke said Daph had better have a 'nip' then and poured out a small, but expensive beer with a great fog of froth on it and said, 'Two-and-a-tanner, ducks.'

'I'll have the same then.'

'That's right, ducks; you've got the same. Two-and-a-tanner. Full of strength, them nips. I lived on them when I had my Charlie.'

The nips were certainly full of something. They left Daph and Richard mildly aware of an off-key expression in one another's faces, but quite incapable of changing it. Daphne ceased to hiccup. Her eyes countermanded his, lustrous and blank. A funny feller . . . she was thinking. Not Mr Right by a long chalk. But she liked him because he was so clean. Too clean in a way for a feller . . .

'Where do you think Bate—Arthur and Rube have gone?'

'You *do* get anxious, don't you!' She was turning the lamp up a fraction. 'Does he worry about you like that? I bet he doesn't! Ooh, my face!' She held her chin up to the mirror and banged hard at her cheeks with a broad greasy puff. 'Thin,' she said; 'I used to go nine-ten—you'd never believe it would you. But what does it matter if you feel all right!' She swayed slightly and Richard said, 'Come on, you had better sit down. Your face is O.K.'

'You like it?' she enquired.
'Adore it.'
She regarded him suspiciously.
'B-bloody men,' she said with feeling.
'*Well* . . . !'
'All the same,' declared Daphne. She retreated to the sofa and threw herself down. 'Who are you anyway?'
With his head feeling most peculiar, like a tremendous sunflower about to burst from its bud into flaming petals, and his eyes seeing everything through a bright, though uncertain, nimbus reflected by this dizzy blooming, Richard said, 'Mr Right . . . I hope . . .'
'Ahhhh . . .' murmured Daphne, not without tenderness. 'You'd like to be wouldn't you. But you're not, you know!'
'Oh, who am I then?' he asked, his hand at her breast.
'You're Dick,' she answered, 'and if you ask me, you're just like the rest! Nice Dick,' she added inconsistently. 'No . . . no . . . !'
'But, darling . . .'
Her breasts were the merest cone-shaped ghosts of the fulness his desires demanded; little, formal budding mounds; the breasts of a Clouet lady, feverishly warm, yet comfortless. His hand considered them, curiously and fearfully. All his actions were now conducted with as much precision as he could muster. He felt fatuous and dizzy and gallant and accomplished all at the same time. *Very* accomplished. He also was able to regard all these aspects of himself with a peculiar detachment, as though they were the component behaviour of somebody else. Such an attitude had its drawbacks, since he at once began to form judgments which inevitably lead to his being conscience-stricken. When one has successfully scuttled commonsense, it seems only fair that one's conscience should go under as well. Nothing is as humiliating as to be rather tight and yet to be able to appreciate the extent of one's shortcomings. Where was the blushful Hippocrene? Certainly not in the half-gallon of sourish bitter he had swallowed. There was no magic in that; no gaiety. He was even wise enough to realise that its sum effect was more or less that of a tripwire. He hoped that Mrs Rooke wasn't just about to make one

of her over-understanding entrances, because his affections had veered strikingly in the last ten minutes and he now decided that he would very much like to make love to Daphne. She should be his Dowson-girl and there was in truth that unhealthy narcotic-smirched, bitter-skinned, transiently-fleshed feeling about her narrow body which invited a comparison with a very special cigarette.

She smelt strongly and sweetly of hot art-silk and tepid talcum-powder. If she had had a mind, making love to her could only have been an intellectual delight, an extension of that taste normally directed to fondling small ivories. As it was, she lacked not only the intelligence but the passion requisite for her entire absence of morals. Now and then, when the need to do so occurred to her, she returned Richard's caresses with a kiss or two. Once she put up her hand and gently squeezed the nape of his neck in her thin, cold, painted fingers. Sometimes she said, 'pardon' for no earthly reason at all. Emboldened by the impersonal stillness she manufactured, the brightness of her stare and the fact that she continued to say, 'Nice Dick' over and over again, he swept her down in his arms until they were sprawling full length on the slippery sofa.

The next thing he remembered was a stinging blackness in place of the exciting sunflower in his brain, and they were standing up, one at each end of the mantelpiece, panting slightly and glaring at one another in the foetid half-light. Daphne's hands flew about her person, patting and tapping it in a brittle frenzy as if a bit of it might have snapped off. Now and then she muttered, 'men' in a tone which was a mixture of tolerant indignation, making it quite clear that although she found their behaviour revolting, she did realise is was an infirmity indigenous to their sex and that if one got too near these, otherwise fairly reasonable creatures, then one either had to put up with their quirks, or defend oneself as best one could. She was sure that Mr Right, when he came along, would be an exception and sink *his* energies in a nice little chicken-farm.

'Perhaps you'll be good enough to find my friend,' she said with enormous refinement, and drew a new lipstick mouth. 'Give 'em an inch and they go a mile,' she added very generally, making it clear again that Richard wasn't to feel the blame particularly.

But he apologised all the same.

'Really,' Daphne said. 'Nobody's asking you to say things you don't mean, I'm sure!' You can call it 'uman nature if you like, but 'uman nature has to be checked. Whatever do you think the world would be like if we all gave in to 'uman nature . . . ?'

Just then Rube returned with Bateson following closely behind her.

Daphne at once fell back on her earlier rôle of hen-like concern. '*There* you are, Rube,' she said. 'Wherever have you been?' Knotting her orange knitted scarf, she nagged on and on with Rube rather enjoying all this solicitude. Rube's face glistened; her eyes were starry and daring, and as often as she sought to screw her lips together in some kind of acceptable composure, they parted softly revealing a generous allocation of extremely white and irregular teeth. Daphne fixed a pink felt halo on the back of her head, squeezed her little dead fingers into damp gloves and sniffed.

Bateson appraised the situation expertly and correctly. He was looking as smooth as a cat after cream; a much-indulged, dearly-beloved cat. His eyelids were half-lowered giving him an expression of sagacious peace. He propelled Rube forward gently, patting her bottom in a small gesture of dismissal which contrived to be proprietary, loving and avuncular all at the same time, so giving her an option on the last should the other attitudes offend her. As it happened, Rube relished all three sensations and was smirking like a calf in a clover field.

'When you two have *quite* finished . . .' Daphne said primly —which gave cause for an unreasonable burst of laughter from Bateson. He stepped forward and gave Daphne a slap as well. She froze with astonishment, then, uttering an extraordinary yelp she flung herself into Rube's arms. Together they rocked and shrieked. Bateson watched for a second or so, perplexed by the hysteria the most innocent of his actions always seemed to precipitate where women were concerned, never realising that in spite of all the psychologists propound it is the male with the minimum of understanding of the female complexity that delights it most. 'Come on,' he said, and that was how Richard and he left them. Daphne steadied herself sufficiently to call out, 'And I should get back to them searchlights just *as soon as you can.*' This convulsed them afresh.

'What on earth . . .' Richard began, but his voice was drowned in the bedlam of the public bar, through which they had to pass. Mrs Rooke, balancing on a chair, was ringing a handbell and bawling 'Time!' Her vast satin-covered bosom shone with fecund promise. Behind her the silver doilies and upturned gin bottles winked. 'Cheerio, ducks,' she yelled. Her bell wanged merrily.

'Oh God!' breathed Richard when the icy night cut him off from all this, 'so that was "The Case . . .".'

'That certainly was,' Bateson said, who was drunker than he knew. He stepped out, determined but unsteady, both conditions increasing as he strode along. He praised the English inn. He repeated the Belloc-Chesterton arguments for it as his own. Now and then he sang in a light, gay voice which carried for miles over the frozen beet fields. Richard was able to walk perfectly, but his head rang with an unpleasant coming and going reverberation, like a gong being sounded behind a busy swing door. He remembered that the last food he had eaten was in the gun-room at Sheldon, which caused him in turn to think of that other part of the day, so oddly divorced from the present, when Sir Paul had probed in the gentlest possible manner into those aspects of his personality which hadn't been obvious to that penetrating mind. What would Sir Paul think now, Richard wondered, to see Bateson and himself rolling along the dear old English road . . . ? But Bateson was in a gossipy mood.

'You know all about the Belle and the Winner, I suppose?'

'About their once being in love do you mean? I think so. Wasn't it you who first told me?'

'I might have: I'm not quite sure,' said Bateson cautiously. 'Abelard and Helloish—that's what they were known as. It must have been all the blackboards and eashels.'

'How could you know?' laughed Richard. 'You weren't even born!'

Bateson became mildly belligerent. 'How do I know? I'll *tell* you how I know, Dick you old T-Thomas. The Belle told me.'

He began to sing loudly, 'Ding-dong bell, Pussy's in the well . . .' and a country youth, escorting his girl home, thrust a protective arm in front of her as they passed. 'Goodnight,' Bateson called, but got no reply.

This silent criticism sobered him up a bit, because when Richard, dragging the subject back to Miss Bellingham, said, 'But I thought you and she weren't getting on so well . . .' Bateson answered simply:

'We aren't; you're absolutely right. But we *did*. I tell you, when I first showed up at Copdock I was the b-bloody blue-eyed boy! She doted on me—she's doting a bit on you at the moment I notice—Might have gone on if I hadn't suddenly got the hang of her little game. Anyway, I couldn't stand her hours.'

'But the Winner,' insisted Richard; 'how does he come into it?'

Bateson was about to make an ordinary statement here, when an exciting hypothesis explaining the entire relationship between Miss Bellingham and her staff suddenly presented itself to him. So exciting, in fact, was it, that he grew vague and incoherent once more in the telling of it.

'Don't you see,' he said, speaking loudly, but none the more distinctly because of that, 'the Winner was the forerunner—no, that's not what I mean—he's the thingummy—the *prototype*,' he all but shouted, dragging the word up from the fuddled ponds of his vocabulary. 'That's what he is, the prototype. Don't you see, it explains everything! It explains why all the masters taken on by the Belle have one thing in common and why she's always been so willing to let other considerations than mere academic qualifications sway her judgment. And why, if it comes to that, why she never employs a woman or two about the place. We could really do with a homely body for some of those younger kids. No, I'll tell you why not. It's because the greatest, most important testimonial for a job at Copdock is to have a nice fresh face. A *gentlemanly* face, mind you; that's essential. Why, I bet if you could see all the staff the Belle's had in her clutches since she started the place in the year dot, you'd have one of the fanciest collections of darlin' bhoys you could meet anywhere!'

This was so preposterous and yet such an 'un-Bateson' statement for Bateson to make that Richard stifled his objections to hear what would fallow. 'Including poor old M'Tooley and poor old Canon Ribbs?' he asked sceptically.

'What do you know about M'Tooley?' demanded Bateson. 'You don't know anything. He came to Copdock when he was twenty-five—which was just half of what he is now. There happens to be a photograph of him among all that muck in the Belle's study. He wasn't a bad type. Gingery and merry.'

'And the Canon?'

'They had high hopes for the Canon,' Bateson said. 'Deaneries and things—until *she* put a stop to them.'

'How?'

Bateson made a fancy kick at a puff of loose snow before answering, missed it, and slithered ignominiously to a foolish sitting position at the side of the road. He accepted this as evidence of his abnormal state and tramped on with a rather crestfallen air. He grew lugubrious.

'The same way she stopped the rest of them from getting on,' he said. 'She sucked his blood. The Belle wasn't interested in seeing how far these protégés of hers could go. She wanted them by her all the time. I suppose that was the truth of the matter—still is. The best way to keep a car at home is to empty its tank. You can then sit in it and have a nice cosy chat without having to worry about the view going by. She's been siphoning all the go out of the poor devils she employs for years. She's a lady spider, that smart old woman! She's a naughty old vampire; a leech. Why do you think the Winner never cleared off years ago? M'Tooley as well? M'Tooley's pretty hot stuff, you know—it's all there, boy.' Bateson tapped his temple. 'People used to come after M'Tooley and *beg* him to take things. They wanted him badly at Oriel. I'm told he used to contribute to *Symposium* and was offered the editorship when Danvers—was that the name? You'll know more about that sort of stuff than I do—anyway, when the last editor died. But do you think he could move? Of *course* not. Stuck, boy, that's what he was. Drained by the Reverend Mother MacCree. All passion spent and not even a spot of loose change left to jingle in his pocket. So what is he now? C-classics c-cum scripture at Copdock! And not even any more little confidences behind the door of the sherry-cupboard!'

'Is it true that she wanted to marry the Winner?'

'There's nothing very complimentary about the idea which ever way you look at it if it isn't.'

'They . . . they were lovers, do you think?' Richard asked, his curiosity overcoming the enormity of such a question.

'Did they go to bed together—is that what you mean? Well, according to all accounts, and I see no reason to disbelieve them, they did. Then the future Mrs W. came along and rescued the poor old Winner—*young* Winner then, sorry—from a fate worse than death.'

'He'd have married Miss Bellingham?'

'I suppose so, the poor bloody necrophilist.'

Mildly ashamed of himself for wishing to dig down and uncover even more of the mouldering fragments of such antique affections, Richard then asked about Mrs Winsley. He had always been able to see what fascination had once existed in that Royal Doulton little figure, the white skin covered by the lilac silk, the excessively pretty colours of her mouth and eyes and hair, the obedience inherent in all her dolly-dolly movements, which, in spite of their insistence on pastel shades, hinted at warmer, darker tones at a deeper level, like hyacinth flowers. It was women like Mrs Winsley who made young men feel good. Later, it was their experience and not their innocence which went *en travestie*. In middle age, of course, they were inclined to make their husbands feel sick. The same flatteringly malleable feminity which had proved to be so complimentary to the male ego when both were young, was apt to persist as a reproach when it dragged on into middle age. This was exactly what had happened to the Winsleys. Their married life had been more lover-like than most of their friends were willing to admit, and it had only been during the last few years that what Winsley described as 'Minna's girlishness' had turned him against her. That shrill spinster excitement rising up so uncontrollably whenever she enthused—how *could* she? he marvelled irritably—after all that their life together had been! 'You silly bitch!' he bawled after her one day, for no apparent reason that she could put a name to. And that had marked the beginning of their next stage; his bullying. Now there wasn't a thing that she could do right, nor any part of all that fragile armoury of love of hers which he did not hurl back with repulsion. Richard could see that she might, at times, be irritating. It was beyond his powers of uncharitableness to appreciate how entirely she could be hated. Fortunately, the truly sensitive are rarely soppy. She suffered, of course, from her husband's spleenish onslaughts, but not nearly to such a degree as her swimming china-bright eyes might suggest. She was puzzled rather than grieved. 'Cadman's getting so peculiar,' she confessed to Miss Ribbs and added that it really was 'rather a foxer'—her Daddy's term. Miss Ribbs, for whom life was better than the cinema every time, absorbed this latest reel of it glassily.

'She was a Waldinfield,' Bateson said. 'It's a wonder somebody hasn't told you *that* before now.'

'She's pretty—or perhaps I mean—nicer than you'd expect her to be. Her sort, I really mean.'

Fatigue was rapidly overtaking Bateson. The long tramp, the determination he had put into the evening, his own helpless loquacity; these things bundled one upon another began to weigh him down like clumsy garments impeding the movements of his graceful body. He yawned openly and continuously.

'Yes she is,' he agreed. 'Oh, *Gawd* . . . ! It's a long time since I felt like this. Last Thursday to be exact. Poor Mrs Winner, she used to worry about me! I think she imagines all the four-ale bars are full of greasy old Fagins. B-bad company I suppose is what she'd call it. Well anything was preferable to squatting in Common-Room watching Canon Ribbs listening to a prom. How did you get on with your paper-doll?'

Startled, Richard answered, 'Oh all right.' In the thick grey light he felt Bateson studying him and realised that he was genuinely curious about this. In fact, that Bateson actually longed to know. In Bateson's case, however, there was little need for words. Richard could see that the basis of his weariness wasn't what he had had to drink, or the pennant of chatter he had maintained all the way to, and all the way back, from the 'Case is Altered', but the aftermath of love.

In Stourfriston the church clock chimed a quarter-to-eleven. A solitary figure was parading the market place like a tourist doing the arena at Arles. At first they identified it with a local policeman on his rounds, but something in the way the precise head was frequently turned to observe some shop corner or the water-spouts gripped by gargoyles on the roof of the church and the reflective attitude generally when the figure paused, caused Bateson to start hard with his smudgy eyes.

'M'Tooley . . .' he said softly.

Although it was impossible for the figure to have heard, or even see them from where it stood by the dark angle made by the church porch, it moved out at once into the empty, but well-lit square and walked briskly across to them. It was Mr M'Tooley.

'Hallo,' he said; 'it should be ill-met by moonlight, except that it's nice to see you and there doesn't happen to be a moon!'

'Getting a breather?' Bateson asked with forced casualness.

'We've been playing bézique,' stated Mr M'Tooley, as though that explained everything. 'In fact we've only just stopped.' He made it sound distinctly daring. 'Then I came out to get a breather, as you say. Have you ever noticed Stourfriston by night; *particularly* I mean? All the beautiful worn old plaster-work high up over the shops and the big porches over the doors which become quite elegant again when one can't see to read the doctors' and dentists' plates nailed all over them. It hasn't changed a bit, you know, since I first came to it. . . . Not a scrap.' He glanced at them in turn. In the soft late evening light the steep bald head and gingery, badly-shaved jaw had the guileless evanescence of a fading fresco. 'Did you have a good day at Sheldon?' he asked, turning to Richard and Richard remembered afterwards that it was the first time someone had made an enquiry about his activities in that direction without the faint *tink!* of their inquisitiveness accompanying it.

'Oh excellent, thanks.'

'Miss Bellingham is delighted with the arrangement . . .'

'Oh . . . ?' This time they both turned and stared at Mr M'Tooley, but Mr M'Tooley, walking a little aside and a little apart, noticed nothing. When he went ahead to unlock the side door of Copdock, Batson muttered, 'The fellow's a monk; a natural, bloody monk . . .'

When he had locked the door from the inside, Mr M'Tooley

swung the key from its iron ring for a thoughtful second or two, then said, 'Bateson, I may as well let you have this now.'

'Now . . . ?'

'For 'rounds' tomorrow night. It is your turn isn't it?'

'Oh yes; of course.'

Mr M'Tooley laid the tips of his stubby, ill-kept fingers against the tired red skin of his eyes and rubbed softly in a languid gesture of abnegation. 'Call it a day,' he said.

'You can say that again!' Bateson favoured Americanisms, and in a way the peculiarly brash element of the poetry in them suited him.

Mr M'Tooley, who had begun to climb the stairs, turned and looked suddenly frightened, almost shocked. 'What . . . ?' he demanded. And then, 'Oh, I see . . .' as the harmless vacuity in the faces of a couple of beery, wintry young men was conveyed to him. He said no more. The transitory, nibbled-away, faded-Giotto look returned to possess him and when he creaked away into the darkness of the staff wing it was like a shade withdrawing.

The mild interest of stumbling upon what Bateson had described as 'one of Danny-boy's cat-that-walks-by-itself acts' was swiftly superseded by a far more repellent sensation. Darwin, the caretaker, in one of his fruitless attempts 'to get forward', as he called it, had decided that gone eleven at night was a favourable time to rootle clinkers from the bowels of the Heath Robinson arrangement in the boiler-room. He was also in charge of some simple, though protracted, task in the kitchen. Since he was never known to shut a door after him the mingled stenches of soot and boiling marrow-bones belched fitfully up through the stair-well. Bateson's lips parted and his eyes closed. 'I thought I could be sick, and now I know,' he said.

Upstairs, in his own room, with the skull from Dunwich as sole witness, he was.

Richard spent a futile hour before sleeping going over in his mind the treacherous successes which had lured him on to so complete a frustration. The image of Daphne trolled through his thoughts. He dropped off with the bemused idea of her lying rigidly beside him like an acquiescent pipe-cleaner.

13

Mr Winsley gave Mr M'Tooley three minutes before saying Grace. Using such a scale of tolerance it might be estimated that he would have allowed Richard two minutes, perhaps, and wouldn't have waited for Bateson at all. He certainly wasn't anxious nor even irritated as he gave a last look in the direction of the door for Mr M'Tooley before doling out porridge from a vast dull grey can. Grey steam from the porridge settled on his spectacles. He plobbed it uncertainly into dull grey plates. The porridge too was grey, though more oleaginous than viscous, slipping from the scoop with every reluctance. An exciting, rather merry whirling noise followed his passing of each full plate.

'No whizzing!' he shouted.

And at once the noise ceased and the thick plates passed decorously from hand to hand.

'Who whizzed?' demanded Mr Winsley, slightly beside himself. 'Did you whizz?'

'Me, sir?'

'I'm talking to Funnell. He knows who I'm talking to.'

'Oh *me*, sir! *No*, sir.'

'Well who did—somebody did. I won't have it, do you hear? That's the way fine plates get cracked. Has anybody seen anything of Mr M'Tooley?'

'Me, sir?'

'You've seen him, Funnell?'

'No, sir. I just thought you were asking me if I'd seen him, sir.'

Mr Winsley removed his spectacles and peered all round the long, thin H of trestle tables which constituted the dining-hall. He wasn't as yet apprehensive, but on the other hand, he wasn't quite happy. He had conceded three minutes and it was now a quarter past eight. The rods of cold sunshine made him blink unbearably.

'Pink-eye,' explained Funnell to his neighbour, observing this. 'It's a disease.'

Richard leant forward and said, 'Shut up, Funnell.'

'Yes, sir.'

Bateson then entered and took his place and said, ' 'Morning, Mr Winsley. 'Morning all.' The greeting was acknowledged with a faint slobbery, porridgy titter, not entirely without affection. Bateson either missed breakfast or he was very late for it. No amount of remonstrance, not even when it came from the highest level, had ever managed to cure this shortcoming. His conviction that breakfast was an offensive beginning to any day had the seal set on it that moment when his own plate of porridge, helped on its way by a dozen busy hands, arrived before him like a lukewarm quoit. He closed his eyes and ate.

'Mr M'Tooley said nothing to you about not coming down to breakfast I suppose, Mr Bateson?'

Bateson, for whom for once the prospect of three hours on a rugby field presented no delight, looked startled. He hadn't a hangover, in fact his head and his stomach shared the impression of a tremendous clarity. Instead a delicate fatigue had set in, an exquisite listlessness so unconnected with food, or for desire for conversation, that he was at great pains not to disturb it. Two mouthfuls of porridge told him how wise he was being to stand firm in this intention. The nauseous yapping of the boys at his end of the table decided him to close his ears, so when the Winner's bewildered enquiry came to him he was practically senseless. M'Tooley? Breakfast? What on earth was the old man nattering about! Perhaps it was something to do with last night. . . . Somewhat resentfully, he let a trickle of intelligence seep through into the delicious vacuum of his brain.

'It's perfectly all right,' he said. 'I've got the key for 'rounds' tonight.'

'Then you've seen Mr M'Tooley?'

'Oh yes,' Bateson said comfortably, still thinking of their meeting the night before.

Mr Winsley didn't look so much relieved, as mildly angry. All this obtuseness! He could hardly blame Bateson, not in front of the school anyway. 'You come to my study after Prayers, Funnell!' The beastly, sniggering creature! He'd change all this soon.

'*Me*, sir?' Funnell, who had been sawing his way through

a wedge of practically incinerated liver with, what was for him, exemplary fortitude, was outraged. 'Just because the old bastard had to have *some*body to wallop with his elevenses!' he told Sellars, his neighbour, furiously.

They all met half an hour later in Big School for Prayers. The boys sat on three sides of a square which was completed by a dais on which Mr Winsley sat with the other masters a little to the rear of him. Canon Ribbs conducted Prayers. The Canon didn't live in the School. He was the Rector of Stourfriston and the combining of a little teaching with his normal parish duties was generally thought to be a kindness shown to Miss Bellingham, since the reason for his doing it could scarcely be financial, the Canon being notoriously well-off. He wore his dignity with an air of Tractarian splendour and the more sophisticated boys assured each other that he was retained by the Belle entirely because of his *distingué* lint-white locks and vintage Balliol accent (1893–6), which had disarmed in their time an entire legion of well-trained, though ill-bred, busybodies such as Ministry of Education inspectors. Anything lying within the nature of that kind of trouble, and it was the Canon who coped. Or should there be difficulties in any of the neighbouring parishes, it was still the Canon, this time in his capacity of Rural Dean, who smoothed them out. 'Pouring oil on troubled vestries,' was how Lindsay, an extraordinarily odd boy whom one wouldn't have expected to have found at Copdock at all, described it.

Lindsay was one of a handful of boys who had stayed on at the school after the preparatory period, so justifying the brochure, which boasted that highly qualified staff would be able, because of the exclusive nature of the establishment, to guide a child from his earliest schooldays up to the standard required for University Entrance. Most parents didn't trust Miss Bellingham that far and took care to withdraw their sons when they became old enough to go to March—if they could afford it—or to the local Grammar School if they could not. Although there was some injustice in this—since both Mr Winsley and Miss Bellingham were well able to get results when they wanted them—such defections had their consolations. It meant that the Sixth was so small that the few boys of whom it comprised received what amounted to a year and a half's excellent private tutoring. Only a boy who was a fool could muff his entrance examination after such privileged treatment. The names of those who had succeeded, with the names of the Colleges which had benefited in brackets beside them, were painted in gold letters on a light-oak board, hanging in Big School. Lindsay's had just been added. 'Sidney-Sussex 1939' it said, a trifle more glowingly than the rest. Lindsay, in this pleasant limbo in which he now found himself, between the teachers and the taught, was amusing himself during prayers with a little private game called 'Catching the Canon's Eye'. The Canon, thought Lindsay, was looking anxious this morning. So was the Winner. He glanced around rapidly. And so were they all decided Lindsay—except Mr M'Tooley, and he was mystifyingly absent. At that moment Lindsay scored a point. The Canon stared straight at him. Lindsay stared straight back. Disconcerted, the Canon's gaze fled to Queen Alexandra, pausing to absorb the sepia panache of her photographed jewels before its interest winged on and came to rest on the gas brackets. Not El Greco, thought Lindsay unkindly, seeing the Canon's upturned eyeballs; not even Holman Hunt, though varnished hard-boiled eggs would not be an improper comparison.

They sang a hymn by Mrs Hemans, the boys' voices promoting the bathos of the words to a level of exquisite absurdity. Macro-Webb, one of Lindsay's companions in the Sixth, strummed out the accompaniment on an ancient instrument by Grover and Grover which had once had pride of place in the old Copdock House drawing-room. The Canon's beautifully shaved jowls quivered as he joined in.

Mr Winsley mouthed gibberish. The words of the hymn crawled about on the white page of his hymnbook like insects and no vestige of their meaning reached him. He was obsessed by the possible fate of Mr M'Tooley. So ridiculous to oversleep he told himself; so worrying for other people! M'Tooley hadn't gone to bed late last night—in fact he'd gone up before the rest of them. And he'd seemed quite happy; quite the same, that is, since nobody could call him a happy man and any lowering of his natural low spirits would tend to reveal him as positively morose. No, he hadn't been morose, Mr Winsley told himself. Rather the reverse if anything. Supposing—no: he mustn't even think such things . . . Anyway, M'Tooley was a Catholic or at least an Anglo-Catholic, and that was nearly as bad, and any suggestion that he might . . . Mr Winsley strove valiantly with the hymn. Why had the damned thing got hundreds of verses! Why hadn't he slipped upstairs to see for himself between breakfast and Big School? Why was Lindsay winking—perhaps he wasn't. Everything was so indistinct this morning. His eyes were playing him up again. It was these spectacles. He'd have to get bi-focals after all. Was Minna right in saying that Dessy (Why did she call him that? Such a disgusting abbreviation) was getting a bit, well, peculiar? He hadn't actually noticed such a thing himself, although that was nothing to go by. It was a good thing in his estimation not to have time to dwell on the derangements of others. His thoughts wandered helplessly on, and when it came to the point where it was his duty to dismiss the school to its various classrooms, his mouth dried up and he was unable to utter a sound.

The Fourth in particular were delighted. First Mr M'Tooley's glaring absence and now the Winner gawping like a fish. They turned to smirk at one another, plainly enchanted by the prospect of a day of confusion. But such hopes were short-lived. Before he had quite realised it himself and with that suppressed gift for strategy which belonged to the *manqué* side of his nature, Mr Winsley was deploying what remained of his forces. There would be no games, he announced; instead Mr Bateson would take over the Fourth for an extra period of maths.

A token groan for the cancelled rugger—no one was over-eager to strip in an unheated pavilion, nor to separate themselves from mud later with nearly cold water—was speedily turned into a more genuine grief at the thought of the extra maths. Only Bateson himself was truly pleased. After the evening at the 'Case is Altered' he felt what he called, 'fragile'. The idea of a morning spent sitting in Mr M'Tooley's chair was infinitely preferable to plodding up and down a soggy pitch in the company of twenty horrid yelling boys.

'Fourth and Fifth to the North Room then, and you, Lindsay, you can carry on with what we were doing in the Sixth yesterday, only I should miss Book Three of The Faery Queen and continue where it says, 'It often falls, in course of common life'—I think on page two hundred.' Mr Winsley was now in huge command of the situation. 'This afternoon,' he said, 'if we are still shorthanded, the Fourth and the Fifth will divide; the Fifth to go on as usual with Mr Brand—Agrarian Disputes, isn't it?' He snuffled, pleased with this instance of what he termed, 'keeping a finger on the pulse', 'and the Fourth can do their prep in class instead of after supper. All right?' He looked up and down the rows of vapid or meditating faces. He smiled and his dentures flashed a confidence he was far from feeling.

Richard, who had listened to all this in only a desultory fashion, suddenly realised that there had been no mention of what he was to do.

'Silly old fool,' he muttered to Bateson, as he edged his way to the front of the noisily dispersing school, 'He's left me out.'

Bateson grinned laconically. Things, he implied so far as he himself was concerned at any rate, were perfect.

The Canon and Mr Winsley descended from the dais.

'Ah, Brand,' said the Canon. 'Er, 'morning. *Much* warmer, don't you think! Mr Winsley's just been telling me that poor old M'Tooley's feeling a bit groggy—A naval term, wouldn't you think, Cadman? The poor fellow's probably had an extra tot of rum when they were sea-sick . . . Fascinating these scraps of slang which penetrate our general usage . . .' He sniffed himself to an apologetic stop. Mr Winsley was looking hard at him and Richard fancied that he saw an unspoken decision concluded between the two pairs of moist weak eyes. At the door Mr Winsley turned and said, 'You coming too, Brand?' which Richard, correctly, interpreted as an order. He joined them in the entrance hall.

Canon Ribbs displayed his celebrated tact.

'You're not in class or anything—er—Brand? No, I thought not. Be a good man and scout out just what *is* keeping Mr M'Tooley, will you?'

Richard looked at Mr Winsley. Mr Winsley's expression gave not the least hint of his intense anxiety.

'Yes, do, Brand,' he said. 'Perhaps you'd have time to come back and tell us just what has happened. Ask him if my wife can get him anything. Poor old chap . . . he does work, you know, Canon . . .'

As he went away, Richard heard the Canon remark, 'I thought he was just a bit peaky last night. His bézique was certainly below par . . .' The Canon's index finger was fumbling its way round the appreciable space existing between his neck and his dog-collar, like a dredger clearing a moat.

'Settling down all right, Cadman?' he enquired when they had the room to themselves.

Mr Winsley was judicial.

'I *think* so . . .' he said slowly.

'Well, I hand it to Freda——'

Mr Winsley found this more than familiar.

'Miss Bellingham has always been a very able judge of character,' he declared loftily.

'She has; she has,' agreed Canon Ribbs at once. Any suspicion of asperity in others immediately acted as a stimulant to his own perfectly svelte manners; manners in themselves so devastating that they usually ended up by leaving him in control of the most irate situations. He had a particular reason for giving them full rein this morning. Something very odd was happening, or had happened, at Copdock and he was intensely curious to know exactly what. 'You forget, Caddie, that it wasn't *me* who joined the staff for the first time last Christmas!' he scolded charmingly.

'No, no. Of course not. I didn't mean that. You'll have to forgive me. It's all this M'Tooley business. It's making me fretful—I never lose my temper as you know. It's this *casualness*. I couldn't say anything in front of that boy, but M'Tooley *is* casual. Never once has he told me what he is thinking! He *looks* ill, but is he? He's never said so. You know how I always get a bit hipped with—with irresponsible behaviour!'

'Oh, come,' the Canon said. He remembered his official rôle in the world, and made a deliberate move towards the milk of human kindness. 'Not "irresponsible", Caddie; not at least until we know . . .'

The frightened look reappeared on Mr Winsley's face. Whatever it was he prayed God it wouldn't get into the newspapers. When Richard came back just five minutes later both he and they seemed to be meeting afresh after a whole lifetime apart. Shock had stripped Richard's features of all trace of their usual expression and had left in place of it, a flat, colourless immaturity against which the shape of his beard showed up in patchy stains. Mr Winsley and the Canon listened very exactly to what he said, so there was no need for him to repeat what he had had the greatest difficulty in mumbling the first time.

The door to Mr M'Tooley's room was a poor little arrangement, narrow and flimsy, like the door to a broom-cupboard. Richard knocked on it three times and waited as many minutes before he tried its small dented brass nob. He did so very gently because Mr M'Tooley's room emanated a sacrosanctity so pronounced, it filled all the passage outside and could even be felt on the narrow staircase which led up to the room and nowhere else. On this particular morning, however, the room would have emanated something more suffocating than sanctity, had not Mr M'Tooley discovered an early use for the rolls of gummed paper they were selling at the local stationer's as a protection against bomb-blasted windows. Nothing happened when Richard tried the knob, except a small papery creak. He knocked again, loudly this time—aggressively—like somebody in Macbeth and the silence, returning, was heartbreaking. After this he just turned the knob and pushed. There was a crisp tearing noise. He pushed harder, leaning his entire weight against the panel, and was precipitated into the room and the world-obliterating fumes which Mr M'Tooley had purchased for exactly three shillings. He had pasted-up the chimney, the door and the windows and Richard rushed back choking, the gas following in his wake like an importunate despair for whom one surrender was not enough. At the bottom of the little staircase he took his jacket off, muffled it against his face, ran back to the room and managed to wrench its large sash window open. The beautiful, stimulating, cold, but living, day poured in.

Mr M'Tooley lay neatly in his bed dressed in fresh-looking pyjamas. His eyes were closed and their lashes made thick faded gingery crescents above each polished cheek-bone. The red rubber tube dangled from the gas arm above his head, but the nozzle through which he had sucked oblivion had fallen down behind the bedhead and although his lips were still slightly parted, they could have been so in a faint smile. There was no other suggestion of his end. A half-glass of water and a bottle of Gee's cough linctus on the bedside table and M.R. James's *Suffolk and Norfolk* open at 'Jurmin, Botolph and Withburga', the pages still under his hand, only emphasized the essential ordinariness of his departure. The only disfigurement of any kind in the room, excepting the red tube which normally led from the main to the ring on which he made his early morning tea, was the sticky brown paper everywhere; though here again, one felt it was only out of consideration for others that it had been applied, since Mr M'Tooley must have known it was unessential to his lonely decision. He hadn't locked the door. He hadn't written a letter. Only one small fib separated him from his usual behaviour. He had said he was going to bed early and he hadn't. He had slipped out into the brilliant January night and taken a last look at the Perpendicular majesty of Stourfriston church. The winter cold and the moon-bright stone had produced the catharsis he required. Not quite certain why he was doing it, but absolutely assured in the doing itself, he put three shillings in the meter, his best linen pyjamas on, wound his watch and read himself to—death.

*

'It will be apparent—I very much trust that it will be apparent, gentlemen, that for the sake of human charity, as well as for the law, I am bound to seek answers to questions which in themselves may occur to you as frivolous.' The coroner motioned towards Mr Winsley and the handful of other people sitting in the front row of chairs set out before the mayor's desk. The considerable number of questions he had already asked, instead of throwing a light on Mr M'Tooley's suicide, only made it appear the more incomprehensible. The coroner drummed a restrained tattoo on the blotter with white, bloodless fingers. Those who hid their grief presumably didn't want charity anyway, he was thinking. But the general opinion was that the law should be as Christian as respectability allowed in such matters and he would do his best to prove that Mr M'Tooley was mad when he did it.

'On the twenty-eighth,' he recommenced gently, 'Mr M'Tooley supervised in the dining-room—quite naturally, would you say?'

'Oh, quite.' Mr Winsley dragged his attention from the smoky oil painting of a hirsute alderman which was the chief ornament of the mayor's parlour.

'Then, that same evening, he dined alone?'

Mr Winsley took this critically. 'He didn't have to. That was how he preferred it. Darwin, he's the odd-job man, generally took a tray up to Mr M'Tooley's room.'

'There was nothing different about the room? It was just as it was? Darwin isn't present . . . ?'

'Should he be . . . ? I didn't realise . . .'

'It doesn't matter if I can accept it that you asked him about the room.'

'He said it was just the same.'

'He didn't notice the gummed paper, or that letters were being burnt?'

'No, nothing. Letters could not be destroyed anyway—at least I don't *think* they could, as the gas-fire is fixed in front of the grate.'

'And,' insisted the coroner, 'you remain convinced that Mr M'Tooley wasn't in any sort of trouble . . . ?'

'I am not convinced of that. What I believe I said to your earlier enquiry was that *I* had no suspicion that he could have been—er—troubled.'

'Then you think that he might have been?'

'I think nothing. Why should I? That he *was* troubled is unquestionable—to have done what he did—but I have no notion of what troubled him.' It was now obvious that Mr Winsley was mildly enjoying himself.

The coroner turned on the Canon.

'I have it that at eight-ten, or thereabouts, Mr M'Tooley came down to join you for cards?' There was a distinct innuendo in the way he pronounced the word 'cards'. It jolted the Canon severely, as it was intended to do, making him recall that Mr Elgin, the coroner, was Scotch and Presbyterian, and that he had been an advocate before he came south to be a solicitor. The Canon saw his poor little pleasures opened up to the most heinous interpretations and he himself made a byword, though for what he couldn't be certain. It would be Tranby Croft all over again.

'We never played for money, you know,' he declared unhappily.

This gave the coroner a chance to lighten the dragging proceedings with a faint quip.

'No one is suggesting, Canon, that the gentleman concerned took this sad way out because of his misfortunes at bézique...'

Bateson, sitting behind, made a choking noise. The Canon twitched, amused, though hardly mollified. It's all very well, he was thinking, but if this gets out it *will* look extraordinary—especially so soon after Evensong ... He bent his head round gradually and there, sure enough, was the lank representative of the *Courier* scribbling it all down.

'Do you remember what you talked about as you played?'

'Archaeology,' replied the Canon promptly. 'Mr M'Tooley was very keen, as you know.' This was a reference to the fact that Mr Elgin, the coroner, also belonged to the High Suffolk Archaeological Society and since Mr M'Tooley's presence had been a familiar one at all the Society's digs, excursions and meetings, Mr Elgin must have known him quite well and that his present manner of speaking of him as total stranger was both irritating and uncalled for. 'We discussed the possible opening of the Parham tumulus, I remember. M'Tooley said he thought . . .'

'Did you discuss other members of the staff?'

'What——? Er, no; of course not. We were in the Common Room.'

'You were all together ... I see ...'

'Oh no; we weren't,' said the Canon hurriedly. 'I merely meant to explain that it isn't our custom to—well—er—gossip in the Common Room.'

But Mr Elgin by-passed this faint rebuke. It was the earlier part of the Canon's statement which intrigued him.

'Then, Canon. I am wrong in believing that *all* the staff *were* present?'

The Canon was astonished. 'Quite wrong. Who is maintaining that it was?'

'Oh nobody. But I have been left with that inference.'

The Canon was waspish. 'Through no fault of mine, I assure

you. And, anyway, I have always understood that inference was something one was more likely to gather than be left with.'

Mr Elgin regarded the room with brown, sad, puppy eyes, in a silent appeal that recriminations, even where they were mildly justified, should be dropped. It was a wretched affair this, and the sooner it was dealt with and filed away the better.

'All I wish to say, Canon, is that until this moment I have continued to believe that when Mr M'Tooley went up to bed early he left all of you still sitting in Common Room and that was the last any of you saw of him. But in fact he only said goodnight to Mr Winsley and yourself—is that it?'

'That is correct.'

'In which case you will agree with me that you may not have been the last persons to see him alive?'

At this point, armed with Bateson's agonised permission to speak given by his raising his eyebrows to a fantastic height and pursing his lips grimly, Richard said, 'Excuse me . . .' only to be frustrated by Mr Winsley's lengthy explanation of what 'rounds' were and that it was Mr M'Tooley's night for making them and that so far as *he* knew they had been made quite properly and, although it was still moderately early, no boy had encountered Mr M'Tooley as he went from room to room, quietly fixing doors and windows and seeing that all was safe.

'Mr——?' the coroner asked after this rigmarole. 'You wished to add something?'

'Brand—Richard Brand. Yes. I think that we, Mr Bateson and myself must have been the last people to speak to Mr M'Tooley.' He looked round to see if Bateson approved of this way of committing themselves. Bateson, from his seat on what seemed to be a municipal version of a small plush throne, moved his head scarcely perceptibly. Richard went on to describe the meeting near the church and their dull and unremarkable talk and last of all, the unambiguous and quite ordinary manner in which they had all said goodnight.

It was Mr Winsley and not the coroner who took exception to all this and he was furious. Up to five minutes before he had been congratulating himself on the superior way he had conducted himself and forced the others to conduct themselves in the whole affair. In his own mind he had even contrived to reduce the tragedy to manageable proportions. It was a retirement of sorts, he told himself. There was no one to blame, least of all M'Tooley, for the extreme tact of whose withdrawal from scenes he had found untenable, Mr Winsley had nothing but the profoundest admiration. No mess, no fuss; an enigma of human behaviour to which heaven alone had the answer, an answer which, so far as he was concerned, heaven was welcome to keep. There was altogether too much prying into things these days. An affair as regretful as this should slide away into decent obscurity. The number of questions already asked had surprised him. He had always understood that in a matter like this an inquest was more of a formality than anything else. After all, there was the doctor's report and the police statement. Wasn't that enough? What had Brand's bicycle ride to Sheldon to do with it? And why did that filthy little man from the local paper have to gobble up every syllable with his nasty chewed pencil and stare at them as though they were murderers? One good thing about Herr Hitler was that his government exercised some guidance over what should be put into the newspapers.

'And you returned to Copdock School about halfpast-six?'
'About then.'
'So in fact you had been absent the entire day?'
'I had been absent the entire day.'
'Please don't repeat my words. Just confine yourself to "yes" or "no".'
'Sorry.'
'That's all right.'
'Then you went out again, this time drinking with Mr Bateson?' Mr Elgin said 'drrrinking' and the reproachful stare from his mournful eyes made it no secret that his duty alone obliged him to stir up this nest of vice, and nothing else.

'We did have a drink—at Stokely.' Richard was aware of Bateson's wholehearted, though mute, approval as he said this.

This time it was Mr Elgin's turn to apologise.

'I'm only trying to get a fairly complete picture of the evening,' he said. 'Where did you say you drank? Which public-house, I mean?'

'Stokely. It's called *The Case is Altered.*'

Richard, without looking round, knew that Bateson was

staring hard at the coroner as he said this, in an effort to discover if the name conveyed anything beyond the fact that it described just a small village inn where anyone might have gone for a talk and a pint. It was much more than this, of course. Bateson had heard quite enough of *The Case*'s reputation not to have been surprised at what had happened, only a sense of justification. He recalled how grateful he had been that rumour hadn't lied; to that gratitude he could now add further thanks—rumour hadn't spread either. It was quite obvious as he looked at the faces of Mr Elgin and Mr Winsley that they were both very willing to invest *The Case is Altered* with a folksy innocence and see it as a rural tavern with roses round the door.

Mr Elgin passed on quickly to the last few questions. The entire affair, so far as he could see, persisted in being undramatic. Nothing had come of the investigation except everybody giving their account of Mr M'Tooley's mild eccentricities. These little quirks when they were added up still did not constitute even one complete side of his nature. They were the harmless, unhideable extremities of a confused nature. Everybody knew of them and so when the Canon spoke of Mr M'Tooley's habit of going into Retreat for part of the Easter holidays—a thing which struck the Canon as fantastic—or Mr. Winsley of his bizarre enjoyment of jazz, records of which he played on an ancient gramophone and was even reported to dance to by himself in the solitariness of his room; of his refusal to speak of a translation of Catullus, a brilliant piece of work undertaken in his youth which still sold and had produced for him year after year a sprinkling of meagre royalties and his air of overwhelming self-sufficiency which had made it so impossible to offer him anything, whether it was in the realm of help or affection; they weren't really adding to a fuller account of Desmond M'Tooley, but giving hackneyed repetition to facts already famous. Desmond Vincent M'Tooley, aged fifty-one, of Copdock House School, Stourfriston, Suffolk, with motives that remained reticent, had plainly killed himself. There was no mitigating madness and Mr Elgin unwillingly returned a verdict of *felo-de-se*. Then they all rose and went out into the beautiful sunshine.

The varieties of human experience, when they press too

hard upon each other, are inclined to bring about a hankering for nice dull ordinary things and good plain company. Friends who, although not cast off, have had to take fourth or fifth place to the latest excitements, are welcome again. After all, old friends *are* old friends if only because of their power to put up with occasional cavalier treatment. Their thread of love can be dropped for a week or a month or a year. Any pain they might feel in the first place is soon compensated by the conviction that they are good, yet neglected, and so in a way, martyrs.

Mary had not yet thought herself into the martyr stage. Goodness was one of the things about herself she found vaguely hypocritical. But she genuinely and desperately felt herself neglected. She would have been greatly comforted if she could have known how much Richard longed to be with her at that moment. He needed her presence to drive from his mind a horribly-swelling suggestion that the world was some sort of distorting glass and that wherever he looked he would only see what was defective or inharmonious. Famous, gifted people like Sir Paul Abbott were at heart miseries, tarts were prigs, Bateson was a lout and as for Copdock, his coming there was like taking a header into polluted water in which unspeakable odds and ends drifted, some of them, like the death of Mr M'Tooley, actually entangling him in a situation which was pitiful, yet at the same time disgusting, and which he resented.

Outwardly, however, he was tremendously polite. He walked along between the Canon and Mr Winsley feeling remote and detached. Bateson kept pace beside them in a rather deliberate way, his tilted face and the stiff, absorbed, leggy manner in which he moved reminiscent of a borzoi. The Canon was thinking: well, *that's* over. Then, as he thought of Richard: poor boy, *that's* a good start to a new post! And poor M'Tooley, of course!—who had, after all, done his best towards exonerating them all from entertaining guilty self-accusations where he had been concerned. Did not everything in his destruction point to it being a purely private matter? His death was stoical, as had been his life. We are *not* to blame ourselves, reflected the Canon, although this did nothing to dispel a conviction that so far as himself was concerned, he may have contributed to Mr M'Tooley's distress by not listening to everything he said. 'Yes, yes,' he used to say, and when Mr M'Tooley went on too long about Premonstratensians and Cluniacs. Even, 'Yes, yes, yes, yes.' It had not been kind. The Canon felt a tinge of remorse.

Gulls flung their thrilling whiteness against the sky.

'Must be rough in your part of the world,' Bateson remarked self-consciously because he felt that somebody had to say something.

'You find Lafney cold, Brand?' enquired Mr Winsley with elaborate courtesy. His small pointed feet went tip, tip, tip, over the coagulated snow. Without waiting for an answer and looking straight ahead, he said: 'I have heard from the Vicar of St James-the-Less, Mr Ilif—'

'Father Ilif,' said the Canon.

'Father Ilif, of course—thank you, Canon, and there is I am happy to say no question of there being any difficulty about the—er—funeral. I mean it will be a proper one. The entire school won't need to be there, of course. But the Sixth might be present. Bateson, you will go: myself, the Canon . . . Miss Bellingham, I suppose . . .'

'Oh, will Miss Bellingham be going?' Richard was so surprised that the question burst from him before he could stop it. The idea of her leaving her room, especially after all the recent talk of her being so ill, struck him as apocalyptic.

'You won't be I'm afraid, Brand,' said Mr Winsley evasively. 'Someone will have to be left in charge. The service will be at eleven. The best thing will be to have everybody together in Big School—but we can discuss all this another time.'

'Oh, yes.'

'There is one other thing, Brand,' said Mr Winsley slowly. They had walked a little ahead of the others and were almost to the huge Victorian front door of Copdock, where Darwin was blackleading the scrapers and breathing on a massive brass plate which announced the school and Miss Bellingham's credentials—*Miss Freda Bellingham, M.A.(Oxon.), D. Litt., Principal.* 'Morning, Darwin. Yes, it's this eternal question of succession—a heartless one, you might think to raise at the present moment—but even when we mourn we may not slacken! Life goes on, Brand. We must have a little talk about your geography. It was one of the subjects you put in your application, wasn't it?'

'Yes, but . . .'

Mr Winsley mistook diffidence for delicacy Also he felt a great need to clear himself of the last traces of his indebtedness to Mr M'Tooley . . . 'You would be surprised, Brand, how many people leave their jobs with the unalterable opinion that now that they have, er—departed, it will be impossible to replace them. I'm not saying this of poor Mr M'Tooley, of course. He and I were great chums—great chums! But I like to think of life as a pail of water—just a picturesque description, you understand, to point my particular philosophy—into which one thrusts a finger. The water rises, but do you see it? Hardly. You take your finger away and what happens? Nothing. The surface is left cold and blank and—er—impressionless. So it is with us—with all of us. Our vanity mustn't deceive us into believing that we leave our mark.'

'I don't quite agree . . .'

'What?'

They had reached the hall, which seemed to be full of telegrams.

'I mean that if you carry humility to the point in your story, it really isn't humility any longer. It's pessimism. Or that is what I should call it.'

The narrow gold rims to Mr Winsley's spectacles flickered with a peculiar animus of their own. The small whitening tuft of grizzled hair showed wet at the roots when he removed his hat. He was getting angry and trying not to be, a familiar dilemma for him, but a dilemma all the same. He had never been able to get the better of these miserable little spurts of temper.

'Better pessimism than *conceit,* Brand!'

And seeing Richard's bewilderment.

'Oh, say no more now. This morning—the whole week, if it comes to that—has been too much for us.'

'That's all right, sir.'

It wasn't all right. In fact it was most unfortunate. Mr Winsley turned cerise. His eyes, much magnified, became brilliant with the huge hauteur of small men.

'*I* am not apologising to *you,* Brand.'

The Canon and Bateson, sensing a row, made an elaborate business of wiping their feet. Mr Winsley, taking small, slow steps, disappeared. Richard would have hurried away as well but just as he was about to do so the Canon put out one of his fat white hands, which looked so much like milk-fed chicken's flesh, and drew him towards the drawing-room. With the other hand he propelled Bateson. 'Come in here,' he said pacifically. Then, while struggling with the sherry bottle in which, like dole from a fairy purse, there were always just about three drinks and never more, he added, 'We're hardly likely to help one another at such a sad time if we let ourselves get distraught, are we! Brand, dear boy, do you see another sherry glass anywhere—I always thought there were six—a mistake obviously. Well never mind. Have yours in this.' He slopped a finger of wine into a small tumbler from which he had evicted a few late snowdrops. 'Come to think of it, Brand, I *do* recall your dear father now. You remember how at first I thought we could not have met? Well we did and it was at Lacey-King's last archi-deaconal at Bury in 'twenty-seven'. Could it have been Admiral Crawford who introduced us?'

'He was dead by then.'

The Canon passed one well-kept old white hand slowly over the back of the other and produced a dry papery sound. His too-kind gaze travelled from Richard to Bateson and then to the window. A complicated piece of farm machinery was being towed slowly by. The room darkened, the windows jerked and throbbed and an intense forlornness draped itself damply over the sofas and chairs like antimacassars.

'And your dear lady mother, Brand, she is well?'

'Oh quite—thanks.'

The Canon slid the sherry between his teeth and said, 'She will be delighted when she hears of the improvement in your position.'

'I don't know that she will be "delighted",' said Richard. 'It's not as if I'd achieved anything. It's not even certain that I'll have the House anyway, not with Mr Winsley in his present mood.'

'But you would like it . . .?' Canon Ribbs insisted gently.

'Why do *you* teach?' Bateson asked suddenly. He didn't even attempt to disguise the unfeeling note in his voice.

The Canon was caught off guard and replied in an over-jolly manner, 'What's this you're asking, Bateson? Why do I teach? Now if you'd asked me a question like that in the ordinary way I might have been able to answer you. But your question isn't ordinary, is it . . .? You don't want my reasons, but my motives. That's it, isn't it? Well, dear boy, I'll tell you something—something I have always believed to be absolutely true. It is that our motives are our own—providing they are noble, of course. They are the well-head of our actions and so of our happiness.'

'Our unhappiness, too,' said Bateson, remembering Mr M'Tooley.

'I shall agree with you there, Bateson, although all this is not answering your question, which is, "why do I teach?" Shall we say that I teach because I have a weakness for inculcation? It is hardly a hidden weakness . . . you are seeing it now!' The Canon smiled broadly, revealing his beautifully preserved incisors, strong and long and the colour of watery gold.

'Well, you're lucky,' Bateson said shortly. 'I came to the conclusion long ago that I can't teach and never will. I might provide a sort of pattern to mimic, but that's about all.'

'Exactly,' insisted the Canon enthusiastically. 'You say "mimic" because you are modest, dear boy. Oh yes you are!' he repeated somewhat coyly, though Bateson had shown no sign of refusing the compliment. 'Why, your work here has been simply splendid, simply splendid . . .'

Annoyed and embarrassed, Bateson retorted, 'Well *I* don't think so.'

'Of course not,' the Canon snuffled. The pink skin just above the corners of his mouth expanded reminiscently. 'I remember once being asked to Church House by dear Randall Davidson. It was just after my "Pulpit Attitudes" had made its own little stir in the world—oh long before your time—Yes, what is it, Lindsay?'

'It's Miss Bellingham, sir.'

'Yes?'

'She would like to see you.'

'Me, Lindsay? Now?'

'Yes, sir. You and Mr Winsley as soon as possible.'

The Canon concealed his pleasure.

'Are you to take an answer back to Miss Bellingham?'

Lindsay may not have heard this. He was affecting what he considered to be a becoming languor, one hand against the door-post, and his eyes fascinated by the dirty turkey-work carpet. Then he looked up suddenly, which was the other part of the game, the brilliant darkness of his gaze all set to bewilder the Canon. But the Canon had turned and was busily gathering together all the notes he had taken for the inquest and the full force of Lindsay's ambiguous amusement ricocheted and struck instead the astonished Bateson, who blushed a complete and even damask. Lindsay blanched and fled.

'Odd boy,' said the Canon, missing all this. 'Why on earth he couldn't wait for an answer I don't know! It means I shall have to trail up all those stairs. Where was I? What was I saying . . .? Oh yes, Randall Davidson. What a shame. It was an incident that would have illustrated my point perfectly. Never mind. It will keep, I suppose. Look, why don't you both come along and have a bite at the Rectory soon? Do.' At the door he turned and said, 'If you can squeeze anything more out of that bottle, *do*.'

'You'll take it, I suppose?' said Bateson, when they were alone.

Richard hesitated. 'What would it mean?'

'I think she gave him three hundred.'

'I could hardly expect that; not straight off.'

'Oh for God's sake do stop being so damned considerate. You'll have to do poor old M'Tooley's work won't you? Put your hand out and keep it out. Incidentally, have you noticed anything peculiar about Lindsay?'

'Lindsay? No. Why?'

'Oh nothing. How about another little trip to "The Case"?'

★

Sometime between Tuesday and Thursday Mr M'Tooley's body was smuggled out of Copdock House and taken to a small chapel at the undertakers. On Friday he was buried. The boys maintained an aloof and incurious silence about the whole business. Their instincts were those of animals when it came to death. They clung together in little romping groups, carefully averting their minds from the horror and keeping well out of the way of all the various officials connected with it. They were neither shy nor respectful. They were disgusted. On the day before the funeral, when the snow had quite gone and the roads were disclosed in strips of an unbearable liquorice blackness, a barrel-organ played with wild merriment in the street below Big School. That same evening Mr M'Tooley's relations began to arrive. Darwin showed them into the drawing-room. Mr Winsley, receiving them, thought how strange it was that in all the years he had worked with Desmond M'Tooley he had never gained the remotest idea of his background. Being basically uncharitable he had decided that it must either be a necessarily apologetic one, or because Mr M'Tooley was unmarried, he must also be unrelated. The distinction of the mourners, however, obliged him to amend both conclusions. And Mr M'Tooley himself, bolstered up on the formal regret of his family, regained a little of the respect of which the manner of his death had deprived him. The M'Tooleys didn't seem to mind very much. Under the lantern in the hall they made loud neighing 'goodnights' and went off quite equably to the local Trust House, where beds had been booked for them. None of them asked to see Mr M'Tooley's room and one of them, a Dr Osmund M'Tooley-Browne more than implied that it was a pity that his nephew had done away with himself in January since it was not the best of months to come from County Cork. Had it been May he might have combined his respects with a short tour of the Suffolk Wool churches, which he had long desired to see. On Friday it rained steadily, so Miss Bellingham didn't go to the funeral. Everybody else did, however, including nine of the older boys. Lindsay stayed behind to help Richard keep order in Big School. They sat side by side on the dais, Richard, depressed rather than sad, and Lindsay, narcissistically reading his own name and achievement over and over again on the scholarship board and thinking how pleasant it was to be eighteen and clever and going to the University. Rain spattered and stung the windows. Lindsay heard it and thought it utterly delightful. The whole school read or wrote solemnly.

At six Miss Bellingham sent for Richard and offered him Mr M'Tooley's house. Unlike Mr Winsley, she didn't seem to expect any particular demonstration of gratitude, but appeared relieved to have settled the matter. Her only comments on Mr M'Tooley himself were surprising but brief.

'He died ages ago really.'

'A great deal has certainly happened since Sunday,' Richard agreed.

'You don't seem to understand me. I mean ages—actual years, if you like.'

'Oh—I see . . .'

She twisted her old, elaborate head and took a quivering glance and said rather grudgingly, 'Why I believe you do!'

'What you are actually saying is that something died in Mr M'Tooley a long time before . . .'

'That's a fault!' Miss Bellingham cried in a claiming way, like somebody winning a point in a game. 'It's a horrible didactic thing you all have! Thank God I was born in an age which traded in nuances and not in amateur psychology! How did you get on with Pauly?'

'Very well indeed. We made a good start with the library.'

'Sheldon's frightfully pretty, don't you think? Was it all muck and dust? I shouldn't wonder. The Penchants are a rubbishy couple.'

'No. It looked remarkably straight.'

'Shall you be going again soon?'

'We arranged every Sunday, except those on which I have tables-duty. I was going to ask you, will my—will this change cause any difficulty?'

'Why ever should it!'

Miss Bellingham rose from her chair and trailed across to the window, miraculously supported on her tiny feet. 'Do your best,' she said. 'Get what you can out of Sheldon—don't hesitate. Those places only exist for the pickings. Tell Darwin I want my milk.'

He was nearly out of the door when she demanded, 'Don't you know how much more you are going to get? Caddie and I have been talking and we think—two-twenty.'

Richard felt a reckless anger spurting through him in swift indignant flames. He longed to be absolutely gross, to shout at her, 'two-bloody-twenty!' and then stare at her astonishment. Except, of course, there wouldn't be any astonishment. His fury with her meanness—all of their meanness, because the whole set-up groaned with the words scrimp and scrape— would have no effect upon her whatsoever. Neither had his momentary bewilderment. 'It's an ill wind . . .' she reminded him, which was true enough. A week ago a change in his job would have been unimaginable. He wrote to Mary, hesitating between her and his mother because of feeling the need only to say something on paper;

My dear,

Now this really is the limit. What do you think? I've succeeded poor old M'T.—you will have seen all about that in the local rag I expect. I won't go into it now—and have become a 'housemaster'—except of course there isn't a house! It's the same job with knobs on, one of the knobs being £220.

How are you? Is Mrs Crawford any better? I do hope so. Our snow has gone and what is even better, the wind has shifted from my side of the school for the first time since I came here.

I can't help thinking of our funny afternoon in the museum —by funny I mean strange. There is something else: I have a need for you. Oh, not when I'm 'down' or anything like that. In fact absolutely the opposite. Unlike most people, it's when I'm cock-a-hoop that my judgement goes. When I'm depressed I'm ghastly sane. This sounds rather mean, as though I'm attributing you with the qualities of a wet blanket, which is miserable rot. Could it be because of all these old fogies who have (here 'us' was heavily scratched out) me in their clutches. Fogey number one is out of favour you may be pleased to know, though not me with *her*. I still get all her tittle-tattle and advice, not to mention her questions. God! her questions . . . Wanted to know who you were. I had a brainwave. I said (read the next bit slowly, lento . . . len . . . to . . .) '*my fiancée.*' The Belle said absolutely nothing at all. Just sat rolling her eyes left-right, right-left like a dreadful old doll. It was a terrible fib, but it needn't be. What do you think?—beyond this being the coolest proposal since Friga's. But it is this coolness, this marbly commonsense which is *my* proof. In spite of all the poetry to the contrary I'm not at all so sure that love should be a form of enthusiasm—or enthusiasm a form of love, if it comes to that. Dearest, I shall be home at half-term for a whole day some time the week after next, Thursday I think, although it hasn't been settled yet, when I shall press upon you the advantages latent in a cold and calculating heart. I have done one or two pretty silly things lately. They would disgust you by their being just this. Let's get all this off our chests when we meet. I feel it should all be *talked*.

Conversely, a note from Quennie—you know, brief, smart and Italianate. Everybody says, 'what beautiful handwriting your brother has . . .' Of course he has. Everything Quentin does has to be beautiful; it's really rather horrible. For instance he enquires, quite beautifully, 'what *did* happen to your poor Mr M'Tooley? The *Times* account is so sketchy.' You may have noticed how Quennie reads a paper; like someone taking a dose of salts. He gulps it all down, then shakes because it's so beastly! Pretends he isn't a bit interested in Sir P. 'Have you done your dusting at Sheldon? I've just got hold of *Miss Trembath's Revenge* and, my dear, it's *so* boring. The utterest bosh, not to say pastiche.' I couldn't disagree because I haven't managed to read this recent-ish Abbott, but Quennie can't be quite right because D. MacCarthy was tremendously praising. Talking of reading, Mummie has just sent me a thing called *Gone with the Wind* and I can't put it down, as they say. Nor for that matter can I pick it up—not without bracing myself. It's ten million words long at least. Good though. You'd like it.

Tomorrow to the Corn Exchange to learn how to fit gas masks. Bateson's supposed to be coming with me. He's always rather fascinated by this sort of thing. I'm not, needless to say.

Don't forget, don't be conclusive about anything in this letter until we have talked. Thursday week, I think, but I'll let you know.

Bestest love,
Richard.

14

It must have been in March that people whose duties in the world were of the most ordinary kind became finally convinced that a time limit had been set even upon ordinariness. The days were tightening up. However there was a quite frightening absence of despair, and history will carry the curious imprint of a civilized continent observing with a fatalistic leisureliness the unhurried protocol of a magnificent summer. The spring, too, was glorious. There was a correctness, a rightness in every flowering day, in the way the swallows swung in dark arpeggios all along the telegraph wires, in the prolific pear blossom and in the blameless skies. There was, everywhere, a dogged determination to be graceful, to enjoy the current hour and to cock a summery snook at Nemesis. Fairytale state visits were arranged. The Lebruns, endearingly stolid and looking like the proprietors of a thoroughly-recommended family hotel, arrived in London to drive in carriages with the King and Queen to Covent Garden, where Constant Lambert conducted *The Sleeping Princess*. The King and Queen fulfilled to perfection their mannered rôle and, seen against the politicians and the dictators, were like Hilliard figures who had somehow wandered into a Breughel beanfeast. They assumed a vivid quintessence of human dignity and contrived to be prim and brilliant, urbane and gay all at the same instant. While Hitler, who was fifty, was identifying himself with the image of Alexander, these two small glittering figures were forced to carry the hopefulness of half the world.

Paris, Prague, London and Rome had never looked so beautiful. Even Berlin, perennially festooned as it was with snaking black banners, presenting a neo-Edwardian vista along the banks of the Spree which was not without its charm. It hardly ever rained. People danced a good deal. There was a positive attitude to pleasure, yet no wildness, no hedonism. Perhaps there was an elegant fatalism like this when the legions withdrew. Perhaps there was the same kind of thankfulness then when a day closed without a glimpse of the hurrying horde.

The Government did all they could with what they had, and nobody suspected how little that was. The tension had a peculiar effect on the weather. It was warm blue and gold for day after day, but however hot it became, the mood for the whole year was that of a fine autumn. Melancholy was seeded by the sunshine and crept gently into every action.

Mrs Crawford, who all through March had been getting more and more agitated by the way things were going, decided on the second of April that she was better and would get up. She took great care to make it clear that it was a feeling of duty and not any great improvement in her health which allowed her to do this. Her first action was to look out the little inlaid box in which she had stowed away her V.A.D. insignia in 1919. The badges and clips and epaulet things were now heaped on the tray on her dressing-table. She fondled them as lovingly as other women might fondle pearls. All the newspapers were spread open at the Bip Pares kind of map which has pincer arrows and ominous shading. Mr Yockery found it a terrible trial to have his Crockford-y gossip buried under appallingly well-informed explanations of the Polish Corridor, Memel, the strategic importance of Tirana and other such information. Smirking feebly to excuse his inattention, he turned his thoughts to such genuinely important things as whether the re-establishment of pre-Reformation *mensae* was really a good policy, or whether the Faculty ought to discourage the practice; whether the porch roof was worth re-crenellating, or whether it might crumble into the responsibility of his successor. All the A.R.P. pamphlets, the government white-papers etcetera which Mrs Crawford passed on to him, he thrust straight into the tortoise-stove in the vestry.

Mrs Crawford had put on a good deal of weight in the nine weeks she had been in bed, but other than this she was much her old self. Her skin had tightened and was a polished dullrose colour. Her eyes swam brightly through one or other of her lorgnettes. Hibble, ever quick to appreciate the changing conditions of her employment, now began to hover behind Mrs Crawford like a cringing A.D.C.

★

Miss Bellingham on the other hand, now that there was not the least possible doubt of there being a war, shrank and decayed visibly. 'I have come to the end of Time', she thought as the international fears multiplied. And this was true indeed where her world was concerned. Limping on for twenty or so years after its first dreadful bludgeoning, it was now to receive its *coup de grâce*. The sheer certainty was too much for her. Somehow she'd dragged herself on through the poor crippled decades of the twenties and thirties, hanging on grimly to what she believed in, the tatters and scantlings of her culture. But now that even these were to be swept away she felt she had no energy left to even contemplate the bravest of brave new worlds. She stopped listening to the news on the London Regional programme and asked that the *Manchester Guardian* should no longer be brought up to her. And Mr Winsley, watchful as a pullet, noted dismally that the old gleam of interest, not to say interference, no longer pierced through the grey cataracts of her vision. Her eyes would follow him as he fidgeted about her room. On and on he would elaborate, plans, plans, plans. And it would always end up with her saying, 'Do what you like. For God's sake, Caddie, do what you like!'

'I don't think you even try to listen,' he accused her wrathfully one day, after he had dwelt at length on his pet theme of having only two houses in the School, and so making it unnecessary for them to appoint a successor to Mr M'Tooley, and hence saving a clear three hundred pounds.

'I'm certainly not hanging on your lips, Caddie, if that's what you mean.'

'Then you really don't have any objection to young Brand being put in charge of Montessori and Bloomfield?—Incidentally, we shall have to drop one name. I suppose it will have to be Bloomfield. What do you think?'

'It's more what does Mr Brand think, isn't it?'

She jabbed away at her hair provokingly.

'It's nothing to do with Brand at this stage is it?'

'How you snap, Caddie,' Miss Bellingham said. 'You are getting a snapper! And you're looking awful. Don't you get your sleep?'

'I'm all right,' he said furiously. '*Please,* Freda; can't you just let me know what you really think about all this? It's really most frightfully important.'

At this Miss Bellingham released her broad dark smile and let the seconds tick themselves away before she replied. When the silence had been stretched to the limit of Mr Winsley's exasperation, she said, 'He won't do.' She said it quite simply, enjoying the confusion three such small words set up.

Mr Winsley tilted his pallid, naked face until his eyes lost focus in their bewilderment. Then he grew as indignant as he could be. Memories of earlier tussles came back to him, and of little victories in which he had worsted her. Why should she be making it difficult for him now? What was her game? She hadn't raised the least objection for instance when he'd switched all the classrooms round—and he'd known the time when it would have been as much as anyone's life was worth just to shift a desk. Then it was only last week that she'd ordered him not to bring the accounts up to her, but to get on with them himself. If she was willing to trust him that far, why should she mind him calling Brand a housemaster, particularly when she knew the title meant absolutely nothing anyway.

'He's not—not good enough? Is that what you mean?'

She pretended to consider. 'Not really. Although it's not his actual worth which I'm taking into account.'

'What then?' He tugged one of the buttony heart-shaped chairs round and crouched down on it. I shall have to keep calm, he was telling himself. Perfectly, perfectly calm. There'd been precedent enough for her obstinacy before, Heaven knew! He opened his fingers in a fan. 'Take the pros,' he said. 'One—' He tucked in his thumb.

'Start with the cons,' Miss Bellingham demanded. She held up her own hand and it fluttered weakly like a rag. 'One. He's too young—*miles* too young!'

'M'Tooley was only twenty—'

'Get Desmond out of your head, Caddie. If you'll forgive my saying so, working on comparisons has always been your greatest mistake.'

'Very well,' Mr Winsley said, pointedly not taking offence. 'First his age. Brand is twenty-four, that is young I agree. And he's not brilliant. I agree again. But there is one very important thing we haven't mentioned. The boy can teach. I've watched him. I know.'

She waggled her head with insulting tolerance—the more so as she watched him trying to assert himself. She knew he recognised this aspect of her condescension, and that he had even found it flattering once. It was her technique of demoting people of their standing—particularly the standing they had in their own eyes—and sending them back to being gauchely charming creatures without a mind of their own. Mr Winsley fought to retain his dignity.

'Listen, Freda,'—fearing to sound over-peremptory, he had added her name as an afterthought—'look at it this way. We can go on with the boarders. You've said so yourself. But it isn't worth it, so wouldn't it be best to limit the intake to forty say—and only of prep age—then we could make up two houses—'

'Why two with only forty boys?'

'Competition. They would create a proper rivalry; some sort of loyalty pole . . .'

He was interrupted by a gust of her rough unobstructed mirth. 'Loyalty pole!' she shouted. 'Oh, Caddie, you are a funny boy!'

He had been rather proud of this term—he'd discovered it in *The Times Educational Supplement,* although it had settled long enough in his subconscious for him to regard it as his own—so now he was extraordinarily angry. 'You don't care about Copdock any more,' he accused her bitterly.

'How right you are,' Miss Bellingham declared. 'You're absolutely right, although we won't go into all that now. Let me see, it's Mr Brand we're discussing, isn't it?' She swung her eyes up to meet his, a gesture which in a young and beautiful woman would have been irresistible, but coming as it did from her, had about the same effect as if he'd got the glad-eye from a mummy. 'But before we go on, you really must understand, Caddie, I don't hate Copdock. Only a fool would hate something which had claimed the best part of their life. It would be too defeating. Oh, I *am* disappointed! I don't deny that. But even my disappointment's an historical affair. We don't have to kid ourselves about that surely! But, Mr Brand. Let's deal with him. How shall you treat him when I am dead—is that it? Next year, I take it, you'll be standing over my grave in the municipal cemetery whining, "Please, Freda , we want four dozen pencils from Rowney's and do you mind if we change Montessori back to Bloomfield because we're fightng the Italians".'

'Freda, please . . .'

'Very well,' she said, 'Mr Brand—although I actually call him Richard. There are quite a dozen good reasons why you shouldn't pin your hopes to Dick Brand.'

'You're going to tell me that he'll be called-up.'

'I wasn't, but he will. But can't you think of another reason?'

He blinked at her with his colourless uncomprehending eyes.

'You're not the only bidder, Caddie—Surely you don't think that?'

He pretended to her playfulness. 'I know! he's been offered some other job. That's it, isn't it?'

'You're getting warm. Pauly wants him.'

'What—?'

'Ah, so I have surprised you! Well haven't you ever heard of an amanuensis? They're so hard to come by it seems. They have to be more than a typist and less than a friend. Well, what do you say? Don't you think our Mr Brand is just the—ticket?'

Mr Winsley made small helpless gestures with his hands and rocked on the balls of his feet. 'Freda,' he said when he could, 'Freda, we have just got to get all this straight. Aren't we each looking at Copdock from different angles? Mine is that the School has a future. Yours seems to be that it has proved to be a failure.'

'Thank you, Caddie.'

'Oh, don't misunderstand me. *I* always did believe in you—never forget it. I have believed in you even more than you have believed in yourself. It is important to remember this,' he scolded, 'because it makes all the difference. You may, in your present mood of self-depreciation—I can't call it humility, Freda, because you know it wouldn't be true—you may think it right and proper to sit in this room and shrug your shoulders at your life's work. At *our* life's work, Freda! But you seem to forget the triumphs . . .'

He was about to catalogue these when she stayed him with a small forlorn gesture.

'Caddie, please; no speechifying. And while we're about it, no diversions either. Just let's be reasonable. Pauly's home. For good. He won't go off again, that side of it is all over. And he's obviously got to have some kind of secretary and he's met

Richard and got used to him, and they get on fine together, so why should *we* be unreasonable! Pauly says how about two-fifty and his keep, and I say perfect. And you would too, except you're too damn miserable to say anything. Also I'm not so sure the young man is cut out for schoolmastering anyway—in spite of what you think. If you're really set on rejuvenating Copdock the first thing you'll have to do is get hold of some qualified staff. Even the ironmongers will demand that. And while you're about it you'd better get old-ish men, because, whatever you say, there *is* going to be a war, then Bateson will go and what will poor Caddie do then, poor thing!'

Mr Winsley flopped back against his chair, drew his trousers up and showed black socks and porridge-coloured pants, spread his hands over his knees in the manner of someone making small headway with a difficult child, and said.

'Look, Freda, Let's put it this way. You—and I don't wish to sound presumptuous—you have made up your mind about the war. I haven't. So far as I am concerned it is just your latest and and worst hypothesis, although we'll allow it, if only for the sake of argument. Well, there's a war. So what? Is the Government going to wreck the educational system of the country by grabbing all the schoolmasters? Of course not. There will be deferments. Bateson will go—there has never been any doubt about that—but Brand will be sure to be deferred. Freda, do try and understand; I need Brand. You point out that he is unqualified. Well I've thought of all that. I've even done something about it. Canon Ribbs has been more than helpful. He's willing to coach Brand privately through an external degree.

'Is he. And what does Brand say?'

'He'll be delighted naturally.'

'Of course, of course,' she crowed. 'But you haven't asked him?'

'Not yet, no.'

'And this is what you would like me to tell Pauly?'

Mr Winsley looked relieved. 'It is the truth after all. Sir Paul is sure to understand.'

'No.'

'What?'

'I said no.'

'But you've got to explain, Freda.'

'Why have I "got" to do anything?'

He jumped to his feet. His lips worked, but no words came. His face grew white and damp as it always did when he was in a passion, and when at last he could speak he found he was almost shouting. Miss Bellingham put her hands to her ears, a roguish gesture she had correctly assumed he would find irritating.

'Why shouldn't you explain to Sir Paul?' he demanded. 'Just why shouldn't you! Why should I stand in this room listening to you being frivolous about things to which we have devoted our entire lives!'

'Frivolous . . . ?' she repeated slowly, so that the word carried a ribbon sound. 'How very strange! Speaking for myself, I can hardly think of a time when I was less frivolous.' She rocked her flaring white head to and fro, saddened, though not by his rage. 'And another thing,' she went on, 'just because I don't talk about it I don't want you to go away thinking that poor Dessy's dying was a little matter to me. A sort of disaster *en passant*. I felt it, Caddie. Horribly, truly; I felt it. I still do. Do you know why poor Dessy died? Shall I tell you? You think he was smothered in the gas, don't you! No, Caddie. Desmond M'Tooley was smothered by the overwhelming realisation of his own stagnation. Sometimes, Caddie, as I sit up here in this room—my nurse's room it was—I think I can smell the stench which comes from the dissolution of all our intentions. *Fine* intentions, Caddie—or have you forgotten? No matter. I write letters, I open books, I search for Brahms on the wireless. Sometimes I drink—though not as I used to in the old days. And why? Just to stave off the corruption, Caddie —that's all.'

She pulled herself up to an easier position and leant out of the chair towards him. Speaking softly and with less malice, she said, 'Promise you won't fly at me, Caddie—no, *promise* . . .'

His mouth warped into a little grin.

'First of all, you do know that it's yours, don't you? You aren't going to insult me by thinking of me as the sort of old woman who plays ducks and drakes with codicils are you? I said you should have it and so you shall. That is a certainty. Only it belongs to me until the day I'm carried out of it. *Then* it comes to you. Now I'll tell you what you should do—are you listening? When it comes to you, *sell it.*'

He started like a person who is nearer to the edge of a precipice than he had anticipated.

'Sell . . . *Copdock*?'

'Why not? Sell it and retire,' she advised brutally. 'You're sixty aren't you? Do you want to go on for ever?'

That did it. He turned on her with that feline indignation which could easily outstrip her own. She bowed her head under his torrential memories. At last they became too much for her and she broke in with,

'I sometimes wonder how you can lose your temper with me when you stand to lose so very much more . . .'

She had her satisfaction in seeing his anxiety work itself up to his collar, a dull red flush creeping out of his shirt and up to his hair-line.

'I have your word, Freda, you just gave it me,' he said shakily.

'I never thought the day would come when I'd ever be sorry for Minna,' Miss Bellingham said abstractly. 'But now I see that it would be quite easy for me to be. I think you are boring me.'

'I'm sorry—terribly, terribly sorry.'

'Let's leave it at that!'

'Very well.'

'And begin again. And don't imagine I'm bringing the subject up afresh just to be provoking. I have to make a decision —you understand? I've already kept Pauly waiting a whole week.'

'A week? You never said . . .'

'No, well, I've been thinking about it. You see, Caddie, *I* don't fly off the handle. I'm only mad; I'm not unreasonable.'

'What do you mean?'

'Exactly what I've been saying, That it would be the best thing for Mr Brand—call him that, shall we—more businesslike—far and away the best thing.'

He watched her expertly, estimating by all the little involuntary twitches and starts of her body just how far he dare go.

How much he could get away with. 'For Sir Paul . . .' he asked.

She drew herself up sharply at that.

'For Mr Brand, Caddie. surely.'

'You know, Freda,' he said, rather as if he were giving advice to a romantically-inclined fifth-former, 'there's not one of us who is not without his dreams. And for those of us who are old, there is the recollection of them. We all want, or wanted to be poets and painters. I did myself when I was at Oxford. Perhaps I never told you, but I read Meredith with the best of them and spent good money on German oleographs of the *Primavera* to hang above my fireplace. I also sent long verses in the manner of Lascelles Abercrombie to the New English—or was it the Savoy? I forget. But it was all a phase, although my pride hardly allowed me to admit it. Couldn't it be the same with Brand? Shouldn't we keep our heads? —Romanticism, Freda—it's so catching.'

'And Dessy? Was that romanticism?'

'Yes,' he answered slowly and consideringly.

'And me—I'm a romantic? Me, at my age?'

He plunged gallantly.

'You are the greatest romantic of us all, Freda!'

Then he began to sneeze and complain, whacking pocket after pocket in a desperate search for his hankerchief. 'My cold is much worse. I shouldn't be here, should I. You'll get it.'

'It's settled then,' she said surprisingly.

'Settled—what is?'

'Richard's future, of course! I take it that we're not likely to put anything in the way if he should like the idea of working for Pauly? And now you can set about getting a properly qualified man in his place and start running Copdock according to this new idea of yours!'

'What you don't seem to realise, Freda,' Mr Winsley said with enormous control, 'is what I could do without your knowing it. Just because I come to you with my suggestions—my hopes, if you like—it doesn't mean that I'm some sort of supplicant!'

She gave her loud, indecorous laugh and said, 'Hoity-toity!'

'It's true. You know it.'

'I've written to Pauly.'

He suppressed his indignation and replied in a thin cold tone, 'How many times have we not had this kind of conversation, Freda? How often have we not discussed every aspect of a subject only to discover at the end that there is not the faintest hope of your preconceived notions being swayed? Since you have written a letter to Sir Paul, why ask me about it. Indeed, why ask me anything!'

'Ah, but I haven't posted it. Shall I? That's the thing.'

'Do. Why not? You are obviously all out to cut the ground from under young Brand's feet. If you are determined to ruin him by pushing him in *that* direction. . . .'

'I'll not have innuendo from you, Caddie! I take it that by "ground" you mean this school?'

'Yes, this school,' he said very deliberately, feeling for the first time in his life that he was standing up for his own property. Suddenly there was no longer any need for him to think of her—of anyone. Copdock was his. His passion for it made it so.

She pursued him with waspish enquiries.

'What about his prospects, Caddie? Have you given any thought to them?'

He explained, but she wasn't listening. Pursuing her own line of thought, she mused aloud in a confused mumble in which he picked out, 'No—no; best for Pauly to ask him. Less peculiar if it comes from him. He could ask on Sunday. Richard could finish term at Easter. Let him off. More ordinary like that. Less collusive. Is that what I mean? No, not collusive at all. Where have my tablets gone to now? No? Blast. Caddie, where are my tablets?'

He handed them to her. They were on her cluttered little desk. 'And then?' he asked.

'Then what?'

'Our young Mr Brand will have to refuse, won't he?'

'Oh—why will he?'

'Because whatever his failings he doesn't happen to be a confidence trickster. What, apply for a post, get it, settle in—then throw it all up in a matter of weeks! No, Freda, our Mr Brand is hardly likely to do that! He'd be mad for one thing.'

'Never mind the madness,' she said. But the other things you mention—what are they?—only formalities. You might spoil your entire life just for the sake of doing what they call 'the right thing.' In fact, you would, Caddie; you're the type. No, *should* the question arise—you know, Brand thinking that he's letting us down—I shall make it absolutely plain that we are quite pleased for him to go.'

'He'll smell a rat,' Mr Winsley sneered.

'Why? Oh, I see,' she said, staring at him hard. He was frigid. 'I must be going, Freda. There are the reports to vet.' At the door he turned and added simply, 'Do let's see reason in all this.'

She observed him unblinkingly.

'Reason, Caddie—or your point of view?'

15

ON Easter Monday Richard walked the long way round from The Portway to Meridian House. The sea was massed in a solid cobalt wall tipped with coalers and minnow-like brigs. On a height stood St Prolixia's, its grizzled tower partly eclipsed by the Meridian catalpa tree. Gulls made white slashes in the even blue. Although it was warm, there were few holiday-makers braving the beach, Lafney not being the kind of place to be taken in by a premature brush with summer. The trippers who were sitting at all crouched in shelters, but most of them packed the small coffee-shops made resentfully busy by the Bank Holiday. A playful wind made sudden skirmishes from the east and cracked the bright canvas of abandoned deck-chairs like pistol shots. Feathery fleck stung Richard's face. There were two narrow look-out towers on the sea-wall. Midway between them, and walking slowly in his direction, he saw Mary.

'Hullo. I was just on my way. I suppose I'm late?'

She shook her head. 'No. Early if anything. No, I just walked. I somehow thought you would be coming the sea way.'

'Do you really fancy the marshes?'

'Is that what we said?'

'It is what you said.'

'I've changed my mind. Do you know what I'd really like to

do? I'd like to walk about in London through squares and side-streets—they're always deserted on Bank Holidays—Berkeley Street, or Chelsea. Or, better still, those rather shabby literary streets behind Kingsway. Just walk on and on calmly reading plaques and knowing nobody.'

'Would Ipswich do?'

'Ipswich? Oh, my dear . . . Ipswich!'

'Plaques and streets and strangers,' he reminded her.

'I wouldn't be so sure about the last. Anyway, it would mean ringing Mummy, who'll think it odd to say the least.'

They drifted vaguely away from the fall and the hush of the sea. The morning train from Liverpool Street rushed past the golf course and gave a long isolated whoop. The sun went in and the temporary nature of the sea's rash gaiety became at once apparent. *Luxe, calme et volupte* it had beguilingly suggested, but shallowly it proved. For only just beneath the sudden glitter were the cold, grey, workaday fathoms of the dull Northern waters. The North Sea is more than a waste; more than a barrier. It is the gigantic distillation of all European regret, a chilly waterway for the passage of even chillier doctrines. Its sound is negative. From the golden promontory of East Anglia to the desiccated coat of Scandinavia it mutters, 'no . . . thou shalt not . . .' Those who have lived by it for generations have perfected an aptitude for rejection. Its astringent winds are unforgiving and treat human carelessness unkindly. Its influence is just as strong as that of the Mediterranean, but in a reverse ratio. It has reined in the blood, checked enthusiasm and diluted the warm and compassionate Eastern faith to suit its own cool conventions. In its protestant strength it has become the exact complement to the tolerant southern waters; the icy bight against the lake of wine.

Geography has much to answer for. Usually when he was led to question things, Richard was inclined only to look within himself, but lately he had taken to seeing his personal problem stated in terms of air, bricks and mortar, dialect; the ingredients which made Lafney Lafney and set it apart from any other small seaside town with a pebble beach, three or four thousand inhabitants and a group of eccentrically segregated classes. Lafney, in fact, was beginning to have a closet-like effect on him. When he was away from it, it became a token of security. When he was home it almost suffocated him. The sea had always given him a rather thrilling kind of sadness. It had invented for him a melancholy which he'd welcomed at first, because it had seemed to him right at the time that anyone who wanted to write should also want to be a bit miserable. Now that he saw how ridiculous this was, he found that the sea-melancholy had become a habit too ingrained to break away from. To change his humour he would have to change his sea. Perhaps, he thought, taking a last look across the beach, it's too late. Where ever I live now I'll most likely be the same. Some people got away, adopting a climate, even if they still clung to their nationality. Sir Paul had, for although Suffolk born and bred, he had contrived to make himself as Italian as a Medici. There was not a drop of North Sea puritanism in Sir Paul's veins. Mrs Crawford could sneer how she liked about what she called 'arty expatriots', but she and her kind could never understand that amongst them, Sir Paul at least had been truly baptised back into a broader, more generous European culture. All of which reminded Richard how that ever since that first snowy Sunday in the white drawing-room, Sheldon had acted on him like intellectual yeast.

Mary saw that he was gravely eyeing her. They were near Boot's. An avalanche of holiday trifles; sunglasses, spools of film, soap, cosmetics, little brass ladies with clappers in their crinolines, indecent rubbery tubes and sepia view-cards spilt down in a flood. There was also a huge pile of gummed paper for people to stick on their windows to stop flying glass lacerating them if bombing began. Nodding her head towards this, Mary said,

'Every day is like a last day. Although I don't suppose such a thought occurs to most people. Look at them all laughing and eating buns! They're like stoics on a day-trip refusing to believe that the next queue they join will lead to destruction.'

'We're not in the queue then?' he asked, amused.

'I wish I could believe that we were not. But at least we give some thought to what is likely to happen.'

'Perhaps *they* aren't as unconscious as we imagine.'

'Oh they are, Richard—why you've only got to look at them!'

'To be honest, I don't given it much thought myself.'

She glanced at him obscurely. They had paused and were standing in the middle of the path, and the promenading holiday-makers were having to break their ranks and flow by on either side. The two of them made a sombre island in such a jolly river. The last half-an-hour had brought the last trainload in and all the residents out. The crowds jogged along, seeming to defeat enjoyment by the very effort they made to maintain it. In the gutter a trio of street musicians were playing 'One Day My Prince Will Come' on piano-accordions. A fair young man limped about and the pennies clanked grudgingly into his can. The mother-of-pearl facings on the instruments glittered and shone. Across the street, on the wall of the newly-erected cinema, a huge poster showed Anna Neagle, her cheeks bunched out on pads, in the film *Sixty Glorious Years*. A monoplane crackled boisterously in from the sea.

'Let's get away, if it's only for a day or two,' she said, plunging suddenly with something which had lain fallow in her mind for weeks.

Richard steered her out of the crowd before he replied, then he said, 'I have always been willing, darling you should know that. There are no, well, difficulties if you like, with me.'

'Do I make the difficulties then?'

'Not make. Have.'

They were descending the gritty Town Steps.

'My mother I suppose you mean? She's been ill. She had a slight stroke.'

'I know; I'm sorry.'

Mary hesitated at the verge of disloyalty to her mother, then said with a rush, 'It's been ghastly, Richard. Awful. Horrible! She insisted on staying in bed the whole winter. Then the news began to get worse and, well, she got excited about it and began to get better. You know what an old flagwaver she is. Well she got up and came down one morning just as though nothing had happened—and absolutely *full* of talk about A.R.P. and her organising this and that, and about it being such a pity that my father was dead. . . . Now there's a meeting of something or other at Meridian every day and although it's a quite terrible thing to say, I'm convinced that Mummy's just longing for the war.'

His fingers gripped her arm, guiding her through the crowd.

'How—how long have you got, Richard?'

'School starts again on the second.'

He was cautious and she noticed it. 'Then you're free till then?' she persisted.

He hesitated. 'Not quite . . . I did promise I'd go on with the work at Sheldon.'

'Oh——'

'It's only on Sunday,' he hastened to add. 'I can't quite expect Sir Paul to give up what he's doing just because Copdock's on holiday, can I?'

'Can't you? You weren't at Sheldon yesterday.'

'Only because yesterday happened to be Easter Day. I heard a rumour that the Belle was going over. You can imagine the fuss at Copdock if she did. She's not supposed to have stepped outside the School for the last ten years!'

'I suppose we do have to talk about her and Copdock?'

Caught slightly off his guard, he said resentfully, 'Sorry. Forgot you didn't like her. You don't, do you?'

'I've never even seen her, but I shouldn't think I'd like her from what I've heard of her. Or, if it comes to that, her me!'

'What would you say if I told you that she wants me to be Sir Paul's secretary?'

Mary stopped dead.

'You'd live there—at Sheldon?'

'Indeed I should.'

'And you're going to . . . ?'

'It's not completely fixed, but that's the idea. That is why I've got to see Sir Paul. To discuss it.' Misinterpreting her silence, he added, 'Wonderful, isn't it! And even if there is a war, a few months or years at Sheldon doing real literary work is going to help me a damn sight more than wasting my time at Copdock.'

Mary did not answer. It was all too unanswerable. Even more than his worldly blindness, Richard's feckless aptitude for slipping into other people's plans was beginning to make her feel sick. She didn't see that for him the serious times had not yet arrived, that his dilettantism—like all dilettantism—sprang from the belief that life hadn't really started and that there would be time enough and to spare to do all that he ought to do. But never *now*. It was always one day, some day. . . .

Risking his anger she answered, 'I shouldn't, Richard. I—I just shouldn't.'

He was heartily rude. 'You weren't asked,' he said.

She swallowed this and repeated quietly, 'I just shouldn't—that's all.'

They sank on a seat inscribed, 'G.R.—M.R. 1910–1935'. Now there was a positive indication of summer beating up momentarily from the warm oak slats and from the salty concrete. Litter—crisp-bags, cigarette cartons, bits of newspaper—was urged along by a ground-raking breeze. Far away the street musicians played the 'Minstrel Boy'. They sat near to each other, their need to be together overcoming their differences. A little gap existed between their bodies, but it was face-saving, fraudulent and merely emphasized the attraction they had for each other which was fastly resolving itself into something mindless and physical. Mary, feeling hollow and insubstantial, as though she had missed a meal, noted Richard's hands spread heavily, one on each thigh. He looked at the sea through screwed-up lashes. It was at that moment—she recalled it often afterwards, vividly and unmistakably—that her idea of marrying him died. And not even with grief, but more with a sense of limitless relief.

Richard on the other hand, driven on by what he thought was expected of him and by some simpler urgency, was thinking, 'what we have come to is sad mostly because we can't talk. All the time we fail to communicate. How could we put up with each other if we didn't talk?' Fatuously he said, 'Well, a penny for them?'

'Oh Dick . . .'

The gap vanished. For a second—people were in sight—her head touched his and his mouth pressed awkwardly against her temple.

'Oh my dear,' she said, straightening herself, 'you see what love does to me!' Laugh it off as she would, she still saw them, the Rectory children and herself on apoplectic ponies skirmishing down the gorse path to the beach in search of amber. She tried to shut all this out by concentrating on the swirl of spiral iron steps on the nearest look-out tower and the bunting snapping round the weather-boarded yacht-club. But what finally dragged her back to the present was a raucously cheerful voice saying,

'Of course you'll like her. What, Rube! She's one of the best! My friend Rube's ever such a good sort. One of the best is Rube . . .'

A thin girl was approaching, feverishly summery in a pink linen suit and clumsy white wedged-heeled shoes. There was a sailor with her and they were walking side by side with an obviously regretful independence, the sailor's shiny bland moon of a face was expressionless as it assessed the girl. Richard, looking up too at that moment, was startled to see Daphne coming towards him and staring straight at him. He saw the sailor's fat naked neck and the sailor's arm bumping tentatively against Daphne's flank. The arm was like the stuffed arm of a great toy in its hot serge sleeve. Daphne's body prinked and wriggled as she chattered. At the seat all their eyes met. For a split second Daphne gazed at Richard with what amounted to a cheerful wonderment as she sorted him out expertly from all those fellers and chaps of hers. Then, with the barest distension of her eyes, she indicated that she had managed to fix the name, the place and the occasion to him. He thought, oh my God, she's going to speak —But of course, she knew better than that. She had never been that kind of fool! She merely looked and saw, and the titillating effect the encounter had on her did not become apparent until she had gone some yards. Then, clutching at the sailor, she let herself go in a brief shriek of amusement—which the sailor must have taken for encouragement because when they moved on, his arm was bent round her waist in an inquisitive bolster.

'Well, and what was there so funny about us?'

'Us?' He pretended not to understand.

'I thought it was us.'

'Are we funny then?' he asked lamely.

'Not remotely at the moment I shouldn't have thought.'

'Then they must have been laughing at themselves.'

Mary said hmm! to that. 'Just look at them; I shouldn't think laughter was their emotion!'

'As a matter of fact I wasn't taking much notice,' he lied.

'Were you thinking of the school?'

He nodded. It was true in its way. He never quite stopped thinking of Copdock, and Copdock included the ancillary considerations of Sheldon and his own work. 'It's been rather a peculiar term one way and another.'

'It must have been. What . . . what really happened?'

'Oh, about poor old Mr M'Tooley do you mean? He gassed himself. Just that.'

'Did you get on with him?'

'Oh yes. Of course. Although he wasn't exactly a friend you know.'

'But you liked him?'

'Very much—we all did.'

'Then—then why?'

Richard shrugged. 'It was all in the newspapers. None of us knew any more than that.'

'I see. Poor man,' she said very gently, wanting to know more, but unwilling to run the risk of seeming too inquisitive. She didn't believe Richard. He was like Quentin, always so careful with information. Always content to let sleeping dogs lie. They both took precautions in getting their facts without making it look as if they rummaged for them. She sighed. This refusal to discuss things which Quentin and he cultivated stripped life of its intimacy. She loathed it. It was insulting, like offering her only an adaptation of his attention; the aspect of his attention he considered most suitable for her to understand.

They walked slowly back to Meridian past coach-loads of trippers being tipped into the market place.

'Quenny home, did you say, Richard?'

'No. He's staying with Munsen-Orle—you know, that funny friend of his. They're in London somewhere. As a matter of fact, we're all supposed to be rather fed-up with Quenny for not coming home for Easter.'

'Only supposed to be?'

'Uh-huh. In the same way that we're not supposed to be surprised if he manages to stay in Lafney more than four days together.'

Mary smiled and said, 'Poor Quentin! He's the kind of person one misses.'

'No.'

'No?'

'Good Lord, no. You don't *miss* people like Quentin. Even Mummy doesn't *miss* him. He's so—so detached. No that's not the word. So irrelative, yes that is what I mean.'

Somehow this vague talk of Quentin had the effect of drawing off their irritation with each other. He was a scapegoat and they dumped their differences on to him cheerfully. Meridian then came abruptly into view, filling up the end of the lane importantly with a panache of chimneys, finials and catalpa shadows. The clock on the church tower struck twelve noisily. Mary fiddled with her watch. She said, 'Hibble's away.'

'Hibble—away?'

'Well, and what's so odd about that? Hibble goes away every Easter Monday. She goes to see her sister.'

'Didn't even know she had a sister.'

'She has two, but one lives in Australia. The one she goes to see she describes as a "Norwich woman". Look, dear, forget Ipswich and London and all that nonsense. Let's be beautiful and rational. Come in and have a drink.'

Silence greeted them in the cold flagged hall. The silence was like a little fog, hard to breath in. When Mary called out 'Mother' the silence puffed itself up as if it was outraged.

'Perhaps *she's* gone to the back-streets of Kingsway.'

She glanced at him and saw that he was surveying himself in the pier-glass fixed to the huge branching hat-rack. Then she saw the note.

> '*Such a glorious day,*' it said, '*so Father Y. has persuaded me to take him to Long Melford (see church). Made up minds at last moment. Taken motor. Leave garage doors open so we don't have to get out. Back for dinner. Dinner better be scratch. M.*
>
> *P.S. Coastal Evacuation committee fixed for 22nd. Tell Edwina if you see her—tell her it's important. Fed cat.*'

She handed it to Richard, who said mockingly, 'Goodness, what gay sparks!'

'Would you like to have lunch in the garden?'

'Mad—and uncomfortable, but let's.'

'Hadn't you better telephone Edwina?'

'I left them with an impression of indefiniteness.'
'That's settled then.'
They went in the kitchen and she began to collect things. 'Apples,' she said, 'cold chicken, bread and cake. Cake? Well we'll take it anyway. And wine—I think there's something like half a bottle of Sauterne in that bottom cupboard. Cheese, apples—no, I said apples. What a mixture!'

New honeysuckle streamed off the stable roof. New grass lifted in the orchard and showed dull blue shadows. The wall corner they chose would have been stiflingly airless on a really warm day, but now it nursed a blissful patch of stillness under the wind. They sprawled on old punt cushions which struck colder than the grass. Plum blossom drifted against the torn white breast of the chicken and floated on the wine. The apples still had loft dust in the crevasses of their wizened skins and the spoons and forks soaked up the light and looked precious and rare.

When they were settled, Mary said, 'You must wonder why I didn't answer your letter . . . ? I couldn't, my dear. I had to see you first.'

'You didn't want to write, "no"?'

'I could not have *written* "no".'

'But you can say it. You are saying it. And do you know why you're saying it? It's because you don't want to give up all this!' He waved his arm to include the house and the trees and the small perfect stable-buildings. 'It's a kingdom. You're somebody here and if you gave it up all the local biddies would say that you were mad—particularly if you gave it up for somebody like me. And there is something else. You would be showing them all that you have it in you to love—and you have, you know!' he threw at her.

'Have I?' she asked wonderingly. 'Do you want me, Richard? Is it really myself that you are demanding?'

'It would mean that you must want me too.'

'It is something which has never been in doubt, has it?—Although you drag the admission from me whenever you can. Perhaps you have never quite believed me. You have certainly never quite trusted me.'

'That isn't true. If I doubt, I doubt myself. I can't see myself. Never have been able to. I am reflected in other people all the time. Sometimes I try to make up all these reflections into a whole me, but I can't.'

She tried to be casual. 'There's nothing to worry about in that. It is really rather a kind way to behave. Only a brute would want to blunder about the world not caring how his personality affected other people.'

Richard didn't answer. She watched his strong brown fingers crack open the pink joint of a chicken-leg. His nails glistened with fat and it occurred to her, grotesquely, how it was that the body could sustain its appetites when the mind was in turmoil. Poised between a fascinated revulsion and an intense tenderness she saw his teeth busy at the bone and the line of bewildered absorption in his almost closed eyes. For all this, she knew he tasted nothing. 'Then,' he said—and still capable, she noticed with unhappy amusement, of nicking away at the silvery white meat—'you won't—you can't marry me? Is that it?'

'How could we, Dick . . .'

'You won't!' He shrugged his shoulders violently as if he could slough kindness like a skin.

'It is only because I can't that I won't. You are too near to me. It's not your fault, but I can only see you out of focus. It's because we've been so close all our lives. There's no judgment. I'm too old to do anything without judgment now.'

This made him laugh.

'When was it you began to see me all blurred? Come on—you've got to tell me! At Christmas? The Martello Tower day? Don't tell me you were thinking in such terms then. You were way ahead of me if you were!'

'No,' she answered remotely. 'No, not then exactly. I saw myself that day. I counted myself up—arithmetically if you like. I had never done that before. I wanted to see what I was and if I dared love you.'

'And so now the grand total has proved too much for you? I was bizarre—excessive? In fact you found it in damn bad taste, because it didn't fit in with your life in this house and your being Miss Crawford of Lafney. You and your mother have both got along so well on the rationed out affection you've been used to that when the real thing comes along it only strikes you as vulgar! Why not admit it—you're happier as you are?'

'You seem to be forgetting that when I got the grand total, as you call it, I had to include, not only myself, but you as well.'

He caught at her full meaning. 'What is it that you know about me? I thought you said I was a blur? How have I become so transparent all at once?'

'Darling, you seem to think I'm searching for your failings. Can't you see it's your goodness which intrigues me?'

Happier now, he said, 'My *goodness*?'

They both laughed then, each willing to drag themselves free from this awkward analysis, but for different reasons. Their bickering had the effect of drawing them together. Some unconscious influence, perhaps the way in which they shifted to keep in the warmth of the weak April sun, brought their bodies round so that instead of sitting *vis-à-vis*, they made an angle of nearness at one corner of the picnic cloth. Like figures in a Giorgione landscape, they constituted a pulsating nearness, connected, yet untouching. Richard sprawled stiffly in half-profile. His legs made a long, indignant L away from Mary's drooping shoulders and the scrunched-up folds of her skirt sweeping around her on the grass. Her hands were pressed against the ground for support. Reaching out, Richard covered the hand nearest him with his own. There was a slight ungraceful tumble as she leaned back in an effort to establish her shoulder against his. This recklessness had all sorts of consequences, chiefly in her mind. But a more immediate result of her losing her balance caused her to forget these for the moment.

'Oh my dear, all over your shirt! It's my fault. I am sorry!'

'Where?'

She touched the place on his shirt where the wine was ringing out in a wider and wider circle. He pressed her hand down until the moist cold disc made by the wine disappeared, conquered by the warmth of her palm on his chest. He kissed her.

At what point does innocence begin its cancerous gnawing at self-respect? Triteness being so frequently true, perhaps it *is* better to have loved and lost than never to have loved at all ...

Yet for all that, it is supposed to be the recollections of sexual experience which at the last make up the greater reproach amongst the weaknesses of an ordinary life. A few look back on this side of their existence with self-congratulation; more with complacency. But whatever affirmations about such things publicly, it is fairly certain that more tears are shed on earth over what has been withheld than for what has been given—however rashly or incautiously. What comfort is there in a view of love as the betraying worm, when a view *without* love is so writhing, so etiolated that it merely grows into a worm of a more shameful breed? Virginity—except in the instance of the religious nature, in whose case it is never neglected, never retreated from or left to seethe and proliferate in its own fungus-like loneliness—repels when it doesn't ravish. Its progress from all that is desired to all that is detested is rapid and sure. Calling it purity doesn't help, since purity implies insistence and determination of a sort—also the chance to have been impure.

Mary knew that she was now seeing Richard with a far greater confidence than at any time before and that with this confidence came an equality which had recognisable roots in their common innocence. Intellectually as well as in the nuance aspects of his not quite reputable charm, in his being so young, and, most of all, in his variety of selfishness, he exceeded her in every way. Even ten years ago, when she had been Richard's age, she had never had the necessary restlessness to shine. He shone. It was the thing about him which fascinated her. Quentin shone too, but more luridly. Richard, though, went on reminding her of the young man at the ridiculous hunt ball when she was eighteen. Her wanting him seemed to have something to do with that brief incident. Perhaps it was true and people *did* comb the world for those unconsciously similar to their first lovers. Giving herself to Richard was, in her imagination, desperately like giving herself to that fair, unintroduced young man *then*. Except, the thing which made her desirable then, filled her with fear now. The historic absence of love becomes a disfigurement. Mary knew it. Being so complete, all she could offer would be some kind of incompleteness. And what she dreaded more than anything else was the sight of herself pursuing desire beyond the reaches of her own self-respect. She couldn't marry him. It grew more and more obvious that his offer of marriage contained no real consideration of it. Yet for months now she hadn't been able to bear the thought of any other woman being anywhere near him. Even Miss Bellingham worried her—that tenacious old creature! She moved until it was her face and not her hand which was pressed against the wine-stain on his shirt.

The sharp, locked angle of the bloomy wall stretched smooth naked plum-wood branches along with it, each branch transfixed to lanes of crumbling pink mortar. Further down were more fruit-espaliers. Her eyes followed the pattern of nodular twigs, blackened thongs and sagging wires abstractly. She heard Richard saying, contritely,

'How we kill ourselves when we talk . . .'

'We do, don't we.'

He kissed her cheek and her mouth.

'It was your living I wanted,' he said sadly. 'Surely you can see that it is your refusal to live which is so . . . so horrible? Surely you can see that? You take sides with the past. Things like this house. And when you say you want your life, what you mean is that you want your routine. Your friend Helen has been making you sensible.'

'My friend Helen, as you call her, wants me to burn my boats!'

'You never said. Good old Helen.'

'You think I've not gone into things, don't you? I have. I've thought of everything.'

'What is it that you look for in me—and cannot find?' he asked slowly.

'I shan't answer that. Instead I'll say that what attracts you in me is my "stillness". I think it's something men often look for in women. Later on they come to hate it. You would hate me for it.'

Except for his saying, 'How critical you are! I'm never that critical about you—' he refused to be serious about the rest of her argument. Instead he took her in his arms. The fretful surface of her ordinary world grew still and placid and the giving in to simple physical impulses revealed to her mental depths she knew she need never enter again. In quite overwhelming control now, she slipped from his arms and jumped up lightly from the bruised grass. The monoplane they had seen hovering earlier over the sea, was now entering the small wall-locked universe of Meridian. It circled, then throbbed out of consciousness. Mr Gilder, who sold whelks and whiting from a handcart, yelped abruptly far down on the roadway. It was a fruit-stone of a moment, engraved all over with minute conceits. Fainter still came the sound of children on the beach, each cry muted and purling and climbing into the air like a tendril. All this against the claiming silence in which Richard released her and the faint purposeful slurring of their shoes on the gravel as they each attempted to take for granted the enormity of the intention which led them to Meridian House. Only when they came to the rosewood snake of the banister rail, and he saw the pretty shallow treads winging up into darkness, did Richard say.

'This will destroy us—you do realise that?'

'Will it?' she asked lightly. Her wonder was momentarily transferred to the extraordinary intimacy of her home. Destroy us? she was about to repeat, staring about her at the prim suffocatingly familiar rooms. She had a vision of her mother and Mr Yockery. They were stomping into country-house gardens—uninvited, of course. They were fact-finding in churches; toiling away, dragging up the coconut matting to find matrices and being insolent to vergers—characters they always reckoned fair game. In the vestries Mr Yockery would nose into the registers to see exactly what was going on in a particular parish, and while he was doing this her mother would be fluffing out her bangs in the choirboys' mirror. They would lunch at the local Trust House, where yet another kind of insolence would be found for the waiter. All this time the Alvis would be resting, not unlike a smart shrine, in the stripy shadow of nude beech trees. Her mother would then find that her vertigo was about to come on so she would lumber into the Alvis to rest and to smoke a Kensitas cigarette . . .

'I suppose they will be out until dinner as they said?' Richard asked.

'Of course. When they go out it takes them all day.'

Meridian then, as if correctly interpreting their separate anxieties, adroitly reversed its message. For all the meaning the stepped set of Francis Towne water-colours on the staircase wall might have had for Mary—and she had seen them every day of her life—they could have arrived from Gimpel Fils that very morning. The frosted bell-shades on the electric light bulbs bloomed above her head like unfamiliar flowers. But for Richard it all became easily comprehensible. He was at the door of her bedroom and he found it neither strange, nor startling, nor out of the ordinary. When the door opened, alarm was suggested by yards and yards of filmy muslin bellying in from the window. He crossed and closed the sash.

'Darling, I had no idea; you can see for miles. Arroby Bay— the Martello—the lighthouse on Hare Island. How lovely!' He opened the window again, leaned out and saw the shutters, and pulled them to. A fine zebra darkness rode across their bodies and across the bed. It drew alternating parallels of desire and doubt across their faces. She heard his breathing, soft and regular, yet tearing into the quietness. He remained at the window with his back to her and said, 'If I went away this minute you could be absolutely free; wholly yourself.'

'No, don't go. Not now.'

'Then you do want me. You still might marry me?'

She laughed, casting into the sound all the embarrassment of her overwhelming sanity. Half-jokingly she asked, 'Darling what on earth is it that you want—some kind of knightliness? And for me some kind of submission? Oh Richard!'

'You know I would go on loving you,' he insisted stubbornly.

'I wasn't doubting that side of things. I was thinking of marriage itself. Its routine, or whatever you like to call it. You would hate it wouldn't you . . .'

'Is that what Helen said? She told you that too?'

'You're worried about Helen, aren't you! No, that happens to be my own conclusion.'

'In that case we're both of us mad!'

He turned to her and drew her uncertainly into his arms.

'Perhaps we are. Then, her voice burying itself against his shoulder, 'I shall never mind, Richard darling; ever, ever, ever. Can you understand? I shall never see us as two fools—or worse'.

Then she drew away and removed her necklace, her not very good, though still not imitation, pearls; the too-dutiful little warm tweed-rubbed pearls which carried with them all which Lafney had expected of her. They made her 'Miss Crawford.' They slithered with angry animation across the polished surface of her dressing-table. She stepped out of her shoes. Then with a half-choking protest at what she suddenly decided was an ugly, deliberate preparation, she vanished into the narrow additional dressing-room where there was nothing but shelves and shelves of books on Naval History and a spiky pile of jaunty French shoe-trees and hangers.

When she returned she found him sitting on her bed with his jacket off looking oddly, touchingly uncouth. He took her hands in his and she had a wild, almost ribald recollection of an Italian painting she had once seen in which a thin nervous Adam led a not so repentant Eve out of Eden.

In the unusually warm afternoon sunshine the crowded polyanthus down below in the fussy Meridian borders circulated their smell of musky, earthy velvet. In the house, the rooms, spoilt but still beautiful, ran into one another with aplomb and rectitude. Both garden and house exacted a security, a smug peace from the world.

Mary had always imagined that love, the act of love, was cloudy, sheltered; that with it ordinary comprehension died. Its deliberate brightness wracked her. She longed for the shades, the incomprehension, the warm, sweet, helpless indefiniteness she had hoped it to be. Her fingers dug themselves into the soft relaxed flesh of Richard's arms so harshly that the hurt they gave was transmuted back to her in a pleading repetition of his name. The name, she saw, made no sense to him. He wheeled above her, white and deft as a bird, and with the same absence of pity. Presently she allied herself to his wild flouting of regard and was shocked to find that it was not until she had done this that tenderness crept in.

★

He woke stealthily, appreciating the conditions attached to waking, but hesitant to accept them. His left arm was as cold as stone. And as unfeeling. He tried to draw it in, to re-unite it to himself, but nothing happened, except a tiny thread of pain—hardly pain at all—the minute and wayward protest of a nerve. The arm which was his, but was dead, ran across the pillows like stripped willow, damply cold and clean. Mary's head laid across it. Her mouth was compressed and mildly distorted with sleep. The skin near her temples glistened. The arm at last came free. She did not wake. He kissed her breast and still she did not wake. I have loved, he thought. His hand rested at the timorous softness of her waist. With closed eyes, scarcely breathing, she asked.

'What is the time, darling? Can you see?'

He saw it on her own watch which she still wore.

'Twenty-to-five?' she echoed in alarm.

They hung together, trying to work out such an hour; to make it reasonable, believable. Twenty-to-five when? On what day? In what year? In whose lifetime? They were eaten up by the silence. He began to kiss her again and it seemed no more than a second later that St Prolixia's chimed five.

When Richard had gone downstairs Mary flew around getting her room how it usually was. Everything in it looked violated. The mounted sheepskin rugs her father had brought back from Tasmania were rucked into ranges. The silk lampshades were rakish. Books, ornaments—all seemed to have been disturbed. But nothing confronted her with resentment. instead there was a gay, wilful insolence in the disorder. She opened the shutters. Richard walked on the terrace. His hair was blown up in a crest. Every now and then he looked up, but carefully not at her window. At last she ran from the bedroom to reach him and there in the first hall encountered the contained figure of Mr Yockery.

'Ha! Where's the fire, eh?' He blocked her way jocosely.

'Dick's in the garden,' her mother said, heaving herself up the three front steps. Lorgnettes swung convulsively from her chain, still pregnant with all they had magnified. The car seat had caused her skirt to concertina up. Other than this she looked wonderfully well-kept. Both she and Mr Yockery were strung-up by the day's proceedings to a pitch of mildly malicious levity. 'Did you give him some lunch? You did? Good. We had a lovely time.'

Over her mother's shoulder Mary saw Richard coming in

from the terrace. They had not surprised him. He had seen the Alvis turn in from the road. 'Everything's changed . . . everything's different!' he'd felt like shouting at them, because of the complacency of their jolting bodies. 'Why do you behave as though you are coming back to the same old smug situation?' He looked at Mary, enclosed like him in the ruthless weakness of after-love, knowing himself to be fragile, yet not vulnerable. They were a honeycomb. They held the sun of Lafney and were drained of its sediment. Mrs Crawford however, only saw them as they had been. She dumped her fur on a chest and demanded tea. Her make-up lay in silver lines in the deep crevasses of her stout handsome face. She and Mr Yockery were exchanging looks of an appalling tolerance. Their 'understanding', Mary saw, was being brought into play. Richard said he must go. Mrs Crawford's broad shoulders swung round.

'Go? My dear boy . . .'

'I think so, Mrs Crawford.'

She looked at him, telling herself, 'sweet'. Then she pushed him into the compartment of her mind she kept for basically harmless young men of her on-furlough-from-Africa kind. She prided herself that she knew his type and its stagnating decency. Safe as houses.

'You won't forget to tell your mother about that meeting!'

But it was Mr Yockery who had the last word.

'What do you think? We passed Quentin. He was just leaving the station. Waved us on, or we'd have given him a lift . . .'

★

At the gate, or just before they got to it—Mary had walked down from the house with him—they kissed for the last time. She was being infinitely right and just; he understood that. But she had defeated him. He had convinced her of desire only. She still retained her code, and her code, trivial as it might seem to him to be, excluded her complete acceptance of him. She had once thought of marriage and now would never think of it again—with him at anyrate. It was all past anger or argument. His chief feeling was a buried, incommunicable sadness. The sadness reached up from his stomach into his throat, like the sadness children experience when other children shrug them off.

'You ought to go. Won't they be waiting for you?'

She said, 'Yes they will.'

'And will I be waiting for you?—I ask because you have grown so clairvoyant in such matters.'

'Let me see,' she said, playing his game. 'No, Dick darling, my glass somehow tells me that you might not be.'

'You're sure—?'

'I am—and you will be. One day.'

'Goodbye then.'

He pressed her hands which hung heavily in his.

A few yards past the swing-gate which led to the back of Meridian, he thought he heard his own name. He turned quickly and saw a fat gull landing with prodigious dignity on the groundsel-fringed wall.

16

EDWINA was destroying a mosaic. The mosaic, crab-pink and macaroni-grey, stretched for some feet before the front door of The Portway. Frosts and moles had buckled it, but it was not for such a reason that Edwina was prising it up. For years she had loathed it with all her heart. The house was empty. Good, she had thought selfishly. Dick had gone off somewhere. It would have been all the same if she had got a proper lunch. Florence Crawford wouldn't call; not now. She glanced at her watch. Gone five! She shovelled up the last pailful of hideous clinking tesserae. When she looked round it was to see with amazement that Quentin stood just behind her. He was poking the damp, wormy scar where the mosaic had been with the ferrule of his umbrella. It may have been the umbrella which made her think of Quentin as an undergraduate again. Whatever it was, for the moment she was quite overwhelmed by the sight of the touchingly youthful figure he made with his black hair thrust out in a sheltering eave above his neat pale forehead and his not very good suit tangled into Quentin's own special brand of elegance.

'Quenny! You never said.'

'I didn't know.'
'But how wonderful!'
'Where's Dick? He is home isn't he?'
'Not at the moment. He's with Mary Crawford.'
Quentin looked relieved.

'But what are you doing, Mum? When did you decide to become an archaeologist? Has Father Yock been getting at you? And, if I may say so, what a mess!'

Edwina, looking at the bed upon which the mosaic had lain, a black indecent bed, blindly proliferous with rushing insects and crawling convolvulous runners, was apt to agree.

'Worse than before?' she asked.

Quentin scrawled his name in the dirt, then scrabbled it out with revulsion. He considered. 'Perhaps not. But what now?'

'Shingle. But I'm not going to do that today. I'd better get tea. Stella's in Ipswich, but she's coming home about seven and Richard—but I told you about Richard, didn't I?'

'You said he was at Meridian.'

Edwina realised that Quentin wished to be certain about this. Was there something to be explained to Richard then? Something which could have brought Quentin home so suddenly?

She looked at him carefully when she thought he wouldn't notice. He waited in the stamp-size morning-room and she saw him reduced by the three receding arches of the doors which led from the kitchen, a narrow Orpen young man who was choosing for reasons of his own to present only his shadow to the world. She bustled through in a manner calculated to make him irritable—he was always more expansive when he was rattled—dumped the tray down and herself beside it.

'Now,' she demanded, 'Why are you home like this, Quenny —without a word to anyone?'

'Don't I often?' he protested, which was true enough.

'How is Mr Munsen-Orle?' Edwina persisted.

'Frightfully well. He sends you his love.'

'Goodness, does he!'

'It may have been his respects. Mum, supposing I left March; what would you say?'

'Well supposing you did?' Edwina answered, playing for time.

'You wouldn't mind . . .?'

'I'd mind terribly. But as it would mean that you'd got a better post it would be silly of, wouldn't it? You see, March has become familiar to me, darling. And you are getting on so well there.'

She sensed his mind working in some schoolmasterly way as though he were making an effort to reframe an already over-simplified question to a rather limited intelligence. Edwina had endured this kind of thing before and found it maddening. But she was so shaken by what Quentin said next that she made no effort to be anything other than the slight booby he occasionally made her out to be.

'We'll put it this way shall we darling. If I gave up teaching altogether—would you mind?'

Then Richard walked in. He hardly seemed to see Quentin, who at once began to invent a hasty resentment that his being in Lafney wasn't a greater surprise to more people.

Immediately Edwina had left the room to get a cup for Richard, Quentin said, 'I've got to see you. It's urgent.'

'Oh—?'

'You've got to be serious.'

'I'm as serious today as I'll ever be.'

Quentin queried this. Anyway, beyond making sure of his attention at this point, Richard's life interested him very little. His own apprehensions and hopes soared to such a fantastic precedence over the plans of other people it made him see life intensely personally. It wasn't quite selfishness. That would be a crude interpretation of his inverted interests. His preoccupation with being Quentin tallied with the preoccupation of an artist at a certain pitch of creativity. In his way he was producing himself. Every stop, every nuance of the Quentin manual had to be extended and sounded to its ultimate advantage. He was the least self-apologetic individual that could possibly be met with. Eventually, life being what it is, Quentin's present tolerable gaiety, his fascinatingly strung-up, over-exposed individualism would warp. Go awry. At forty he would most likely be detestable. It was only the fact that Quentin himself occasionally showed signs of knowing that such a thing could happen which lent him a sort of pathos in the eyes of certain people—Mary especially. In fact, if she were truthful with herself she would agree that it was Quentin who had made her have second thoughts about Richard. But now Quentin was looking at Richard and seeing that he was not quite the same. Something had happened. Richard had changed. Quentin was intrigued.

'Could you put off what you were doing this evening, Dick?'

'Easily. I had no intentions.'

'Aren't you what they used to call "sought after"?'

'Who have you been talking to—some ghastly old gossip?'

'No—not unless that is your idea of Sir Paul.'

'Richard was going to see Sir Paul about something or other tomorrow, weren't you Richard,' Edwina said, returning with another plate and cup.

Richard, staring straight past his mother at Quentin, said quietly. 'That's right. I'm going to Sheldon on the early train. Sir Paul is offering me a job.'

Even more quietly, the pianissimo of altercation, Quentin replied, 'I'm here to talk about that. There has been some kind of alteration—although I did understand nothing had been absolutely fixed.'

He rose and balanced himself on the revolving piano-stool. He played a smart little Milhaud tune. 'Munsen-Orle adores Milhaud already,' he explained. His fingers faltered wittily.

'Do you mean that there is no need for me to go to Sheldon—again?' Richard asked, heavily, but still not loudly.

'No actual *need*—since you put it like that,' Quentin said, still playing. 'I like the bit where it goes into the major, don't you . . .' He hummed.

Edwina, with high percipience for her, said soothingly, 'Look, boys, let's all have drinks. Then you can both go off for a walk somewhere and discuss all this properly. Stella is coming back to supper.' She added this to cheer herself up. It had been so lovely working on the path . . . So lovely to see Quentin standing there like that. But now . . . Her fingers worked uncontrollably against the carved rails of her chair.

Quentin and Richard saw that she was upset and at once were ready with their nonsensical comfort. But she shrugged them both off and hurried into the kitchen and took refuge in what had once been the rectory cook's basket-chair, where she wept a little and loathed both her sons with a temporary fury. There was Florence Crawford, she told herself, hanging grimly on to her child as though she were a lifebuoy, while she had to put up with Stella, Dick and Quentin using her home for a stamping-ground every week-end. She longed passionately to be left alone with her own futility. Never mind what cleverer people thought. No longer to be organised by Stella, nor disorganised by the boys.

In the morning-room Richard was asking, 'How did you meet? When?'

'We were introduced in the usual way by John Munsen-Orle.'

'On Tuesday? In London?'

'Yes, why?'

'And did you say at Munsen-Orle's club?'

'I didn't. But that was where we met. It's the Sheridan in Bruton Street.'

'I know.'

'You've been there?'

'No. Wasn't Sir Paul surprised to meet my brother like that?'

'I suppose he was—although he takes precautions not to be surprised at anything, doesn't he?'

'You're finding him out rather soon aren't you.'

Quentin didn't answer. His hands continued to fly across the keys, but without striking a note. Their reflection lashed about, white and antic in the lid. At last he said, 'Let us both be careful not to take a stand on a false intention. If you really meant to go through with it and all this comes as a disappointment to you, then all well and good. I can say that I'm sorry and that it is one of those things—and you can curse me if you like. I *do* happen to be going through with it, you see, Dick. It does have meaning for me, which, if you're honest, is more than you could ever say.'

'So he thought I was shallow?'

Quentin stopped his phantom strumming and turned round

abruptly. 'Good God no! He was full of your praises. The man's beholden to you. You've helped him no end. But he's looking for friendship, not librarianship—if I may put it that way. And—'

'Yes?'

'Well, he heard that you had other plans—that you might be getting married, for instance.'

'Who in Hell's name told him that?'

'A colleague, shall we say—'

'Not—not the Winner?'

Quentin nodded. 'Right first time.'

'But *how*—?'

'Partly because Mr Winsley got that impression when you brought Mary along to some party or other at Copdock, and partly from what old Yockers told him when they met at the Archaeological Society. They were both at the House or something in the year dot, so they find plenty to chat about.

'Is that all?'

'Oh no. One last thing—rather a nice thing really. Apparently your being Sir Paul's secretary was Miss Bellingham's idea. As soon as Mr Winsley heard of it he went straight over to Sheldon and put his own spoke in. He wants you for Copdock. In fact he's got great new ideas for the school. In a way, as you can see, Sir Paul had very little choice.'

Then the telephone rang. Small spurts of an imperative bell splashed across the conversation. Edwina left to answer it. The telephone stood on a bracket in the hall. She returned at once and said, 'It's for you, Richard.'

Analysing later what had at first had seemed to him mere coincidence, Richard understood that events do, at times, have a tinder quality. They leap the distances between situations, connecting them with a flame which unites them in a mutual climax. Mr Winsley's voice jumped in the receiver. The nasal, 'Ah Brand' contained a note of self-indulgence—the telephone had always been a luxury where Mr Winsley was concerned. He spoke rapidly, but with care.

'At first I thought I ought to write,' he said, 'but letters, as you know, take time. It is going to be a great shock, dear boy—'

There was a satisfying pause before he spoke the sentence

which contained for him the most dreadful sequence of syllables on earth; 'It is my unhappy duty to tell you that Miss Bellingham has died.' He had rehearsed these few words at different times throughout his life, sometimes inserting euphemisms such as 'passed on', 'entered her rest', 'passed away', etc. But unfortunately, as in so many instances of premeditated distress, when the moment actually did come Mr Winsley discovered that all his worst fears had already been indulged. Since eight that morning, when he had entered her room and found her already hours dead—though appearing much the same as usual—he'd had to positively goad himself into an appropriate outward grief.

'You will never know—no one will—just what Miss Bellingham meant to me. And mine is only the personal loss. Who is there left nowadays to take the place of ladies like Miss Bellingham in the field of education . . .?'

'Shall I come over to Copdock? Would that help?'

'Oh, no, no, no.'

'I am dreadfully sorry.'

'She would have celebrated her eighty-seventh birthday on August the third.'

'She had a very long life.'

'And a brilliant one,' Mr Winsley reminded him.

'Oh, indeed.'

'*Many* have much to thank her for.'

'I'm sure.'

'She was devoted to you. Your interests were much in her mind at the last.' Mr Winsley's voice sounded strangled.

Richard was silent.

'Well I'd better ring off, there's a great deal to do. But I wanted you to know particularly. Miss Bellingham—' Mr Winsley's words suffered glottal confusions—'She had been planning great things. Great things . . . She was longing to reform the School. It was her dream to do so. *You*, I may add, my dear Brand, came into those plans very fully.'

'I do? I mean I did?'

A smirk was somehow conveyed. 'Present tense, Brand! Is it not our duty to carry out what she would have planned had Heaven been merciful?'

'Perhaps it is. I'm very glad she liked me. I liked her. She was a—' Words failed Richard. 'She was a great character,' he concluded weakly.

Mr Winsley gave the impression of frothing over at his end of the telephone. 'She was a *genius*,' he corrected severely.

The talk in the morning-room ceased abruptly as Richard hung up. He glanced in and saw their faces—Stella's too; she had returned home—taut with expectancy. He hesitated, then walked quietly on up the stairs to his own room. In the wastepaper basket was Bateson's brief note and the crumpled Suffolk Regiment recruiting instructions he had enclosed. He smoothed them out and filled them up without any feeling at all. The sea hissed over the shingle and the spring fishermen clumped by below. Searchlights came out to play. He walked to the window to watch them and heard again the faint, clever discords of Quentin's new party-piece. Then he sat down and wrote, 'Dear Bateson', crossed it out and put instead, 'Dear Tom.' And even when he'd done all this St Prolixia's was only just striking six.